Table of Contents

The Z Redemption
Daniel Wetta

"….a tense international thriller in the best sense of the word. In his debut novel, the Author has made his mark and, if he continues writing the rest of the Trilogy in this manner, could well be on the way to standing up there in the ranks next to masters such as Eric Van Lustbader and Christopher Reich." - Cate Agosta, Cate's Book Nut Hut, http://www.catesbooknuthut.wordpress.com/2013/6

"Daniel Wetta's thriller, *The Z Redemption*, is a novel with sweep, perspective, and heart. He has captured modern Mexico in all of its glory and heartbreak and created a work that throbs with action….Wetta's debut novel is a triumph!" - Nancy Stancill, Author, *Saving Texas,* publisher Black Rose Writing (Amazon review)

"A well-crafted novel that is as action packed as it is heartbreaking, *The Z Redemption* is a fast paced, edgy tale that hits the ground running and never lets up….A fascinating read from beginning to end, *The Z Redemption* will leave you not only with a feeling of having been on a dizzying ride, but of having learned something important about the world we live in along the way." - Paige Mitchell, Goodreads reviewer, http://www.goodreads.com/review/show/682684543

The Z Redemption

Author: Daniel Wetta

Edited by Bob Selfe

Published by Daniel Wetta Publishing
Second Edition
Copyright 2015 Daniel Wetta

First released and copyrighted in 2013

Please visit author website and blog at
http://www.danielwetta.com

Prologue

Prologue
Monterrey, Mexico
Monday

David didn't want one of those moments in slow motion again where on the other side was either death or another lucky escape. Yet he foresaw this coming as soon as he saw the man ascending the steps to the roof. He carried an assault weapon. It looked like an AK-47. God! There was Ana on the edge of the building, ready to drop the six stories to the sidewalk by grabbing the fast-rope and zipping down. They had both seen the armed man and the two women with pistols appearing on the security monitor mounted over the door opening to the roof. Ana was doing something strange given that they were out of time. She was standing on the small platform by the rope, and she was spreading her arms wide overhead. It was the Z distress signal.

Who can help us now? he wondered.

"Hurry, David!" she urged. She leaned forward as if she were going to leap from the roof, but she jumped to the rope and descended quickly to the ground. Her months of Z training showed in her execution. She wanted to be out of the way for David to follow.

Being aware of all details around him at once affirmed for David that the laws of psychological physics were taking hold. This was an experience he had lived before. Time was slowing down for him. Put another way, he was moving faster and perceiving more within the same units of time. It was an effect produced by the stress of knowing that he was about to die.

The man coming up to the roof, of course, had to be El Gato, even if he did look like a banker in that dark suit. Who else could it be? A banker and two female assistants in business suits with weapons drawn? No, this was El Gato, a top commander in the Cartel of Sinaloa, coming to take care of personal business with David. David should not be surprised. He had invited this, hadn't he?

1

What he found most remarkable was his reaction in the middle of this developing drama, when Ana raised her arms above her head: *God, she is uncommonly beautiful!* Only he thought it in Spanish: *Dios, ella es extraordinariamente hermosa!*

For David, this is the moment that stopped: Ana was about to descend; the door to the roof was about to open; and David was about to put himself between Ana and the gun pointed towards her. He really had no options. David knew that once again he would be making his own leap, one that determined life or death, as he had been forced to do in other situations. But he was older now, and there was something about this time that felt very different, and it did not feel good.

Chapter 1: The Tip Over the Edge

Monterrey, Mexico
Monday

Before they first made love, Ana told him to take her to his place so that she could prepare him for war and make him shoot cannons. He wasn't exactly sure what she meant, but he was already in love and so did what she said. David fired inside her with gringo bravado that night. Four years and a revolution later, he was happy to be on the front lines with her. He was an old cannon, nearly sixty-two years old now, but she gave him fresh powder each encounter. More than once in bed, they finished celebrating a climax of explosions with happy shouts of victory while collapsing in laughter against the headboard from the noisy exuberance of their efforts. She was twenty-two years younger, and though he had lived a life of hemispheric intrigues, Ana was the one who showed him roads that he had never traveled. He adored her more than ever.

That first time was four years ago. The sex was always hot and bright white, even as the days in Mexico turned black and nervous around them. True lovers and close families held each other tightly. They gathered and partied only with friends known a long time. No one went to the bars and clubs after midnight anymore, except the ones who got killed or disappeared.

He was waiting for Ana now on this dry and unusually hot morning in early February on the roof of the sixth floor of the office building which Ana owned in the museum district of central Monterrey, close to the terminal of the Santa Lucía River. He was standing by the scaffolding which the Zs had built to hold the fast-rope that trailed to the ground at the corner of the building. It had been a silly thing to do, but the evening before, David had felt vigorous; and even though the demonstrators were everywhere in the street and were still crowding into the Macroplaza, he grabbed the end of the rope from the ground and climbed all the way up in the dark. He used the Navy Seal method of using his legs and feet to

3

create holds in the rope so that he could rest in intervals and not burn the muscles in his arms. He had the gloves on, and when he got to the top, he grabbed the scaffolding and swung himself onto the roof and rested. He relished the physical condition that he was still in. The exertion and the warm breezes of the evening lulled him almost to sleep despite the loud speeches of the people in the Macroplaza. They were rallying support for the coup through the microphones on the temporary stage that had been erected in front of the Governor's Palace.

Earlier that afternoon, David, Ana, and Enrique ate takeout in the office, out of view of everyone, before Ana went home to her family. Enrique had brought the Chinese dinner to them because Ana and David would have been instantly recognizable. They shouldn't be seen eating together in an intimate way in Mexico. Ana was married and they were celebrities.

Ana owned the building and leased out the other offices, but since the military coup just two days prior, hardly anyone had come into the building. The coup had taken place late on Friday afternoon. They had come together with Enrique on Sunday afternoon to work. There would have been few office tenants who would have come there on a weekend anyway. They had spent a lot of time on the roof during the weekend because from there they could watch the demonstrations. Just across the street a CNN Mexico crew had placed television cameras on top of another six-story building, and from time to time they did broadcasts to give an aerial view of the happenings in Monterrey. They also snuck in a couple of shots of David and Ana on the roof.

David and Ana had become celebrities of rare kind in Mexico because of their work. They directed the company that funded the paramilitary group trying to protect citizens from the violence of the drug cartels in Mexico. The company was named "Z," in reference to the Spanish word, "zorro," meaning, "fox." Ana had founded the company, and David was its CEO, a mostly symbolic position because he did part-time undercover projects for the CIA, and he ran a security consulting firm for international corporations. Enrique was the first lieutenant of the Zs and functioned similarly to a chief operations officer. He headed all the cells that operated in the cities and in the rural areas of Mexico. The growth in membership of the

Zs under their leadership in the past three years had been extraordinary.

The government can't protect the people, David told himself when he reflected on it. *The Mexicans have to turn to others for safety, sometimes even to the drug cartels in the remote mountainous areas. In the large cities, the people trust the Zs even more than the Army. The cartels have bought the governments. The Army is often outgunned by them.*

David observed during the weekend how often people on the street looked up to the roof because they hoped to see Ana there. Many had seen her on television on the roof with him. When she wasn't on the roof, people would call for her in the hope that she was in her office and would come out. When they did see her with David on the roof, they urged her to join the speakers in the Macroplaza. Everyone in Monterrey knew her building and its proximity to el Museo de Historia Mexicana, the Museum of Mexican History. Even before the recent civil disruptions and the coup, Ana's building was an informal tourist attraction. Inside was the national headquarters of the Zs. These fit young men and women in their black pants and shirts were plentiful in the central district of Monterrey. They made their presence known as public guardians around the museums, theaters, river walk, and government buildings.

David liked Ana's way of flirting with her admirers in the crowds. The situation in Mexico was tense, so she tried to relax people. Responding to their invitations to come with them to the Macroplaza, she laughed and waved them on, shouting, "Adelante! Maybe later! Viva México!" On a couple of occasions, a Z, observing these exchanges, grabbed the rope that dangled at the corner of the building and climbed athletically to the top to give people a show. This lightened things and garnered applause and cheers. When David saw the young man do this, he felt competitive inside. He waited until the cover of night to make his own climb, and he did it unnoticed. *It's just as well,* he thought to himself this next morning. He was a lot slower, but he was very happy he could do it.

It was still too early in the morning to know how many people would be returning to work in Monterrey and throughout Mexico on this Monday. A bank leased half of the first floor in the building. So far David hadn't seen signs of life there. He had shouldered through growing crowds in the streets to get to the office. Traffic was stalled everywhere, and he had to park some fifteen or sixteen blocks away. Enrique was going to bring Ana to work. David was anxious to see them to talk about the call he had received that morning from a contact in the Drug Enforcement Agency. That call was a game changer.

The building had elevators, but David opted for the athletic urban sprint, as he called bounding the stairs. The phone call had made him feel cautious, so he decided to wear the ballistic vest that he kept stored in an office closet. But first he went to the roof because he wanted to see what was happening in the city and to see if he could feel in his skin what the day might bring. He saw on his phone that he could still pick up the internet from Ana's office suite. That was a relief. He had wondered if communication via phone service, internet, radio, and television would continue.

When he opened the door to the roof at the top of the stairwell, the shadow of something new caught his eye. Enrique had ordered that a security monitor be installed above the door on the outside of the structure that housed the stairs. David hadn't noticed the cameras on the way up, but on the roof he saw the split screen with two different sections of the stairs on the black-and-white monitor. The installation company had done a good job of concealing the cameras in the stairwell.

"We're spending time up here, and people know we're here. We're even on television on this roof, and let's face it, we have plenty of enemies. We need to be ready if someone is coming," Enrique had insisted.

The monitor was set in an open metal casing to protect it from the weather. *One thing about Enrique: he always follows through quickly with his promises*, David thought. He loved the young man like a son.

He walked over to the corner of the roof where the housing for the fast-rope was located. The rope consisted of eight braided strands of assault static line with an eye splice. The splice looped around a steel beam that extended from the scaffolding erected atop the roof. A person climbing from the ground to the roof could reach for a brace of the scaffolding and pull himself to a small platform there. On the platform was a metal utility chest containing training equipment, gloves, and other accessories.

The Zs trained for urban combat without weapons. They raced up dozens of flights of steps, jumped down from one section of stairs to another, leaped across spaces between roofs of close buildings, shimmied along cables and wires, ran sideways along walls, swung from beams, dove through open windows, and hop-scotched across the hoods and roofs of moving cars on the training field. And, of course, they flipped, backwards and forwards.

This fast-rope on Ana's building was what Enrique had wanted as a distinguishing icon for their Monterrey offices. Ana had a gym on the first floor with every conceivable piece of equipment and free weights, so that when the young Z guards desired, they could exercise there any time of day or night. Climbing or descending the fast-rope provided extra exercise.

Ana enjoyed using the rope. David remembered that originally Ana had taken the Z training at the facility near Monterrey so she could get in shape and have a taste of what urban combat might be like. The training focused on disarming and disabling aggressors who had weapons. Disabling could be to the point of death if that were necessary. Ana had developed the Rules of Life for the Zs. She had been influenced by the peace and victims' rights movements, especially the group, "No Más Sangre" (No More Blood). Under the rules, the Zs committed themselves to protect and serve without the use of firearms, as much as reasonably possible. The rules derived from a philosophy that blood is precious and that life should be enjoyed in peace and enriched through fraternity.

David remembered the time when Ana had first informed him that she was going to take the Z training. She had asked him which was the most essential skill that had best served him all his life. He became unsettled when he realized that she was transforming from a leader behind a computer to one who would put herself physically in the firing lines. First, he answered her that in no way was she going to take the training. They fought for three days, but she was stone-head stubborn. He knew that she would do it regardless of his feelings and regardless of their love. When finally he told her that the essential skill was jumping, she was surprised, and he insisted this was true.

"You have to jump," he told her. "You have to leap as high as a man's head. You have to jump from roofs, across roofs, onto roofs, from one car-top to another, from one building story to another, and from a tree branch to the ground. You have to become rubber and roll, so you break no bones. You almost have to fly. This is what I call jumping. This is the essential skill."

She didn't expect that answer. She had a fear of heights, but after months of falling attached to bungee cords from towers, diving from cliffs into water, plummeting onto nets, landing and bouncing on trampolines, running and jumping, and more running and jumping, she began to understand what David really had been telling her. She hadn't exercised much since her teenage years of swimming with her father, and the three months of intense Z training literally almost killed her, but then she could do it.

She could jump without fear. David had told her to learn to fly, and now she knew what he meant.

He glanced at his watch and saw that it was 8:30 a.m. He was becoming restless because Ana and Enrique still hadn't arrived. It was becoming very warm in the sunshine on the roof. He walked to the roof's edge at the front of the building. He recognized a few office workers entering the main entrance below, including the branch manager of the bank.

Apparently some people plan to work today, he thought. *That's a good sign!*

He reflected on something Ana had said the previous day about his blog activities. Tens of thousands of people subscribed to receive his blog articles. He had begun it months earlier for the purpose of flushing out El Gato. To capture this leader in the Cartel of Sinaloa would definitely be a footnote in the pages of history unfolding in Mexico. David taunted El Gato in his blog postings. He addressed personal messages to him as if there were no doubt that he was a real person. Most people thought he was a myth and that his work really had been done by a number of different leaders of the cartel. David's research had convinced him that El Gato was real and that he had worked his way up over the course of years to be second in command of the Cartel of Sinaloa. He suspected that he was the cartel leader who quietly coordinated the successful openings of new distribution centers and plazas in the United States for the trafficking of meth, cocaine, and marijuana.

Whoever El Gato was, David had determined that he was a murderous man of incalculable ego. Once this man understood that he, David Wilson James, was the author of so much investigation against him, he would want a face-to-face confrontation. El Gato, if he were real, had hidden for years behind myth. David was flushing him out of hiding and putting El Gato in the public eye. The man would have to be pissed!

Ana was the one who came up with the idea of appearing on the roof of her building while the demonstrations were going on.

"It would make sense for us to be there," she had reasoned with David. "Our office is in view of the Macroplaza where so much of the action in Monterrey is taking place, and it would seem natural that the leaders of the Zs would observe happenings from there."

But David had other concerns about the roof this morning. If El Gato were coming, he and Ana would be there alone with him, away from crowds, and they would be easy targets. He realized that the public images of David and Ana as idealistic gringo and celebrated housewife of causes were perfect fodder for someone like El Gato to believe that they would be naïve and stupid enough to put themselves on an open roof top. That's precisely what they were doing, stupidly or not. He didn't worry much about this until he had received that call in the early morning.

Ana and David were always unarmed because they lived by the Z Rules of Life. So now David did a quick assessment of the roof. The cooling towers, fans, and satellite dishes made excellent hiding places and shields from bullets, but only if they had time to reach them before someone would help them. Enrique had been right about the need for security cameras. Those could give them precious time in an emergency. David knew that there were Zs watching the doors to the building for anything suspicious. The fact that CNN Mexico had decided to broadcast from the only other roof top with a clear view of theirs worked out as a plus. Yes, their coverage meant people knew where they were, but the television crew could summon help if they saw anything happening. *And if push comes to shove,* David thought, *I can always jump and fly in a crunch.* His lifelong skill always felt reassuring to him.

But in light of what he had learned that morning, he regretted that he and Ana had let their whereabouts be so publicly known.

Think about it, David, he told himself. *You've been goading a cartel boss trying to hide from public view, and you've been reckless in your obsession to prove that he exists. It's one thing to endanger yourself, but you've put Ana in danger.*

9

Indeed, there was actual reason to believe that El Gato might not only be real but that he might be in Monterrey! This morning the acquaintance from the DEA had given David a stunning piece of information relating to El Gato that seemed to be a confirmation of David's theory. He knew what Ana would say when he told her about it. She'd worry for his safety. He remembered now to go to the office and put on his vest before she arrived. He had to admit even to himself that he was possibly in danger.

And Ana too! Damn, where is she? he wondered.

He had received the ballistic vest a year before through a contact in the Central Intelligence Agency. He didn't work for the agency directly anymore. He did freelance contract security or intelligence work for them and for other governmental agencies in the United States and Mexico. He also did security consulting for international corporations in Mexico. However, under orders from the President of the United States, the Director of the CIA reluctantly approved one of these new-model vests for David. The President, known to David as Donnie, was Donald Austin Blair. He happened to be the college roommate and close friend of David all the years since undergraduate school at The College of William and Mary, much to the annoyance of the CIA Director. David had had the luck-of-the-draw at William and Mary to be the roommate of the son of the then-Governor of Virginia.

The President appreciated the special projects in Mexico which David had been doing. In addition to the CIA, David worked also with the Drug Enforcement Agency and the FBI. He knew the danger David was in as more and more people became aware of him. David had given up undercover work and was working publicly with Eduardo Ortiz and Ana Valdez. The vest had been developed by a private company contracted with the CIA. It had performed extremely well in ballistic testing, taking multiple hits at close range even from AK-47 semi-automatic rifles. It was constructed with a new composite of titanium and ceramic squares enclosed in experimental, synthetic fiber material. It was light-weight, flexible, and reasonably cool for vests worn under shirts. After several executives and consultants from the United States were assassinated or kidnapped by drug cartels in Mexico, the President directed that one of these vests be sent to David.

"He needs it," the President had said to the CIA Director. "They don't shoot you with nine millimeter pistols very often in Mexico. They riddle you with shots from AR-15s and AK-47s. I want him to have a chance."

David put the vest on in a bathroom in Ana's office suite. He hadn't worn it before. He had only tried it on when he first received it, and then he kept it in a closet in the office. The vest extended several inches below his belly button, so he tucked it in his pants and pulled his black T shirt over his head. He looked at himself in the mirror. *Incredible, it isn't really bulky at all,* he thought. He checked himself out. He was trim and athletic from a lifetime of gymnastics and running. His cropped white hair contrasted nicely with the black outfit he was wearing. He thought of Ana, how beautiful and young she looked at forty, and then he observed his mature face and wondered how she could love him with such passion.

Whatever! I don't know why, but I take it, he thought, observing himself with slight amusement in the mirror.

He spent a few minutes looking at websites on a desktop computer in the office, but then he felt antsy and curious about how the vest would feel outside in the heat. He cut off the computer and went back to the roof. Just before he shut off the computer, he saw some images again of the bags that were left in the front of the Governor's Palace in the Macroplaza just a week before. This made him feel sick in his stomach. He pushed himself away and headed for the rooftop.

Outside, the rising temperature and the bright of day didn't dispel the images in his mind. He couldn't stop himself from remembering the incident which had sent the whole nation over the edge just a week before. *A tipping point*, he thought. It seemed like a thousand years ago now. Perhaps if it had been the only horrific incident, the spiral of events leading to the coup would never have happened. The problem was that Mexico had just experienced six years of the cruelest, most revolting kinds of human trauma. When this particular atrocity happened, the people of Mexico went crazy in a hysteria of rage. They piled into the streets to demand justice for the victims. There seldom was justice for these crimes, and the people were sick to death of impunity. The country was ripe for radical change. This, in fact, had emboldened the plotters of the coup to make their move.

11

The eight dark-brown plastic garbage bags had probably been in the Macroplaza five or six hours when the school girls arrived. No one had bothered to examine them despite the fact that the bags had no place there whatsoever. It wasn't a trash pick-up point. The bags had been left across the Macroplaza from the Governor's Palace before the grounds crew arrived to clean the area for the tourists of the day. The bags were near the steps that descended to a small city park.

The school teachers who were chaperoning the girls assembled them in that park so they could visit the monuments and read the commemorations there. They were fourth graders in school uniforms of light blue skirts and white blouses. Each girl held hands with the one ahead and behind her, and they all walked in a line from the park up the steps. The girls would be in the first tour of the Governor's Palace that day. They were early. They were singing and laughing, but when they got to the top of the steps, they saw a dark liquid coming from one of the bags beside them. It looked like the bag had split from the heat of the unusually warm morning sun. A teacher close to the bag thought she saw a dead animal in it. Curious, she poked the split of the bag with a stick to open it a bit more.

A human head rolled out, that of a child. A nearby professional photographer who was shooting pictures of fashion models heard the screams of the children. He snapped images of the terrified and hysterical school girls in the next moments as they began to understand what was in the bags. The pictures accompanied headline stories on internet news pages and in newspapers throughout the world.

The eight bags contained fifty-four heads. The victims were twenty-six women, twelve children and sixteen men. None so far had been identified. Because of the presence of women and children, there were theories that the people were migrants who had been riding atop the trains from Central America on the way to their land of dreams, the United States. Thousands attempted this every year. All the train riders were vulnerable to the attacks of the cartels, who kidnapped them for small ransoms from their families back home or who drafted them into slavery for prostitution or other work of the cartels. The Zetas, in particular, in this region of the country were active in this line of business.

Often things went wrong. When things went wrong, the simplest solution for the cartels was to kill the captives. Leaving their dismembered bodies or severed heads in public places also was a signature of the cartel meant to impress other cartels, public officials, and the Armed Forces not to interfere with their activities.

David was feeling horrible remembering the traumatized school girls and the victims when Ana and Enrique finally appeared on the rooftop monitor. He was glad to be distracted from his disquieting feelings. The cameras which Enrique had arranged to be installed were located inconspicuously between the first and second floor stair landings and on the last one. David watched Ana and Enrique disappear from view after they reached the second floor and then reappear just before opening the door.

Ana surreptitiously blew David a kiss from the doorway before coming out where she might be seen by others. Enrique hung in the open doorway.

"Good morning, darling," Ana said. "It took us forever to get here! Enrique said you would be on the roof." She laughed.

"Buenos días," Enrique called. "I'm going back down to check with the men in the street. I have a couple of guys checking who comes in and out of the building. I see the bank will be opening. I noticed employees going in there."

"Yeah, I think so," replied David. The building could be entered from front and rear glass-door entrances opening to a central lobby with opposing rows of elevators. The bank was a tenant on one side of the building on the first floor, and on the other side, the gym and other lessors occupied office space. It was customary to have Z guards at both entrances.

David wanted to include Enrique in the discussion that he would have with Ana about El Gato, but Enrique bounded down the steps in his hurry to check security downstairs. For years after this, David remembered the irony of this small exchange of words about the bank employees. It foreshadowed a mistake that led to their lives being altered forever. David later found that events of the next few hours also had roots in his life fifty years earlier. All of it changed the course of history for two countries.

When David turned to speak to Ana, she had already walked over to the corner of the roof by the fast-rope scaffolding. She was waving to people below. When she noticed David looking at her, she

13

nodded her head in the direction of the CNN Mexico crew on the rooftop across the street. Laughing, she told him, "Do something, baby. I think their television cameras are on us now."

So David went to the metal utility box by the scaffolding and began rummaging. He saw that it contained a few pairs of gloves, a first aid kit, flash lights, and even a pair of boots that Ana sometimes wore when using the rope. He noticed that Ana was wearing small boots and jeans this morning. She seemed prepared to have a day in the streets, if necessary.

He was about to tell Ana about the call he had received concerning El Gato that morning when she noticed the thickness under David's black T shirt.

"Cariño, you're wearing your vest! I'm so glad, but what brought this about?"

"I got a call this morning from a DEA contact. He reported that someone who lives in Monterrey and who works for the Sinaloa cartel has been informing the Federal Police. The Feds have been paying this cartel guy well to talk. One of the Feds in police intelligence is a reader of my blogs. He's familiar with the work I've done on El Gato and the supply routes of the Sinaloa cartel which I've traced in the United States. He heard something of concern that he thought would interest me, and he passed this information to the DEA. The DEA, of course, has been working secretly in Mexico with the Federal Police. The cartel informant reported that a major Sinaloa boss arrived in town yesterday to do what he called 'personal business.' That's all, but the point of interest was that he called the boss, 'El Gato'."

"Oh my God, David! Who is this source? Someone reliable?" Ana asked.

David shrugged. "I guess he's considered so. The DEA tells me that the informant is someone close to a guy called 'El Contador,' the accountant for the Monterrey plaza in the Cartel of Sinaloa."

"Then El Gato not only is real, David, but he's here for you! What else could 'personal business' mean?"

David shrugged in a manner to display calm. "We can't be sure of anything, Ana, but I knew that when you came, and I gave you this news, that I had better be wearing the vest, or you would start in on me. But I really think it would be a good idea for you to be somewhere else. I'm starting to have a strong feeling that something might happen today."

It seemed like the craziness began just as he finished these words to Ana, but later David remembered that a few more minutes passed as they discussed plans. He recalled that he and Ana were going to go inside to their offices when they first saw the images of the banker and his two female associates coming up the stairs.

At that moment he and Ana were standing by the scaffolding when they saw the three on the monitor. They were on the lower level of the staircase. The camera there displayed a man in a dark suit and two females carrying handbags. The women also wore professional clothing as if they worked in a corporate office or bank. The man was carrying a brief case. They began to climb steadily and they disappeared from the first camera's view.

"Ana, why would anyone from the bank be coming up the steps?" David remembered asking.

"They're not dressed like the people in the bank, David, or any of the tenants I know," Ana responded. "The bank employees and executives wear those burgundy uniforms."

"Shit!" David said. "Ana, put on your gloves!"

Ana was already digging through the utility box. She grabbed a pair and threw them to David, and then she found a pair for herself. She pulled on her gloves. They looked at the monitor. No people.

"They're taking too long. They're doing something," Ana said.

David saw his radio lying where he had set it on the roof, a little closer to the door, and he began moving towards it. He wasn't sure that he would have time to make a call.

He picked it up, and then he saw Ana do something strange. She stood on the scaffolding platform and raised her arms skyward in a wide "V", which was the Z signal that something was wrong. Then she turned to him, and her eyes grew big. She was looking past him at the monitor, which showed that the man and the women were on the last landing before reaching the door.

"David! He's got a rifle! There's no time! Come here!"

David swirled to look at the monitor. When he saw them, he backed quickly towards the rope because he knew Ana wouldn't go down unless she thought he was coming.

"Go, Ana! Go! I'm behind you!" he shouted to her. But he knew that if he followed her, the assassins would simply run to the scaffolding and fire down on them.

He saw her stand on the platform and begin to reach for the rope.

"Hurry, David!" Ana yelled.

At that moment the door began to open. David turned his head so he could see Ana begin her fast descent through the corner of one eye while still observing the door. The man came out with the first of the ladies just behind him. David saw him looking at Ana as he emerged. He came out with his rifle already partially raised, so he might be able to fire a shot at her before she got out of view.

David had a lifetime of experience in quick-second assessments. He knew what he had to do, and that was to fly.

But first he hurled the radio at the man to throw off his aim toward Ana. The radio struck the man's head with a forceful thud. *That was successful,* David thought with relief. Now Ana was gone, and the man had a grimace of pain and surprise. David, the "Z," took to flight, his trajectory and attack calculated.

Hope this fucking jacket works, he thought. From a short run toward the attacker, he leaped, throwing his legs out to his left and getting his body horizontal to the man. The guy was short, thankfully, so it wasn't difficult to be at his neck level. The first woman behind him was squeezing out of the door to the man's right side. At that point everything was perfect. David puffed his chest to draw the man's fire there because the man would react instinctively to the largest surface area of the body hurling towards him. David would strike the man's larynx with his right hand. His left foot would break the woman's face. The force of his flying body would push her against the other woman behind her.

In his mind time and sensory perception continued to be distorted to his favor. The man and the first woman seemed magnified to David. He saw the expression of fury on the man's face. He even thought that he was seeing the bullets firing from the man's assault rifle. It was an AK-47. He saw the nine-millimeter pistol that the woman had, but she hadn't yet raised her arm. He thought she looked confused. In this slow-motion view, David observed himself flying closer to them from his jump. He felt a self-assuredness about what he was doing.

16

But suddenly the strength of the force of the bullets on his chest surprised him. They were diminishing the power of his leap. He realized that the trajectory of his body was falling short. He plodded to the roof top on his right side. For a moment, he still saw all three of his assailants, but then darkness began to engulf his consciousness. He heard, "crack, crack, crack!" He felt his life becoming faint, but in his mind he thought the cracks sounded like, "Uno, dos, tres."

He was almost gone now, but he saw El Gato fall to the ground near him and also the two female companions. The second woman had emerged from the doorway behind the other and had been hit. He fought desperately to maintain consciousness, but his chest constricted in terrible pain, and he slipped deeper into the darkness.

He thought of Ana. She hated to see blood, he remembered, but he was seeing blood streaming from El Gato's head.

It has to be El Gato, he thought. *Who shot him?*

In the moment before the darkness snuffed him out, when David struggled to see the face of his assailant clearly, he had the shock of his life. He recognized the man. He knew who El Gato was!

This can't be possible! This simply can't be! God, am I really going to my grave with this last insanity? Then there was total darkness.

Across the street, Enrique Santos had noticed the man and the women in the dark business suits as they came up the block to the entrance of Ana's building. He presumed that they worked in the bank, but he watched them because they were attractive people. The man carried a large black briefcase. Enrique saw that the two Zs standing at the door to the building exchanged words with the man, and then they let him and the women pass inside.

All is well, he thought. *They work in the bank.*

He checked his phone for messages for a minute, but when he put it in his pocket, something caught his attention on the roof. There was Ana standing on the platform with her arms upward in a "V." Then she jumped to the fast-rope and began descending rapidly.

17

Enrique snapped to action. When he began running towards where Ana would land, he heard the gunfire on the roof, then distinctly three cracks from a rifle behind and above him. Absolute silence followed as even the people in the street hushed. Everyone was gazing upward, trying to determine from where the gunshots had originated.

Ana hit the ground just as Enrique got there. Trying not to sound hysterical, she shouted, "Enrique! I think they shot David! He didn't come down. He jumped, Enrique, he flew towards them! I knew he would do that! Oh my God, Enrique, we have to help him!"

Enrique felt his stomach sicken. He took off towards the entrance to the office building. Young men in black outfits, Zs, were already hustling to join him. He yelled back to Ana, "Stay down here, Ana! We'll take care of it! Stay here!"

Frantic with anxiety, Ana turned in circles. She looked at the roof of the building across the street from hers but could see nothing from her angle. As soon as Enrique disappeared into her office building, she pushed through the crowd and ran to the stairway inside it. She started up to the roof, as Enrique and the Zs had done.

She prayed in her mind, *God! Mi amor, please live! Please live, David!*

But a sickening discovery awaited her on one of the stair landings. There was an open briefcase with indentations for parts of an assault rifle. She had seen these before. They were built to hold weapon parts which an assassin could assemble quickly. She drew a sharp breath and hurried to the roof.

Chapter 2 Stepping through the Ruins of Love

Mazatlán, México
1986

Ana Sofía Valdez was a child who loved deeply and was loved deeply, and she had been born with a generous and compassionate heart. As she became a beautiful young lady, she responded to her increasingly curvaceous body by dressing in romantic style. Maybe it was because she was the last of six girls, or because her mother bore such heavy responsibilities of a large family of means, or because her father was an older and kind gentleman experienced in life, that young Ana had such an old soul. She loved old-fashioned, romantic, Hollywood movies; happy endings; ball room dancing; love ballads; and older, tender boys.

In Spanish the verb describing being born is in the active voice. It's something a person does, not something happening to a person. The beautiful way of saying that her mother gave birth to her in Spanish is that her mother, Lili, gave Ana to light. Mothers do that in Mexico. They give their children to light.

Lili came to work in the housewares store that Ana's father, Javier, started in the historic downtown section of Mazatlán. She was seventeen and he was thirty-nine. Once Javier met Lili, he was a man in love all his life. He married a young beautiful girl with common sense and reserve, a perfect person to manage the large family he wanted to have once he got established financially. In the first months before children, Javier came home at lunch every day and made love to his wife. After the children arrived, he came home to have lunch every day with his family, a tradition seldom breached. He adored each of his daughters, and he couldn't believe his good fortune to have six of them. The last of them was Ana, and she was the first daughter to look like him. Definitely she inherited his love of the classics, education, the arts, and all things Mexican. She also had something that delighted Javier to the end of his days: a voracious appetite to devour life and to experience the untried.

Ana attributed her romantic yearnings and love of life to this father whom she adored. He was the man of her life, and as a child she never expected that she would ever find a man as wonderful as her dad when she grew up.

She fell in love for the first time at fifteen in a way that she had never imagined.

It happened during the break in the school year when the children and teachers had holiday around Easter time. Ana's home town, Mazatlán, attracted about one hundred thousand college students from Arizona, Texas, and California each year during the week of spring break, and many couples from the United States brought their children. They came for the seemingly limitless beaches. Mexico's longest stretch of uninterrupted beaches ranged north from Mazatlán, and in this time of year the weather was perfect with hardly any rain and daytime temperatures in the eighties.

For Ana, the international mixture of people on the miles-long malecón (boardwalk) was part of her daily life. Always she was aware of people from other countries, not only the USA, Canada, and Europe, but from Latin America too, and even Japan. Strolling the beaches to the sands of the El Cid resort or along the broad, colored boardwalk of the main road which was the spine of the city, Ana heard primarily English and Spanish. Between conversing with tourists in English and watching Hollywood movies, she became so accustomed to English that sometimes in the city she had to focus whether she was hearing English or Spanish. She spent most of her time on a neighborhood beach near her father's store and a few hotels, bars, and restaurants. This small stretch of sand about four blocks long was as much home to her as her own street, and it never looked any different.

Until the summer she was fifteen.

What seemed different to Ana then were the young men on the beach. In truth, it was Ana who had changed. She had developed a woman's body. She was suddenly as adult in her body as she was socially mature. Now boys her own age and older men were doing double takes when they saw her. They thought she was older, perhaps twenty. When in her Catholic school uniform, she wore her hair in a ponytail and looked like the young girl she was, but when the school day ended, she let her dark brown hair fall long and straight. For the fiestas she occasionally wore red lipstick and a little mascara, although her long thick eyelashes didn't really require any. In this particular spring, for the first time Ana became aware that men and boys had hungry eyes for her.

The same happened with her best friend, Claudia, who lived just three blocks from Ana. She also had a metamorphosis that year. Claudia's long hair was coal black. She stood a little taller than Ana, but she was still a short young woman.

It was the Saturday morning before Easter Sunday when Ana first noticed a particular young man who made her feel funny in her body. She and Claudia had walked down to the beach from their homes to watch the people who were jamming the ocean front. He caught Ana's eye because he was huge. He had to be 1.90 meters (about six foot three). His shoulders were broad and his chest a perfect "V" with hard, rounded pectoral muscles. He dwarfed the older couple with him. Because of the resemblance he had to the woman, Ana thought that he was probably with his parents. His surf-blonde hair cascaded over his forehead and partially obscured one of his ice-blue eyes. Once, when he glanced her way, Ana thought, *Without a doubt he's a gringo. Wow, how old is he?*

He looked like he could be in college, but his baby face suggested that he might be high school age. Standing with the couple on the beach, he pointed to the mountains in the distance and then to some of the restaurants along the beach as if he had been exploring earlier and was now pointing out some features of the area. The man and the woman were dressed in shorts and shirt, like Ana and Claudia, but the boy wore only yellow bathing shorts. Ana was about to show him to Claudia, but then she discovered that Claudia was already admiring him. They both giggled. When Ana looked back, the boy was staring at her, but then he gazed vaguely above Ana and turned his head as if he had been looking at something beyond her. But Ana knew his blue eyes had lingered on her. She could feel it in the quickening of her heart.

It was becoming late in the morning. After a few minutes, the boy and the couple sauntered farther up the beach. They seemed to look at everything with tourist eyes. Soon they were lost in the throngs of people.

On the following Monday morning, Ana, her sister Rosie, Claudia, and a handful of young boys and girls from the neighborhood met up on the beach to swim. Nearby was an outdoor restaurant that served fish and shrimp, and the odor from its grills surfed atop the ocean breezes to the kids. After playing in the waves, they hurried, starving, to the restaurant. Ana threw a shirt over her bathing suit and carried her sandals to the steps leading from the sand to the deck of the restaurant. She was with Claudia and another girl friend. When she stopped to put on her sandals, she noticed the boy from the previous Saturday. He was standing there looking at the men tending the grill on the deck and at the bar where all the rich, delicious condiments for fish tacos were set. Seeing his demeanor of indecision, Ana became emboldened to help him. She walked over to him.

"These are the best tacos you've had in your life," she told him. "They're easy to fix, and you can put in them anything you want. The standard plate is three tacos. I recommend that you start with that, although you look like you would have no problem eating more!" She said this and then gulped with surprise at her own forwardness. She reddened when he turned those blue eyes on her. She saw that he wasn't that old. He was just big.

"Oh, good, you speak English," he answered. "And thank you! God, this smells so good! I came over here because the food called to me on the beach."

She had never heard an accent like his. He was definitely from the United States, but he spoke English words more drawn out than she had heard before.

"Yes, me too! You can join us if you want," Ana told him. "I'll show you how to fix the tacos and tell you what the condiments are, if you don't know. Are you ready to eat?"

"Yes, ma'am, I'm always ready to eat," he answered. "Very nice of you to offer. Yes, I would love to join you."

Ma'am? What's that? Is that like señorita? Ana wondered. *He seems nice and polite. I'll just ask him how old he is and where he's from.*

"I'm Ana," she said. "A pleasure to meet you!" She held out her hand.

His big hand swallowed hers, and by the nervous way he held it, she could tell that he liked her. She liked the way he looked directly into her eyes.

"Well, my name is James," he said, "and I'm here on vacation with my parents. They're back in the hotel room and still asleep, I think."

"Where are you from, James?" Ana asked, trying to sound casual instead of breathless.

"A little town in Georgia, a little country town," he replied.

"Well, I live here, and I don't know much about Georgia. Come sit with us, and I'll hear a little more about it."

"Okay," James agreed and then added, "Do your friends speak English, because I don't know Spanish."

Ana giggled. "My friend Claudia, my sister and the other girls speak English fairly well. The boys, not so good."

Ana found a table on the wooden deck overlooking the beach. Her sister and Claudia sat staring wide-eyed at the giant James. They were intimidated by his size at first, but Ana became relaxed, so they relaxed also as Ana ordered for her and James. When the tacos came, she took his hand and led him to the condiments bar where she told him to add salsa, guacamole, cilantro, lettuce, tomato, and onions with mahi-mahi. Back at the table, James scoffed down the tacos and wanted more before the girls had hardly begun to eat. "Wow!" they said, but they liked his appetite for Mexican food, and they encouraged him to get more. He went to refill by himself.

The biggest surprise for the girls was to find out that James was only sixteen years old and a sophomore in high school. Claudia and Rosie observed how James looked at Ana when they all talked. His eyes were for Ana. He almost forgot that they were there. Sometimes he looked at them as he was speaking, but it seemed like an embarrassed afterthought.

When Ana finished eating, she reached down out of habit into her beach bag and found a lighter and set it on the table. She retrieved her pack of cigarettes and pulled one out. Suddenly she stopped and looked at James.

"Oh my God!" she said. "I forgot my manners. Would you care for one?"

James shifted in his seat and said, "Well, I don't smoke. I'm on the football team in my school, and so I have to have plenty of oxygen in my lungs. Can't drink or smoke. I'm trying to get an athletic scholarship to college, trying to go to Georgia Tech, so I need to play good football. That means I have to be at my best.

Thanks, anyway, Ana." Then he glanced around at the people seated on the deck and smiled and said, "Looks like everyone in Mexico smokes."

Ana suddenly regretted revealing her habit. She had been smoking since she was twelve. She began to put her cigarettes back, saying, "Well, I don't really need to smoke right now," but James had already picked up her lighter and was trying to ignite it. He was fumbling. Ana quickly put the cigarette in her mouth. She was amazed that he was going to light it for her, just like in the movies! Finally the lighter ignited. With a shaking hand, he brought the flame to the cigarette, at first a little too far up from the tip, but Ana maneuvered so that it would light. She took a happy puff. Claudia and Rosie saw the clumsy gesture and stifled their smiles. The restaurant speakers began blaring Van Morrison's "Brown Eyed Girl."

"Gracias," said Ana.

"De nada," James answered, staring at her. He was awkwardly silent a few moments, looking indecisive as if he should say something or not. Finally he brought his head close to Ana's and spoke low so the others couldn't hear.

"I'm sorry. My hands were shaking. I'm a little nervous. To tell you the truth, I think you're the most beautiful girl I've ever seen in my life!" he told her.

Ana felt like the rest of the world suddenly disappeared and only she and James existed. Blood rushed to her cheeks, and her heart pounded exuberantly. No young man had ever said that to her before. Many of her boy friends in the neighborhood and school had begun to stare at her recently as if they were noticing for the first time that Ana had left her little-girl body and had slipped into a woman's. Yet here was this gringo kid, blonde and handsome and with the muscular body of a telenovela star, saying he had never seen anyone more beautiful! She couldn't find words to speak.

The pause became awkward, and then James said, "I'm sorry, I hope I didn't embarrass…"

"No!" Ana interrupted. "It's just that…I didn't know what to say…no one told me that before. Thank you, James, that was very sweet. And I think you're very cute."

"Sha la la la la la, you, my brown eyed girl…" played the song over the speakers.

24

James broke into his big Georgia grin. His eyes glistened happily.

"This is my favorite song of all time," he said.

Sometimes pure innocence permeates first romance. Until she met David a quarter century later, Ana never experienced again that queasiness in her stomach, that nervousness, that sense of immortality that someone feels in those rare first loves or in the love shared by true soulmates who somehow find one another against hopeless odds. For Ana, the memories of that week were bookended by James' astonishing confession of Ana's beauty and the horrifying tragedy that brought the week to a sudden end. In between those events, the memories of Ana's first love came to mind as if she were looking at crinkled Polaroid photographs: laughing with James, holding his hand, and embracing him in the caresses of the wind, sun, and sea mist - always with Claudia or another friend nearby. The young Mexican girls were never completely alone with a boy. Normally, the encounters that Ana and James had would begin with Ana seeing James first in a group. Later they paired off to talk alone while Ana's friends kept a discreet distance away.

There were times during the week when James had to go on excursions with his parents. He hated these because all he really wanted to do was to be with Ana. There was a brief moment on the beach once when James' parents met Ana. They received one of those clumsy introductions that teenagers make to acknowledge the adult world but showing clearly that they feel it's a world irrelevant to their lives. James hustled Ana away after the brief exchange of pleasantries, leaving his parents shaking their heads as they left. Ana looked back and waved goodbye to them. She sent an apology with her charming smile.

On the last day they were together, the Friday of that week, they didn't really know that it would be the last time. They did know that their time together was drawing close to the end, and they were feeling edgy about it. Ana and James were with Claudia on the beach. Ana asked James if he would like to see the house where she lived, saying the three of them could walk there.

"Maybe you can say hello to my mom," Ana said. She hoped that after James left, they would write letters to each other. She knew that for this to happen, Ana's parents would want to have met him.

So on the slow stroll to Ana's house, James was already beginning to feel reminiscent, and he talked about how wonderful the week had been, that it had been the best week of his life; and that he thought the Mexicans were so cool and had been so nice to him; and did Ana think that the Mexicans liked the Americans, really?

"Well, yes, gringo (which was the nickname she had given him that week), with some reservations," she answered him. "You have to understand that people in your country are very ignorant about the Mexican people. They think we all ride burros. We feel like Americans can be arrogant, like they believe the United States is the most important country on earth. Sometimes the United States takes away the lands and resources of other countries whenever they feel like it. Think also about the name of your country, the United States of America. For example, I bet you don't know that our country is not Mexico, but the United Mexican States. We have thirty-one states and a federal district like your District of Columbia. Actually, we're America too. The United States refers to itself as America and forgets that the other countries of the continent, including Canada, are also America."

"Whoa, wait a minute!" James protested. He had become used to Ana's strong convictions during the week, and he was smiling, but he felt a little taken aback. He explained that he came from Georgia, which was in the South, and that the Georgians were conservative people who loved God and their country, and that the flag of the United States was sacred and inspirational to them.

"Maybe you're right about people not knowing so much about Mexico, but where in the world do you get the notion that the United States takes lands away from people and does what it wants?"

"Oh my God, gringo!" Ana replied. "Do you know the history of your country? You took away all the lands of the native peoples who were there. You brought over slaves to sustain the economy of the entire South until just a little over a hundred years ago. You constantly cheated other peoples, like the Indians from whom you bought Manhattan so cheaply. Your country also purchased from the French the Louisiana territory for hardly anything. Your people believed in 'manifest destiny,' that God Himself felt that your country should extend from the Atlantic to the Pacific oceans, and they used this notion to invade Mexico and take away half of our country!"

26

"What the heck are you talking about?" James asked incredulously.

They had crossed over now to Ana's street and had stopped in front of the produce stand which Ana had annihilated a couple of years before, when she had tried to drive her father's Jeep. It had been rebuilt with money from Ana's father. The owner of the stand, Señor Moreno, saw Ana, Claudia, and the big gringo kid. After staring at James curiously a few moments, he gave Ana a look that asked, *Is everything okay*? Ana gave a wave and a bright smile back, and Señor Moreno returned to his customer.

Ana pulled Claudia closer to her. The Mexican girls liked to be close. Both looked up high to James and laughed. Ana felt relaxed. To her it was fun to debate. She did it with her parents, who hoped she would become a lawyer. She continued with James, but she smiled at him reassuringly.

"This is what I know, gringo," Ana answered. "Everyone in your country studies history, but they don't understand the history. Maybe you remember the war with Mexico that began in 1846? I think it isn't covered in depth in your school books. Probably this war is regarded as a small event in which you had to fight Mexicans because people in the Texas territory were rebelling and your government reacted by annexing Texas. But many Texans wanted to be independent from both the United States and Mexico. In fact, for ten years Texas was an independent republic. Your government just took Texas in 1845 and then looked for an excuse to invade Mexico."

James was at a disadvantage because he couldn't remember what he had studied about this time in the history of the United States. He just shook his head as if what Ana was saying didn't make sense. He was irritated with himself for his ignorance.

But Ana was having fun, and she persisted: "Do you realize that Mexico included the territory called New Mexico, and that's the land which is now Texas, Arizona, New Mexico, California and other states? All this belonged to Mexico, gringo. Then in 1846 and 1847 your troops invaded Mexico and fought against brave Mexican soldiers, and they came all the way to Mexico City! But let me tell you, that devil, Santa Anna, was the General of the Mexican Army. He actually defeated the United States Army in a fierce battle near Monterrey, but for some reason, on the evening before the dawn in

27

which he could have advanced and wiped out the rest of the United States' forces, he withdrew and retreated. After that, the war didn't go so well for us. When the United States Army arrived in Mexico City, leaders negotiated a truce that called for the New Mexico territory to go to the United States. Almost all Mexicans believe that Santa Anna had been bribed into agreeing to this. He was a constant scoundrel in our history, and we blame him for the theft of our lands. And, gringo, the land that went to the United States was half of Mexico!"

They had begun walking again, and James didn't know how to answer this. He didn't have any facts with which to contradict her. To him Ana's command of history was amazing, especially because she was younger than he. She seemed older; she looked older; and he had to remind himself the entire week that she was only fifteen.

He stopped their walk to give Claudia some money to go back to the produce stand to get them some orange juice, because he had something he wanted to do with Ana.

So he said, "Maybe they teach a different history in this country. I don't want to talk about this anymore."

But Ana wanted to continue her story. "Let me finish," she said to James. She had been surprised that he had interrupted to ask her friend to go back to the stand. James chuckled because in the past week he had learned that Ana was going to finish all her stories.

"The reason we were almost able to defeat you in Mexico is because of the Irish who helped us," she began.

And there James let out an exclamation because his mother was Irish. Now Ana had regained his attention completely.

"The Irish?"

"Yes, gringo, the Irish. You know about the potato famine in Ireland?"

That he did. He had heard his mother speak of it.

"Well," Ana continued, "it began in 1845 and lasted six years. It killed over a million of the Irish people, and over a million Irish left their country in those years and fled to other nations, mostly to the United States, but also to Canada and Mexico. Of course, your people are not too welcoming when other peoples come to your country to live. They forget that their own grandparents were immigrants. There was much prejudice against the Irish.

28

"But your government needed troops to fight the war against Mexico. So they conscripted young Irish men, and they gave them the worst jobs. The generals didn't believe that the Irish were very smart. They held that they were just belligerent drunks. They thought they would use the Irish for muscle and let them pull the cannons. They worked them hard and put them in the most menial positions. On the march to Texas, your officers mistreated the Irish so badly, beating them, putting them in stockades for the slightest infractions, ridiculing them, that by the time they arrived in Texas, many of the Irish troops deserted and came over to fight on the Mexican side! And, gringo, your generals made a big mistake, because the Irish were very smart, and they had been trained well to fire the cannons with precision. So when they fought against the United States in Monterrey, even though our cannons were so outdated compared to yours, the Mexican artillery fired by the Irish decimated the United States' troops. If Santa Anna had finished that battle like a proper general, the Mexicans would have defeated the United States in that war!"

Now James was stunned. That information just seemed crazy to him, and he would definitely verify it later. However, he was stunned more by Ana herself and the force of her personality. Her animated way of speaking excited him. He felt his strong body be weakened by her beauty and comeliness. He had managed to focus on what she had been telling him, but her dark eyes and curvy body and self-assuredness electrified him.

He had an intention when they began the walk, but his opportunity was fading because Ana kept talking. Knowing that time was short, he glanced up the street to verify that Claudia was still occupied chatting with Señor Moreno at the produce stand while she was buying the juice.

Ana looked towards Claudia too, but something strange caught her eye. She saw the same black Ford Bronco that had driven down her street just a couple of minutes before. It was making a second pass. She had noticed it because of its darkened windows and its slow cruise. It rode past them again.

She pushed her unease to the back of her mind and turned back to James to see what response he would have to what she had told him about the Irish. He was staring at her with a look that she couldn't decipher. Suddenly, he pulled her to him, bent down and kissed her on the lips! She was completely off guard. The kiss lasted just seconds, but it was her first adult one.

She liked it. Looking up at him, she thought that he was beautiful. She felt a rush of joy, and she lit a big smile. Then she came up against him and pulled his neck down for another kiss. She broke away shortly because she worried that Claudia might see. She saw the look of happiness and relief in James' eyes to find that she liked him in a special way. At the produce stand, Claudia was just receiving the three juice bottles and probably hadn't seen them kiss.

Ana began to shake and noticed James trembling a little as well. She thought that neither of them wanted to speak and break the spell of magic surrounding their first kisses.

But then she had a strange feeling of guilt that in their growing excitement for each other the past days, she and James might have excluded Claudia too much. So she called out to her and met her to take the juices. When they resumed the walk, Ana didn't really hear what they were saying to each other. She was in heaven, and because her mind was back on the kisses, and because Claudia actually *had* seen them kiss and was also distracted, neither girl noticed when they walked about a block past Ana's house.

"Oh my God," Ana laughed. "We went too far! We passed my house."

She heard Claudia giggling as she noticed on the sidewalk ahead, about a block away, her neighbor Arturo talking to two young guys as they exited a parked automobile. She saw Arturo occasionally in the neighborhood. Usually he was with these guys. What was catching her attention now, however, was something that seemed ominous: the black Ford Bronco rounded the corner and cruised slowly toward Arturo and his friends. Just as the Bronco got beside the boys, it stopped.

Ana's father had warned her many times not to have anything to do with Arturo or his family. Arturo was the seventeen-year-old son of the boss of the Sinaloa cartel. That man stayed in the mountains and oversaw the production of marijuana crops. He employed the locals there who otherwise wouldn't have jobs. But he had set up his wife and family in Mazatlán in this nice neighborhood where Ana lived. He wanted to give them somewhat a normal life, and, hopefully, some anonymity. He left them protection in the form of bodyguards who accompanied them everywhere. The boys with Arturo were two of them.

"Wait!" Ana commanded James and Claudia. "Something isn't right!"

Precisely at that moment, the large flatbed Army truck that carried soldiers from the Ninth Reserve rounded the corner behind the Bronco. Just as Ana saw young men jumping out of the Bronco with weapons, she heard the first pops of gun fire. The two young men with Arturo reacted by trying to extract something from underneath their shirts, but both suddenly jerked spastically to the ground. Then Ana saw the soldiers on the back of the truck opening fire. The popping noises escalated to a continuous curtain of sound. One of the three guys from the Bronco fell to the sidewalk, but one of the other two grabbed Arturo and began dragging him backwards towards the Bronco. The soldiers fired furiously at the vehicle now, which suddenly lurched forward with a squeal of tires. All this happened before Ana, Claudia, and James could comprehend what was happening and react.

The house that they stood in front of had a two-meter high concrete wall with an opening where a cement walkway led to its front porch. James gathered the two girls in his big arms and hustled them through the opening. He pulled them down against the inside of the wall. A couple of shots hit the opposing wall of the entrance and sent cement chips flying. James shifted his body to shield the girls behind him along the wall. His frame was so huge and they were so small that he formed a perfect shelter for them. Ana and Claudia huddled while Ana kept whispering, "Oh my God! Oh my God!"

The Bronco kept advancing until it screeched to a halt at a point in the street where the three could see it through the opening of the wall. Through the window of the passenger side, a young man was firing an automatic rifle non-stop at the army truck behind them. Someone from the driver's side was doing the same. Ana, Claudia, and James could see the Bronco rocking from the impact of the bullets hitting the rear of the truck. More chips were flying off the cement wall and striking their faces.

James turned and pushed the girls' heads to the grass and told them to lie prone. He then got down and wiggled infantry-style on his elbows to the end of the wall. Summoning courage, he stuck his head out to look behind them down the street to see what was happening.

He quickly ducked back behind the wall. He had seen that one of the men from the truck was lying on the sidewalk, but one still had Arturo by the neck. That man was pulling Arturo towards the Bronco. He had a pistol extended towards the army truck. James realized that the driver in the Bronco was trying to wait long enough for the man to pull Arturo there and get inside. The guy was advancing backward, hugging the wall. He had only been maybe fifteen feet away when James saw him.

"Back! Back!" James commanded the girls in a whisper. "Stay close to the wall!"

The guys in the Bronco had been too busy firing at the soldiers in the truck down the street to notice them.

The girls wiggled backwards, keeping their eyes on James. He scooted a few feet into the yard and grabbed a large decorative rock from a circle of rocks around a palm tree. Then he returned and posted himself next to the wall opening. He posed in a crouching position.

Ana began to understand what he was going to do and said a silent prayer.

Just as the back of the young man dragging Arturo appeared at the opening of the wall, James raised up. With a fierce blow from his right hand, James smashed the rock into ear, temple, and jaw of the man holding Arturo. Ana could hear bones breaking. The power of his blow sent the young man crumpling to the ground. His arm went limp and his pistol glided across the sidewalk. Instantly, James grabbed Arturo's arm and swung him to the ground behind him, snug up against the wall.

A hellish fury of gunfire erupted after that towards the Bronco and the young man sprawled on the sidewalk. After what had to be three or four minutes, there was no more sound from the Bronco. The ensuing silence was so absolute that it seemed there wasn't even a single sound in the entire city. Then the Army truck began slowly advancing. Ana heard the thuds of boots on the sidewalk and weapons clacking as soldiers ran towards the Bronco. They were approaching quickly.

"Manos arriba!" Ana shouted out, in case Arturo couldn't speak English. Then she yelled, "Raise your arms!" All four of them behind the wall put their arms over their heads.

As she heard the soldiers just on the other side of the wall, Ana screamed as loudly as she could:

"No disparen! No disparen! Somos niños! No tenemos armas! (Don't shoot! Don't shoot! We're children! We don't have weapons!)."

Through the opening of the wall, they saw a handful of soldiers split off, with weapons drawn, and run to both sides of the Ford Bronco. They yanked open the doors and the bodies spilled out. One soldier pulled the body of the young man whom James had hit out of view on the sidewalk. Then several soldiers jumped through the wall opening with weapons drawn, pointing in both directions of the wall. That's when they saw the four kids with the raised arms.

The soldiers stood silently a few moments sizing up the situation. They all wore full face masks, and they seemed twice their normal size from the bulk of their uniforms and equipment. They were terrifying in their demeanor. But Ana was looking in their eyes, and she saw that they also were young and afraid. She saw their eyes move quickly from her to Claudia and Arturo and James, finally fixing on James with looks of confusion.

So Ana realized that she needed to clarify for them.

In Spanish she said, "The big guy is James. He's my friend. He's a gringo tourist staying with his parents in a hotel on the beach, and we were just walking with him on my street to show him my home."

One of the soldiers nodded in comprehension. He looked at Arturo and said, "Hola, Arturo. Are you okay?"

"Sí," Arturo answered, apparently not surprised the soldier knew his name. "I'm a little scared."

A couple of masked soldiers chuckled, and they lowered their weapons.

The speaking soldier said to Ana, "Pues, el gringo es un heroe, verdad? (Well, the gringo is a hero, right?)"

"Sí, lo es," Ana answered. Her entire body was trembling from the experience. "He is. He's an incredible hero." She glanced at James and saw that he sat also trembling against the wall. The excitement had caught up with him.

Arturo looked pale. His voice quivered as he asked the soldier, "Are my mother and sisters okay?"

Another of the soldiers had been speaking on a radio, and when he heard Arturo, he answered, "Our soldiers are with them. They went into the house and found them safe. I just confirmed."

Arturo began to shake his head.

"And my guys, my guards?"

The original soldier who spoke said, "I'm afraid they're gone, hermano."

Ana was sitting now with her back against the wall. James and Claudia had taken their places on either side of her. Claudia began sobbing.

Arturo's emotion transformed into anger and resolve. Arturo told the soldier, "We have to leave Mexico. I'm the son of the boss. They'll come for me again and again. They know us now. They'll want to kill my family, my mother, my sisters. They'll want to capture me and torture me and cut me up and send my pieces to my father. This is what they do."

James' eyes grew wide. Ana took his hand and squeezed it desperately tight.

The soldier said nothing. He just looked at Arturo.

Arturo stared back at him a few moments and then said, "You know where my father is, verdad?"

The soldier made a slight nod.

"Well, you tell him our time here is up. He has to get his family out now. Right now!"

Then with a nod Arturo indicated Ana, Claudia, and James. He told the soldier, "Take them through the house there and out the back to the other street, and take them home. I don't want these girls and this brave guy from the United States to see the mess out there. Make sure they get home. Please do this."

"Sí, claro" responded the soldier, and he began to give orders to the other men. There were sirens now in the distance from city police cars coming to the scene and the shouts and loud conversations of neighbors feeling safe to venture from their homes.

But on the ground against the wall, Ana understood that she had just seen her childhood take its last breath. Its death arrived in split moments. In her heart she resolved that joy and love were treasures that she would guard and fiercely protect all her life. She now would

34

bear an adult knowledge of how the world worked. She saw that the world can lose innocence and grace in mere seconds. She thought that God had just given her a glimpse of her future burdens. From that very moment, Ana knew that she would give her life, if she must, to resist the kind of evil that says it's okay to cut up a beautiful young person as a way to murder a father's soul.

Chapter 3 Magic Time

Richmond, Virginia
1957 to 1959

David Wilson James was born all good-hearted in the South in
the last year of the 1940s, loved by his mama, raised by his grandma
while his mama worked, and praised by his daddy every time he
brought home good grades from parochial school, which he always
did. In every photograph he was an honor student in his Catholic
uniform. Always he wore his blue honor-roll ribbon. He was curly-
golden-haired cute and probably for this reason an irresistible target
for all the older boys in his neighborhood to pick a fight. They were
bigger and meaner. Maybe they got the best of David, but he always
fought back hard and took a piece of them with him when he went
down. This, of course, meant that vengeance was due, so the cycle of
fights perpetuated. David endured them from grades three through
eight, the last grade in St. Stephen's school. Then David began going
to public school for the first time. The uniform was gone, the honor-
roll ribbon also, and the fights became pointless.

During school hours at Saint Stephen's, David had protection.
This was because each year the boys joined gangs led by charismatic
kids who were good fighters, and David figured out who looked the
toughest in the beginning of each school year. In retrospect, these
were innocent gangs. Their main purpose was to give the boys
something to do at recess. David joined Duke Schneider's gang in
eighth grade, which was opposed by the perennial gang of Randy
Miles. Not much happened in these gangs except to hang around the
parking lot in front of the school. Occasionally the bad mouthing
between gangs led to fights, which were nothing more than very bad
wrestling resulting in a bloody nose here and there. More frightening
than the boys in the other gang were the nuns who would punish
them severely for fighting by requiring them to write a monotonous
sentence two hundred times. That was hell.

Twenty-five years later David had his first experiences with the cartels in Mexico. He saw the poor kids in barrios run by gangs. The first time he realized that these children were the same age that he was when he was in the gangs of his youth, he felt shocked. How had the world come to this? These kids had guns, and the protection they sought was protection from being killed. The contrast between his childhood and the childhoods of some of the kids in Mexico was so stark, yet for some reason he related to how the Mexican muchachos felt. He couldn't explain it. It was irrational. His boyhood was innocent. When David reflected on his life at sixty-two years old, the covert things he had done when he worked in Mexico and other places in Latin America seemed a distortion of the life he began in a world far away and long gone. Yet somehow when he plodded through these darkest times of his life, an innocent ten-year old boy peered outward with hope from the corner of his heart.

Maybe it's because I continued my childhood adventures, David mused at times.

He grew up in the 1950s, enchanted by the magic and the morality of the early years of television. He learned in black and white. There was good and there was evil. Good triumphed in the end, always. The television programming helped him develop his inner moral compass. He also understood with certainty that by living right, the good guy got the beautiful girl in the end.

David loved the pretty girls and would be forever a hero to win them. He was ten when he first began living adventures as he lay in bed at night, postponing sleep as long as he could. He developed a persona called The Fox. Into the early morning hours David imagined stories about the Fox. Dressed in black-red pants and black shirt, he was a youth of bold character. He wore a mask to protect his identity when he worked. He was the Fox because he was clever and intelligent. He used tricks, subterfuge and smooth talking rather than brute force to defeat his enemies. The stealthy Fox liked to help the downtrodden. He rescued the bullied. He found the stolen, prized possessions taken from people by thieves. He solved mysteries for victimized people desperate to know who caused their misfortune.

The Fox didn't act alone. His equal partner from the very beginning was a beautiful young neighbor in his imaginary world, who fought by his side in all confrontations, who loved him with fierce loyalty, and who frequently saved him at the last minute from a certain end. He eventually came to call this girl Annie, named in honor of the great love who rode into his real life that year. She was a person he could trust completely. To each other they vowed loyalty to death. He and his partner had certain unusual powers, including the ability to fly. They invented weapons that helped them escape danger, such as guns firing electrical charges which would stun and disable opponents. They had time machines to zip them away from whatever impending calamity. Their favorite means of transportation were bicycles that could fly. David and Annie were always smarter than their enemies. One always showed up to help out the other whenever one was on the short side of the fight.

How David met the real-life Annie and her twin brother Roberto began like this:

One afternoon after school, when David was ten, a special package arrived in his mailbox. His godmother, Aunt Jenny, had sent him this gift for his upcoming birthday. When he opened it, he thought it was the most sophisticated and elegant gift he had ever received. It was a tan leather wallet, like a grown-up would have, except that there was a relief of a horse on the front cover. It was a true cowboy wallet. Inside were secret folds and compartments. Best of all, it held a new twenty dollar bill.

David could hardly contain himself! He wanted to show it off, so he grabbed his bicycle and rode to friends' houses. However, everyone was either off with his mom somewhere or had to do homework and couldn't come to the door until it was done.

Behind all the homes on David's side of the street was a long grassy field that was part of a broad tract of land serving as a right-of-way for huge steel power towers that delivered electricity from the Virginia utility company to the surging neighborhoods and commercial development in the west end of Richmond. The right-of-way extended miles, cutting a field that crossed suburban streets and thoroughfares. Directly beyond the field behind the homes on David's street, just past the electrical towers, were "the woods," a stretch of forest bisected by a creek. The woods actually separated the back yards of houses in that subdivision by a respectful distance. The terrain in the woods was hilly and in places formed ravines and small cliffs that dropped off to the creek. The woods were where the neighborhood children spent a lot of their free time. It was a perfect place for cowboy and Indian fights, Civil War skirmishes, army battles, and hideouts for the Fox. Later it was ideal for first kisses and smokes.

So on this particular afternoon, unsuccessful at finding friends, David rode his bike to the field and bumped across it in a diagonal line towards the woods and arrived at its edge almost directly behind Winston Hamrick's house. Winston was the bully of the street. He always had a special itch to torment David. At this moment, David intended to drop his bike and walk down to the creek. He laid his bicycle on its side on the ground and ventured a little ways into the trees. He could see the creek from where he was. Not far was one of the neighborhood gathering spots, a little beach of sand at the base of a precipitous dirt embankment with exposed tree roots reflecting in the running stream. There was no one there, but a few moments later he heard young male voices approaching from deeper in the woods. These included the prematurely deep voice of Winston Hamrick.

Just great, David thought, and he started to walk back towards his bicycle. As soon as he got to the clearing of the field, Winston and his friends, Ernie and Pete, emerged also, at a distance just two backyards from Winston's house and directly in the path to David's home. David considered what to do. If he rode away from them, he would look like he was afraid of them. If he rode towards them, he knew the three would rush his bicycle and pull him off. So David opted simply to stand his ground quietly beside his bicycle. Once the boys saw him, they glared and began stalking in his direction.

As he expected, the three boys approached and posted themselves in a circle around David. Winston spat on the ground and then stepped up close to David's body and demanded, "What are you doing in my yard?"

David nearly laughed, but he checked himself and said, "What are you talking about? This isn't your yard!"

"Yes it is, asshole" Winston replied. "There's my house right there."

"This is a state right-of-way," said David, recalling something his father had told him. "Our properties don't come to this field."

"Listen, smart ass, if I play in this field and say it's my yard, then it's my yard." Winston retorted.

"Okay, okay, fine" said David. "I just stopped here to walk to the creek. No big deal."

Winston punched his right index finger hard into David's chest. "Keep outta my yard, wuss."

David pushed his arm down, and Winston dug his finger back into his chest. David slapped it down again. This time Winston pushed David backwards into Pete, who grabbed his arms and pulled them behind David. David began to twist and turn forcefully and managed to pull Pete to the ground with him. They rolled in a wrestling grip until David felt a kick in his side, then another, and then Winston was sitting on top of him with Pete while Ernie circled around puffing.

"Big men, three against one," protested David. "You can't even do your own fighting, Winston. Get off me!"

"What are you gonna to do about it? You shouldn't have been in my yard," said Winston.

Ernie noticed David's new wallet on the ground beside them.

"Hey, look at that!" Ernie yelled. Seeing it, David tried to twist on his side so he could reach it, but Ernie ran and scooped it up.

"Man, oh man! We got twenty big ones in here!" Ernie shouted to the others.

"Let me see!" Winston replied. He jumped up, and Pete did as well.

David launched himself up and hurled himself at Ernie, but Ernie tossed the wallet over David's head to Winston. David used his momentum to bump Ernie to the ground, and then he spun around and ran towards Winston. But Winston had already done his quick inspection of the wallet, and, holding it in the air, he began running towards his house. David took off after him, but from his place on the ground, Ernie managed to extend an arm to grab David's ankle, crashing David hard into the field. Now Ernie was up and running with Pete directly behind Winston, who had the wallet with the horse relief on the cover. Thrusting himself up with his arms, David shot into top speed in chase. He was the fastest runner in the neighborhood and was quickly gaining ground on the boys, but they managed to get inside Winston's back door and lock it. Through the open screened windows in the back of the house, David could see and hear the boys run, laughing hysterically, as they first locked the front door and then came back to the windows to call out to David.

"Thanks for the nice wallet!" Winston shouted.

"And for the twenty bucks!" added Ernie.

David was furious, and, face pressed against the screens in the windows, shouted his demands for his wallet's return, but the boys responded by ridiculing him. David reconnoitered the outside of the house, looking for some unexpected entry. There were no cars in the driveway, which meant neither of Winston's parents was home yet. He could think of no neighbor in whose court he could make an appeal for justice, and he certainly didn't want to go running home to his mother about it. So after about twenty minutes, fuming, David jogged back to his bicycle and rode home to regroup and think about what his next step would be.

He spent a near-sleepless night, upset and angry. In his bed he tried to formulate a plan, and he made several but rejected all of them. He was too emotional. He wanted Winston not to be in his life. Why should he have to go through this kind of bullying all the time, he wondered. What he needed was a way to put an end to it once and for all. He didn't like to fight, at least not in real life.

The next day was a Wednesday, and he decided that he might take some action after school in the afternoon. Winston came to the bus stop just as the bus was arriving, and he selected a seat far from David. But upon arrival at school, David was able to catch up to him, and he calmly demanded, "I want my wallet back."

"What wallet?" Winston answered and then turned into his classroom.

That afternoon David got off the school bus first and ran home so he could put on his casual clothes quickly. His mother tried to make conversation, but David got out the door, jumped on his bike, and sped down the field behind Winston's house. He rode the bike into the woods, where he hid it behind a tree. He crouched down to peer up the slight slope of the land towards Winston's house. He had a decent hiding place and felt he had stationed himself there so quickly that Winston hadn't noticed him. Winston's father was away at work, and he saw Winston's mom leave with Winston, perhaps to go grocery shopping or on some sort of errand that Winston didn't want to attend.

Once the car was out of view, David walked his bicycle a little ways back into the field and sat down in an area of high brown grass so he could study Winston's house from afar and think. Like all the houses in the neighborhood, it was a brick bungalow with one back door on the house and screened windows. Winston's parents had converted an attic space upstairs into a bedroom for him. On the roof were two dormer windows facing the field, just like on David's house, except that David's house still had an unfinished attic. David liked to go out the upstairs windows onto the roof at night to look at the stars and in the daytime to have a more aerial view of the comings and goings of the neighborhood. The roof was A-shaped and sloped to the top of the first floor. The roof wasn't terribly high, and when David felt daring and wanted to impress the kids in his yard, he would jump to the ground from the base of the roof. Now, when David looked at one of the dormer windows on Winston's house, he thought to himself that his wallet was somewhere in that bedroom beyond the window.

And it was precisely at that moment when time jumped track, and chance punched David's ticket to a destiny that not even he could imagine: It was this moment when David first saw Annie and Roberto.

Some memories of childhood take on mystical qualities through the years. Memory and imagination mix together to make some necessary enhancement of truth, some improvement, some correction to promote a moral lesson, or some interpretation of the event later in life to explain its purpose. So it was with many of David's childhood memories.

But the particular moment when Annie and Roberto came into his life was the instant from which he marked a major change in the course of his destiny. Every time he remembered this, his heart ached with melancholy and longing. It was the first time he ever heard Spanish. The boy and girl in their magnificent outfits sung commands to their horses with such joy that he was enchanted. His memory of this played like a movie: He saw himself rising to stand beside his prone bicycle in the high grass of the field when he heard them. He watched his head turn slowly to find them. He saw his eyes at the instant he first saw Annie and Roberto. His eyes reflected bright, orange flames behind the image of a boy and girl on horses. David later assumed that he had witnessed in his eyes a baptism into a new life that he had never foreseen.

There were five of them living in three creatures: boy-and-horse, girl-and-horse, and dog. Boy-and-horse and girl-and-horse had bodies bent in the center forming letter "Cs". They were a union of human and animal prancing sideways in a circle around the black Labrador. The dog yelped joyously as it chased first one horse then the other. The horses extended their heads low to tease their little friend closer. They stayed just out of range of the hot breath of the dog with each charge that the canine made at them. The noses of the dog and horses almost kissed, but the horses maintained a whiff of distance from the breath of the barking animal. The horses high-stepped in the exhilaration of the circular dance with the dog. They dropped their hooves with a precise snap of the knees as if to show they were aware of their own grace and special place in the world.

The children and animals were a distance of two football fields in the right-of-way of the power lines just beyond a road that bisected the neighborhood. The boy and girl looked small on the animals, but they were very much in command. They orchestrated the dance of the horses and the charge of the dog. David thought they must all hear some inner music that he couldn't. Their playful dance moved slowly in a spiral towards him.

Suddenly the children saw David, first the girl and then the boy. They stopped their play. The boy rode his horse beside the girl, and even the dog turned as they all stared at David. He saw how gorgeous they were, the horses, the dog, and the slightly older children. Even at eighty yards, David discerned the luminosity of the kids' dark eyes. David could see that the boy was very handsome with coal-black hair lying forward and thick to frame his oval face. The lithe girl sat up tall, her hair the same color as the boy's. Colorfully decorated with purple and red flowers, her hair hung in two braids nearly to her waist. David thought that they looked older than he by a year or two. The boy wore black pants, long, brown leather boots, a black shirt with silver metallic designs, and a wide dark belt. He had a round, black hat strapped to his back. His horse was a rich brown with a close, black mane, a full black tail, and legs that were black beneath the knees.

The girl wore brown leather chaps, brown boots, a dark brown shirt buttoned to her neck, and a circular brown hat with a narrow brim and black ribbon that circled and dangled behind the hat. Her horse was silver gray with dull, irregular black splotches running through its coat; but its intriguing, black face formed beautiful symmetry with its black tail. David thought that the girl and her horse were breathtaking.

43

The girl said something to the boy, then both issued commands to their horses. To David's astonishment, they began to gallop straight towards him with the dog at their heels. He felt the ground below his feet vibrate under the muscular power of the horses' legs, and he heard the muted plod of their hooves on the grass. They paused momentarily at the bisecting street, then, with a little bit of that sideways dance, they clacked loudly across the rock and tar surface. Before the snorting noise of their approach, David felt intimidated. He stood his bicycle up. He tried to appear casual, but he wanted a means of escape if it became necessary. As the children approached, he formed a conclusion about them. He had seen photographs in his fourth-grade geography text book of children who looked and dressed like this boy and girl.

They're from Mexico, he realized.

In his geography class he had learned that on earth there were two billion persons, but all the persons of colorful costumes in different nations in his textbook pictures seemed as many light years away from him as the galaxies that he viewed through his telescope. So this reality of two Mexican children on magical horses galloping towards him in his familiar Virginia neighborhood was strange and unsettling. He heard his heart pounding. Yet other than to stand his bicycle against him, David didn't move. He didn't want to appear afraid.

The children pulled their horses to pause a respectful distance away. Then they approached David slowly, but the horses still showed their spirit by craning their necks from side to side in broad sweeps. They snorted the desire to play more. The boy's horse neighed an alarm about David's presence, so the boy calmed him as he got closer to David.

"Buenos, amigo!" the boy said to David. "Hi!"

"Hola!" said the girl.

Up close, David saw the girl's sweet and amused countenance. It took him two seconds to realize that she was the most beautiful girl he had ever seen, even prettier than Marilyn Monroe or Sophia Loren, he thought.

"Um, hi," David answered awkwardly, and then he tried to compose himself. He said, "Man, your horses are so cool! I saw you playing with your dog. I didn't know horses could dance like that! I mean, in the westerns I just see them either hitched to a post or

44

galloping real fast. I never saw horses look like they were having so much fun."

The boy was the first to answer. "You're just not used to being around horses. They're full of happiness and dance if you treat them well. These are Lusitano horses. They're a breed originally from Portugal, and they train these horses to be in bull fights. The horses tease the bulls and keep away from them just like ours were doing with the dog."

"Bull fights!" David exclaimed. "No kidding! I read about those in my geography class, about how they have those in Spain!"

"Yes, and in Mexico," said the girl. She sat up proudly. "Mexico is where we're from, and we brought our horses with us from there."

David's eyes opened wide. "You rode them here?"

The boy and girl looked at each other and burst out laughing. It wasn't a mean laugh but one of enjoyment. David felt the silliness of his mistake.

"No, amigo, we brought them here in a trailer behind our family's truck. When our father moved us here, we told him we wouldn't come unless he let us bring our horses from our ranch in Mexico. He was sent here by his business to start a new cement company in Virginia. He's part owner of the biggest cement company in the world, which started in our city in Mexico and is owned by our family. By the way, I'm Roberto, and this is my sister, Annie."

"Oh! Well, I'm David, glad to meet you! You're brother and sister?"

"We're twins," Annie answered. Then she said, "In our country, your name would be pronounced 'Dah-veedth.'"

"Cool," David answered, "but your name doesn't sound very Mexican. I know other Annies, and we even have a famous cowgirl named Annie Oakley."

Annie giggled. "Well, sí, you're correct," she replied. "My real name is Ana Sofía, but I just thought it would be easier for everyone here to say Annie."

"But how come you speak English?" David wanted to know. "I thought you spoke Spanish in Mexico."

"Sí, we do. Hablamos español. But many people in the city where we live speak English because we do so much business with the United States. In our family everyone speaks English: our parents, our aunts and uncles, and our cousins. They teach it in our schools in Monterrey. We hear it on United States television, and we watch Hollywood movies all the time."

"I didn't know that," David answered. He was marveling at Annie's prettiness so much that he was struggling to focus on what she said. "How old are you?"

"We're twelve," Roberto replied.

"Oh, well, I'll be eleven in November," David said. He wanted to seem more grown up, especially for Annie.

She looked as if she could tell that David was impressed with her and liked it. She asked, "Why were you just sitting here in the field?"

"Oh…" The question snapped David back to reality. He felt the pain again of his humiliation by Winston, and he was unsure whether he wanted to share this yet with his new friends. But he felt the friendliness of Annie and Roberto so he decided to explain.

Keeping a wary eye on the horses, David wondered how he sensibly could begin the story of the unprovoked attack by Winston and his two friends that resulted in the theft of his wallet and no justice later. So he put the story in the context of the history of fights with Winston and his friends. He described the kind of fights that never exceeded a bruise or two on the arm or chest but that always provoked anxiety within him. He talked about his aggravation that he couldn't simply enjoy a day playing with friends without the possibility of having a stupid fight that he never wanted.

While he was talking, Annie dismounted her horse and brought him over to David. She took his hand and put it above the horse's nose and showed David how to pat him. The whole time she looked quietly in David's eyes and listened intently. It was a simple gesture to relax him. Even as he continued talking, he could feel inside that he not only trusted the horse, but he trusted this girl immensely. It was as if she were trying to soothe him more than the horse. It worked.

David went on to tell them about the kids who lived in the neighborhood; about what they liked to play; and about how they pretended their bicycles were horses when they reenacted westerns. He told them about their cap guns and BB guns and water guns, about their army battles that ranged across the yards and vacant dirt lots of the subdivision, and about their bicycle explorations through

46

parts of Richmond that they never told their parents they explored. Finally, David told them about how he liked to pretend he was a hero called the Fox. He had even gone so far as to ask his grandmother to make a custom-made Fox outfit for him. He wore it sometimes in the neighborhood, and he liked to aggravate Winston by never admitting that it was he in the costume, although it was so obvious. He decided to withhold the part of the story about the Fox's girl companion who was a co-adventurer.

When he finished talking about the Fox, Roberto whistled to his horse and shouted a command. The animal reared on its hind legs and neighed loudly. He looked huge! Roberto sat triumphantly atop, as if to show that David had just encountered a real-life hero.

"You're showing off for our new friend, Roberto!" Annie cried out to her brother.

"I'm a Mexican hero!" explained Roberto with a laugh. "I've come to win back all the land that the United States stole from our country!" Roberto patted his horse and calmed him into standing relatively still again.

David didn't understand. "What are you talking about?"

But Annie answered so Roberto couldn't speak. She said, "Mexico used to own all the territory which is now California, Arizona, Texas, and New Mexico. Your country invaded us and sent its army all the way to Mexico City and then took half our country away from us. You don't know this?" She asked it in a polite way.

"No," David replied skeptically. "When did this happen?" He had never seen anything about this on television nor had heard about it in school.

Roberto answered, "It was a few years before your Civil War. Most Americans don't seem to know about it, but we talk about it in Mexico."

David felt uncomfortable. He thought his companions might be mistaken, but he was enchanted by them, especially Annie, and he didn't want to get into anything that would detract from the good feelings he was having.

"I'm sorry, I didn't know that," he said. "Well, anyway, I've been thinking about how to go into Winston's house and find my wallet. I want to go in dressed as the Fox, and I wish I could do something to make him leave me alone. That's what I want."

47

That statement hung in the air a few moments. Annie and Roberto looked at one another in some silent communication. Then Roberto said, "Our uncle always says that every house has its secrets, and if you need to quiet someone, you find in their home what they don't want you to know."

David looked blankly at him, trying to understand the relevance of the statement. "I don't get it," he said.

"Well, amigo, if you want this to stop, you might find the way to do it inside his home."

Annie said, "Roberto, I think our uncle was speaking figuratively, not necessarily meaning inside the actual home."

David just felt confused. He wasn't sure what Roberto meant by his uncle's wisdom, but he felt that perhaps Roberto had a more sophisticated understanding of tactics than he. Judging by the looks that Roberto exchanged with his sister, he might be skilled in complicity.

"And what's the point of going in dressed as the Fox?" asked Annie. "Just to make this kid mad?"

"Well, I don't know exactly," David said. "I feel braver when I'm dressed like him, and in the costume I can say and do things that I can't when I'm just myself. I really have just been thinking about going in his house when no one is home. If I wear the costume, I can always deny it was me if anyone sees me, even if people are sure it's me. I wear it sometimes, and Winston makes fun of me, but I never admit that it's me, and this makes Winston just furious."

"Isn't it against the law to go in someone's house when they don't give permission?" Annie asked.

"Well, yes, I suppose," David replied, "but I can do it when they don't know I'm in there. I want to get my wallet back. I guess there's some risk."

"Which is what makes this so much fun!" Roberto added. At that moment David knew he had friends who were going to help him.

David saw Annie nodding to herself in thought, and then her face produced a beautiful smile.

She said, "David and Roberto, I have an excellent idea!"

The next afternoon, after Winston and his mother had been gone from the house about ten minutes, the Fox pulled loose the screen that covered the dining room window which looked out on the back yard. With the screen removed, he was able easily to pull himself inside the house. Once in the dining room, the Fox heard the large window fan in the parents' bedroom that was drawing a slight breeze through the house. Like all the belt-driven window fans of its day, it made a loud clattering noise that drowned out many other sounds. It was late September and still uncomfortably warm in Virginia. He saw that the Hamricks had left open the side door of the house, but the screen door to it was latched with a hook. People left their houses unlocked often in those times, and the open door might be an indication that Winston's mother didn't expect for them to be gone long.

He would work quickly. He was good at being observant when necessary. He took a minute to survey the rooms of the first floor which only included two small bedrooms, one tiny bathroom, a kitchen, the little dining room, and the living room which had the door to the side porch and the front door. Next to the front door was another door on the opposing wall. It opened to a stairwell ascending to Winston's bedroom.

He had planned that first he would find dresser drawers where Winston might have hidden the wallet. He went upstairs and reviewed the bedroom. He saw the furniture piece he expected. It had four drawers. He rummaged through the clothing in each one but discovered nothing at first.

Then he noticed something that made him smile. He would come back to it.

He went to the closet. This took more time because he had to feel in each pants pocket, and there were a lot of pants hanging. Next, he had to go through the shirt pockets and then through the storage boxes on the floor. It was all neat and tidy due to Winston's mother's obsession with orderliness. He found no wallet.

He went to the bed and looked under, and there wasn't anything there, not even dust balls or an errant shoe. The bedspread covered the pillow, so he felt underneath and struck something hard. He pulled it out. Pay dirt! It was the horse wallet, and, indeed, the twenty dollar bill was still inside!

Now he had something else to do so he took the pillow case off the pillow, replaced the pillow underneath the bedspread, and smoothed the bed. He returned to the drawers and put the articles which he had found so amusing earlier in the pillow case.

Outside, from their hiding place in the woods, the other two were watching the house. They could see the empty driveway beside the house, and they saw also later when the Hamricks' car returned and Winston and his mother got out.

"Okay, trouble now," Annie said. "Just as we hoped!"

In the house the Fox heard Winston's mom scream. She sounded like she was in the dining room. Then he heard the sound of feet running up the stairs. He shut the drawer and ran to the dormer window and pushed it up. There was a screen with two simple prongs to unhook, which he did, and the screen fell out on the roof.

"What the...?" the Fox heard behind him. He turned and saw Winston at the top of the stairs. His face was beet red. Then, recovering from surprise and becoming angry, Winston shouted, "James, I'm going to kill you!" He was using David's last name. Winston dashed towards him.

But the Fox was fast and already on the roof. When Winston was about to follow and pull himself through the window, he stopped dead in his tracks. He saw a brown horse standing beside the house directly below. The Fox was already sitting on the edge of the roof, and then he dropped onto the bare back of the horse, a distance of less than five feet. Winston heard his mother on the back porch. She was screaming, "Get that horse out of here right now!"

"Shit," Winston muttered, and he pulled himself all the way out to the roof. The Fox was bent over the neck of the horse. He was saying something to it. He had a pillow case in his hand.

"You're not fooling me, James! I know that's you! So, big guy, you got a horse! Big deal!" Winston screamed.

Not even acknowledging Winston, the Fox kicked the horse with his heels, and they took off in a gallop towards the field. Winston was spitting mad. But as he watched the Fox ride off at full speed, he saw David riding his bicycle towards him! David had a look of astonishment on his face as the Fox raced by him on the horse. David had come from the direction of the woods, and now he was watching as the Fox rode the horse over the street which intersected the field.

Winston looked first at David, then at the Fox, then at David again.

"James, who is that?" Winston demanded.

"I don't know! He was wearing a mask," David shouted back.

Winston's mother ventured further into the yard now and looked up at Winston on the roof. "Who was that Winston? I know you know who that was."

"I don't, Mom" he said with frustration. "He was up in my room and ran out when I came up here."

David rode his bicycle up to Winston's mother. "I don't know who that was either, Mrs. Hamrick," he said innocently. "Maybe you better check inside to see if he took anything."

David saw a flicker of worry cross her face, and she hurried back into the kitchen.

"Shit," Winston muttered to himself as he thought of something. He turned and slid quickly through the window into his bedroom.

From the edge of the woods, Annie watched and laughed to herself as she saw the Fox, her brother, gallop by. She wanted to stand and let out a whoop of excitement that her plan had executed so smoothly. What secrets had her brother tossed into that pillow case, she wondered as he passed. However, it was important not to be seen, so she picked up her bicycle and headed deeper into the woods to an undeveloped lot that led to the street. She walked her bicycle to the road, mounted it, and started the ride home to her neighborhood next to the Franklin Farm, where people had large lots and horses. She had seen David in triumph in Winston's yard and had seen the confusion on the faces of Winston and his mother, and so her beautiful face displayed a satisfied grin all the way home. She couldn't wait to ask Roberto about the secrets he had found inside Winston's house. Then she wanted to call David.

When she and David finally talked, they told the story over to each other several times. When Roberto got on the line, he said to David, "Well, amigo, I'll have a surprise waiting for you at your bus stop in the morning." No matter how much David begged, Roberto wouldn't reveal the surprise. He did tell David that he had his wallet and his money and that he would return these to him the next afternoon after school.

"What secrets did you find in the house?" David asked, referring to the quote of Roberto's uncle.

"That's part of the surprise," Roberto answered. "For now, let me just say that it's crazy how organized Winston's mother is. She must be just a little loco."

They arranged a meeting place in the woods for the Friday afternoon so David could receive his wallet. Roberto and Annie would ride there on their bikes.

That night when he got into his bed, David said his prayers to the Virgin Mary and to Jesus. He felt especially anxious. He had done something daring, something maybe illegal, and something that, no doubt, would stir up his enemy. He didn't know what would await him at the bus stop in the morning.

Friday morning arrived. David felt nervous and irritable. His mom delayed him a couple of minutes from going to the bus stop by asking him to watch his two-year old brother in the play pen while she got something from the attic. Then a slice of toast with jelly splattered his school uniform pants, and his mother took forever rubbing it out with a wet dishcloth. Every little thing seemed to delay his exit. When at last he could leave, heavy book-bag strapped to his back, he walked in a near run up the hill to the bus stop.

As David approached, he saw the neighborhood kids standing by a tree in the corner yard at the stop. They were jabbering excitedly. As he got closer, he saw that the kids were looking at items stuck to the tree trunk. They were also shouting to a boy sitting on the street at the edge of the lot. The boy's distinctive white hair let David know that it was Winston.

When David got to where everyone was, he had a clear view of the tree. At head level in the trunk was carved "Winston's" in large letters. Below that were nailed four articles of clothing. Below those was carved the signature: "The Fox."

His friend Janet saw him and ran up to him. "Did you do it?" she demanded, laughing. "I know you did it!"

"Did what?" David asked. "I didn't do anything!"

"Yes you did!" she said, and now the others congregated around David as he inspected what was on the tree.

Under Winston's name, slashed in the bark of the tree, were hung four pair of boys' underpants. All had pictures of Roy Rogers, a popular cowboy television star and balladeer. A couple had pictures of Roy with his wife, and the title under the picture said, "Roy Rogers and Dale Evans." In each of them had been stitched a name label by the highly organized mother who lived on the street. She was the only mother who would think it would be necessary to stitch a name in underpants. So there in each one, beside the pictures of Roy Rogers and Dale Evans, was a label bearing the name of Winston Hamrick.

David looked over at Winston, who sat staring at the street. He saw in the back of his white shirt collar the distinctive rectangular lump that was on all his shirts. It was the Winston Hamrick name label sewn on the inside.

Oh my God! was all David could think. The Fox had entered Winston's room and had found the perfect embarrassment to punish him for the humiliation David felt while his wallet was in Winston's possession.

"Hey, Winston," Janet called. "Who should give you your clothes back? David or the Fox?"

David thought of all the times Winston had made fun of him when he was in his Fox costume. Now he understood that the costume didn't hand him this victory. It had come through complicity with the help of an imposter. Cleverness and the assistance of friends could bestow a lot of power, David realized.

You're stuck in a hard place, Winston, David observed. *You really don't want to tell everyone that I did this. It would mean that I've bested you in a clever way. Yet if you say that someone else did it, you're admitting that there's a different Fox who is not me. I bet this last one worries you more. Who was the bold Fox who came to your house on a horse to retrieve what you stole? Worse yet for you, this Fox is a friend of your enemy!*

The success of the scheme to retrieve the wallet warmed David's heart like an answered prayer. Winston's response to Janet's question was silence. The Fox was a hero not to be challenged.

Winston continued being quiet after that, and he slowly faded from view and memory. He switched to public school in the seventh grade. He made friends somewhere outside of their neighborhood and was seldom seen. By the time that David entered high school, the Hamricks had moved to another city, and David never heard anything about Winston again. Still, David never forgot this early experience with meanness. He remembered how exhausting it was to live with it daily and how trying to deal with the meanness provoked too much anxiety.

One day after he had become aware of the evil and injustice that exist in the world, David had a revelation: He should be proud of himself. What he had done those years of his childhood when he felt so anxious was to stand up to injustice. Why should he let himself feel so sad about those memories? As he grew older he saw that good people often didn't want to confront evil. They wanted to pretend that it didn't exist or that it could be transformed by kindness easily. Whole nations did this. In the face of evil they isolated or looked the other way.

David matured into a life of complicity, double identities, and physical prowess. He learned to jump and to fly and to ride horses. He wore masks of aliases, and he deceived entire countries at times. Terrible things happened to him, and he spent thirty years in darkness, but always innocence lay in a corner of his heart. His youthful spirit gave him the energy to do what he did in life, which was to help the victims of meanness. He was old before he pieced together all the adventures of his life into coherent meaning. Ana was the one who set his life's design in front of him with clarity.

"You think I turned you into the Fox in Mexico," Ana told him once, "but you've been the Fox all your life. You use your hands and feet as weapons instead of a gun. You use your cleverness in strategic ways. You're quick at thinking ahead. What distinguishes you from many other intelligent men, however, is that you move through the world with the vulnerability of an exposed and caring heart."

She thought that way because she loved him, David believed, but he did hear the truth in her words. There were so many blessings in his life and so much irony. All his blessings flowed from the strong women who loved him: his mom, Annie Ortiz, Julie (his wife of thirty years), and Ana Valdez. The irony derived from the women who were bookends to his life. Annie was the Mexican named Ana Sofía in his youth. Ana was the Mexican named Ana Sofía now in his older years.

When he was a kid he had invented a girl to share adventures with him. He felt her presence his entire life.

Chapter 4 The Darkness of the Past

Monterrey, México
Monday

If he thought about his age, the number seemed big: sixty-two. Other than that, the only reminder David had of aging was when he saw his face in the mirror. He definitely had a mature face, but a lifetime of gymnastics, martial arts, Krav Maga, yoga, jumping, running, stunts, and weight machine work had given him the physically fit body of a much younger man. He still had muscles.

As a kid he dreamed of flying, and so he learned to fly somewhat like a flying squirrel does, by jumping. He used whatever aid might help him, be it ropes, cords, tree branches, monkey bars, or trampolines. He especially loved taking his bicycle airborne. He took any dirt hill, embankment, or ditch as an opportunity to soar and become one with his bike. In high school he led his team to several state titles in gymnastics. He shone in vault, high bar, and trampoline events. He was in the air so much that his friends in high school and college just came to think of him as a flyer. Sometimes with pure joy he shouted to them, "Let's fly!" Then he might go airborne to a different level stair landing, or maybe he just did a backward flip in the air. These were things he did all his life in such a natural way that it never seemed immature to anyone who knew him. He could fly at fifty, at sixty, and his friends the same age just accepted it through the years as nothing unusual for David. He was a flyer.

David couldn't believe it when Ana told him that she had decided to begin jumping. She was pushing forty, for heaven's sake, and she smoked. She told him she wanted to do the Z training. She surprised and intrigued him constantly. David felt certain that she would have cardiac arrest within her first week. The only physical exercise she did of which he was aware was dancing. Ana danced all the time including long before she met David, but he had no idea the juice she put into her salsas and lambadas until they began dancing together and he experienced her amazing endurance. She could dance at killer, cardiopulmonary levels for hours. In fact, as the evenings of dance wore on, Ana laughed about dancing until dawn, but David would finally slump in a chair and watch her continue with some unsuspecting partner who had sauntered to the dance floor.

He might have picked up another clue about Ana's physical condition if he had thought about their times making love. Her sweet, Latina body curved and hugged his form and received his thrusts with equal passion. She could tease, circle, and sway in another kind of marathon dance that would send them on multiple tours of the four corners of their bed. Sometimes they spilled onto the floor and laughed until their sides hurt. When that was over, dripping with sweat, they propped their backs against the side of the bed and leaned against each other until one could help the other stand. When they had sex like this, Ana didn't feel the need to smoke for hours. She complained to David that he made her forget her addiction so that she never enjoyed the pleasures of smoking after sex. David told her that he didn't feel the need to move for hours.

He went to watch her a couple of times when she was in the training camp on the ranch owned by Eduardo Ortiz. It was a hilly retreat where the Zs had a boot camp for the building of bodies and the molding of heroes. This particular one, a little northwest of Monterrey, looked like a Hollywood set with false buildings several stories high, each with stairs. There were automobiles and truck bodies to run across, steel towers for bungee jumping, trampolines, rope structures for scaling, trees for climbing, and fitness trails coursing through thick forest. In the forest, two steel cables were strung one over the other across a wide stream. One cable was to walk on, and the other, overhead, was for holding. There were two high places where rickety wooden foot bridges strung by ropes were the only passages across ravines.

David watched Ana do bungee jumping, which really was preparation for developing the courage to jump off buildings. On another occasion he watched her practice bouncing straight up and down on the trampoline. Her objective was to propel herself in a controlled fashion as high as possible and then to land with precision on the same spot each time she had a bounce. On a third occasion, David saw Ana do this type of trampoline jumping after she had improved to an advanced level. He noted that after weeks of training, Ana had toned leg muscles, and her knees flexed and tolerated the landings quite well.

But Ana impressed David the most in the urban environment training. This entailed jumping from one building roof to another; dropping from stair steps to stair landings; running across the tops of cars, buses, and trucks; and using ropes to scale buildings. These activities mirrored a sport called "free running" in the cities, and it was a young person's sport. Seeing Ana doing this at forty years old just made him all the more desperate for her. He saw that she brought heart to everything she did. He did these same exercises, but he had done them a lifetime.

Then came this present moment when Ana stepped off the sixth-floor roof of the office building in Monterrey and grabbed a rope to escape a man and two women who came to fire guns at them. Because he had seen her train, David made an immediate assessment that Ana knew what she was doing and would make it quickly to the ground. Therefore, he made his own decision to leap through the gunfire and rush the three who had come to assassinate them. He couldn't risk that Ana might still be vulnerable on a rope with a shooter training on her from above.

This was another of those time-standing-still moments. He had thrown the radio and had hit the man's head. He took a running leap, pulling his legs up to head height. As he flew through the air, he heard his thoughts: *Put right side parallel to the ground. Push chest forward to draw the enemy's attention and aim.* David knew it would be a natural, instinctive thing for the man to shoot at the largest area of the object flying towards him. His launch had gone perfectly. He had estimated the distance and thrust needed with precision, but the surprise was the powerful backward push on him from the rain of bullets that riveted the body armor. He hadn't factored that in.

I'm getting too much resistance from the bullets. I'm going down. He'll shoot me on the ground, David thought.

He landed with a painful thud on the roof. His right shoulder and arm took hard blows. His chest hurt like hell, and he expected that the shooter would soon put an end to the pain he was feeling. But suddenly he saw the man and then the two women drop to the concrete in front of him after their heads jerked from bullets that had been fired from behind him.

Someone is shooting them from the CNN Mexico location behind me! He had a flash of memory about Ana requesting protection from the Army. *She took some things into her own hands,* David guessed. *Someone shooting from that other building must be Mexican Army.*

What he saw was that the man shooting at him went backward forcefully against the open door from which the women had emerged. He bounced and fell forward, his face landing in front of David's. Then David quickly forgot his pain as he had the shock of his life. El Gato had come, and David knew who he was! He recognized him after nearly forty years!

The immediate giveaway was the unique, bluish, star-shaped birthmark on his left forehead just at the hairline! For many years David had been searching for this man at Eduardo's request, but, unlike Eduardo, David had never expected that he would still be alive. His hair was still as jet black as when David knew him as a young man. His body looked still in good shape. Despite the blood running from the man's forehead down his face, David recognized the man. It was Roberto! Roberto looked weathered as if he had spent much life outdoors, but the resemblance of this man to the friend of David's youth was impossible to deny.

Another pain shot through his chest suddenly, stronger than before. David gasped. It felt like every rib was snapping, and he could hardly suck in a breath. *It's from the bullets hitting the vest,* he thought, *or possibly because I've just seen Roberto take a bullet to the top of his head and fall beside me, and I'm in some kind of physical shock.*

Now he felt too hot. Everything around him darkened. He struggled to maintain consciousness in order to observe as much as he could. The darkness intensified until there was nothing but a gaseous circle of black approaching, and he became sucked into it. When he did, the pain stopped. He felt like he was swirling in an atmospheric whirlpool, and then Roberto swept in with him. They were opposite each other, going around and around. He had a troubling thought: *Maybe I'm traveling to eternity with El Gato! But if I'm here in the black cyclone with this author of a thousand deaths, then my own redemption must be unlikely! Why am I here with him?*

58

He heard weird chants in his head, almost as if they were being sung:

We all go round and round,
round in the circles of life.
We start at the beginning
and end where we start.
We understand life
through circles of thought.

They were whirling at a nauseating pace.

Circles of life must be completed. I'm back with Roberto again. Maybe redemption is not possible when forgiveness doesn't exist.

David stared into Roberto's eyes. The mischievous light he remembered in the eyes of the twelve-year-old boy on horseback fifty years earlier had extinguished. Now Roberto, the lieutenant in the Cartel of Sinaloa, glowered back at him with eyes cold and stone black.

This made him think: *Roberto is the reason why this is taking place! I'm swirling in his storm! Has he come to avenge ancient and present scores? Does he want me to know it's he who came to kill me?*

David struggled to understand what was happening in his body because he didn't want to die. He wasn't breathing, but he could hear. He remembered that it was said that after death the senses leave the body at different times, and the last sense to go would be hearing. He felt nothing in his body, but he felt sensations and emotions in his mind. Something was off about time, like it was out of sequence. He heard the helicopter landing on the roof, but then later he heard the soldier summoning the helicopter on his radio. He heard boots running, and later he felt people jerking him; then he heard boots running again. What language were they speaking? He could understand them, but the language came to him sometimes in English and sometimes in Spanish.

Finally, he spun into the center of the whirlpool where blackness totally consumed him. All the spinning stopped, and for an instant there was total calm and quiet. Then the crazy thing happened: David could see through his closed eyelids! The pain was gone; he couldn't move; he couldn't breathe; but he could see and hear. He was on the ground facing the door on the roof which opened to the stairwell of the building. He could see Roberto lying there bleeding from the head, and the bodies of the two young ladies lay just beyond. Even though he could hear the soldiers on the roof and the approaching helicopter, now he saw none of that. His field of view only encompassed the bodies before him and the door to the roof just beyond. Then, once the door to the roof began to open, even the shouts of the soldiers, the sound of their scuffing boots, and the groan of the helicopter disappeared.

Yes, he observed, *the door is opening. This is like the sensation I have when I know I'm dreaming, and I know what will happen next in the dream. I know who will come out the door!*

And she did.

It was her, the same girl he had first created when he was around six or seven years old to be his partner in evening adventures. He summoned her every night to keep from falling asleep because he hated going to school. Postponing the morning gave him a long reprieve. He could count on her to come. When he first began to envision her, she looked different on different nights. Yet David felt her inside him, always the same person, always his true companion. He felt comforted the minute he saw her. She was his true partner in all senses, his social equal, his blood sister, his loyal friend to the death. So how fitting that now she would visit him at the time of his dying!

First El Gato, and now this! Does death unravel all mysteries, he wondered?

After he had met Annie when he was ten, he liked to imagine that this girl he had nightly adventures with looked like Annie. This time when she came through the door on the roof, she was dressed in a brown robe with a sash of rope around the waist and a hood over her head. He couldn't see her face well at first, but then she pulled the hood back and shook free her long hair. She gave him the gorgeous smile that he remembered so well. She looked like Annie did when she was twelve years old! Her eyes glistened. She was obviously happy to see him. She sidestepped the other bodies and came to David, knelt beside him, and kissed him on the cheek.

David wanted to speak to her, but he couldn't, so she said, "All you have to do is think. I can hear you."

So he thought a big smile for her. He wanted to tell her about Roberto. He looked over at him so she would follow his gaze.

"I feel all your emotions," she said to David. He saw this, because as soon as he looked at Roberto, she suddenly clutched her chest, and tears came to her eyes. Then she reached and caressed David's cheek with the back of her hand as if to remove the tears he would have had.

She's soothing me, he thought. *She knows the betrayal I feel when I look at Roberto.*

"I've come to show you things, "she told him. "For you to understand, you have to trust me and let me be the one to lead the journey. This time I'm real, and I'm the one giving you life. Do you comprehend? This time you're in my mind and I'm dreaming you. We're going to take a trip back fifty years and look at things you saw but didn't see. This has to do with Annie and Roberto."

This surprised him a little. He thought, *She looks like Annie, but she's not Annie. I imagine her, right?*

She nodded because she heard him. Then she continued, "Annie and Roberto saved you from an ordinary life, but you were so charmed by the magic of what they could do that you didn't see important things. These are things that have festered deep inside you since then. They're the source of the dark feelings you've had for years. The feelings have distracted you. Instead of being in control, you've been like a ball inside a pinball machine, bouncing in different directions when it hits obstacles and energized by flippers operated by people who love to play games. Now you're in Mexico, crazy in love with Ana! How did you get here, David? Why are you here? Do you know your trajectory?"

"I don't have a clue!" he answered. Now he felt frustrated and nervous. "I don't know what's happening, whether I'm dying or already dead. I don't know what happened to Ana. She climbed down from the roof. I don't know who shot this frigging monster of a person who came to kill me, as he has killed hundreds or thousands of people. He turns out to be my childhood friend, Roberto! Now you're here, and I'm wondering if you're really just a part of me and I'm talking to myself! You ask me if I know my trajectory? Right now I don't understand anything!"

"Then let's begin," she answered, noting his frustration. He watched as she rose and untied the sash to her robe. She began to

61

transform herself, and suddenly she assumed the fleshy form of the twenty-two-year-old woman who had conquered his heart and kept it until she died. It was Annie, looking just as she did the last time he saw her. The shapeless monk's robe disintegrated, and Annie's comely, adult body poured into tight black jeans. She was the young Mexican woman he had loved desperately. He recalled those last moments when he stared at her and admired how she was dressed: her jeans, her three-inch black heels, her white blouse that showed the tops of her tanned, round breasts. Those promised the sweetness of seduction. He remembered the lilac smell of her hair which fell straight and long to her waist.

Annie looked exactly like that standing beside the Corvette in the crisp light of the sun forty years earlier. She was laughing then, teasing him because she was going to drive his car for the first time but saying that she would show him how to really drive. The car had a gear shift. It was 1970, but the car was a first generation Corvette, a 1961 convertible. The top was down, there came a breeze from a passing eighteen wheeler, her hair blew in front of her face, and an instant later…

David flushed the thought away immediately. He focused on the lovely girl in front of him now.

"Oh God, Annie! " David exclaimed, feeling desperate because of the confusion of emotions in his heart. He had never expected to see her again, of course, yet there she was in front of him. This was some kind of a miracle, and he wanted her to please, please explain to him what was happening.

Annie turned her eyes to El Gato. She shook her head sadly. "Roberto. Mi hermano, la otra mitad de mi alma. (My brother, the other half of my soul.) He doesn't look the way I expected."

"Annie, this is not the Roberto I knew," David said to her. "And he certainly isn't the other half of you! This man is the anti-Christ. What happened to him? How did he change so much? Do you know? Please tell me!"

When she looked back at him, David's mind sped through hundreds of memories of victims he had seen through the years in Mexico, Colombia, and parts of Texas. He wanted to show Annie what he had seen. The victims were dead from cartel violence. They weren't only young people killed by rival cartels. Many were older people. Some were innocents, just ordinary people, casualties of flying bullets, fire bombs, grenades, car bombs, and burnings. They included lawyers, judges, policemen, soldiers, politicians, mayors, governors, school teachers, journalists, artists, and musicians. They were high school kids buying marijuana from someone a rival drug gang didn't like.

He saw all the bodies, their blood forming streams along the sidewalk curbs. He remembered the bodies left in car trunks or shot to pieces at the steering wheel. Some were found in vacant lots or trash deposits. David remembered going to remote desert areas and finding "fosas" where hundreds of bodies were boiled in acid or burned so that there would be no trace of their former lives. Everywhere David went in his dark years, he touched blood, bone, cartilage, connective tissue, parts of brains, and vital organs.

He remembered most vividly the burned bodies, partially cremated. Each was an ashy reminder of a person still in the clothes that he was wearing when he had been a person alive; a person with parents, spouses, brothers and sisters, friends, and cousins; a person with a lifetime of Christmas celebrations, music, parties, little successes and daily frustrations, good choices, and bad ones, like the ones that got him killed.

The victims who bothered him the most were "las personas desaparecidas (the disappeared persons)." These were tens of thousands of people carried off. There never was found a trace of them again. Sometimes the kidnappings were bold, in broad daylight, even in places of business. That had happened to David's friend, Israel, who had been kidnapped right off the car lot where he worked as a Volvo sales person by three armed young men who had pushed him into their SUV and had driven off into the busy traffic of Monterrey.

Where was the American anti-kidnapping consultant who was whisked away from a restaurant when he was the speaker at an anti-kidnapping conference with city officials in Saltillo? Where was the mother pulled from her minivan in front of a convenience store while her two little boys screamed from their car seats? Where were the young parents getting into their car in their garage one morning as they prepared to go to work while the sitter was already in the home with the children?

No one knew where they were. Daily life in the world that David roamed was punctuated by people with guns who appeared out of nowhere, kidnapped, murdered, disappeared, and never got caught.

What role had Roberto played in all this? How much of the blood was on his hands? The people were sick of it: the blood, the lack of justice, the complete absence of protection from their police and the city, state, and federal governments. They had poured into the streets to take matters into their own hands, to stop the bloodshed, to put an end to impunity, and to insist on a world civilized and just.

Knowing now who Roberto was and what he had done made him sick. David's heart wept a sob of grief that caught in his throat.

"Do you know all this, Annie? How did this happen? How did Roberto become a monster who was behind some of these things?"

"He was going crazy even before I died," Annie answered him. She was holding her throat. "Watch!" she commanded. "You'll remember what I show you, but you'll have to face what you don't want to remember!"

It felt like a dream again, like watching a video of his youth from fifty years earlier. He saw the three of them, beginning when they met in the field and first became friends and planned the Fox adventure to avenge the theft of David's wallet.

They looked so innocent in the early years. Annie and Roberto were almost two years older than David, and they went to a private school, but they were just one grade ahead of him. He could see them in their school, almost always together, Roberto trailing the halls behind his sister. They were dark, beautiful children in a sea of fair-skinned, shiny-eyed scholars bustling to their classes. Mexicans in Virginia were rare in those years. Though Annie and Roberto spoke English well, they had moved to the South just a century after the abolition of slavery and still in the times of segregation. Some English there couldn't be understood by foreigners.

There was a lot of old tobacco money in Richmond. In those years the city was conservative and Protestant. It was run by a network of old boys: bankers, lawyers and investment advisors, some of whom still spoke of the South as if there still were a chance it would rise again to secede from the Union to uphold states' rights.

After all, Richmond had been the capitol of the Confederacy. The statues and shrines to Confederate leaders and the museums commemorating the nation's Civil War and the southern men and women who had fought and died for the South were all over the city. So, although clever and sophisticated for their young ages, Annie and Roberto very much needed a friend like David to help them learn the unwritten codes of conduct in a place where social relationships were defined by race, creed, sex, and money; and cues of behavior were delivered through elegant sentences, long slow smiles, and arched eyebrows.

David knew the geography of the city because he rode his bicycle through all its quarters. Annie and Roberto put him on a horse and taught him to ride, but David led them on bicycle adventures all over the city. The twins' father, Eduardo, traveled internationally more and more in those years. He also had important political connections in Mexico demanding his presence from time to time. He wanted his wife and children to remain in one place, Richmond, so the twins might have stability, continuity, and international experience during their most formative years. So in those early years, although he was younger, David led the twins in the Saturday morning explorations of the University of Richmond campus, the boulders in the James River where they sunned, the downtown department stores and movie theaters, the city's most famous ice cream parlor, and the new suburban shopping centers.

David was enjoying watching these years that Annie was making him recall. He felt physically present in each memory. It seemed that he lived years in a matter of minutes. Annie had put him as an observer looking at his life from a space outside of time.

He saw himself back in his neighborhood woods with Roberto and Annie. He was stealing glances at Roberto. It was the first time that he had begun to notice how his friends' bodies were changing quickly as they aged ahead of him. Roberto was swinging back and forth on a rope over the creek. His arm muscles formed a range of mountains as he clung to the rope. David admired Roberto's body. Roberto was strong and gracefully athletic, a natural gymnast, and he had Mexican swagger. David wanted to be built like Roberto: broad shouldered and muscular, not skinny, as he was. Roberto was like an older brother in those early years of their friendship, and David wanted to be like him.

He saw Annie's body change far beyond what he could imagine. From a pretty Mexican girl, she suddenly matured into a young woman with a breathtaking figure. David remembered in school studying myths of women so sumptuous that grown men of all nations would go to combat to win them. That's what he came to think of Annie. When he met her she already showed the promise of what she was to become, but the change in Annie came swiftly, leaving David feeling far behind, still a boy in the woods. Yet Annie was unimpressed by her beauty. She was confident, not because she was exquisitely gorgeous, but because she trusted her gifts of intelligence and acuity. She knew what she wanted in life from the earliest years of high school. She would make her mark in the world in international law and trade, and, especially, she would work to open up the world markets to Mexico. She talked about this when she was only fourteen.

David checked his mood: *Yes, I see my giddiness around them.*

As he remembered more, David observed how Roberto and Annie had influenced him. They taught him conversational Spanish, which he later took in high school, and horseback riding. Annie in particular shaped his dreams. From the first day of meeting her, he kept inside the secret of wanting to be her boyfriend and wanting to seem older to her. Annie's sweet sophistication and openness to adventure swept him away. None of the girls he met in the schools which he attended had a prayer of attracting him like Annie. He saw that she loved him like a little brother because she was so much more adult in her body and personality than he. She received the attention of older boys, boys who seemed like men to David. But he saw plainly how fortunate he had felt to have the attention and friendship of this Mexican brother and sister, and how much their friendship had enriched his life.

But just when David was beginning to relax about recalling his childhood in this extraordinary way, something changed. Annie reached over to him and placed a hand on his head. It felt as if she were peeling off images in his mind to reveal layers below surface memories. *What's Annie doing to me now?* He wondered. He felt raw in his skin.

Suddenly they were older, and when David looked at Roberto he saw something new: Roberto hardly ever took his eyes off his sister. He responded to her every movement, every statement, every glance, with a kind of dance that seemed to...*attend* her. Roberto watched his sister's eyes to anticipate what she might say or do next. When she suggested something be done, he jumped to it. He was solicitous, seeking her approval. David looked at Annie. Was she oblivious to Roberto's behavior or simply ignoring it? Clearly, she did enjoy being the one to lead. That David could see.

There was something else though, something creepy. Roberto controlled access to Annie. Even when they were in groups of people, Roberto stationed himself within Annie's space and didn't permit people to be physically close, especially boys, but even some girls. He did this in very subtle and smooth ways. David saw this now. He was witnessing countless times when the three of them were around groups of kids. Roberto was a master of access to his sister. With respect to David, he didn't impose himself physically as much. David guessed that this was because he was no competitor for Annie's attentions like the older boys.

That came later.

For her part, Annie seemed fine around Roberto as long as she decided what to do. David wondered now: *Was this a manipulation by Roberto, to allow his sister to feel in control while he controlled what was important to him?* On occasions David noticed that Annie rebelled and insisted on being with someone whom Roberto was trying to block. When this happened, it was obvious from her face that she was very annoyed with Roberto's intrusions. She punished him by slipping away on her own with whomever she wanted.

What about me and Roberto? When did things change? David wondered. He focused and began to review the relationship that he and Roberto had through the years.

He recalled a time when he was around twelve years old that he walked to Roberto's house to visit him. He hadn't thought about this incident in many years, and now he began to relive it. When no one answered the door of Roberto's home, David walked to the stables on the property behind the house. There he found Roberto grooming his horse. The night before, David had seen on a television western a cowboy and an Indian cut their hands and mix their blood in order to become blood brothers. Explaining this to Roberto, David took his hand and made a cut in Roberto's index finger with his pocket knife. Then he did the same with his own and smeared their blood together.

Roberto told him that he was honored by this ritual, and that David also could be very proud because now he had Mexican blood. David felt his heart beat fast because he idolized Roberto, and Roberto was accepting him as a brother! From that time forward,

Roberto was attentive to David in a way similar to how he was with Annie. Considering that the boys didn't attend the same school and had some exclusive friends and activities, it was surprising how much time the two spent together through the middle and high school years.

Roberto was the one who introduced David to gymnastics and encouraged him to join the team in high school. Roberto liked the outdoors. He liked challenging his body. On their weekend bicycle rides through the city, Roberto pushed David for the lead as both pumped their legs to keep up with the city traffic. In the woods, Roberto challenged David to race through the rooted trails. He dared him to jump his bike over the creeks with him to see who made the farthest mark on the other side.

Sometimes others were with them, including Annie, who held her own in these contests, but David and Roberto were usually the ones to beat. David did have other friends from his own school, the closest being one who had started with him in kindergarten, but he saw that Roberto was always the big brother to him, always the one paying special attention, always spurring him to try something new.

But… as they got older, David began to notice, Roberto's suggestions about their activities more and more did not include Annie.

And he understood why: *It was because Roberto couldn't tolerate my crush on his sister.*

It was clear. Roberto watched their eyes: David, with his silly puppy eyes every time he looked at Annie; Annie, with eyes amused and tolerant in return; Roberto, with eyes wary and….*jealous? Yes, jealous, assessing, and calculating.*

David had such a crush on Annie and was so focused on getting her to like him that he had never noticed back then the coldness in Roberto's handsome, black eyes whenever David, or any other guy, had Annie's attention for a few minutes. David had been blind to the wide-open eyes of Roberto.

Now that David had this insight, every memory confirmed it. Roberto tried to possess them. In this he was more successful with David than with Annie. David now realized that he had mistaken Roberto's possessiveness as fond attachment from the friend whom he idolized. What Roberto felt about David might have been friendship at first, but later the relationship was about control.

However, Roberto was far less successful in manipulating Annie. David saw clearly that as the years passed, Annie's impatience with her brother's impositions grew. But their relationship was complex. They had a lot of private communication in play, much of it nonverbal. As they got older, the twins developed an unacknowledged conflict of power. They had secrets that were only theirs. Sometimes Annie's eyes issued warnings to her brother: *Back off, I know what you're doing.* When the tension between them became obvious to others, Annie vacated the stage.

David remembered a car ride with the twins when he was fifteen and they had their drivers' licenses. They had obtained theirs a little more than a year before David got his. Eduardo bought them a new red Mustang convertible to share. At first, the three of them were in it often together, with David cramped in the small back seat. Later, one twin or the other used the car. Annie especially relished its availability as her rare opportunity to do anything not involving Roberto. David also saw that Roberto liked to take David in the car when he wanted to get him away from his sister.

In this particular memory, David was in the back seat of the Mustang with Myra, a girl his age from the neighborhood. It was one Friday night soon after the twins had first received the car. The four of them went to Bill's Barbecue, where everyone in Richmond hung out before and after going to movies. David noted the tense silence in the front seat on the way there. When they arrived, Annie asked David and Myra to get the order for all of them while she went to the bathroom. Immediately, Roberto said that he needed to go as well. David and Myra got the order. As he and Myra carried the meals from the counter to a booth, he saw Roberto and Annie in the hallway leading to the restrooms. They obviously were arguing. Annie's face was flushed. She stopped speaking when she saw David, and she put a distracted smile on her face and followed David and Myra to the booth. Roberto trailed behind. When they all sat down, Annie took the seat next to David, which she never did. She always sat beside her brother. She was making a statement to Roberto. *Perhaps,* David thought, *she wanted to be able to look directly at Roberto and continue their argument silently with her eyes.* This left Roberto and Myra opposite them. The twins maintained a stone-cold silence, eating, while David and Maya tried to keep conversation going; but their effort fell flat in the tension.

David had forgotten this incident, but its recall unburied a frightening revelation about Roberto and Annie, a memory he had stuffed all the years since.

He had heard snatches of the argument between Annie and Roberto when he had passed by them on the way to the booth with their food. He didn't comprehend the argument at the time, or perhaps he hadn't wanted to look too deeply into its implications. But suddenly Annie's words sounded in his ears in fragments, like an AM radio station at night, fading in and out through static. There was no mistaking the fury in Annie's voice, however:

"If you ever touch… if you ever so much as put a foot in my bedroom again at night… I'm going back to Mexico… I'm telling our father everything, everything you've done, everything you've said. I don't care what the consequences are. Do you understand me?"

David stopped cold. He shut down the memories. He made the screen go blank. If he could have at that moment, he would have sat upright on the roof. He felt a knot of anxiety in his stomach. He wanted to vomit.

Where is she? Damn it, where is Annie?

He cleared his mind of Annie's projections so that he could return to the present and see what field of view he now had on the roof. He sought Annie and discovered that she was still there, kneeling beside him.

He saw in her face that she was embarrassed. She returned his gaze, and then, with the saddest expression, she directed her eyes to Roberto. When she did this, David felt Annie's heart inside him. Suddenly David understood what Annie was going through back in those days. Through Annie's heart he discovered that, in spite of everything that had occurred between her and Roberto, she wanted to believe that her brother had an original kernel of goodness, but that later mental illness brought on the evil that he displayed first to her, and then to the world. Because of her belief in Roberto's young innocence, she had a tolerance for Roberto which David would never be able to feel from that time forward. He was too dangerous.

But now David could feel all the burdens Annie carried in her short life because of her brother. She had loved him but was horrified by him. She had condemned him but wanted to forgive him. She had anguished that others would find out about his secret perversions. She had poured exhausting energy into presenting a

70

normal face to the world. She had stockpiled hope that things would change, but her disenchantment as Roberto worsened through the years nearly killed her. Then after she did die, she interceded through prayer for her brother's victims.

What? I don't understand that last one, Annie, David thought.

"You can't understand this until you confront what you don't want to confront, David. You know what I'm talking about. I insist that do this. Unless you do it, you have no future. You'll die here on this tarmac. You have to remember it and look at it. After you're done, I'll ask you a simple question. Your answer to the question is what will determine if you live or die."

David understood perfectly well what she wanted him to do.

Please, Annie, this can't possibly help. What's the point? Don't make me do this!

But Annie persisted, "You're going to have to finish what you started, David. You don't get an easy way out. This is why I'm here. This is why I came. This is why you brought me here, really. Deep down you understand that you have to remember, and you have to settle things with my brother and with yourself. What started with us as children now must be settled by you. We're all the same stardust, David. There's no single present life that's not entwined with the past and future lives of all others. All the living hearts that ever were, and ever will be, beat to the rhythm of one life. Roberto and I came from Mexico and entered your world. You took us in your heart. Everything that has happened has led to this moment on this roof. Now you lie here beside my brother, a destiny together that began fifty years ago. Like you, David, he's dying. What you do now decides for both of you."

He was horrified. *More of the completion of the circle of life,* he thought bitterly. *She wants me to remember the accident.*

He still didn't want to remember the moment Annie died. He had never wanted to remember. It was horrible. Since that day, he had blocked it from his mind, isolated it, locked it in a steel compartment of his subconscious, and discarded the key. Every time in the past when he even got close to the memory, the unbearable feelings of guilt and despair returned with a vengeance. He was a wreck of a soul when she died. He knew that the accident had broken Roberto also.

It's true, David thought. *I destroyed two souls. No, three, counting my own.*

He didn't see Roberto much after Annie died. He hadn't wanted to face him. Roberto reminded him of Annie. It was too painful. In his heart, David realized that Roberto blamed him, but he never expected his friend might want to kill him.

The big difference between me and Roberto, David observed, *is that somehow I redeemed my soul, but Roberto never did.*

He was going to have to do it.

Chapter 5: The Dream of Being Alive

Monterrey, México
Monday

David considered everything he had just seen and felt. He began to feel ready to do what Annie wanted. He nodded slightly to her. Just as he did, a terrible, rhythmic pain accompanied an awful pressure in his chest. He tried to suck in a breath so he could shout, but the breath never came. Instead, he fell through a hole that opened up beneath him.

He dropped with a thud into the driver's seat of his 1961 Corvette. He turned to look at Annie who was sitting in the passenger seat beside him. It was a cheery, sunny Friday afternoon in June, 1970. The top was down, and he was having fun shifting through the gears on Route 250 as they sped up the gently ascending highway to the mountains around Charlottesville. Annie had graduated from Radcliffe College in Boston the weekend before at the top of her class. It was the first year that the graduates of Radcliffe had joint degrees with Harvard. David still had a year to go to graduate from William and Mary where he was majoring in business, and he had come home for the summer. Roberto had scraped by at the University of Virginia in Charlottesville, also in business studies. Like David, he had to complete another year to graduate, because of dropping some courses, which had put him behind a year. Roberto had partied a lot and had smoked a lot of dope. He wasn't in Charlottesville now. He had attended Annie's graduation with their parents and had flown back to Mexico with them. Annie had lied. She had told her parents that she would celebrate for a week in the Bahamas with some of her friends, but after they left, she went to Richmond instead.

David had never gotten Annie out of his heart. He wrote her and campaigned for her vigorously while she was in Radcliffe. Annie liked this and wrote him back, not as often, but she looked forward to his letters. David begged her to come see him in the summertime, but she went to Mexico the first two summers, back to the family ranch where her father had settled again with her mother. She had had boyfriends at Radcliffe, and she wrote David about the social life in Boston. David felt like a simple Virginia boy in comparison, but at least she kept writing him back. During junior year, Annie's letters didn't mention boyfriends, but they did express a lot of personal interest in what David was doing.

He wondered, *Was it a change in her attitude?* He clung to the hope of her love. He kept writing her.

The summer after her junior year, Annie remained in Boston and took courses that would help her succeed in the law school that she wanted to attend. She intended to go to law school in Mexico City. She came to visit Richmond twice that summer and stayed with David and his parents. The visits were two long weekends marked by soul-bearing conversations during walks in parks along the James River. David could feel Annie growing closer to him, but he had an instinct not to push anything past the friendship level just yet. He knew that Annie was aware that he loved her. For the first time, he thought he might be getting to her. He made a point to speak only Spanish to her, even when she answered him in English. To him, Spanish was always a poetry of words that spoke from the heart instead of the mind. It was a language her heart would hear.

Then this past March of 1970 on spring break, Annie surprised him. She shocked him, really. She asked to come to visit him in Richmond when he would be home. This time his parents were away on a cruise to the Western Caribbean, which took them, ironically, to Cozumel, Mexico, as one of the stops.

On their first day together in March, David and Annie drove to places they used to visit in Richmond where they had ridden bicycles as kids. They went downtown and to some of the newer shopping centers that had sprung up. They drove to some boulders in the James River near the Huguenot Bridge. They stepped out into the water and talked a long time. Afterwards, the two laid back on the flat, stony surfaces of the boulders warmed by the spring sun to let their skin absorb heat.

When they returned to David's house, it finally happened. The sun had dipped below the horizon, and it was twilight inside the house. They were standing in the living room as David tried to think about what they might do next. Annie came up and pressed herself against him and said softly, "You're a good guy."

Then, as natural as a lover who had been with him for years, she raised up and kissed him. Her kiss was long and sweet and moist. She pushed her body tight against his. Her body was comfortable and yearning. She draped her arms around the back of his neck and tenderly tickled his sensitive skin. It shot him to the moon. When she broke the kiss, she kept her lips tantalizingly close to his. He felt like they were floating in space. She whispered softly, "You're good," and she kissed his lips lightly. Then she whispered again, "So good," and kissed his neck. She repeated whispering his goodness while kissing him lightly on his cheeks, his lips, and his ears. His heavy breathing encouraged her to deliver even more ultra-light kisses. He wanted to undress her. His trembling fingers sought the top buttons of her blouse. He fumbled because her kisses destroyed his focus.

He could see her in the deepening twilight when she pulled back and smiled. It was the smile of a tease. She got back just far enough that he could observe her undress. She did it slowly. He was crazy hard with excitement. He was so far gone that he didn't even remember to start taking off his clothes.

When she finally pulled her blouse away from her chest, a new light of amusement entered her eyes when she saw how he gaped at her big breasts that were swelling above her lacy white bra. She held his eyes while she pulled down her shorts slowly. Very slowly. Her abdomen was wide and flat. Her hips curved behind her to the breath-stealing, high and round bottom that Latina women have.

Annie giggled softly because she loved seeing David paralyzed with that wide-eyed boy look on his face. Slipping off her white bikini panties, she returned fully naked to him and began to undress him slowly and provocatively. Suddenly David went desperately out of control. His chest rubbing against her breasts put an unquenchable urgency into his upright cock. He pushed it between her legs. He kissed her with all the years of love that he had bottled inside himself. He let his hands adore her bottom; then he ran them up and down her back to consume the entire softness of her.

Finally, David let escape a loud moan of desire. He scooped Annie in his arms and carried her to his bedroom, kissing her the whole way. When they got to the bed, she gave herself to him as if she had been his all her life.

They made love over two hours and climaxed together. They fell asleep holding each other in a buzz of warmth. When David awoke, he was famished and hot. He left the bed and went naked to the kitchen where he got a huge bowl of ice cream. She was awake when he returned to the bed. Annie laughed and hit him when he pretended that he wouldn't give her any. They devoured the ice cream, and when they were done, he kissed her with ice cream lips. They warmed again and made love, and when they climaxed together this second time, David's sperm swam deep inside her, and one found the egg.

Later David found out that in Boston, by the first week in June, Annie hadn't had a period. Her gynecologist confirmed what she already knew. She was pregnant. This wasn't news that would go down well with her traditional Mexican family. She would never consider abortion, so she decided that she should do the right thing, which was to keep this secret until she could see David in person again and tell him first.

David called her a couple of times during the weeks she was back in Boston. He wanted to go there to be at Annie's graduation.

"Maybe not such a good idea, David," Annie told him by phone. "God, I wish you could come! But Roberto and my parents are coming. Things are so tense between me and Roberto right now. I just want to enjoy my graduation, and it will be hard enough to do that with him there. If you're around, I think it will be very obvious that we love each other and even that we sleep together. I want to prepare the family for that, especially Roberto."

"You aren't ashamed of it, are you, Annie?" David asked her.

"Of course not, Sweetie! Roberto is a problem for me. His moods take such wild swings, and there's always tension in the family when he's around. He and my father butt heads in very bad ways. He's very jealous of you. It's weird, I know. I think it's because of all the drugs he's using. I'll talk with you more about this later. I've a better idea. I'll come to Virginia to spend some days with you after graduation and before I go to Mexico! Then maybe this summer you can come and spend some time at the ranch with me!"

David accepted this plan cheerfully. Things had deteriorated between him and Roberto in the last couple of years as Roberto became more and more a pot head, and he didn't savor being around him anyway. He loved knowing that Annie wanted to be with him

76

before going to Mexico and that she had invited him to come to her home there. That was a good sign. He didn't know at the time that if he went to the graduation, Annie would be dealing also with hiding her pregnancy until she had the right time to tell everyone.

David's parents were at home when Annie visited this time. David gave her his bedroom, and he took a room upstairs which had been finished in the attic. She arrived in the Richmond airport in the late afternoon. After settling her things in the house and chatting briefly with David's parents, she and David went to a romantically-lit Italian restaurant. There Annie broke the news to David.

He could tell that she was nervous. She ordered an appetizer as her dinner, and she declined wine when David suggested it. He studied her face curiously as she made small talk and kept looking around the room. Finally, she looked him directly in the eyes, and he could tell that she was going to get to the heart of something troubling her.

"So, honey, I guess this time we won't have as much opportunity as we did on my last visit…to….," and she smiled. "Well, your parents are home."

David relaxed into a laugh. *Was that what was bothering her?* He replied, "Well, there may be ways we'll be able to be together like that."

Annie looked surprised. "Really? David, what have you planned?"

"I have us at a bed-and-breakfast in Charlottesville tomorrow night, if you would like that. Your brother isn't in town. It's so pretty there. We could take a walk on one of the nature trails tomorrow in the mountains," he answered.

He saw her heart melt. "God, David, I love that! What a great thing to do!" she said. "I just want to have some quiet time with you."

He beamed.

She continued, "David, when we made love the last time I was here, it was just beautiful. We were sweetly tender with each other. I wanted to tell you that it was the best time of my life. It was so special. We made love, and…"

Her voice was trembling a little. David noticed her cheeks reddening. He saw her struggle to continue speaking. Then a light of understanding passed through his heart. He leaned across the table to

Annie and took her hand. He said softly, "Yes, Annie, we did. And tonight you're trying to tell me that you're pregnant."

She jumped back, and tears shot to her dark eyes. "Yes!" she whispered. "David! Oh my God, you can hear my heart! You're like my real twin!"

Without any hesitation David reached across the table to take both her hands. He squeezed them tightly.

"I knew somehow. Listen to me, Annie. I've completely adored you since that first day I saw you on your horse and we were children. Almost all my life I've loved you. For me, you're a miracle, the meaning in my life. I've chased you and chased you and always knew that one day you would love me. Then the first time we made love…well, to me it makes perfect sense that you would get pregnant by me right away. I've saved my love for you a long, long time. So whatever happens going forward, I'm all in with you."

He saw immediately that she had expected this reaction from him. She asked him to come to her side of the table in the booth. When he did, she brought to his lips the gift of her warmest kiss. His cheeks got wet with her tears. She stopped and gave him a lovely, liquid smile, and then she kissed him again. David reached across the table and moved his plate and silverware in front of him so he could remain by her side.

Annie smiled happily the whole dinner.

"I'm not surprised by you at all!" she told him. "Your reaction to this news. You're a wonderful guy, David! You're all about romance and dreams and magic and possibility and second chances and goodness and optimism and doing the right thing. You're the Fox, for God's sake!"

And she laughed.

Early the next morning, they left Richmond for Charlottesville. It was a pleasant morning. It would be hot in the afternoon, so David lowered the black top of his Corvette convertible. He had loved these cars since the mid-1960s when the Beach Boys sang about them in their car songs and had a picture of one on an album cover. With money he had put aside in a car fund for years, he bought this older one from a friend just a month earlier. It was Roman Red with a fuel injection option and a four-speed shift. Annie was thrilled to see it. She loved speed and she loved sports cars. They weren't far down the highway when she began to beg David to let her drive. He

78

playfully teased her at first, telling her that there was no way he would let anyone else drive his car. That game lasted about fifteen minutes. Then he gave in and said that they would switch drivers at Zion Crossroads. A small service station was there with snack items. They would pull over, get some drinks, and Annie would drive the car into Charlottesville.

"You'll look so impressive driving this baby," David told her.

Laughing, Annie agreed to the deal. "Am I the baby, or is the car?" she asked.

But the deal went south when they passed a road sign that said Zion Crossroads was still thirty-four miles away. Annie declared that she wouldn't wait that long. She reprimanded him that David didn't inform her properly how far away their stop was.

How happy and silly they were is what David remembered about those final moments. He couldn't wait to arrive in Charlottesville and carry his gorgeous, pregnant, Mexican girlfriend into their room and ravish her body with kisses. God, it was going to be so much fun to be in this car of his dreams as a passenger and with the woman of his dreams driving! He would savor the day all over his skin and feel this happiness in the sunlight, in the breezes, and in the smells of the mountains while they sped along the road.

They were joking about something when David impetuously decided to pull over on the shoulder. Looking in the side mirror, he saw a tractor-trailer far behind in the distance. He opened his door and began to walk behind the car. He told Annie to hurry to change places. She had to walk around too because of the gear box between the two seats in the car. She opened her door but waited for David to come, and then she stood and kissed him. David looked back and saw the approaching truck. He gave Annie an affectionate little push to hurry her around the car and get in the driver's seat. Annie walked around the front of the car to the other side, but the driver's door was opened. This slowed her just a minute, so she decided to stand in front of the opened door until the truck passed. David was standing by the passenger seat. His door was also open, but he was on the inside of the door. Annie was looking at him, smiling, looking absolutely lovely, as the truck rushed past with a gust of wind, and her hair blew in her face. Annie then made her planned move to step quickly around the door. She got farther out on the shoulder towards the road.

He saw everything that happened.

All of a sudden a car was there. It had been tailgating the truck and hadn't been visible before. It was driving close to the shoulder on the right. It struck the door of the Corvette and tossed Annie into the air. The Corvette swung sharply around from the force of the impact as if on a pivot. The opened door on his side threw David across the rear of the car. He had heard the ugly metallic crack of the collision and had seen Annie airborne, thrown like a rag doll. The driver who struck his Corvette slammed his breaks. The car skidded into the ditch ahead and rolled on its side. Where it came to a rest, Annie lay just a few feet away.

He tasted blood in his mouth, but he pushed himself up, and he ran to where Annie was lying. "No, no, no, no, no! Annie! Annie!" he screamed as he ran. He dropped beside her on his knees, but he could tell from the peculiar way her body was twisted that she was no longer with him. He heard shouts and other screams. He saw someone struggling to get out of the other car. There were people running to him from other vehicles that had stopped. He pulled Annie desperately into his arms and held her, and as he cried her name over and over, the force of his sobs broke his heart into pieces.

There was too much pain!

David was horrified all over again. He wanted to get up and run. He had put this memory out of his mind so many years and had never wanted to revisit it, but now he had just relived it, and with no detail lacking.

He struggled to remove himself from the accident scene and to return to the roof top. He wanted to find Annie. He wanted to demand why she put him through this horror again.

Then he heard the question which she had told him she would ask. "Tell me, why should you live?"

Because I love Ana! He felt like he was shouting this at the top of his lungs. The answer had just poured from his heart without him even thinking about it for a second. *She's my reason for living! I love her like I loved you, Annie. It's as simple as that. We live for love! I have purpose because of her! I make a difference because of her! I want to live because of Ana!*

But there was more. It had to do with why he thought Annie interceded in prayer for her brother's victims. It wasn't Annie who did that. It was he, wanting to redeem himself.

He thought about the long years he had spent doing undercover work for the CIA in Colombia and Mexico. He thought about the things he had seen and the things he had done and how disconnected he had felt from his childhood, when his moral compass pointed either to black or to white. He thought of the years he didn't see his wife and children and even grandchildren.

He was starting to feel the familiar, dark, heavy guilt that had deprived him of joy for years.

Then he had a startling realization: Every single time that he had encountered one of those victims who lay scattered along the paths of his work, his heart had broken. Each heartbreak had been a prayer for the victim and the victim's family. His life efforts were, in fact, intercessions for them. He had never looked at it that way.

He thought, *I've lived too long in my grief. I can't even see my own light.*

He still felt the rhythmic pressure in his chest. The pressure was painful, like sobs that were trapped inside, sobs that would have provided relief. He focused really hard, trying to see Annie. When finally he could see her, she was nodding to him. She looked satisfied with his answer to her question.

She stood up and went to her brother. She knelt beside him and began studying him. As she did, she started to look alarmed.

"Something isn't right about him," she said.

She turned to David and tried to mouth words, but she was fading. She pointed to her brother and appeared to shout to David, but silence came from her lips. She continued fading. She looked frustrated as she disappeared, as if she were failing to show David something important. David tried to hold onto her visage, but he couldn't.

David thought, *If I created her in my mind, I should be able to hold onto her. Wait! Hadn't she said that she came this time on her own, and that she was dreaming me? I'm confused!*

On the roof now, with Annie gone as if the accident had taken her away a second time, only Roberto was in his direct field of view. He began to speak to David. However, David realized that in his mind what he was truly hearing were the echoes of Roberto's tormented life:

"You took my sister. You took her and got her killed. You kept after her for years until she fell in love with you. I told you to leave her alone. I was the only one who could really understand her! She should have been back in Mexico after graduation or at least in the Bahamas, but instead she was in Virginia with you. Why the fuck did you pull the car over on a busy highway and carelessly get her killed? You say you loved her? You grieve her? You know nothing about pain! What you feel is nothing like the grief a twin feels when the other part of him dies and he's left to live alone with half his soul ripped out! We were perfect symmetry. She completed me emotionally, psychologically, and anatomically. You would never understand the… importance… of our union. Her life is gone. You're the one who doesn't deserve a life. You never did!"

David wondered if the force of Roberto's hatred might be sufficient to finish David off on the roof. He considered, *Maybe I'm in hell now with Roberto on this hot roof!*

For years he had believed Roberto was dead, murdered by a drug cartel in a horrific way a short time after Annie's death. Roberto's father had never accepted that his son was dead. But in that one instant of recognition after El Gato fell from his bullet wound, David realized that Annie's twin had been alive all those years. Furthermore, to be where he was now, he had to have lived the darkly productive and satanic life of El Gato.

David had a horrible thought: *Roberto is El Gato! He has been alive all this time! Eduardo was right after all. God, I see him there, dead …but not dead… like me! Blood flowing from his head…but…oh my God, this man might live!*

David could practically smell the putrid fear welling inside him that El Gato would revive.

He might live! So I have to!

He strained to check on himself: his body, his heartbeat, his senses. The effort made him hot. He stopped seeing through closed eyelids. He heard voices all around him. It reminded him of when he was holding Annie right after their accident. He also heard a loud, whirring sound, and a Spanish word sounded in his mind: Helicóptero.

He felt that rhythmic pressure on his chest once more. He struggled to release a sob or to catch one big gasp. He felt air flowing inside him, coming from somewhere else, but he wanted to breathe on his own. His chest hurt awfully. He felt his skin again. There were people touching him, and, yes, someone was pushing on his chest. Someone had removed his bulletproof vest and his shirt. It was God-awful hot, and the roof was burning him. Now he was aware of a blinding light just outside his closed eyelids, a light that hurt; but in seconds the hurt diminished, and he realized he would be able to open his eyes. The noise of the outside world was increasing. All around him there were shouts and commands. Someone yelled excitedly in Spanish, "This other guy is alive!" Suddenly there was a lot of commotion beside him.

Then with joy he heard a very familiar voice shouting in English just above him in a tone of astonishment and exhilaration, "Oh my God, Enrique! He's breathing! He's breathing!"

It was Ana!

"Eyyyyy!" he heard Enrique's voice shout now. It was a gasp of relief. Enrique was close.

David realized, *He's sitting on me!*

David now distinguished more tumult coming from a little distance away and below him. His orientation was returning and he understood exactly where he was: physically on the roof, and very much alive! The uproar he was hearing came from the people in the street, and they were agitated and dealing with some kind of issue below.

"David! David! Darling, can you hear me?" Ana was shouting. Her words came out soaked in tears of happiness and relief.

He felt some people lifting him up. He wanted to let Ana know that he heard her. He opened his eyes. Squinting, he saw her standing there. She threw her hands up to her mouth in prayer pose when she saw him look at her. She yelled with urgency, "David, you're alive! You're going to be okay! I'm here, Enrique is here, and this medical corps is taking you on the helicopter to the hospital! Do you understand?"

He was able to nod and smile a bit to Ana, but then some soldiers whisked him onto a stretcher and began running him to the helicopter. He caught a quick glimpse of Enrique. As they moved him, he heard Ana behind him exclaiming, "Te amo, David, te amo, te amo, te amo!" There was a pause at the helicopter door because some soldiers were lifting up another patient into a bay.

Once they began loading David, he began to feel himself falling asleep. Some alarm inside him told him to resist, and he shook himself to stay conscious. He tried to focus.

Something about the last memory of Annie was still with him. When she died, the baby died too. He had thought about the baby through the years, whether it would have been a boy or girl, and what the child might have done in the world. In a very real sense a piece of him, some of his DNA, some of his stardust, also perished out there beside the highway with his beloved Annie. Maybe this had a lot to do with why he felt so emotional about lives cut short.

Later, when he met Ana, he was struck by the many coincidences of her life with his own. She had the same name as Annie. Her father had been twenty-two years older than her mother, and David was twenty-two years older than Ana. Hearing from her the wonderful stories of her father, David knew that the man loved Ana's mother in the same adoring way that David loved Ana. And Ana loved David with the same sweetness and naturalness that Annie had. Both women loved him in a way that made David feel completely secure in the world, no matter what chaos surrounded him.

They hung David's stretcher in the helicopter bay above the stretcher of the other patient. David felt overpowering exhaustion, and his chest hurt when he breathed. He did his best to answer the questions that the rescuers were asking, but he felt weak and still sleepy. He was so tired that he thought the soldiers were speaking in English to him. He knew that he must be extremely weak because he already understood that the other patient in the helicopter with him was Roberto, and he didn't even have energy to worry about that anymore.

He felt the helicopter lifting, he heard the surge of the power to the engine, and he felt the tilt as it found its direction in the lift off. There was no way he was going to be able to stay awake. He would let himself sleep a few minutes. If he could do that, he might escape his pain and discomfort. But just before he succumbed to the drowsiness, he had a disturbing thought:

Near Charlottesville, Virginia, Annie had died in 1970. Ana was born in 1971 in Mazatlán, Mexico. In between the times of loving those two women, David had lived in a limbo of despair that had darkened his days of life. On both ends of that time line was

Roberto. Now he knew that Roberto had been in between too, ghostlike, dark, and living in shadowy places throughout Mexico. Despite the heat inside the helicopter, David felt a nauseating chill and a foreboding that terrible tragedy was ahead.

Chapter 6: Where Did the Bird Fly?

Monterrey, Mexico
Monday

The wind from the UH-60 Black Hawk helicopter's blades made everyone lower themselves. With tremendous noise the military craft, which had actually been ordered by the Mexican Air Force and used in 2009 against drug traffickers by the Federal Police, lifted up and ascended over the city. On the roof of the building it left behind about a dozen soldiers, Enrique, Ana, and the bodies of the two women who were shot from the building across the street by an Army Special Forces soldier. Ana had worked with an army commander on a plan, which she assumed General Alvarez approved, to provide protection for them on the roof if needed. She advised him that David had been writing investigative pieces to flush out a powerful and unknown cartel leader and that he was more vulnerable on the roof than any other place. Furthermore, she said, she had made the world a more dangerous place for David since she had helped make him well known in Mexico as the head Z, and many more bad people were aware of his existence than before, when he had worked most of his career under cover.

"Plus I know him," she explained. "He'll do anything to save my life or any other person. He'll put his own life completely at risk to save others. He's too valuable to too many people for us to lose him. I love him; the people love him; it's important that he's with us. This is something we just have to do because he'll probably object. He has a tendency to think he's a superman and doesn't often like the idea of receiving any help. So let's do this and keep it between us."

So she made her plan with this commander without consulting David, and the commander seemed easily in agreement with her to implement this without anyone else knowing. All David's friends were loyal to him to the ultimate degree and couldn't be told, even Enrique. *Especially Enrique,* she thought.

What Ana didn't know, but learned later, was that the military commander was working at the private training facility on the property of Eduardo Ortiz at the time of her call. Eduardo was the one who got his old friend General Alvarez to station a Special Forces sharp shooter with the CNN crew in the building across from the one Ana owned.

When the helicopter was gone, Enrique came over to Ana and asked, "Are you okay?" Both of them were so distracted by the emergency with David that they didn't pay attention to the steep ascent of the aircraft as it left them behind.

"Yes, yes, I'm all right. When I came up here behind you and saw him lying there, I was so sure he was dead!" Ana answered him. "God, I was so scared, Enrique! You started doing resuscitation. You knew he was alive?"

Enrique glanced around at the soldiers and then turned to Ana and said, "He looked dead. I thought his heart might have failed due to the pounding his body armor took from so many bullets in the chest. I don't know, Ana, I was just so anxious that my CPR technique was right. He wasn't breathing. Damn, that seemed like forever, but I guess it was just a minute. He was faintly alive when I first got up here, and then he seemed to die. It was like I saw his heart stop, and then I couldn't find a pulse. I had to take off his vest and shirt. I began pushing on his chest and breathing into him."

"Oh my God, we could have lost him, Enrique! Gracias, gracias! I can't believe he wasn't hit anywhere else on his body!" Ana exclaimed.

"Sí. Well, that shooter took out the three of them pretty quickly. I don't think El Gato, or whoever that was, had time to turn his weapon anywhere else. What the hell happened up here, Ana? Why didn't David climb down with you? Do you know who shot these guys?"

"I think a Special Forces soldier. I requested the cover," Ana answered. "Truthfully, when I was on the roof earlier, I only saw what I thought was the CNN Mexico crew on the roof across the street. I recognized the same team from yesterday. Then I noticed someone new there this morning, a big guy. He wore military fatigues. I saw this guy chatting briefly with the television crew; then he disappeared and I wondered where he was. God, Enrique, he came over to this roof when you were working on David! The guy was huge, muscular. He didn't say a word. He just walked over and seemed to inspect the ones he shot by just staring at them a few moments. I saw the Special Forces insignia on his uniform. Then he looked over at me and gave a slight nod, and then he left! I was so nervous about what was happening with David that I didn't say anything to him."

Enrique looked in the sky and couldn't see the helicopter or hear it. Some forensics workers were examining the bodies of the women on the roof who had been shot.

Enrique said, "You should have told me, Ana. Not knowing, I'm issuing different orders to our Z leaders about watching the two of you. We have Zs who are unarmed, and they can put themselves in the line of fire if they don't know that there's danger. I have guys watching the building downstairs. I'm sure what happened here has confused them. Things are chaotic enough. We don't want the Zs to think there are communication problems among their top leadership in Monterrey. You thought I would tell David if I knew, didn't you?"

"I'm sorry, Enrique, yes, I did. It was wrong. You're right. I'm afraid where David is concerned, I'm too much a slave to my heart and fears for his safety. Yes, the three of us have to be completely honest, and I was out of line by not telling both of you. I only admitted yesterday to David that I had asked protection, but I never let him know that I had obtained it."

"Honesty first!" he replied, quoting the first rule of life of a Z from Ana's own code of ethics which she had developed. He saw her face redden with embarrassment, but then Enrique nodded his forgiveness. He was still observing the events in the street below when he had a strange feeling.

It's a mess down there," he said. "A lot of people not working. I assume they're taking David and the other guy to University Hospital?"

Enrique realized that he didn't know where the helicopter was taking David, and he looked to Ana for verification. But she had a look of chagrin on her face, as if embarrassed not to know herself, and she said, "I think that's where. It's the best close medical facility in Monterrey, and they have a heliport on their roof." She hesitated. "The other option is that they could take him to Doctor's Hospital. Oh God, I didn't think to ask!"

Enrique shook his head and said, "Maldito! I didn't ask either. Okay, I'll find him. Hopefully the hospital staffs reported to work. If you're thinking of trying to go one of the hospitals, Ana, it's not a good idea. Too many people can recognize you, and we don't know who could be there. It's easier for me to get around without attracting attention. Besides, I think Rafael has seen you with David enough these past days, don't you? Where is he?"

"At home with the kids," she said. "Nobody is sending their kids to school today. Rafael closed the restaurants today. I think I'll go downstairs to my office. At least the cell phones still work. The service has been sporadic, but they're working at the moment. Maybe you can get some of the guys to take me home later, but right now I want to be available. I want to hear about David by phone, by radio, whatever. Would you try to reach Rafael for me and tell him I'm okay? I don't want to talk to him. Just tell him I'm coming home later today, not to worry, you'll take care of getting me home. Mostly I don't want the kids to worry."

Enrique nodded. "Okay. I'm going to University Hospital. I'll find out where David is. I think walking there is faster. I'll grab some guys and go. I'll get word to you just as soon as I know anything."

He put his arm behind her shoulders and gently began to guide her to the rooftop door. He thought of something, and then he said, "Ana, the Armed Forces took over the Federal Government and the municipal offices in the three largest cities in Mexico. So there's no real Federal Government working, nor city governments in Mexico City, Guadalajara, and Monterrey. The Army and Marines are going to run the bureaucracies I guess. So much shit has been happening these last days so fast. I know we work with General Alvarez…" he meant he knew Ana worked with him.. "but I haven't had a chance even to tell you that I was caught totally off guard by what the Army did. Does it bother you that…"

Ana interrupted him: "…the Armed Forces betrayed their Commander in Chief and are running the country under military leadership?" They had descended the steps and had entered the sixth floor of the building and now stood in the corridor. Soldiers were guarding the stairwell.

"Yes, Enrique, it bothers me, and we have to keep our ears to the pavement. There are lots of reassuring words coming from our

89

friend General Alvarez to calm people. Pledges to protect people. Reassurance that democracy will get restored. He even publicly praises the Zs for their help in preserving order. He has been trying not to characterize this as a coup, but you and I and everyone know this is a military coup in Mexico."

"Sí!" Enrique agreed.

Ana looked up and down the hall. There was no other person in it. She sighed. She admitted her private feelings to Enrique: "There's no way the military took over the government just because people have been in the streets screaming for protection and order and the end to corruption in government and police by the cartels," Ana stated.

She went on to tell Enrique about the last announcement by the Commander of the Fourth Military zone in Monterrey she had seen that morning. The Army and Marines had "friendly custody" of the President and his family, the Secretary of Government, the other Cabinet members, and many of the Deputies and Senators in Mexico City.

Whatever "friendly custody" means, thought Ana.

She told Enrique, "The announcement said that the President and the others are being held now for their own protection. The Presidential Guard obeyed the orders of General Alvarez to quarantine the President and his family at the presidential home in Los Pinos in Mexico City. At the Zócalo, the Army and some Marines of the Navy seized members of all three branches of the Federal Government who were there in the Supreme Court and the governmental buildings. The Army promises order and security for the people who are in the streets, but the commanders want the demonstrators to return to their homes and places of work. The Commander reported that there have been so far just sporadic attacks on the military by the cartels and that the soldiers are cordoning off all areas where large groups of people are gathering to pass them through security check points. They're trying to keep the weapons out."

She started leading them down the hall towards her office. "I'm dying for a cigarette," she said.

She decided to tell Enrique about the phone call she received that morning from General Alvarez. He needed to know that the General believed that the Zs might be useful in intelligence and infiltration of the cartels in addition to the security brigades they formed to protect citizens. She added that the General wanted to see democracy restored, but with elected officials who wouldn't be on the payroll of the cartels. None of the leaders of the coup had interest in governing Mexico on a permanent basis.

"Do you believe that? Do we still trust General Alvarez?" Enrique asked. He had been unnerved by the coup.

Ana shrugged slightly. She was feeling calmer now. "You know, I listened intently to General Alvarez. He tried to speak to me in a reassuring way, but I think he hid private concerns about how long the coup could control the current state of affairs. This is why we have to do our part, Enrique. We have to stay close to the military now, to maintain the dialog, to know what they're doing. We have to influence their actions. We have to watch out for what the United States might do. They're in an uproar up there. We have to get David well. He's our communicator with that country, even with the President. This is so critical."

But Enrique pushed. He wondered other things and wanted to know how Ana would respond. "And what about David and Eduardo? Did they have anything to do with the coup?" He didn't include Ana's name, but he wondered that too.

Internally Ana sighed. Enrique was asking aloud the very questions she had in her own mind. She decided to dodge the question for now. She told Enrique that she had no indication from either of them that they had any foreknowledge of a pending military coup. She knew David would have nothing to do with it.

"But Eduardo has very powerful friends, including General Alvarez and the nation's top Admiral," she continued. "Eduardo also supposedly holds a high post in a rumored coalition of wealthy business leaders in Mexico who believe themselves to be true national patriots. Eduardo loves me like a daughter and trusts me so much, but he's crafty from a lifetime of both political and corporate intrigue. He keeps secrets.

"I'm sure we'll learn a lot more as time goes by. Things are happening quickly. This is why I want to go to my office. I don't know if internet is working…" She pulled her phone from her pants and checked it. "It is. I want to see the reports about what's going on while we still have internet access! Let's get the word out that David is okay. God, I hope he is! We need to know. And we have to put out that you're on top of things, Enrique. You need to be giving orders now. You need to be online as well. It's important for people to hear Z leadership speaking loud and clear! It's important for our military friends to hear the voice of the people and for them to know who is in the hearts of the people." She smiled ironically. "It must continue to be us, the Zs."

"Absolutely, Ana, you're so right! The people of Mexico don't want anymore violence, and the soldiers are the ones with guns!"

"And the narcos," Ana added.

She decided that they had talked long enough. She looked up at him and said, "Enrique, find out about David. Also, get in touch with the units at the border and let me know what's happening there. Which border cities might be having problems? What's happening in the United States since yesterday? Are they talking intervention, and if so, who's talking about it? And so on. If David is okay, we need his help with these issues immediately."

Just then they heard the rat-a-tat of gunfire in the distance. It started in a fury but then settled into volleys that sounded like the shooters were on the move. It sounded a kilometer away.

"God!" Ana said. "Be careful when you're out there. I'll tell you my belief, Enrique," Ana said resolutely. "In its depth this is more than a coup. This is civil war. The Army did it, but the people have been in revolt the past few years. Everyone wants safety and peace, not more blood. Mexico has had civil war since the government declared war on the narcos and brought the Armed Forces in to take out the top cartel leadership. If this isn't civil war, we're on the brink of it. Now the military will have their hands full just being policemen to preserve order while the cartels decide their strategies. If the cartels attack in big ways, it could look like civil war in this country to the gringos in the North, and then we'll really have problems!"

She punched numbers into a keypad and opened one of the double glass doors to her office suite. She paused in the doorway. She had used the office originally for her events planning business, and in the last couple of years she expanded it to include her internet publications businesses as well as the national headquarters for the Zs. It also provided a nice place to get away from Rafael.

Enrique saw her mood to get busy and her concern about David, so he decided to summarize their priorities:

He said, "Okay, your top concerns right now are the status of David; the actions of the Armed Forces, where and when; what the United States is doing; and if the Zs are out there gathering surveillance and trying to preserve calm."

"Perfect," Ana said smiling. "And making sure we keep the communications network operating. We need cell phones, radios, and internet. We need public services restored as soon as possible. We need people to go back home. They're in danger in the streets."

"Okay," Enrique said. "The University Hospital isn't that far away. I'll go find David. I'll call you as soon as I know his status. I'll make sure someone gets you back home later. If you need anything, try to reach me. I'll get the word out to the teams to post reports of calm or unrest at least every hour from their stations."

Ana answered, "Until I hear from you, I'll be in my office reviewing the news websites like El Norte and El Universal, and, especially, CNN Mexico. I'll try to reach General Alvarez by phone again to see if he has news about David, even while you're going to find him in the hospital. I'll look at the Twitter postings for news of cartel activity. The usual things, Enrique," she said. "But let's encourage everyone to publish anything important from their phones so we have instantaneous awareness, okay? Tweets and videos and photos."

"I'll send out the word," said Enrique. He gave her a farewell hug, and he said, "Jesus, I saved our David, and now I don't even know where he is!"

Chapter 7: Eyes of Green, Eyes of Black

Ana's Office in Monterrey
Monday

The sounds of the gunfire in the distance had ceased. From her window she saw more Army presence than before in the street, mostly soldiers and trucks. She felt hungry and physically tired. She was still a little shaky from the fast-rope descent and the emotions of seeing David looking dead on the roof. She wondered how satisfied he must feel knowing that El Gato had been captured. She thought about how happy he would be to be living because he adored her so much, and she also couldn't envision life without him. Before they met, only her children, Rafael Jr. and Paula, brought joy to her life. They were eleven and thirteen years old now.

Ana kept cigarettes and candy bars in her top desk drawer, and she pulled out a chocolate bar. Under some papers she had hidden a small photograph of her and David, and she uncovered it to look at it. They were standing by the river in El Parque Fundidora. They had asked a tourist to take their picture with Ana's camera after Ana had checked to be sure there was no one around whom she recognized. David seized her with both arms around her waist and pulled her up close to him so suddenly that she was laughing with delight in the photograph, and he was beaming, full of love.

That's what you see when you look at this picture, Ana thought. *You see a happy couple with light in their eyes, and you can tell that this is a couple who make love a lot. Our bodies fit together in the natural way that true lovers have when they're not wearing clothes.*

Ana could feel herself becoming turned on thinking of this, so she closed the drawer with a sigh and looked at the photograph of her and Rafael which sat framed on top of her desk. In that picture his eyes were cold and hers were dead, even though both of them were smiling.

Their love died when Ana's third pregnancy terminated. Rafael had no interest in having another child. He was too busy with the chain of healthy salad restaurants he had founded. There were nine of them now in Monterrey, and all Rafael wanted in life was to have his Ensalada Picante restaurants throughout Mexico.

And even in the United States, Ana thought to herself. She rolled her eyes because this was a tag that Rafael added without fail whenever he told anyone his plans. *Rafael, did you even notice I was pregnant?*

Ana and Rafael stopped having sex. It had been ten years. She had no interest in making love with him anymore. As the years passed, he became more and more absent from home because of work. He came home late in the evenings in order to go to bed, but he ate a meal Ana had prepared for him first. Sometimes early in the mornings he took the children to school, and on weekends he carved out some time to do family outings, but mostly he was absent. On rare occasions Rafael made an effort to find out if Ana wanted to make love, but he was always fine when she had an excuse. Ana suspected Rafael might have someone else to do this with. She didn't care. She didn't want to know. She accepted the truth that they just didn't like each other that much.

But Ana was a passionate woman. Sometimes after the kids went to their private school and she didn't have tasks to do, Ana got on the internet in chat sites and talked with men. These were never serious flirtations. Ana knew that Mexico was becoming too dangerous a place to have real encounters with men whom she met on the internet. But there were a couple times when she risked getting on camera with some men she had come to know well. This was how she took care of her sexual desires.

Ana's curiosity about life drove her to be on top of the latest technology, particularly so that she could help her children advance. She loved to find applications that allowed her to locate resource material on the internet. In the afternoons after school, she prepared lessons for her children to complement what they were learning in school. She used the search engines, and she taught her children how to do this as well. She made sure that her kids had the latest computers, video games, and data phones. She became excellent with computer graphics, and although she didn't have an events planning business anymore, she stayed in the center of planned school functions and parties put on by the moms of her children's classmates. She designed invitations, posters, and websites for all these events.

When the social media websites began to become sophisticated with applications and games, Ana hit her stride in using these tools. She spent hours each day on Facebook and Twitter and YouTube, becoming a personality and source of information about music, events, concerts, and the arts, and expressing her opinions. She was funny. She had hundreds of followers on Twitter and Facebook. She didn't realize it at the time, but she was developing the skills with social media that later served her when she began to get involved with the mothers online who had lost sons and daughters because of the narco activities.

She remembered a day when she was crossing the Macroplaza to go to the shops in the Barrio Antiguo a few blocks away. Some mothers in a victims' rights movement had set up tables with signs and brochures in front of the Governor's Palace demanding that the Governor do something about the city police who were working for the cartels and allowing impunity to run rampant for the narcos who killed their children at will. A woman at a table called out to Ana and extended a brochure. Ana paused, then accepted it, not because of the woman's call, but because a little boy about two years old sat in her lap and stared at Ana with the most lucent green eyes she had seen in a Mexican child with dark brown skin and coal black hair. He was stunning and beautiful. Ana complimented the woman on him. She was a brown-skinned woman with dark eyes. She appeared to be about forty. In front of her on the table was a handmade poster that had a picture of a teenage boy and some words describing how he and his father had been innocent victims during a battle between two drug gangs.

"This is your son?" Ana asked, meaning the child. "He has such beautiful green eyes!"

"Yes," the woman answered with a laugh. "His father is from the United States. He's totally a gringo with blonde hair and pale skin and green eyes. As you can see, this little one looks just like me. The only thing his dad gave him is the green in his eyes!"

Ana laughed and smiled at the little boy. "Can I give you a hug?" she asked him. Immediately the little boy broke into a big grin and climbed from his mother's lap and came over to Ana, who squatted down and embraced him happily. "I'm surprised he came over so easily!" Ana said, looking over to the woman.

"He's a loving child, very special. He's a miracle baby for me. After my husband and son were killed…" She looked at the pictures on her poster. "…I was completely destroyed. I had a breakdown. No one could help me, and I was so angry to lose my family. He was my only son, and I lost my husband, a man I had known since I was twelve years old. Everyone in my world was gone. After a couple of years, I met this nice man from the United States. He was working here temporarily for a company where I work. We became involved, and I got pregnant, but I didn't know until after he returned to the United States. We're trying to figure out how to be together now. But this little baby here, this child, really saved my life. I didn't even care that much if I lived, but once he was born and I saw him, my whole life changed. He's nothing but joy for me. I'm so much more peaceful now in this work I do, trying to help others like me who have been destroyed by all this senseless violence in our country."

The child gave Ana a second hug and then returned to his mother's lap. It was as if he understood the conversation. Ana was amazed.

"I lost a child," Ana told the woman. "Not in the way you did. It cost me my husband though. It cost our love. It made my two other children more precious to me than ever. I was so depressed many years. It's funny you stopped me and told me your story. I love a gringo myself and am not with him in the way I would like to be. So we have things in common. I'm a lot like you. I'm trying to help Mexico, too."

Remembering the child's green eyes, Ana thought of David. It brought her back to the here and now. She cut her reminiscing and looked out her office window. *The morning has been just too emotional,* she thought. *I'm a wreck.*

She didn't hear the commotion in the streets or see the imposing mountains rising steeply, green and brown and grey, subdividing the city. She only felt a tide of misty emotions ebbing and flowing inside her. It made her feel unbalanced and dizzy. She stared at a cloudless sky but didn't see it. Instead, she saw there the face of a little baby with black eyes gazing into hers. She felt inside her the force of a tide so strong that she thought it might dash her against the rocks of her life. She saved herself by bursting into sobs. She cried because of her loss, and then she cried for Mexico.

Chapter 8: The Hero

Monterrey, México
Four Years Prior

It was through YouTube that Ana first became aware of David in the world. At the time she saw him on the famous YouTube video, one of those which had gone "viral" and had millions of hits, she was just following random links while bored. It wouldn't have mattered if she hadn't found it, because it turned out that she was destined to meet him anyway. The fact that she saw this added to the mystery of their connection with each other. It was about a year before she met David. At the time, the man's heroism captivated her. Something about him intrigued her in a powerful way.

The video came from a local television broadcast in San Antonio, Texas, a city Ana had visited many times with her family to go shopping. The local television hosts announced that a masked man had thwarted an armed robbery involving gun shots in a convenience store, and the video came from security cameras located in the store. It turned out that the attempted robbery was from Halloween night, just a couple of nights previous.

The outside camera showed a man dressed something like a cat burglar entering the store. There was only one car parked out front, but he hadn't come from a car. An inside camera showed him in the back of the store looking into the beer windows. Besides the sales clerk, he was the only one in the store. The time on the film registered as 11:32 pm. A couple of minutes later the outside camera showed a pickup truck parking in front. Two men wearing ski masks got out and rushed into the store. Inside, the camera showed them pulling out pistols, and one immediately jumped over the counter and punched the sales clerk, an older gentleman, in the head and directed him to the cash registers. The other stood pointing his pistol at the man while casting glances outside. With the gun to his head, the sales clerk opened a register and began removing cash, which the gunman stuffed into his pocket.

At this point, the television news editor slowed the video down. This part of the film showed in the back of the store a shadowy figure crawling swiftly, army style, along the rear wall to the area on the opposite side of the counter, where the sales clerk and the gunman were. The video paused, an arrow pointing to the figure. A newscaster pointed out that it was the costumed cat burglar and that the other gunman was looking outside to the parking lot. The video resumed, and the crawling figure disappeared briefly. But then in the background, suddenly the man dressed in black sprung up! In a single leap he jumped up on the counter behind the others. Knocking over some items on display, he flew into a second leap where he soundly delivered a kick to the head of the gunman holding the clerk. Then he sprung backwards to the floor and pulled both the injured gunman and the sales clerk below the counter with him.

Now the camera showed the other gunman reacting with surprise as he turned from looking out the window. He fired a gunshot over the counter. He then rushed forward to peer at the men on the floor, his arm extended so he could shoot down. When he did, the cat burglar's hand shot up and grabbed his wrist and applied pressure delivering enough pain that the gun dropped from the man's hand. Now the sales clerk was on his feet. Seeing the pistol of the first on the floor, he retrieved it and pointed it down at the gunman who was lying there, out of view of the camera. The man whom the costumed burglar grabbed wrested his arm free and began to run to the door. With his arms, the cat burglar pushed himself over the counter, swinging his legs parallel as he cleared it. He caught the man from behind and, with the momentum of his run, pushed the man's head into the frame of the exit door. That sent the man crumpling to the ground outside on the sidewalk as the cat burglar rode him through the door. Then the costumed figure pushed the man onto his stomach, pulled his arm behind his back, and shoved it upward towards the man's neck as he sat on his back. The outside camera showed him looking back and communicating with the sales clerk in the store. The inside camera showed the sales clerk pointing a pistol at the first man on the floor. Then the video skipped a few minutes, about three, when the outside camera showed a police car arrive. Two officers rushed over to the hero of the story. They relieved him and let him stand. They handcuffed the man on the ground as another police car arrived, and those two officers rushed inside to help the sales clerk.

Ana had shaken her head in disbelief when she saw it and thought, *God, there are still heroes in the world sometimes!* She thought of James from her youth, the gringo kid who had helped to save Arturo from being kidnapped, and she marveled that there were still people who reacted from gut bravery.

The YouTube video was so popular that the cat burglar was interviewed for a few days afterwards on popular morning national news shows in the United States. Ana saw one, and, to her amazement, discovered that he was a white-haired, athletic-looking man in his late fifties. She had assumed he was younger. She learned that he was originally from Virginia. He had visited family there and then was driving across country to Mexico when he stopped to spend a couple of days with some friends who lived in San Antonio. He had stayed there to be at their Halloween party. They lived less than a block from this convenience store. The cat burglar had wanted a particular Mexican beer which had run out at the party. He had decided on a whim to walk to the store to get some more. He said that everyone was laughing at him because he left dressed in costume to go to the store.

When the interviewer called him a hero and asked him where he had learned his skills, he responded, "Well, I've had some martial arts training in the past. But I think the real hero is that sales clerk who had the cojones under that stress to pick up the gun and hold the one man on the floor until the policemen arrived."

The YouTube clip and the subsequent interviews no doubt would have stayed in Ana's mind in the future as one of those extraordinary things that happen sometimes in life. There was one coincidence though that amazed her. This gringo was named David Wilson James. His last name was the same as the first name of the gringo boy who had been so brave in her youth. The synchronicity of this delighted her.

That night after seeing the interview, Ana had an erotic dream that the white-haired handsome man came through her bedroom window. Without saying a word, he stretched himself over her and delivered delicious kisses. He pulled off her silk pajama top and cupped her big breasts in his hands and licked them and kissed them so lightly that she felt she would scream if he didn't enter her. He

101

didn't because she woke up. *Damn!* she thought in English. She slipped her hand inside her panties and touched herself pleasurably. She wanted her breasts kissed exactly like that. She was very wet, and with her husband snoring beside her in the bed, she silently, silently, brought herself to orgasm. She raised up and looked out the window at her city and sighed.

Monterrey is losing its romance and heat, she thought. *Just like I lost mine, a long time ago.*

It was because of the drug wars. The violence began to change everything. As Ana's children grew, there was increasing danger that they could be kidnapped. The drug cartels operating in the city began to diversify for sources of income besides the sale of drugs, and some kidnapped for ransom. They grabbed not just wealthy people but also the middle class. University students were among the favorite targets. The parents would turn over their automobiles and round up as much cash as they could get quickly from friends and other family members to save their sons and daughters. As time ticked away, the cartels sometimes tortured the kids and let the parents know it to rush them. Then even when the ransom got paid, too often they killed their victims anyway. As this kind of violence ratcheted up, the United States Embassy from time to time issued warnings to United States citizens not to travel from the border towns of Nuevo Laredo and Reynosa to Monterrey. Eventually, the embassy sent their staff back home and shut down.

Two cartels in particular began to wage war in Monterrey for the control of territory to the U.S. border: the cartel of Sinaloa and the Zetas, which had been started by former military Special Forces personnel in the early 1990s as a branch of the Gulf cartel. The Zetas were particularly aggressive and vicious and by 2010 had become the largest cartel in Mexico, making its presence felt in nearly every part of the country.

Because the city and state police were so corrupt, many of their members being on the payroll of the cartels, Ana taught her children to call the Army if they were ever in danger. This was nothing unusual. Most Mexicans admired the young people of the army who would sometimes have to make arrests of their mayors or corrupt police. The Army was one of the organizations least tainted by corruption in Mexico, although it was far from perfect. She also taught them that if they were ever together in her SUV and were stopped, at her command they should get out and then run to be beside her, and she would make the decisions for their safety and tell them what to do. But it was important for them to stick with her.

It was these thoughts about her children that helped Ana in her office to stop crying and envisioning the baby she had lost. She looked again at the photograph of her and David and remembered how they met. She shivered from the memory because on that day she nearly lost Rafael Jr.

It had been a hot fall afternoon, and Ana had picked up Paula and Rafael Jr. from school. She was driving home on La Avenida Gonzalitos. Her close friend, Katrina, sat beside her in the front of her SUV, and her children were in the back seat. As usual, the notorious Monterrey traffic was horrible, moving too fast, bumper to bumper. Ana and Katrina were laughing about something, and the children had their earphones in listening to music.

Ana was a natural city driver. To drive in Monterrey requires driving aggressively. Every driver expects that, and not to do it confuses other drivers and causes accidents. At one point as traffic merged into this main thoroughfare, it became stop-and-go. Ana was expert at switching lanes and cutting in close without ever touching another car or being hit. She had her conversation with Katrina while sounding the horn and maneuvering without missing a beat. They were making progress getting home as she approached an overpass crossing above her thoroughfare. She had some music playing on her radio, not too loud. She and Katrina were conversing over the noise of the city. Ana had put down the windows while the traffic was slow so that she could yell at other drivers as she maneuvered from lane to lane. The air-conditioning running in the SUV added to the overall background noise.

Therefore, Ana didn't hear the pops right away or notice that the cars ahead had stopped. It was only when she glanced in her rear view mirror and saw the face of Rafael Jr., looking horrified, that she realized something was wrong. He was pulling out his earplugs from his Ipod. At this moment Paula leaned forward to look at something through the windshield.

Ana snapped to attention. The first thing she noticed was something dangling and wiggling from the overpass ahead. She saw another beside it, and soon she realized she was looking at two young men hanging by ropes tied around their wrists. They were about a block away from the overpass. Then she noticed the men ahead in the street with weapons. They were shooting the hanging boys, which was causing their bodies to wiggle.

"Oh God!" she yelled. She shut off the radio.

Paula and Rafael Jr. began screaming. Ana commanded them to get down on the floor. They didn't immediately, but then as the sound of the gunfire became louder and closer, the children dove to the floorboard.

Katrina sank lower in her seat. "Ana, can you get us out of here?" she asked breathlessly.

Ahead, Ana could see that groups of men were rushing to the cars and pulling the drivers out at gunpoint. They struck some of them as the people got out. Then they were taking the cars, but not far. They were pulling the vehicles into clusters to block all lanes of the thoroughfare. Quickly Ana guessed that one of the drug cartels was setting up an orchestrated blockade of the city streets during rush hour to paralyze Monterrey. They had done this in the past, often seizing tractor trailers or city buses and setting them cross-ways to block all lanes. Sometimes they set vehicles on fire. Often the cartels paralyzed the city with these types of blockades as retribution for the arrest of a ranking cartel leader. But Ana saw that this blockade included the executions she had seen. Looking into her rearview mirror, she saw drivers trying to back up, but they were hitting other vehicles. People were jumping out their cars and running away, no doubt taking their keys with them. She saw a man behind her do this, but someone shot him and ran to his body to retrieve the keys to the vehicle.

Think, Ana, think what to do! She urged herself, and then she thought: *I'm not reacting fast enough!*

She looked for police and saw none. She understood from experience that the police probably knew what was going to happen and had been bought off. They would arrive when it was all over. Later there would be yet another investigation of the police forces, more firings, more announcements that the force would be purified, and then this would happen again.

Ana assessed the situation. In the street now, men who belonged to the cartel were shooting their weapons at the hanging boys or firing them in the air. They wanted to terrify the moms and dads and children in their cars so that they would abandon them and they could get the cars quickly to fortify the blockages.

Ana screamed for everyone to stay down in the car, and she commanded her children not to look. Finally she saw on the overpass ahead soldiers running towards the ropes from which the two boys hung. She saw some soldiers crouch from there to initiate a full gunfire assault on the cartel members below. Suddenly they were firing at the men just in front of her, who returned the fire! Bullets began to ricochet off the sidewalk and the street around her SUV. The noise made her cover her ears. She heard hysterical screaming. It was her children and Katrina.

It was just at this point that some men jerked open all the doors of her car. Before she realized that someone was beside her door, she saw a man pull Katrina from the SUV and throw her to the ground. Someone opened Paula's door. Ana was about to jump out to try to collect her children, but two men were there as she started her move. One pulled her out and carried her to the other side of the SUV. As he did this, the other jumped in behind the wheel. Yet another man yanked Rafael Jr. out as he crouched, terrified, on the rear floorboard. This man jumped into the back seat. Now the SUV lurched forward as the men in the vehicle attempted to escape. It moved just a few meters when fierce shots from the soldiers halted the vehicle.

When Ana had been thrown and released, she saw Paula and Katrina in the adjacent lane. She grabbed Paula and ran forward, pushing Paula and Katrina to take cover behind a car. Ana's SUV was now beside it being pounded with bullets. They hugged each other closely behind the right rear wheel well.

Ana looked desperately for Rafael Jr. It was then to her horror that she where he was. He had panicked, and he was standing in the middle of the road as if in a trance, turning himself around in circles while bullets danced all around him. Ana screamed his name.

From the sidewalk in front of a restaurant, a man came running like lightning. Ana saw him from the corner of her eye, and it registered that he was directing himself towards Rafael Jr. Suddenly a blast of bullets sprayed the front of the car that Ana and Paula and Katrina crouched behind. They ducked, but Ana kept a clear view of her son.

The running man made a powerful leap, and it looked almost like he was flying to Rafael Jr. In mid-air he grabbed the boy and then curved himself so that the two of them would fall on the street, rolling. He held Rafael Jr. as he rolled once, and Rafael was on top of him; and then he rolled again so that the boy was underneath him. Next he spread his body so that he covered the boy entirely and held him still. Even in all the commotion Ana heard the man tell her son not to move or say anything, to play dead. He turned his face towards Ana, and she could see clearly from his eyes that he was telling her to stay put and stay calm. He had Rafael Jr. under control. Ana nodded her acknowledgement. Then in a low voice she told Paula and Katrina not to move a muscle.

It seemed forever that they were all there, still as rabbits freezing in an open field when danger approaches. Eventually, a wave of silence rolled in except for an occasional pop of a gun somewhere distant. When they heard the sound of soldiers running again, she saw the man in the street raise his head to look around. Then he got off Rafael Jr. He pulled the boy up. In a crouching position the two of them ran quickly to Ana.

They were quiet from shock and horror for a moment. Then Rafael Jr. began to cry quietly. When Ana reached for him, he grabbed her tightly. He looked at the man who had saved him and said "Thank you" to him in English. Ana picked up on that. She realized that when the man had commanded her son to be still and not to move, that he had spoken Spanish with a gringo accent. She was about to give him her thanks as well, when suddenly there were soldiers beside them in the street. One said all was clear, but the soldiers still had their weapons drawn were still casting wary looks everywhere around them. Cautiously, Ana and the rest stood up. Ana looked over at her SUV and saw that the glass was shot out, the tires were flat, and there were bullet holes riddling the doors. The men inside were motionless. She shuddered.

Then she turned to the man, who was staring at her in a curious way. She said, "Gracias, gracias, gracias! Thank you for saving my son! I was so scared! I would have run out there! I would have been shot too if you hadn't done that! We both probably would have been shot!" The words and the realization made her break into tears. Katrina and Paula began crying too, raw nerves being unleashed by the relief of survival. Paula took her turn now, holding her little brother against her chest.

The man said in Spanish, "I just finished eating in the restaurant with my friend, and I was standing in the doorway with my cell phone when the shooting began. When I looked up, I saw your son and saw you, and I knew he was in trouble. It was just an instinct to get him down and covered, is all."

"Oh my God, thank you, thank you!" Ana said, still crying. The others repeated this softly.

"It's okay, we're all safe now," the man said. He revolved to look around, as if to confirm what he said. Then he extended his hand to Ana, saying, "By the way, my name is David. A pleasure to meet you!"

She heard his voice and that accent. She had heard this voice before. Now she noticed his white hair and his green eyes. She remembered him from an erotic dream that she had had about a year earlier. She remembered him from an interview on television and a YouTube video she had watched at least ten times. Her eyes became very wide.

"Oh my God!" she said to the man. She might never have remembered his first name, but she remembered his last name.

"Are you David James? Are you the hero I saw on YouTube?" She asked him in English.

Just a few minutes before, David had finished having a late lunch in the restaurant with Eduardo Ortiz, the man who had become the closest thing to another father to him. He regarded him as his Mexican father. He was, in fact, the father of Annie and Roberto. Roberto had long ago disappeared or died, and now David just thought of this man as Annie's father.

After Annie died, David was so wracked with guilt and heartbreak that he could hardly function. He was too heartbroken to face her funeral in Mexico. On the day of her funeral, David passed the day in bed with the cover over his head. He was ashamed to be in contact with Annie's family, one he had known for years. However, in a few months after the accident, David began to feel a new layer

107

of guilt because he didn't attend Annie's funeral, and this tormented him every time he thought about her. Three years after Annie's death, David couldn't bear going through life without asking her parents for forgiveness, particularly Annie's father, Eduardo, So he drove to Monterrey that year and appeared on the Ortiz' doorstep.

Eduardo Ortiz had aged considerably, not only because of Annie's death, but also because his son Roberto had apparently been killed. He was shocked to see David, of course, and he was very reticent with him at first, but very soon he saw how heartbroken David was and how David had blamed himself for his daughter dying, and his heart opened. Annie's father couldn't understand the core reason that David felt so personally responsible for the accident. Obviously, he had loved his daughter very much. Yet to hang his entire life in sadness that he had left the car door open, causing Annie to delay and wait and therefore be struck when the other car hit the door, didn't make complete sense. He felt sorry for this young man who had been as tortured by his daughter's death as he.

Then the next day of the visit, David, with a heart full of pain, told Eduardo the missing part of the story: that he and Annie were expecting a baby and that was the reason Annie hadn't come back directly to Mexico or hadn't gone on the vacation to the Bahamas. She had come to Virginia to tell David in person. And now David told him that he couldn't live another day keeping that secret. He had never told anyone.

But Annie's mother had been sitting there with them, listening. She looked at her husband and David, and she said, "But Annie did tell someone."

The father and David turned to her, incredulous.

"She told me," the mother said. "I was talking to her by phone just before she went to Virginia that last time. I guessed it because she was so preoccupied and nervous and didn't seem herself. She confirmed to me that she was pregnant. She insisted that I not tell anyone until she talked to David and the two informed the family. Unfortunately, Roberto overheard the conversation. I turned, and he was there. He had been listening. He walked away without saying anything. I guess I just felt like I should keep Annie's secret."

This was a stunning revelation for David. When he turned to look at Eduardo, he saw in the man's eyes that the man accepted this news with some understanding of something that he was holding inside him. His expression was one of great puzzlement. There was more to know.

David came back the next year. He came back every year, and he and Annie's father became exceptionally close. Finally, on one of the visits, Eduardo made an astonishing request of David, a request that brought David to Monterrey frequently through the years.

"I don't believe my son is dead," he told David one day. "I believed it for a long time, I think, because it was a tidy ending to a horrible situation. But I feel that Roberto's death was staged. If it was, I've no idea where he is or what he has been doing. We had a big falling out, a big fight, just before he supposedly died. I confronted him in a rage after reading some entries about him in a diary that Annie kept, and he left home. He got some things a couple of days later, and on his way out, he took a volume that Annie had written. I hadn't had a chance to read it before he got it, but it was among her belongings. I still had her diary. He didn't get that. I don't know what was in the volume he took. I've always wondered about it. I think he's out there somewhere. I would like you to find him for me or to find out if he did, indeed, die."

David had sat in stunned silence for a while. The thought that Roberto might be alive had never crossed his mind, even as he learned the circumstances of Roberto's death. He told Eduardo he would do what he could in his limited time. What he realized was that a search for Roberto could easily be incorporated as part of his undercover work in Mexico, Colombia, and the United States, work which very few people knew he did. Not even his wife, Julie.

Now in the Monterrey restaurant, David had finished dining with Annie's father and had said goodbye. He took out his cell phone to make calls before leaving when he heard the shooting begin. Some people in the front of the restaurant began to shout that shooters were taking cars, and David pushed to the front door to see. It was then that he saw Ana and everyone in her vehicle being pulled out. He saw the boy panic and run into the middle of the street as bullets ricocheted around him. So without thinking, he did what he always did. He flew to the boy.

And just now, when to his complete astonishment this beautiful Mexican woman before him asked him if he were David James, he gave a surprised laugh.

109

"Well, I can't believe you know my name. But yes, I'm David James."

"Oh my God!" she exclaimed. "You're that guy in the YouTube video!" Then she accepted his extended hand, and she said, "It's my great honor. I'm Ana."

On hearing her name, David felt his heart stop. For one brief instant he felt like he was looking at Annie, like the last time he had looked in Annie's eyes and had held her so tightly. The instant passed, and then in Ana's watery, profoundly dark brown eyes, he glimpsed the mysteries of his future. He saw his reflection, and he looked like a man already falling in love.

Chapter 9: El Gato

Monterrey and Sinaloa, Mexico
The years leading to Monday

He hadn't been Roberto for three decades. He was nothing like that former person, that shell of a soul who returned to Mexico from the United States in 1970, a lazy kid who wanted to smoke weed, who wanted to fuck his sister. He could hardly remember the early days in Richmond when he seemed to be a normal child, one who made horses dance and who lived adventures with his sister. Once David told him that life soars from exuberance of doing good things, but he never believed this. All he could get now was the satisfaction from completing a job, ticking off another task, checking off one more item on the master plan. An enemy killed, a friend betrayed, check, check. These things didn't bestow him joy, just fuel to keep going.

He didn't understand what he wanted to achieve until once he heard a Mexican writer use the word "narcocontinent." That was it! That's what he was doing. He was developing the narcocontinent of North America. He was sixty-three now. He only needed maybe another twenty years. Central America and Mexico had already fallen. The United States was succumbing faster than he had dreamed. Canada was nothing except asleep at the wheel. It was possible that he might live to see the narcocontinent.

He wasn't fooling himself, of course. There was no unity in Mexico or anywhere in North America among the narcos. The cartels warred savagely with one another over territory. Worse, the fucking Federal Government targeted the capos and chief lieutenants and sent the Armed Forces to eliminate them one by one. With every grave hole there was a job opening for which lower ranking cartel leaders cut off the heads of their competitors. There were frigging blood and body parts all over the cities, and the freaked out citizens had recently found the steel to band together and demand an end to the messiness.

Despite this, what mattered was that, more than ever, elected officials of federal, state, and municipal governments of Mexico had become vassals of the cartels. That subservience was the necessary foundation for the narcocontinent. The provision of illegal goods and services took place in an alternate economy. This required transportation routes by land, sea, and air; and a banking system that washed dirty money through legitimate businesses and services from all sectors of international economies. Restaurants, casinos, real estate, wineries, resorts, car dealerships, jewelry stores, tobacco and alcohol outlets- all were necessary elements of the narco-economy.

It took years, but El Gato came to appreciate the enormity of human capital and scientific knowledge required to support the narco-economy and the macro and micro economic measures required to tinder it. For the marijuana production in Mexico, he called upon horticulturalists and botanists to help him improve the crops in an environment where the seeding and harvesting might have to be relocated suddenly. He needed chemists for expansion and improvements in the production of crystal meth and new synthetic drugs. He hired mechanical and design engineers for the chemical manufacturing plants the cartel built in Guatemala and for the tunnels constantly being constructed between Mexico and the United States. The sophisticated ones had air conditioning, utilities, and freight elevators. He needed military consultants for the weaponry and intelligence operations; communications experts in radio and telecommunications; accountants and business managers, software engineers and network administrators; mechanics for the stolen vehicle fleets; pilots and ship captains; cooks; and tens of thousands of "soldiers", the muscle, the ones who did the day-to-day thug work in the streets.

In the time he had been with it, the Cartel of Sinaloa had expanded its business lines way beyond transport of drugs, so El Gato realized the limiting connotations of the description "narco." He was really thinking of all the corporate activities of the cartel to which he had dedicated his career. These activities included extortion, the levying of taxes and insurance premiums on businesses for protection, kidnapping, identity theft, car theft, art and precious stones theft, and human trafficking. Through the years the corporate organization had to adapt to changing market conditions, changes in technology, and changes in state and national laws. As an executive, he had to be entrepreneurial and open to new ideas. All of this required logistical planning, administrative management, and human resource management.

The latter is especially important because sometimes you have to kill the employees, El Gato mused. *Or they get themselves carelessly killed. Employee turnover is a real problem.*

This meant that the organization continuously had to evaluate the strengths and weaknesses of its employee force so that positions might be filled quickly. Cross training was an absolute must. Fortunately, Mexico had a seemingly endless supply of human capital for entry level positions in the cartel. There was so much poverty still among the youth, with no jobs for them, no hope of education, that the cartels could recruit and replenish their turned-over positions quickly. There was employment mobility. People were always moving up the ladder. In fact, he quite often mused that Mexico would be an economic disaster if it weren't for the jobs and opportunities provided to the country's youth by the cartels.

In the beginning, after he abandoned his family (to spite his father in particular), he quickly observed that short life expectancy characterized the profession he would enter. At first he didn't care about his life that much. Later he liked the adrenalin rush of cheating death. It felt like sport. However, at some point he began to have short-term goals, then long ones. He wanted to live simply to accomplish certain things. He saw that in the cartels, if you accumulated personal history, you became targeted because someone didn't like what you did or for whom you worked. He decided that his best shot at surviving long enough to achieve was to make sure that no one ever knew much about him.

I can't be the son of Eduardo Ortiz. I can't be who I was. Roberto has to die. His footsteps have to lead to a dead end. Literally.

The only person he cared anything about in his family was his mother, and he never wanted her to be in a position to be hurt just because she was his mother. The cartels specialized in sadistic vengeance. Sometimes before they killed you, they tortured your entire family, and killed them, and then made certain that you knew what they had done before they killed you. Sometimes they made you watch. He hated his father, was indifferent to all the other aunts, uncles, and cousins because he didn't grow up around them, but he

113

loved his mother. She had always accepted him unconditionally, even when she learned some of the things he had done, even when she unraveled the relationship he had with Annie. Everyone in the world had betrayed him except his mother. He didn't want her hurt. When he went to work for the cartel, he made sure Roberto died, so that his mother might be safe somewhere beyond Roberto's dead end.

To die in Mexico is so easy. Witnesses saw Roberto purchasing weed on a street corner in Monterrey. They saw the car with dark windows race up to the curb. They watched a couple of young men with pistols jump out and grab Roberto and pull him into the vehicle, and then they saw the car race off. Of course, later no one could remember the descriptions of the muchachos who had taken Roberto or the make of the auto. It was black, and it went that way. The seller of the marijuana fled as soon as he saw the car racing towards them.

Roberto's family was lucky. Roberto didn't simply disappear off the face of the earth like many young Mexican men, leaving his family to wonder for years if he were still alive. In the woods beside a two-lane road winding through the mountains near Santiago, a picturesque town close to Monterrey, a couple of men found a decapitated body burned and wrapped in a blue plastic taupe. The clothing fragments appeared to be from the clothes Roberto was wearing at the time of his abduction. On the body's left hand was a University of Virginia class ring bearing the year of Roberto's graduation. Tagged to his clothing was a narco-message that warned another cartel not to sell drugs in their territory, or their vendors and customers would look like this. The body's head was never found, but the evidence presented so convincingly by the state police to Roberto's family robbed them of any suspicions. They accepted that Roberto was gone. Of course, the police officers handling the investigation were on the payroll of the cartel.

This is what Roberto believed, that his family accepted he had died. He never knew that his father would have doubts about it.

Roberto went to Sinaloa after that. He never found out who the victim was who had been put in his clothing and left in Santiago. Roberto had only been required to give up his ring and his clothing. He stayed a few days in a safe house belonging to the Cartel of the Gulf, but when he had an opportunity to leave unseen, he went out and never came back. He hiked through mountains for two days until he found a road that he knew would lead him out of Nuevo León, the Mexican state which contained Monterrey and Santiago.

In those days the historic Cartel of Sinaloa was the most fabled one of Mexico, with a history going back to the end of the nineteenth century. They grew marijuana in the mountains of their state and received cocaine in the ports on the Pacific for overland transportation into the United States. Inside, Roberto craved history. Not just any history, he wanted to be a part of genuine Mexican history, one with some balls. Roberto's history made him sick now. He had been a University of Virginia pothead, lazy and directionless, and not a dot on any social map in the United States nor Mexico.

Especially he wanted to fast track into management, so he went in as a trigger man. He didn't want to waste time vending marijuana in the city for small cash or trafficking loads across the border for mule pay. He wanted the respect that came with tough jobs. Besides, the trigger men took orders from the top lieutenants. He wanted to be around them, to know what the plans were, to hear who was in favor and who was out. He would start as a sicario. An assassin. He had planned for this by purchasing pistols and semi-automatics and shooting at targets in the mountains around Monterrey.

But it was difficult to gain trust and intelligence within the cartel. Many times the assassins only received instructions pertaining to the target. They were kept on a need-to-know basis. Often he played no role in the surveillance of the victim. He would receive orders to be at a certain place at a specified time, and sometimes he had to go by a photograph to find the target. Worse, he might be joined by as many as five other trigger men when they were after multiple parties. They would pile into a large SUV and fire two or three dozen rounds into the victims. He thought there was excessive overkill. He felt like he wasn't distinguishing himself as a trigger man; he was just one of a gang firing AR-15s or AK-47s. He knew that the cartel had adopted the Colombian model of assassination, except that the sicarios there acted in ones or twos and fired pistols at close range, pulling up to the victims on motorcycles. Individual skills could distinguish a shooter more easily there.

The biggest problem that he faced, however, was that he wasn't from Sinaloa. He wasn't one of the traffickers who had for generations lived in the mountains of the famous outlaw state. They were "people," and he wasn't. Worse, he was educated and stood out from the poor young men who had lived hard lives in the hills and who seldom had gone more than a few years in school. He had felt macho in the United States, virile and strong, but the scrappy, suspicious men he met in the mountains had the genetics of the drug trade. They were naturally murderous, and murderously loyal to their bosses, who were more often than not blood relatives. They had no concept of life expectancies. They looked for ways of living on in the stories and songs of the narcos celebrated in Sinaloa and throughout Mexico.

So he kept quiet. He observed. He listened. He killed. He made himself loyal to his bosses. He demonstrated his commitment with guns and knives. To become comfortable with his first kills, he disassociated himself and imagined he was reading a novel about a cold and remorseless killer. He watched his hands as if seeing the hands of someone else murder or torture. He performed his acts dispassionately, but in step with his ambition. In less time than he imagined, he eliminated most of the longings and memories that remained from his former life. He blotted out his sister's death and the subsequent events at the ranch in Nuevo León.

About a year after he "died," he had a huge surprise. He went one day to an apartment in Culiacán to meet a guy who would give him information about a target. He was ushered into the kitchen to sit at the table across from a powerfully built, middle aged man with a faded tattoo of a python on his neck. He directed Roberto to the kitchen. This man had looked at him curiously in the doorway for a moment, but then indicated to Roberto that he follow. In the kitchen stood a shorter, more slightly built man about the same size as Roberto. When they saw each other, both visibly drew up tall. It took about seven seconds before each understood who the other was, but neither said a word. The other shot a warning look and then glanced down. Roberto appreciated the young man's instincts. It would be best to keep quiet until they could talk.

While he listened to the man with the tattoo, Roberto racked his brain to remember details his father once supplied when talking about the family tree. His father had come from a large family. He had seven brothers and two sisters. One brother moved to Sinaloa when Roberto was a kid, and he knew very little of him. That would have been about twenty years previously. This man in the kitchen was about twenty-four or twenty-five, the same age as Roberto.

116

Once when he looked over at the young man, the other nodded slightly to him. His eyes fixed on the mark on Roberto's forehead. It was his way of communicating that they shared a genetic commonality; namely, similar star-shaped birth marks high on their left temples. Roberto had had a twin sister, but this first cousin standing in the room came close to looking like an identical twin. It was incredible! Roberto understood to his astonishment that he had a relative in Sinaloa after all. The other wore a moustache, and Roberto didn't. They wore their hair a little differently. Their body structure was remarkably similar. They would have a lot to catch up on.

During the meeting, the young man left the room briefly, and afterwards Roberto heard a toilet flush. When he returned, the man slipped a small note into his hand. It had his phone number and his name, Yog. When Roberto called him a couple of days later, their lifelong partnership began. It was a partnership of conspiracies borne from their similar appearance; the kind of conspiracies identical twins might employ for sinister purposes. In the businesses of the cartels, this gave them advantages.

Free of his former life after Roberto died in Monterrey, the construction of a new identity went in fits and false starts for him. He worked it out over time with Yog as they tried different things. At first the black hole of his soul sucked every idea that came to his mind about the character he would assume for the rest of his life. He didn't feel Sinaloense. He wasn't "American." He didn't even feel Mexican, although he looked puro mexicano.

When Eduardo brought his family to the United States, Roberto felt different from every other person he met. He grew up a kid in Virginia in the 1960s, in a land of homogenous white Anglo-Saxon Protestants. His feelings and desires and cultural orientation differed from everyone he met. He was a Mexican "varón," a male, a Mexican child in a white bread world with an English history. His sister adapted through enthusiastic cultural curiosity, but he never did. He clung to her dresses.

His friend David, whom he really enjoyed like a brother at first, wasn't like the genteel and phony people he encountered everywhere in Virginia. Maybe it was because David's family had no money, and the only pretenses David possessed were his many fantasies.

117

Unfortunately, David's most enduring fantasy was about his sister, and that was an intrusion into forbidden space. Unpardonable space.

Thank God for his horse! That horse represented heritage to him. It kept alive the warmth and smells of his previous Mexican ranchero life. The memories provided him some solid ground in the humid, mushy social environment of Virginia.

But in Virginia he did learn how to role play, whether he appreciated this or not at the time. He played the macho and precocious Mexican kid, acting lucky because he had the fortune to come to live in the United States. But as he grew up he judged the USA to be a country which codified its prejudices in mannerisms. The adults smiled at the handsome little Mexican boy, but he knew the people weren't genuine. He was angry a lot. He wanted acceptance and respect for the person he really was. He got it for the person he played.

Yet after the years of living in the states, he also felt foreign when he returned to Mexico. He remembered his life in Mexico as a small child, a life of privilege, but the Mexico he came back to didn't jive at all with the fantasies of his childhood.

He quickly found he had no place at the ranch in Monterrey. His father, Eduardo, couldn't hide his disappointment in the soft and unmotivated son who returned in the summers from Virginia. Roberto knew his father naturally expected his son would be the heir to take the reins of the family business. It was a traditional expectation attached to the first-born male from birth. However, Roberto had little exposure growing up to the business of the ranch, and his traveling father, somehow so involved in both work and politics back home in Mexico, didn't have the time to invest in his son. The Roberto who arrived at the ranch after college was unmolded, directionless, and a pot head. When his uncles came to welcome him home, Roberto saw the puzzlement and disappointment cross their faces after some awkward conversation with Eduardo's prodigal son. He could read what they were thinking: *You're not like your sister.*

By the time Roberto arrived in Sinaloa, his nerves were raw. He had died in Monterrey, and unless he made a mark of usefulness quickly in Sinaloa, he would die again in a much more painful way in a place that was never his own.

118

A couple of weeks after his arrival in Sinaloa, he was sitting in a bar in Culiacán when he heard the lyrics of the old Doors song, "People Are Strange":

"When you're strange,
No one remembers your name.
When you're strange."

That's it! he thought as he banged his fist on the table. *So simple! I don't want anyone to remember my name.*

So he tried never giving his real name. With no name or personal history, the man who was once Roberto easily slipped in and out of the bodies of "las personas desaparecidas" (the disappeared persons) of Mexico. There were tens of thousands of names and histories available from the victims of the cartel wars. As it turned out, he used several identities in the early years. Once he began to have experience, he decided to be a true ghost. He would become invisible to his enemies. He began to create the persona of "the leader with no name, or a thousand names." Later, in the Sinaloa towns and mountains, the myth of this person flourished in the narco culture which glorified imprisoned or dead capos and all the bosses who provided protection and jobs to the people.

He himself fanned the rumors about a cartel cell run by a boss with no name: a man who gave orders without being known. In the stories and ballads that ran through Sinaloa through the years, there were accounts of a boss who fought in the gun battles alongside his men, but none knew which one he was. He was fearless and brave; he had balls the size of pomegranates; and he escaped with his life from impossible ambushes so many times that the people began to refer to him as El Gato, the cat. Before long, the songs known as "narco-corridos" performed by popular Mexican bands and recording artists celebrated the legends of the fierce capo that couldn't be killed nor could be known. He was made of smoke. He was The Cat.

El Gato hired substitutes when he needed them. He rotated actors to impersonate him, attending summits with other bosses, or giving orders, or making some public appearances. When the head of the Sinaloa Cartel eventually began to rely on him as a top lieutenant, he himself was already expert at being shadowy and

119

transient. However, El Gato had achieved something the boss wished that he had; namely, El Gato was more of a position than a person, and a smoky position at that.

His boss was the opposite. He had international notoriety, being named on a national business magazine's list of the world's wealthiest men. That capo's old photos showing him in the prison from which he had escaped adorned the narco websites for years. The man stayed on the move, paying handsomely for the silence of conspirators who knew his whereabouts. On the other hand, El Gato went where he wanted, unknown and unnoticed. For this very reason, he used El Gato to execute some of his high-level strategies, more and more in the United States. El Gato could get around the United States more easily because he wasn't on the radar of the FBI, the CIA, or the DEA. So the anonymity and mobility of The Cat by extension helped his boss accomplish what he wanted to do in the country to the north.

El Gato took great pains to please his boss. The man had known him well for twenty years. The boss knew what El Gato really looked like. He knew about Roberto's former life in the United States, because he once gave El Gato one opportunity to gain his trust, by having him tell his history to him. Except for Yog, El Gato's boss was the only one who knew the identity and whereabouts of El Gato's family in Monterrey. This, in fact, insured El Gato's loyalty to him.

The anonymity of El Gato both confined him and liberated him. It confined him because he had to think constantly about subterfuges and alibis. It liberated him because once in play, anonymity allowed him to move freely, to have discussions with men who didn't know who he was, to hear sometimes what they really were thinking, and to observe the faces and body language of those around him. This was as close to being the Invisible Man as one could be in life, he supposed. Yog was the one person on earth with whom he kept a lot of company, and Yog savored the duplicity and impersonations assigned to him by his cousin as much as El Gato.

As the years passed, El Gato became more sophisticated and experienced in living through the legends which he helped to create about himself. The advancing borders of Sinaloa moved in stride with his achievements. His troops did endure hellish rains of bullets and high body counts, but he inflicted more casualties on his

120

enemies in cruel and terrifying ways. The wealth and power of the Cartel of Sinaloa continued to grow. As a result, the pesos and dollars arrived in quantities that the cartel accountants struggled to launder clean. "Efectivo," cash, was a problem of excess.

El Gato had an important international reason for being a shadowy human being. He wanted the intelligence and law enforcement agencies of the United States to remain clueless regarding who was directing the operations of the cartel at the top. He had lived in the United States. He knew what kind of country it was. It was a country which would use any pretext, like an "unstable" neighbor on its border, to invade and destroy. He knew the CIA, the FBI, and the DEA were infiltrating Mexico like carpenter ants. Their agents and intelligence officers in the U.S. Armed Forces were working with the Mexican government and its military under the guise of helping Mexico to fight organized crime, but in reality to promote the self-interests of the United States.

On two occasions El Gato exposed DEA undercover agents posing as cargo transportation agents to help the cartels move their merchandise through Mexico to the United States. The agents had laundered money for the cartels in order to follow the money trails. El Gato had seen the Bureau of Alcohol, Tobacco, and Firearms stupidly allow the sale of thousands of automatic weapons to Mexican cartels. These strategies backfired and led to more violence not only in Mexico, but also in the USA.

When the violence escalated, growing numbers of people in the U.S. Government and military itched for military intervention in Mexico. They tried to set the stage for invasion by insisting that Mexico was a "failed state," unable to contain the bloodshed that was certain to spill into U.S. cities as the Mexican cartels gained more and more power. In the skies unmanned drones and spy satellites watched movements in Mexico like hawks stalking small rodents. El Gato would never be naïve regarding such activities. He understood well how the United States had provoked Mexico into war in the 1840s so that the United States would have the rationale to invade and seize territory for its expanding country.

But when thinking about the United States and what it might do, El Gato thought hard about the narcocontinent he was building. The border between the United States and Mexico had always been a

121

huge problem. It was the place where the costs of delivery for product tripled.

What if there were no border, and Mexico and the United States were one country? Would it be better if the border were removed, he wondered? *Maybe one nation under God would bestow huge advantages! I'll think about this.*

Sometimes El Gato shook his head in self amazement. Except for his superior, he was the most powerful and decisive leader of the Cartel of Sinaloa, and no one in Mexico or the United States seemed to have figured this out. The government and narco-blogs still had out-of-date organizational charts which missed entire business units of the cartels and which had question marks in many of the positions purporting to show the boss of that unit. He had seen nothing to indicate that there was any intelligence about his work. Yet under his leadership, the Sinaloa centers for the distribution of product in Chicago, Houston, and Atlanta became much stronger. In the past three years he had expanded greatly operations in New York, Washington, Memphis, Tampa, San Francisco, Los Angeles, San Diego, Phoenix, Toronto, Montreal, and Vancouver.

The products were marijuana, cocaine, heroin, and meth. Synthetic marijuana recently had become popular as the demand for organic weed dropped among the high school population. The kids believed that synthetic marijuana wasn't dangerous or addictive. El Gato saw firsthand the naivety of the gringos when he grew up in the United States. They wanted a party high, and they were completely disconnected from the blood and guts of the delivery system that brought them products which were designed to addict. Later in life, El Gato exploited these national characteristics of naivety and short sightedness by addicting hundreds of thousands of people. It meant billions of dollars.

Then all of a sudden one day, a ghost from the past turned up in Mexico, and threatened to make a mess of the work El Gato was doing in the United States. His name was David Wilson James, and somehow he was in Mexico tracking El Gato's path north of the border. Worse, he was insisting that the shadowy legend of El Gato was a real, flesh-and-blood person. El Gato could feel him on his heels, and he knew that destiny would bring David to his ultimate rendezvous, where he would discover that the Roberto both of them

122

knew was still very much alive. The stakes were way too high for El Gato to permit that to happen.

Chapter 10: Santa Muerte

En Route to Monterrey, Mexico
The road to Monday

On the day before El Gato intended to appear on the roof to assassinate David, he was a passenger in a black Lincoln SUV with his driver Yog and the two beautiful women who would accompany him. The women were veteran assassins who had survived three years in the Cartel of Sinaloa. Recruited in Monterrey, they had been university students who spoke fluent English. They were trained in using weapons. In the beginning they worked as seductresses to lure men to places where they could be taken. El Gato saw their value as cover for him when he was Alberto Bernal, the CEO of Bernal Solutions, so he requested them for this mission. They believed they were working for Sr. Bernal, the CEO who was on the payroll of the Cartel of Sinaloa.

On this trip the two women had been taken to a hotel in Laredo, Texas, where they met up with Sr. Bernal. In fact, they first met Yog, believing it was Bernal, and Yog instructed them in their roles for crossing the border back into Mexico. They would pose as corporate managers for Bernal Solutions. When El Gato showed up in their hotel room later, looking so much like Yog, the women felt a confused uneasiness, but they had learned to roll with the dice. They kept quiet and studied the information they needed to know about the business and about the information they should obtain on the trip to Monterrey from Laredo the next morning.

The pre-dawn darkness was surrendering to the coming sun when, dressed in business suits, the four of them boarded a SUV and proceeded directly to the International Bridge. El Gato had been doing business in San Antonio. They used attendance at an electronics exhibition there as a cover for their presence in the United States. El Gato had his passport identifying him as Alberto Bernal, and he had business cards and brochures in the car for his company, Bernal Solutions. It was a wholesaler of medical electronic equipment, with installations in hospitals and physician offices throughout Mexico and the United States, and with headquarters in Mexico City, Monterrey, and Houston. At least that was the façade. Alberto was President and Consultant. In fact, El Gato had become very conversant in the technical language of the medical electronics industry and could be quite convincing. He had in the vehicle customer lists, all of whom could be called to verify the legitimacy of Señor Bernal's company and its services, if that was necessary. However, on that particular morning, no one on the Mexico side of the border required that their vehicle stop for further inspection. They were waved through after a customs officer looked at their passports and faces and glanced in the SUV.

But it had taken hours to get through from the United States side. The USA was sealing the border because of the military takeover in Mexico, and there was mass confusion over who might be allowed to pass. They were allowing Mexican citizens to pass through for the time being. There were demonstrators everywhere, and United States Army troops, and El Gato had been extremely nervous about their passage. Finally, they had been allowed through.

From the border, they drove through the city of Nuevo Laredo and took the toll highway, the "cuota", to Monterrey, a trip of about two hours. Very early in the morning, on instruction from Señor Bernal, one of the women radioed a contact in Monterrey over encrypted frequency and told him to leak to the appropriate person in the Federal Police that El Gato had been verified to be in Monterrey the previous evening to take care of "personal business," and to be certain that David James was informed.

The dusty road out of the city to the cuota was flat, but the toll highway traversed rolling desert tufted with green brush and grass and dry river beds. Farther it began the steep ascent through the grey, brown, and white countryside of the stony mountains buffering Monterrey. It was a boring ride until they hit the mountains, and as they sped their way towards the city, El Gato stared blankly out his window and kept deep in thought. When he traveled, he insisted on quiet, not even music playing. The others listened with headphones, but he wanted to hear anything unusual, such as a rapidly approaching vehicle from behind or anything wrong with the SUV.

One of the women occasionally announced a relevant report on her phone which updated El Gato on the current happenings in

125

Monterrey as they flew along the highway. They learned that Monterrey was a mess. Citizen groups and demonstrators for dozens of causes filled the streets and blocked traffic. On the major thoroughfares in the city, cars crept at a snail's pace bumper to bumper as they tried to push through the crowds. On the secondary roads in the center of Monterrey, downtown, vehicles were at a standstill. Army and federal police stood on corners in the city. Apparently some tried to direct traffic. The Army and Marines had troops and trucks everywhere. Young men and women dressed in black clothing to identify themselves as Zs mixed among the people. All were looking for anyone who had weapons. Citizens immediately reported via Twitter whenever they found a blockade or ran into gunfire, alerting people to stay clear. Some took pictures or videos with their phones of anything unusual. They listed links to videos of confrontations or news reports provided by news organizations like CNN Mexico and Grupo Reforma.

The woman leaned forward to speak to El Gato from the back seat. "Senor Bernal, you wanted to know if David James and Ana Valdez are on television on the roof of that building today," she said. "Yes, they're there."

El Gato grunted. "It's the lure of the trap," he replied. "It's a place clear of all people; a good killing field for us, and a good ambush point for them. What's the environment in that vicinity today? Who is around?"

"The same as yesterday," she replied. "Army and police and Zs everywhere. They're estimating a hundred thousand people in the streets near the Macroplaza."

But there was an expression of surprise on her face when El Gato said it was "a good killing field for us," and he saw it on her face. She turned and tried to act like she hadn't heard, but it was too late. He had made a mistake, and they both knew it.

He shook his head a little and turned to Yog, who was driving. In a lower voice he said, "We need to get our weapons in place. Has to be cars and mommy mini-vans stuck in the street tomorrow if the situation is the same. Want them loaded with a fuckin' arsenal: grenades, AK-47s, the works. I need men and women who look like married couples in the vehicles. We use stolen cars. Weapons hidden on the floor or in the trunks. We'll have the cars in the area where we create the diversion to pull the soldiers from the assassination

126

scene. Has to be a place far enough away where our men can shoot a retreat to the trucks that can get them out. So the trucks have to be in a place where there's a road you can friggin' drive out of the city. We pay whatever it takes to have this route. They blast everyone who gets in the way; especially hit the kids in black. As for us, after the ladies and I do our job on the roof, we leave our weapons and we take off our suits on the way down the stairs. We just go down into the crowd to rendezvous with an exit team in a different place. Before we go on that roof, we'll know there's no one there except David and the Valdez woman."

El Gato stopped and stared out the window. He said to Yog in a hushed tone, "My old friend David might be a Z, but he has just been one lucky son of a whore his whole life. I can't understand how he hooked up with the Valdez woman. She's the one who has really caused us all the fucking problems with these people in the streets, and we never noticed what she was doing until recently. How did that happen? She has turned out to be a worse problem than the Zetas. She's dead. They're both dead. I know this David. Forty years isn't going to change him. He has figured out there's a real El Gato. But he's naïve. He'll believe that El Gato will come on that roof and talk to him. El Gato has nothing to say to him to him. I just need to finish something I should have done forty years ago."

He turned back and looked at the woman. He stared at her to intimidate her. She couldn't take the silence of his look and said nervously, "Sr. Bernal, I don't care about anything except to do the job I'm given. I'm a professional. I like working for you."

Calmly he told her, "I've been interested in this gringo David James because he believes El Gato will come to meet with him. He believes in El Gato like a gringo kid believes in Santa Claus. But he's going to meet me and you and your sleeping sister there. We'll have a date with him." She didn't answer him. She just nodded her understanding.

He turned back around in his seat, and caught his cousin's look. It said, *We'll have to kill these ladies later. We've run our mouths too much. We're not used to working with people in on our discussions. We've fucked up and now we have some turnover for the cartel.*

Since it no longer mattered if the women heard or not, because they would be dead, Yog asked El Gato a question. "Why are they on that roof? Why that building?"

El Gato was annoyed by his own mistakes, and replied irritably, "It's where her fucking office is. We should have burned the place. We should have paid more attention. We're warring over the Monterrey plaza and not noticing important problems. Jesus, the government got overthrown and we didn't see it coming! We're making too many fucking errors."

Now everyone grew silent as they rolled along past the empty land of the huge ranches and dry stream beds in the flat landscape before coming to the mountains. Out the window on the autopista, El Gato saw one of the several small, crude temples to the Virgin that had been set up, little shrines with candles and a statue of the Blessed Lady inside. Some were decorated with fresh flowers. He wondered if there were any shrines to Santa Muerte between Nuevo Laredo and Monterrey.

Santa Muerte. Holy Death. Jesus! he sighed.

He had read recently that she had two million followers in Mexico and the United States, and she was popular among the lower classes and the criminal groups. She was prevalent in Mexico City, but recently had become popular also in Nuevo León, the state dominated by Monterrey. There were even Mexicans in Texas worshiping her. While he was thinking of her, he said a small prayer to her just for the hell of it. He asked to be successful in killing David and Ana. He prayed for his men of the cartel coming to Monterrey to meet with him. He had a plan of action in this time when it felt like the country was up for grabs. Now would be the time to consolidate power and to make some bold moves not only in Mexico, but also in the United States. His ideas depended on the United States not invading. They were going to need the Zetas to pull off what he had in mind, and it was going to be very difficult to run a mission together with their bitter enemies. So he sent a prayer to Santa Muerte that the Zetas would be willing to listen. Then he laughed at himself because of the prayer.

Ahead, he saw the mountains of the Sierra Madre begin to loom closer. Their vehicle was quickly catching up on a convoy of Marines heading to Monterrey. He turned to Yog and he told him, "Just hang back behind them through the mountains. We'll watch them." He glanced back at the women behind, and the one who stayed on her phone was already radioing someone about the location and direction of the convoy. He looked ahead again.

"I'm sure before we arrive to the mountains that there will be a check point by the Marines," he announced. "Everything in stow?" He was referring to the secret compartments under the floor board where they hid their weapons. Everyone self-consciously checked their pockets and bags. Everything was concealed. There were four leather executive brief cases, custom designed for their modular AK-47s, which fit inside a false floorboard compartment. Their Beretta pistols were under their seat. In addition to wearing their business suits, the four had briefcases in the rear of the MKX with falsified documents that would appear related to their positions in Bernal Solutions. El Gato wanted a believable cover, and he had reviewed personally every document for consistency and credibility.

He thought about David again. The truth was that David hadn't been on his radar until a few months previously, when there seemed to be an explosion of Z enrollment and activity in Monterrey, Guadalajara, and Mexico City. Then someone showed him Ana's tweets and blogs, and the video and subsequent interviews of David and the Halloween incident in San Antonio where David had thwarted a robbery. *What the fuck?* he thought when he saw that.

After that, he found that Zs had official tweet sites to report activity in those cities. Those kinds of tweets from other websites and organizations had been going on for a couple of years, but through the coordination efforts of Ana Valdez, the Z sites had developed a national branding, with a Z logo, and a "Like Us" page on Facebook. How crazy, he thought. Not to mention the blogs. There had been numerous blogs on the narcos, one of the most famous being El Blog del Narco, reportedly being run by a university student in Texas. These featured grisly photos of death scenes and were compendiums of news reports from various news organizations throughout Mexico and the United States.

Of course, the blog that interested him the most was the blog that David wrote. He wrote it in English, and Ana Valdez often referenced it in her blog. She translated his into Spanish. The interesting thing to El Gato was that David titled his blog "Cat and Mouse." He wrote intermittently. His blog concentrated on the warfare that had intensified between the Zetas and the Cartel of the

Gulf in Monterrey, and the growing presence there of the Cartel of Sinaloa. David named the Zeta leaders often. However, when he wrote about Sinaloa, he mentioned El Gato's boss, but he ruminated in recent writings that someone else was also functioning as an operations leader and calling a lot of the shots in Mexico and the United States. He attributed this work to one person. David wrote his opinion that the legend of El Gato was real, and that there was one man, an unknown, who executed many of the leader's orders in the United States.

So, El Gato wondered, *why does David write his blog in English?*

The only answer that made sense to him was that David was directing his blog personally to this unknown, someone he believed familiar with the United States. El Gato thought David was fishing, but the last blog was blatant. The last blog was an invitation to the roof top.

David had written it two days earlier when the demonstrations broke out huge in Monterrey and the center of activity was in the Macroplaza. David wrote of his splendid views from the roof top of "the revolution of the people." He encouraged peace and restraint from all sectors. He stated his appreciation that the police, the military, and even the cartels had so far not served up much violence. He asked that everyone listen to the speakers who took to the podiums and to maintain respect for all viewpoints and personal stories. He urged the Armed Forces to transition power back to an uncorrupted democracy. He offered that Z leadership as well as leadership from citizen groups might work with the military in establishing a transitional government. He urged the soldiers and police not to abuse power. When he wrote about the cartels, he appealed by name to the local leaders to help Mexico by calling a cease fire.

Except when he wrote about the Cartel of Sinaloa. There he addressed "the powerful leader represented by El Gato."

"I know you're there," David wrote. "You're real, and you have a lot of bearing on what happens with the United States. It's important we talk."

That had sent a cold charge through El Gato's body. How much could his old gringo nemesis really know about El Gato? He was furious that on this internationally read blog David was putting flesh and blood on the smoky and shadowy skeleton of El Gato. And much worse than that: tying him to the United States!

El Gato imagined David standing in front of him now. *We should talk about what, Fuckhead? You want me to answer your blog so you can confirm I exist? Get an idea where I am? Set up a trap with your friends from the CIA or DEA? Jesus, we're not going to talk. I'm just going to blow you away."*

El Gato shook his head. They had been friends a million years ago. At least, it had started that way. Roberto loved that a gringo looked up to him, a Mexican, with so much respect. Almost all the gringos he met assumed that anyone not from the United States was second class in some way, inferior, less fortunate, someone needing instruction in the right way to live, the right God to believe in. Yet from their first meeting, when Roberto showed his mastery of horses and his physical superiority, David put himself in a role of apprentice to Roberto. It was beautiful. It felt good to be recognized in that way. Roberto loved impressing the doe-eyed David time and again and getting him to do exactly what he wanted.

Their relationship was like that the first couple of years. But later David began to wander into territory reserved only for Roberto. Those doe eyes began to follow Annie's every move. Then all David wanted to talk about was her. David was young, but as they grew, Roberto began to sense he would later have competition for Annie's affections. He didn't think he should even have to explain to David that it was wrong for him to be thinking about Annie. It was betrayal of an unwritten rule that should have been clearly understood. For David, Roberto's sister should be hands off.

Annie was his twin sister, for God's sake! They had shared a bed together until they were six years old. This wasn't because they had to. Their ranch home in Mexico was large and beautiful with several bedrooms, even though they were only a family of four. But Annie and Roberto were close and wanted to share a room. At night time they told each other stories and talked about their day. Their family was innocent. They were just children, and their parents doted on them. The reason for giving them separate bedrooms later had more to do with gender identification, so that Roberto might have boys' toys and clothing and room decorations, and Annie would enjoy her feminine tastes.

Even after they had separate rooms, Roberto used to come to Annie's room at bed time. He would lie beside her or hug her from behind as they chatted. He adored her. She made him feel complete and safe in some way. She was an integral part of his identity.

Her body responded to adolescence first. Roberto became astonished at the changes in his sister. She was eleven when this began, and he noticed her hips and breasts rounding underneath her clothing. A year or so later he felt the changes in his own body and how it began to respond when he would think about his sister.

One night, he believed it was when they were thirteen (he knew that they had already met David), he went to Annie's bedroom to chat with her. Out of habit, he slipped behind her on the bed and held her as they talked, like they had done so many times. She was telling him about someone in school, but he found that he wasn't listening. Instead, he was thinking about how she felt in his arms and how good she smelled after her bath. His cock enlarged and became rock hard and suddenly pressed against her buttocks. She was wearing cotton pajamas and felt it. He moved back quickly, and she turned and looked at him with a strange and puzzled expression. Then she stated in a voice that betrayed her displeasure, "Listen, I'm really sleepy tonight. I thought I could talk, but I see that I need to crash. Do you mind?" Roberto shook his head and quickly left the room.

But he never could forget how his sister looked, so sensual, so beautiful, so grown up. As his voice began to break and deepen and he began to shave and hair began to appear on his chest, he looked at himself long periods of time in the bathroom mirror. He imagined Annie standing naked next to him, so he could think about how they were similar and how they were different. In their faces they resembled each other strongly. Their hair and eyes had the same color, so deep brown they were almost black. Sometimes when Annie went into her bathroom to shower or bathe, he snuck through her bedroom and cracked the bathroom door to look at her. This helped him remember how her body appeared, so he could imagine it beside his when he looked in his mirror in his own bathroom. He had a big cock dangling from a shock of black hair, and he pictured the symmetry of their bodies next to each other, Annie's large breasts projecting outward. If they were to rotate towards each other, he imagined, then her breasts and his upright cock called for a union of their bodies like the fit of perfect puzzle pieces. Their minds, their

132

intuitions, their feelings were always one. They were twins. In the mirror he could see that their bodies were also twins, with male and female symmetry.

He wondered if Annie ever thought about these things. He decided that certainly she must, but she wasn't as daring as he, that she would never risk peering at him in his bathroom. So he let her see him with his shirt off often, or in just his underpants, so she could know how the other part of her body was changing, the part that was him, the part becoming masculine, muscular, more manly. Once, he took a Polaroid photograph of himself naked. The camera pointed to the bathroom mirror, and the flash obscured his face and the top of the picture. He left the picture out where she could see it when he called her to his bedroom and pretended to be occupied in his closet while talking to her. He knew she saw it, but she never said a word.

One day he walked in on a conversation that Annie and their mother were having in the kitchen. He stopped just outside the door to listen, and when he heard, his heart sunk to his stomach, blood rushed to his cheeks, and he felt like it was hard to catch a breath. They were fifteen years old. He heard Annie talking about a seventeen-year-old boy who had asked her to attend the Junior Prom with him. He was a big, blonde, blue eyed gringo on the football team. He was very popular and had his own car. As he listened near the door to the kitchen, Roberto felt hot and sick.

This guy who had asked her out was an impressive kid. Roberto knew that now he had entered into a new phase with his sister, one that he wasn't going to enjoy at all. He was going to have to figure out how to control their world better.

When they first arrived in Virginia, Roberto was all that Annie had, and vice versa. They both had David, of course. Later, the social networks for Annie expanded as she became popular. Roberto had a reflected popularity because of the novelty of being her twin, but Annie was the one who electrified others. People wanted to be around her. She was sweet, funny, and gorgeous, and she made people feel like she truly understood their feelings.

Roberto began to see that he had less time with her. Older boys were moving in on her. At night, after she finished studying, Annie returned calls to girlfriends. The nightly chats of Roberto and Annie became less frequent and shorter. So in that moment outside the kitchen, it became very clear to Roberto that his sister was leaving him behind.

Given that, David's crush on Annie was salt in the wound, and David's emboldening relationship with Annie through time especially infuriated Roberto. He felt a strong betrayal. He thought that he shouldn't have to deal with that from his friend.

The memories were making him upset. *Fuck,* El Gato thought as he stared out the window of the Lincoln SUV. *These memories make me feel like Roberto again.*

He had just relived the moment outside the kitchen as Roberto. That was a person long dead, a victim, not a player with balls like El Gato.

Fuck, fuck, fuck, he thought. And he remembered that things got a lot worse.

His worst nightmare came true because Annie did eventually fall for David, and that was just too personal against him. Roberto suspected that she had feelings for him beginning at the end of high school, but David was a couple of years younger, and for a young woman going off to college, that was a world of difference in time. But by the time of high school graduation the gap between Annie and Roberto became an unbridgeable chasm. She had challenged the stirrings and feelings he had for her. She clearly was disturbed by them, especially after the incident in her bedroom one night when he reached down and touched her while he pushed a kiss on her mouth. She kicked him in his testicles, and, in an enraged whisper, she told him to get out and never put a hand on her again.

A couple of days later he tried to restore some equilibrium between them with an apology, but when he put his hand on her shoulder, Annie reddened with anger and pushed him away. That night they went out with David and Myra to Bill's Barbecue, and there Annie threatened Roberto that she would let their father know that he was touching her.

Jesus!

What really had crushed him that evening, however, was that he saw the looks she gave to David at the table. She looked at him with trust. Roberto knew that she could have an intimacy with David that she used to have with him.

They left David behind when they both went off to college. Somehow Annie got accepted into Radcliffe, which was like being

134

accepted into Harvard. Roberto had done well in high school, but he knew he couldn't get into the New England prep colleges. In fact, he was surprised when he was accepted into the University of Virginia, a difficult school to enter, and he was a foreign national. There were excellent schools in Mexico that either might have attended, but Annie in particular had felt that to continue education in a more international way would benefit them greatly in the future. Their parents had traveled extensively throughout the world, especially their father because of his business, so they understood the desire to go to college in the United States. Eduardo did, however, want both his children to return to Mexico when they finished undergraduate school.

As high school graduation neared, Roberto felt anxious because of his pending separation from Annie. He was also pissed with David. He hated him for the trust and affection that Annie bestowed upon him and withheld from Roberto. Annie had older boyfriends, but Roberto knew Annie's heart and soul. In the future she would fall for David. He began to drink heavily, and in the spring before graduating, he started smoking marijuana.

With that memory, El Gato laughed sadly to himself in the SUV now barreling towards Monterrey. He remembered that in college he had mild interest about the guys who sold him the grass and drugs in Charlottesville. He wondered about the distribution system: where they got the drugs, who supplied them, and if the marijuana in particular had come from Mexico. He wondered how much money these preppy looking boys selling to him in the dorms were making and if they were paying for college that way.

Mostly he was interested in using. He wanted to do well enough academically to stay in school where he could party until his time was up and it was time to go back to Mexico to face some kind of reality he hadn't been a part of in many years. He thought of Annie a lot. He thought of her even as he had a series of girlfriends he didn't really care much about, but they partied with him well. Annie returned maybe one out of three of his calls, and mostly she tried to know how he was doing in school.

He flipped out when Annie first confirmed that she was seeing David. She told him by telephone while he was in Charlottesville. He made up an excuse to get off the line. Then he acted out his furor by destroying his bedroom. After so many years of anticipating the moment, this almost felt scripted. He pulled out some cocaine and used, then sat on the floor with his back against the wall and fantasized about different ways in which David would die.

In his mind now, El Gato looked at Roberto in that memory, sitting against the wall. He hardly recognized that naïve and silly young man he had once been. Roberto was the one who had died. Not David. But in the life of El Gato, he thought, maybe each of the persons he had killed or tortured, in fact, had been David. Maybe there was a little David in each dying man or woman or kid. In all those nearly forty years, there had been so many deaths, uncountable, unknowable, for which he had been executioner either in person or by command to another. To see someone die, to bleed, to swell from beatings, to scream and beg, to burn alive…

Well, he observed in himself, *no reaction to that now.*

How dim did that Roberto sitting against the wall appear: the Roberto who had off handedly wondered about the distribution systems for the drugs he was using would be amazed at the logistics of the international distribution network which he had come to put together over the course of forty years. That Roberto didn't have a clue about the products floating throughout the world on rivers of human blood.

He returned to the ranch outside Monterrey looking forward to having a summer to spend with his sister. He thought that if he were on good behavior, he and Annie might recover some of their old trust and rapport with one another in the natural environment of Mexico. He had been there just a couple of days when he heard his mother take the phone call from Annie when she broke the news that she was going to see David in Virginia and that she wasn't really going on vacation with friends to Bermuda. He never saw it coming when his mother intuited that something was wrong with Annie, and she asked her, "Annie, are you going to see David because you're pregnant?" He listened a few more minutes in shock as it sunk in what had happened, and then he ran to his room. He was furious to the point of vomiting. He did make some heaves in the toilet later, but first he slammed his fist into the wooden headboard of his bed until his knuckles bled.

Two days later, during dinnertime, they received the news that Annie was dead. The uncles and aunts were still coming by to see Roberto and to find out when Annie would return home. There had been so much family celebration and activity that Roberto hadn't yet had private time with his father, which he was dreading. The dinner table fell silent when a servant who had answered the phone whispered something into Eduardo's ear, and he excused himself by saying that he had an urgent call from the United States. From the dining room, the guests heard Eduardo greet David on the phone and then heard his gasp and mournful wail. Roberto's mother and an aunt ran panic-stricken to the room where his father had the phone. Alarmed, they demanded to know what was wrong, and Eduardo, in shock, blurted out that Annie was dead. Everyone at the dining table then rushed to the room. One of Roberto's uncles had to wrest the phone from Eduardo's tight grasp to find out details from David.

Eduardo collapsed to a sitting position on the floor. His eyes darted pitifully from one face to another as if to plea that someone might tell him that he was mistaken, that he had heard the news incorrectly. On the other end of the line, David was sobbing. The information emerged in miserable shards of sentence fragments. Roberto stood back a small distance, listening in shock to his uncle talk to David. He was not believing what he was hearing. He had just absorbed that Annie was pregnant, and now he was hearing that she was dead. It was insane. It was all too fast. She was going to be home in a few days. How could she be dead?

El Gato was feeling edgy and disoriented by these memories when his cousin, driving, tapped his left arm and nodded towards the rear mirror.

Yog announced, "We have company."

El Gato looked back and saw a couple of police cars in the passing lane coming up very fast behind them. The cars raced by them and the Marine convoy as well. They were the Federal Police.

"Eyyy, who is giving *them* orders?" Yog asked sarcastically. "Who's running the fucking country right now?"

"That madre de puta, General Alvarez, is trying to," grumbled El Gato. "But he doesn't know the dogs he has unleashed."

He remembered the demonstrators whom they had seen on the United States side of the border near the international bridges and the military units that were amassing there, plus the Texas state police. "You saw the gringos back at the border, holding up their signs and shouting shit," El Gato told Yog. "Most of them looked like Mexicans. Hell, all the USA border agents are Mexicans. It's a fucked-up world."

He had heard some of the people shouting "Save Mexico!" Others, opposing them, were bellowing, "Protect our border!" Someone was holding up a placard that said, "Alvarez, kill the narcos!" El Gato had even seen forty or fifty robust young men in black pants and shirts. *Gringo Zs*, he thought.

They were becoming more of an annoyance for him, the Zs. They were becoming troublesome, not on the scale of the Zetas, but the problem was that they were making people believe in hope. It was the lack of hope which had driven people to turn to the narco way of life. A dream that Mexico might become a land of opportunity could become an effective weapon against the cartels. Until recently, all the firepower and political rhetoric against the cartels had bounced like bullets off armor. Now, however, organized crime in Mexico was getting some competition for recruits.

Jesus, a Texas band even has a YouTube video about transnational Zs that's popular in both the United States and Mexico, he recalled, shaking his head.

El Gato turned to the women in the back seat. For his own ironic gratification he said, "Did you see the kids in black at the border? They're a bunch of hopping adolescents taking Kung Fu classes. We gotta put some money and guns in their hands and get their priorities straight. At least then we might have some guys who can run and get the work done fast. They're already in shape."

He sat back in his seat. He felt impatient to plan in more detail how they should manage the next day. Halfway to Monterrey there was a service center with fuel, restaurants, and shops. When he saw it ahead, he instructed Yog to pull in there. After they parked, he told the women to go to the rest rooms and then join them in the fast food area for some sandwiches. When they left the Lincoln, he turned to Yog.

"Let's talk about tomorrow," he said.

Yog answered, "I've been thinking about it too. We should talk about the roof top. Maybe we have the same idea."

El Gato returned his cousin's stare and saw that they were thinking the same way.

"You need to shave off your moustache," he told Yog.

Yog nodded and replied, "I can take the ladies to the house in Cumbres if you want. That way you can be in Anáhuac to meet the men coming for the meeting. The women and I can join you later tomorrow afternoon. Don't worry, I can get us there." The references to Cumbres and Anáhuac were to two of the residential communities of Monterrey.

El Gato said, "I'm thinking maybe the ladies don't make it to Anáhuac later."

Yog nodded his understanding and said, "You're sure our favorite couple, David and Ana, will be there again? On top of that building?"

El Gato snorted a sound. "They'll be there. If not, they'll be somewhere we'll know. We'll adapt. Let's eat and get to Monterrey and map out the positions for tomorrow. We have a lot to do."

Looking at his cousin's face, he thought: *With the mustache gone, Yog is my twin.*

He told him, "You can shave when you get to Cumbres. On the way into the city, I'll ride in back with one of the ladies and the other will be up front with you. We'll look like just a pair of happily married couples to anyone checking us out."

The crossing through the mountains on the toll road took about forty minutes. The highway ascends steeply, travels near the top of the range, and then quickly descends with sharp curves to the outskirts of Monterrey. As El Gato had suspected, there was a military checkpoint at the bottom of the last mountain. The traffic backed briefly, but they were waved on after only a cursory perusal by a couple of soldiers who saw the two nicely dressed couples in the Lincoln MKX. It was a dress vehicle, not a huge SUV so often favored by the cartels, and El Gato had selected it for that reason.

In the back seat, as they began to enter the city, El Gato removed his suit jacket and tie and reached for a Tigres fútbol cap. He rarely came to Monterrey because relatives still lived there, and he knew that his father was still alive. He hated his memories. It was impossible to avoid coming there because Monterrey was the most important corporate center in the north of Mexico, and it was the principle intersection of the gun, drug, and cash routes to the USA border. In the past couple of years, Monterrey had also become the urban killing field where the Zeta cartel had succeeded in pushing into Monterrey. The Cartel of the Gulf, allied with the Cartel of

Sinaloa, fought back. They tried to annihilate one another in the most horrible ways imaginable and with no concern for innocent bystanders.

As they sped down the mountain now quickly into the city, El Gato drifted in his mind to his last days at home, when Annie's belongings had arrived at the ranch. A couple of nights later, his father burst into his room after he was asleep. The bedroom door slammed against the wall as his father rushed in, and Roberto jumped upright, frightened by the sudden commotion. He could not see much because only the light of the hallway illuminated the room. His father attacked, screaming names at him. He threw a solid punch into Roberto's jaw, and when Roberto fell back, his father jumped on him and pounded his head with a furious series of blows. His left hand was holding a hard book, and several times the bottom of its binding slammed into Roberto's nose. His face spurt blood on the bed and floor. Dazed, confused, not understanding what was happening, Roberto didn't fight his father back. It would have been difficult to do. His arms were pinned under his father's knees, and he hadn't been able to protect his face with his hands.

His mother flew into the room. She screamed hysterically for her husband to stop. When she began to pull his father away, Roberto finally managed to jump from the bed. He ran into the hall and screamed, "What's wrong, what's wrong, what's wrong? What are you doing?"

"It's her diary, you son of a bitch! It tells everything you did to her, your own sister, you pervert! How can you do this to your own sister? Touching her! She was disgusted by you for years! It's all in here, pages after page. What's the matter with you? How could you do this? How could you do this to your own sister? I want you out of here! Out of here now, you sick, drugged-up piece of shit!"

His father ran out to the hallway to attack him again, but now Roberto had become enraged. He grabbed the journal from his father's hand and threw him hard against the wall. He pushed past his mother to the nightstand beside his bed, grabbed his wallet and his clothes on the floor beside his bed, and ran and locked himself in the bathroom. He quickly put on his clothes, found his car keys in his pocket, and went out into the night. He returned only once a couple of days later when his father wasn't at home to pick up some clothes and personal items. He had a melodramatic encounter with

140

his mother then, but despite her pleas that he stay and consider counseling, he left in a rush. But on his way out of the house, he saw Annie's belongings in the corner of her bedroom. He noticed there a curious looking journal similar to the diary brandished by his father. He instinctively felt he should take it, so he grabbed it and tossed it into the car as he left. He never returned again to the ranch.

A heart lost is a death counted in hell, Roberto told himself.

A couple of weeks later, Roberto died. A black soul emerged from the ashes of the blue taupe left on a roadside in Santiago. It floated unnoticed to Sinaloa. It traveled lightly, carrying a bag that contained the curious journal from Annie's bedroom on the ranch. Now, years later, that journal was cruising through Monterrey inside El Gato's baggage in the back of the SUV. He thought about it as they sped towards the safe house in the city where Yog would let him out. He wondered if anything in it could save his soul.

Chapter 11: Love At All Costs

Downtown Monterrey
Four Years Prior to the Day on the Roof

They stood in the landscape of a violated city, raped by thugs with automatic weapons. David snapped a digital photograph in his mind in that split instant when Ana accepted his extended hand of introduction. Still juiced by rushing adrenalin, David saw the vista from an aerial view somehow, looking down on him and Ana in the center. All about were the twisted madness of tilted cars and trucks with flat tires, windows shot out, and glass shards sparkling in the streets in the afternoon sun. Two bodies at the end of ropes hung dangling from a city overpass. City buildings with doors and windows in pieces opened to uneven sidewalks with dark liquids of oil, gasoline, and blood gathering in pools around human bodies. These were people who had begun an ordinary morning and but had finished life in an extraordinary afternoon with no evening to follow. He saw living people crouching and running, but frozen in place in this photograph of his mind.

The police cars and army vehicles parked blocks away looked abandoned by the uniformed figures running, crouching and pointing weapons. Ana's SUV, full of bullet holes, was close to where David and Ana were standing. Inside, the bodies looked like dummies askew in strange poses. Beside them, Paula, Katrina, and Rafael Jr., locked together in a hug, were staring at Ana and David. Because he found out later that Annie's father, Eduardo, was safe, David imagined one of the cars in this mental picture as Eduardo's, driving away with the elderly gentleman oblivious to what he had left behind.

For David, this action photo in his mind was like a picture taken at the time of his second birth, because the end of this hysteria marked the beginning of a new life: He found Ana and passion like none he had felt before in life.

She had accepted his extended hand and had introduced herself, but then David, in the most natural way, pulled her suddenly to him and hugged her. She took him and held on to him as if bullets were still flying. She held tight and began to sob, and her body shook from nerves because she had just seen her boy nearly killed, and this man had saved him; and because they all might have been lying in the street along with the unfortunate people riddled by bullets and covered in blood. David remembered the raw emotion of their embrace, how it seemed to last forever, how he didn't want to release her, and how he heard the crying of Ana's and Katrina's children. They were venting their relief and horror.

This photograph formed in memory, not pixels, so it was a picture that included noise. He heard the sounds of the city in war then: the shouts of soldiers giving commands, the confused screams and panicky exhortations of people trying to find cover, the thuds of running shoes and boots, and the screeching brakes and revving engines of motor vehicles. Mostly he remembered Ana in his arms that first time. He was holding her for dear life, literally. He recalled the thought he had at that moment: *I haven't held a woman against me this long since Julie died.*

Julie, his wife of twenty-five years, who had died from a brain tumor.

It was crazy, but he noticed the wedding ring on Ana's extended hand just before they hugged. The large diamond set among many small ones reflected the Monterrey sun in bursts of yellow, red, and purple. A moment later she clung to him with the same clutch of desperation in which he had her in his arms.

How strange, the disassociated fragments of thoughts that pass through your mind when something shocking happens to you, David mused. He remembered, as he held Ana forever during those moments just after the gunshots subsided, that he wondered if she had insurance to cover her SUV for the damage done to it. Then he thought how wonderful her hair smelled, and, after that, he wondered would they ever dance under the stars? *Or maybe,* he thought, *she just feels gratitude to an old man who had saved her son.*

They separated when a couple of soldiers ran to Ana's SUV to inspect the lifeless men inside. Katrina, Rafael Jr., and Paula moved next to David and Ana, who gathered her kids in a tight hug of relief

143

that they were still alive. They all stood there, a raw family of sorts, formed from the mud of flesh, metal, and cement left by the urban war around them.

David began to calm, and then he felt angry. *The Mexicans endure these experiences daily,* he reflected. *What would my family and friends back home think if they saw what I just went through?*

He already knew. They would be puzzled and judgmental about the people David lived among, as if somehow they had done something to deserve this. But they also would be worried about him. Just a few short years later they would experience the same horrors when massacres in the streets would start occurring in Chicago and Atlanta and when people would begin disappearing in Laredo. Then all their delusions of public safety would vanish, as it had in Mexico.

That night in his condo in Cumbres in Monterrey, David couldn't sleep. He fixed himself coffee and stood out on his patio to watch the traffic pass by on Avenue Pedro Infante. It was a busy road full of buses, trucks, cars and motorcycles going and returning from the distant parts of the city where people had jobs. He watched also horse-drawn carriages driven by men and women who bought junk or sold barbacoa in the surrounding neighborhoods.

The street in front of him ascended from the valley steeply to the commercial area around Paseo de Los Leones, then up the mountain to the elite neighborhoods with security entrances. The road terminated at a private school that resembled a luxury resort when seen from the distance of David's condo window. It was only when he had walked up there the first time to the guard gates of the school and was greeted by the three barking watch dogs that he discovered that it was a elementary school and not a hotel resort.

One steamy April afternoon, he hiked up the road for exercise. An endless stream of mommies in minivans en route to pick up their children at the school sped up the hill, and then they streamed down again. He had to jump into the brush a couple of times to avoid being struck by these mothers on a mission on this road with narrow shoulders. From the heights of the school there was a breathtaking view of the city and the surrounding mountains. *In the evening the lights of Monterrey would outshine Los Angeles,* David thought. He looked at the classroom windows in the stunning school building.

I wonder if the children know how privileged they are to be receiving such a good bilingual education in a school with one of the best views of Monterrey?

He loved seeing the young Mexican families that populated Cumbres. He always noticed their affectionate closeness and their passion to dress nicely. The children, even the teenagers, had an innocent and loving nature which they demonstrated in the simplicity of holding hands with their parents or walking arm-over-shoulder with their brothers and sisters. He thought about this as he stood on his patio with his coffee at two a.m. the day after he jumped to save Rafael Jr. from bullets chipping pavement in the street around him.

In truth, this war endured by the Mexicans had been breaking his heart for some time. "When you really come to know the Mexicans, you fall in love," he would tell his friends in the United States. He was therefore already a man in love when he met Ana, but he had no clue about the way his life would change once she began loving him.

The condominium building in which David lived had five connecting residential towers, each six stories high, using up three blocks of La Avenida de Pedro Infante. There was one entrance to the parking lot through gates with a guard center attended always by at least two security officers. These were men and women dressed in business suits who stopped any vehicle not bearing a permit sticker. David's parking spot was one close to the guard caseta. The main entrance to the building complex was through a huge lobby with columns and oversized sofas and chairs.

Living alone, David liked to bring his lap top computer to the lobby at all hours of the day and night to enjoy the comings and goings of people while he worked. His explanation to people of his gringo presence was that he researched and invested in securities on the stock exchanges in the United States and Mexico, and that he loved living in Monterrey. This was true, but he also prepared his security work for his consulting business. Wireless internet access was available in the lobby, so some of the residents, particularly the graduate students who lived there, came to the lobby to use their computers without having to pay for access. Also, some of the young professional men with new families did the same as a way of saving money. David loved this because it gave him the opportunity to meet

145

people and to learn how they earned a living in Mexico. The young men and women he met were always curious about him as well. The university students, in particular, asked David many questions concerning investments in the stock market, what life was like in the United States, which would be good universities to attend there, and what were the salaries of professional jobs in that country.

It was in this lobby that David first met Israel and his roommate, Enrique. Israel always sat in the same spot with his computer on one of the sofas directly across from David. He was handsome, in his early twenties, always in a business suit, and very, very serious. He wasn't as friendly with David at first as most, but, after a time, he engaged David in conversations about stock market investments.

After the first couple of months of seeing Israel in the lobby, David noticed that Israel's daily routine changed, and the young man began showing up in the sixth-floor gym and weight room, where David worked out every afternoon. They began to train together. Israel opened up and they became good friends: a young man and a man pushing sixty. Israel's reserve melted. Once, he even asked David how sex was at his age.

"Fucking great," David answered, setting both of them into a fit of laughter that bonded them as friends.

Israel was a law student, as was his roommate, Enrique Santos. Israel also worked as a Volvo salesman at the nearby dealership. That turned out to be the reason why David saw him so often in a business suit. David didn't see Enrique much in the lobby, but soon he also began to come to the gym with Israel, and David began to know him better also. Sometimes, the three grabbed a beer or dinner together after their workouts and showers. The other two guys were young and single, and the weekends were their party times. They would go to the clubs and private parties in Monterrey, which began no earlier than ten p.m. They would invite David. Their invitations were sincere, but David would laugh and wave them on their way, telling them that he didn't want to be the grandfather at the party.

One day David noticed an unusually beautiful young Mexican girl passing through the lobby. He saw her several days in a row. During this same time he didn't see Israel in the lobby or the gym. Just when he was about to become concerned, Israel came into the lobby one afternoon holding hands with the young woman. Smiling,

146

he made a quick introduction to David, and then the couple disappeared into the complex.

That explains everything, David laughed to himself. *Israel has found a love.*

David had business in San Antonio, and he had to return there for a couple weeks where his other home was, a house in the suburbs. On the night before he left to go, he saw Israel pacing quickly to his car in the parking lot. He appeared absorbed and upset and more intense than usual. David shouted a greeting but received only a distracted wave from his friend as he got into his car, exited the security gate, and sped away. It was unusual behavior for Israel. David made a mental note to give him a call while he was away in San Antonio.

He made one which was unanswered, and he left a phone message and then forgot about it. As was his custom when away, David read the Monterrey newspaper, El Norte, on-line every night. Just before returning to Monterrey, he read a chilling article. A young man named Israel Sanchez, age twenty-six, was found dead in a vacant lot. He had been tortured before dying.

God, David thought, *it can't be my friend!*

He didn't remember Israel's last name. He couldn't recall if he had ever asked. The names of people in Mexico could be confusing, and David learned last names when it became necessary, often in his work. Monterrey had four million people, and the name Israel wasn't uncommon. Statistically it didn't seem probable it could be his friend. When he arrived back in his condo, surely he would see Israel's car in the lot.

He returned three days later and didn't see Israel's car in the lot. He raced to Israel's condo and knocked, but it was Enrique who opened the door. He only had to look at Enrique's red, swollen eyes to know that Israel was dead. Stunned, David couldn't move, but Enrique hugged him and told him to come in. Enrique went to a living room sofa and collapsed on it. He pointed to the refrigerator in the kitchen and told David to get them both a beer. David felt sick and didn't want one, but he opened one for Enrique and then sat in a chair opposite him. He didn't say a word. He just waited for Enrique to speak.

"I think it was because of the girl," Enrique said. "He was at work, walking across the Volvo parking lot, when a pickup truck drove up and three guys put him in the truck. At gun point. No one heard from him after that. There was no demand for ransom. They found his body in that vacant lot. They had set him on fire. Who knows what else they did to him." Enrique had new tears in his eyes.

"What the hell!" David gasped.

Silence lingered while Enrique composed himself. David thought of his innocent, young, bright friend being tortured, and he could hardly bear the thought.

"She's gone too," Enrique said finally. "She was married to a cartel guy. She had left him, and Israel didn't know. She only told him a day before he was taken. No one knows where she is."

"Enrique, you've got to be friggin' kidding me," David said, feeling anger rising inside him. Then he had a frightening thought. "Oh my God, was she staying here?"

"Yes," he answered. "Israel met her at a club and fell for her hard, like right away. It was a problem with us. We had a couple of arguments about her. I didn't know anything about her and told him she couldn't stay. He told me she had fought with her parents and was looking for an apartment. It would just be a few days. She had money. Cash. I saw it. Israel thought she was rich. She paid to stay here. She left the day before Israel got taken, right after telling him that she was married and had run from her home. She was becoming scared and nervous just before she left. Israel was freaking out and was looking for her all over the city. He called in sick at work that day, but the next day he went, and shortly after getting there, they got him."

David was quickly ticking off things in his mind. He asked him, "Enrique, what about drugs? Did Israel use? You guys didn't…?" He didn't need to finish it.

"No, no, no, Israel didn't use anything hard. He smoked a little, just at parties, but not much because we're in law school, and it isn't a good idea. But I do think he did a little with her."

David looked around the condominium and saw that there were boxes in the bedrooms down the hall, which relieved him. Enrique noticed him looking and read his mind.

"Yeah, I have to get out of here fast," he told David, knowing that David was already in agreement. "I'm leaving in the morning. I don't know how much they know, but they surely know where Israel lived, and if they know he had a roommate, they're going to think I was in on it, the sheltering of the guy's wife. They might want to teach me a lesson too. I have friends coming to help me move tomorrow morning."

"Damn," David said. He worried how much they knew about Enrique, if he went to school, if he worked, and where. He thought about his contacts in the Mexican Army and decided that they would be receiving his next phone calls as soon as he found a moment away from Enrique. "Yes, you're getting out of here, but now, not tomorrow. You're staying with me tonight."

Enrique didn't argue. "Okay. I've been a little scared."

He took a couple of sips of his beer. David could see his relief. Then he said to David, "Israel's father came here from his home town taking care of things. The burial will be there. He already got Israel's belongings. He's staying at a hotel near the Macroplaza. He's a nice man, totally wrecked by this. I've been staying in his hotel room the past couple of nights."

Thinking of Israel, imagining how devastated his father must be, and seeing Enrique heart broken and scared on the sofa, David could hardly contain the swell of sadness in his chest. He sat beside Enrique and put his arm around him. The room was darkening as the late afternoon sun sank deeper below the horizon. David's tender gesture caused Enrique to cry softly. He hardly moved, while David seethed inside and vowed he would get justice for Israel.

They sat with those emotions for long minutes, then David said, "Come on. Get a few things to bring to my place for tonight, and then you can help me get my stuff in from the car from my trip. You should turn in early so you'll be ready for your move tomorrow." He saw that Enrique was psychologically exhausted and needed someone to tell him what to do. Once Enrique went back into his bedroom, David stepped into the hall and punched a speed dial to a contact in the Mexican Army. He wanted protection for Enrique, and he wanted Israel's killers found. He knew whom to call.

But now on his patio, David set down his coffee and tried to extract himself from those memories. Soon it would be a new day, the first day after he had met Ana Valdez. Traffic was increasing on Pedro Infante as the earliest workers started their work day in the dark. He looked at the yellow-black night sky with its sparseness of stars due to the light haze from the city. He thought about Ana out

149

there, about her eyes, about her body, how she had felt against him, and how desperately they had clung to each other.

The thing about Mexico is the rawness of life, he considered. *The scatter shots of death everywhere impute urgency to live each present moment in full. Is this why I feel so desperate for her?*

Ana was married. He was a generation older. He was a gringo. It was ridiculous to think of a relationship with her. However, he had already lost so many people he loved in life. He wasn't going to lose Enrique, and he wasn't going to live life without Ana being in it in some way. He could hardly wait for the morning to make the phone call he had wanted to make since he said goodbye to her the previous afternoon. He had asked for her cell number, and she had given it to him.

He went back to bed, but in the light of the morning he did his yoga and meditation, tools he used to ward off dark moods or paralyzing depression. He discovered late in life that these worked for him. Then he put the warm Mexican winds of destiny to his back and opened his sails so they would blow him to Ana.

He called her. He asked her for coffee and held his breath waiting for her response. After such an ordeal the previous day, would she want to go out into the streets again? Would she even want to take her children to school? Yet he knew enough about her already to judge that she was a brave woman. As he hoped, she didn't hesitate to say yes, she would love to talk with him more. She picked a Starbuck's in a shopping mall just blocks from where David lived in Cumbres, which was the opposite end of town from where she lived. She said she could do grocery shopping at a supermarket chain there which also had a store in her neighborhood. She would have the branded supermarket bags in the house so nothing would appear strange to her husband Rafael.

David thought about this. *Why would she cover up from her husband that she would be talking again to the man who had saved their child?*

She was just a few minutes late. Later David became accustomed to her being habitually late for everything. She was a busy woman. He saw her approaching from the mall entrance. Like most Mexican women out shopping, she wore high heels, and she paced quickly and noisily. She wore tight jeans and a black blouse revealing magnificent cleavage. She was a woman with big

150

everything: big necklaces, big bracelets and earrings, big breasts, and she walked big. She's barely more than five feet one inch tall, David estimated, but with her high heels she gained proportion.

She saw him waiting near the entrance to the Starbuck's, and for the first time he witnessed what her smile could do. She smiled big and bright, her whole face transformed, radiating an uncommon prettiness that made him think of candy. He noticed the women around Ana making long assessments of her. You could read the thoughts in their faces: She's serious competition. She has got it. He felt suddenly nervous, like he did sometimes before addressing a seminar just as he was about to go on stage.

They got through the awkwardness of placing their orders at the counter. Because of his nerves, he could only handle a tall house coffee, but Ana got a pastry plus a frappuccino caramel, some exotic concoction that might have been related to coffee. She looked around and spotted an inconspicuous table and led them to it. After they settled, Ana looked quietly at David. She smiled to encourage him to speak first.

"Thanks for coming," David began. "I really didn't sleep last night. I kept thinking about what happened yesterday...thinking about you...your family and friend, how you're all doing."

"Oh my God, I cry a river," Ana answered in her animated fashion. He had spoken to her in Spanish, but she kept responding in English, and so he switched languages also.

"David, I'm so upset. This isn't right what we go through. We shouldn't have to live this way. I told my husband Rafael about it all, about what you did. God, he hugged Rafael Jr. and he cry, and he thanks you so much. Rafael Jr. told him you're a hero."

Perhaps that was the reason that Ana didn't want to reveal to Rafael that she was having coffee with him. Maybe her husband was grateful to him, but maybe also he would be jealous because his wife and son had a hero. Maybe Ana was just playing it safe, he thought.

"No, believe me, I'm no hero," David said. "I just saw Rafael Jr. and knew something had to be done. All last night I thought about your children and what they saw. It's terrible. I'm so sorry this happens. It's heartbreaking. You take your kids to the mall or to school, and they have to witness executions and gun battles. I can't imagine moms and dads in the United States bearing these horrors. Childhood should be a time of innocence."

151

"I want this for them, to have innocence," Ana agreed. "But there's no innocent way in this country. All leads to violence and corruption. Our leaders can't arrive in positions of power without being corrupt, and once in power, it's all about self-enrichment. Meanwhile, every day the ordinary people risk their lives just going on the streets. The parents have to fear constantly for their children. Do you know, David, my kids have never spent the night at the homes of their friends? I let their friends stay at our house but never permit mine to stay in someone else's home. I can't trust anyone. You don't know who might have some problems, and your kids are at their house. When I take my kids to the mall, I'm always with them. Now Paula is like a pre-teen. She wants to run in a group in the mall with the kids, but I give her a cell phone and make her call me every half hour. When they go to a movie in the mall, I go and sit in the back behind her."

She took a couple of sips of her coffee while looking at him directly in the eyes. He could see his reflection in them across the table. Then she said to him:

"No, David, you're not telling the truth. You're a hero. I know a little about you, and I've seen you be a hero two times now. So tell me one thing. Why are you here in Monterrey? Do you know, I watched the video of you stopping the robbery in that convenience store in San Antonio, and several of the interviews with you later. That was a while ago, and I admired you so much. I sighed because I know Mexico needs heroes. That's the only thing that will save us now. We need heroes, brave people, true leaders, people for the kids to want to be like, people besides fútbol stars. God, even some of them work with the narcos. It seems like all the celebrities we like fall, connected with the delinquents, or victims of them. So when I see you, I realize this is what we need. I look around me, wondering where they are, the heroes, and I know they're here but no one leads them. The people are cynical about everything because all is corruption. I think about these things so much. Then yesterday, when my own son almost dies, you of all people come, like you're flying in the air to him. I can't believe it! I knew who you were when I saw you. I think about this all last night. Why is this man here in Monterrey?"

Ana's accent and the way she expressed herself in English with so much emotion charmed David. He relaxed and began to talk about himself.

"I live here about half the year," he said. "I have a condominium here in Cumbres, just a few blocks from here. The other part of the year I live in San Antonio, where I have a small house a little out in the country. Originally I'm from Richmond, Virginia. I've been coming to Monterrey many years for a couple of reasons. I love the city. God, it's beautiful here. I love the people. I have a close friend here who is much like a father to me. My own father passed away several years ago. This gentleman's wife died a couple of years ago. He owns a ranch outside Apodaca, and he's getting older now. I help him with things, mostly administrative duties and management of their homestead." He wondered how this was sounding because the "administrative duties" required the vitality of young men, which both he and Eduardo had. He could see that Ana was listening intently.

"The family of this man owns one of the largest cement companies in the world, and it was founded here in Monterrey. When I was a boy, the couple moved to Virginia to open a cement plant in Richmond. They brought their children, and I became close friends with them. The man opened plants throughout the world…"

"Is this the Ortiz family? Eduardo Ortiz? Ortiz Cement?" Ana interrupted.

David was surprised. "Sí," he answered. "You know this family?"

"Everyone in Mexico knows who they are," Ana replied. "The other cement business here was a client of mine. I had a company doing large corporation event planning here in Monterrey. Eduardo Ortiz is a heavy player also in Mexican politics."

David now realized that Ana might be connected in Monterrey. He would need to be careful what he might say to her until he knew her better. He continued, "Tragically, both children died."

"Oh my God, yes, I remember!" Ana said. "His son was kidnapped and killed. That was big news. I don't remember about any other children."

"Well, Ana, it was very sad. His son had a twin sister. In fact, I was beginning to date her when she was in an automobile accident

153

with me in Virginia and was killed. This was just a month before her brother died."

Ana sucked in an audible breath. "David!"

He saw how quickly tears came to her eyes.

"Lo siento mucho!" Her emotion came out in Spanish this time. Then she reverted to English. "I'm so sorry! That's awful!" She seemed not to know what else to say and was silent. David saw that her sadness was sincere. They both sipped their coffees. Then she said quietly, "Well, I guess I can see how such a thing might bond you to this man. It's amazing. You've had a relationship all these years?"

"Pretty much. I was so ashamed of the accident and felt so guilty. I blamed myself and stayed away from Eduardo and his wife three years before coming to Monterrey to see them. The accident wasn't really my fault, but I was young and had never suffered tragedy before. I didn't do so well with it. When I came here that first time, we shared a lot of stories, and then Eduardo and I grew close. We've worked together on projects through the years."

"And this is why you come to Monterrey now? To help the Ortiz family?"

David nodded and then added, "Well, yes, but I do have other work here. I have a private consulting company for international corporations in matters of security, mostly in Latin America, especially in Mexico, and especially here in Monterrey where so many companies are located. I've scaled back my work some, and I select the projects that I take on so I can do a few things I like." He didn't mention work he did with the military in both the United States and Mexico nor Eduardo Ortiz's collaboration with him on some of this. He didn't bring up his years in the CIA when he worked in Mexico, Central America, and South America.

She was nodding, listening, and then she softly asked the question he hoped she would ask. "You never married?"

David smiled and said, "Oh yes, I did. I married Julie when I was twenty-seven. She was a Richmond girl, a dental hygienist. We had a good marriage. Our first daughter, Katie Danielle, came when I was twenty-nine. Then when I was thirty-one our second daughter was born, Anna Marie."

154

Ana inhaled sharply. "Oh my God, David! I have the same name as your daughter!" She laughed. "Except my middle name is different."

This caught David off guard. He set down his cup and stared at Ana. He really hadn't thought of that. Then he told her, "Well, there's another coincidence. The daughter of Eduardo Ortiz, whom I loved, was named Ana Sofía. But she called herself Annie."

She had a strange look on her face, and the moment started to feel like it was becoming awkward.

He continued, "Well, I suppose Ana is a fairly common name in Mexico. Our daughter was named Anna Marie after her great grandmother on my father's side."

He wanted to change the subject. He decided he should speak more about his career. Would that be safer for his feelings? He hesitated, trying to decide what exactly to tell her. He felt the familiar darkness inside him that he experienced every time he thought about the insane years he spent in Colombia and El Salvador. He felt guilt about so many things. What he had seen. What he had done. How he hadn't been at home much of the time with his family. How he had missed so much of his daughters' growing up. He decided to skim the surface of those years.

"Years ago I used to work with the Central Intelligence Agency, doing some intelligence work in Central America and South America. Julie and I moved to Williamsburg in Virginia where the CIA had a small base called Camp Peary. It was a little town, very nice place for the kids to grow up. Safe. I was away all the time. About a year after our youngest daughter was born, I wanted more control over my travels and work, so I accepted a position in charge of security for an oil company.

"I was still traveling more than I wanted. So it fell to Julie to do the bulk of the raising of the girls. She did a wonderful job with them, always involved with them in school and in their out-of-school activities, driving them to sports events, girl scouts, all of that. I used to miss them so much and regretted all the traveling. I didn't really know how to get out of it. Raising a family and trying to be prepared to send kids to college is so expensive, so I guess I just did what I felt I had to do. Julie was sweet, always supportive. She seemed tireless. She was always there, always doing, and I just kind of took it for granted. It never occurred to me she might not be there some day.

"So I still wanted to try to have more control over how, where, and when I worked. I thought having my own company would help me with that, so when I was forty-two I started my own private consulting business for security. I did well. I worked very hard."

Jesus! he thought. *I wanted to have more control over my work? I made that sound like something from a resume. Do I tell her that after Annie died and the baby that I wanted to kill people? That I wanted to kill myself? That I married a good woman and thought she would be a good cover for my life in espionage? That she deserved so much more than what I gave her? That it took decades for me to find the goodness in myself?*

He shook the thoughts from his head and continued.

"Both of my daughters went to college, but my wife died the year before Anna Marie graduated from hers. I was busy as usual, and then we got the devastating news that Julie had breast cancer. She died just four months after we found out. This was seven years ago."

Again Ana got watery eyes, and seeing this, David fought his own eyes trying to fill. He thought, *Wow, this woman really does cry a river!* He thought that seeing someone with tears in their eyes was like seeing someone yawn. It made you do it. Then, trying to keep his voice even, he continued: "The thing is, life goes on. Both Katie and Anna Marie married Richmond guys, great guys, and both have children. Katie has two girls and Anna Marie has a little boy."

Ana looked surprised and said, "So you're a grandfather?" The question was more of an exclamation. Her pretty smile lit her face, and she began laughing. "No way!" she said. "I mean, I see you have white hair, but I've seen you jumping! I would never think of you as a grandfather! You're in such good shape! Seriously? Oh my God, do you mind if I ask how many years you have?" She asked it in English but in the Spanish way of expressing age.

David chuckled and answered in the same manner, "I have fifty-eight."

"Wow," Ana teased. "I have thirty-six years, so I guess I'm just a little older than your daughters."

Oh great, David thought. *The arithmetic of these numbers really suck. She's going to think of me as her father. Damn, David, why are*

156

you even thinking about this anyway? This is a married woman, maybe even happily married.

He sank back in his chair, the rhythm of the conversation now flowing to Ana. He passed the baton by asking her to tell him something of her life. He wanted to relax.

To his surprise, she spoke first about Mexico and Monterrey. She conveyed tremendous passion and pride in her country, its people, and the cities of her birth, education and career. She knew her place in the world. She was an international woman who spoke English in a charming way, and he learned that she conversed also in Italian. While Ana talked, she moved her hands constantly as if they held brushes to paint her life on a canvas in front of them. Her animated spirit lifted his mood. He saw that Ana wasn't just a narrator of life events, she was a gifted story teller. She punctuated her tales with uncommon perceptions and observations. She built suspense. David listened and found himself falling into the enchanted labyrinth of Ana's life.

He had to focus because he was distracted by her expressive eyes. He loved her eyes. Somehow her dark eyes emitted colors. Little laugh lines spreading from the outer corners were the only visible signs of Ana's aging. David could see in her eyes the life of privilege and graciousness which she had lived. She looked kind. When she laughed, her eyes lit from within. She tossed her head back and threw her body in a posture of delight, but she never looked silly. She had the composure of a woman used to being prominent in society.

She finally got around to talking about her husband, and David paid special attention. Her first comments about Rafael seemed a little like marketing press releases. He was an intelligent entrepreneur in a growing network of well-known salad franchises which he had founded. He was a hard-working man providing for his family, but he was never at home because he felt the restaurants couldn't run well without his frequent presence. Still, David sensed something off in Ana's emotion about Rafael. So after she had talked at some length about her life, David returned to the topic of Rafael. He looked for a subtle way to ask what he wanted to know, but the question just blurted out of his mouth.

"So, do you love your husband?" He reddened immediately. *God, I can't believe I asked her that!*

157

She wasn't put off by the question at all. "Let me tell you something, David," Ana responded. He learned through time that this was the way Ana often introduced a subject. When she said, "Let me tell you something" or "Let me tell you this," he would be in for a long but charming dissertation. It was as much fun to watch Ana tell her stories as it was to hear them.

"Let me tell you something, David," she said. "My love for Rafael is like this: Sometimes there's a beautiful glass ornament which gets dropped, and on the floor it shatters into ten thousand little pieces. This can't be fixed. This is my love for Rafael. It's broken like that, and there's no way ever to repair it. Once love and trust are broken in that way, it's gone forever, and only the memory remains. No, I have no love for Rafael like a man and wife should have. We're partners because we have children together, and he is to me like a brother who is nothing at all similar to me. I feel a loyalty only because he and I share the same children. He has hurt me too many times, and now I don't even care. We live different lives in the same house."

David felt a small amount of shame that he was silently rejoicing to hear this. He decided not to comment. They didn't know each other well, and he wanted to earn her friendship. Besides, he understood completely what Ana felt towards Rafael. He kept his eyes on her, but he could hear his thoughts.

God, beautiful woman, you make me feel in my heart everything that's inside yours! It's like we have the same emotional DNA. What is it about you that makes me feel so connected to you? Is it that you're a wonderful story teller? I feel like I knew you even when you were a child. When you speak your body moves like you're dancing. I want to dance with you! I would love this!

Time was flying. David saw by the way Ana glanced at her watch a couple of times that soon she would announce that she would have to leave. Finally she glanced at her watch with a disappointed look and said to him, "God, I don't want to go, David, but I have to. I love talking to you. It's just that I have to do the grocery shopping, then pick up the kids a little later from school, and I always do homework with Rafael Jr. because he's a little devil who will try to do anything except his work!"

David mulled how he should say goodbye when Ana stood up. So he got up and walked over to her, and before he could make any other move, she looked up at him and then kissed his cheek. She told David, "You're twenty-two years older than me, and my father was twenty-two years older than my mother. They were so in love. I adored my father." She said that in a natural and unembarrassed way. He felt like he was levitating from the floor.

She picked up her oversized pocket bag and smiled. She said, "Call me again. I want to see your condo in Cumbres. I'm sure it's lovely and has a great view. Until then! Hasta luego, haha! Spanish!" Then she walked big away from him.

Chapter 12: I Will Make You Shoot Cannons

Cumbres
Four Years Prior to the Day on the Roof

David called her the next morning. He was nervous, but to his
relief the conversation flowed relaxed and funny. This emboldened
him to put it out there.

"So....I want to show you my place, but what I really hope is
that you'll let me take you to dinner and we can talk a little more.
Ana, are you able to be out of the house in the evening and we might
find a restaurant hidden from your life?"

She laughed mischievously. "You would think in a city as big as
Monterrey that would be possible, but my footprints are all over this
town. I'm not sure that I have a place to hide with you!"

Her tone was welcoming, even if her words were discouraging,
and David was ready. "Well, I live a bit of a clandestine life, and I
have a secret place a bit out of town up the mountains where you can
see Monterrey from the opposite end of town where you live. I
guarantee discretion and safety if you would trust me to let me show
you this astonishing place. And let me assure you, the drive there is
half the fun." He held his breath.

"Hmmm, you're tempting me," was her answer.

David pressed. He told her the area, not the restaurant, and she
admitted that she didn't go there or think that she would know
anyone in those outskirts of the city. They chatted long enough for
Ana to overcome her anxiety about being seen, and she accepted.

Ana's problem was what to tell Rafael. With the help of her best
friend, Katrina, who was single, she developed the alibi of going
with her on an overnight girl's trip to Katrina's cousin's inn in the
mountains south of Santiago for a weekend of relaxation. In fact, the
true plan was that she would have dinner with David and then go to
Katrina's house in Monterrey.

Ana agreed to meet David at his place in Cumbres because he
had a guest parking space she could use. She could leave her rental

car near the guard station next to his. He was standing beside his black Corvette convertible when she arrived. She laughed as she emerged from her car, saying that she needed a cigarette before they left for the restaurant.

David's hands shook as he lit her cigarette. He couldn't help it. He felt like a nervous kid on a first date. It embarrassed him. He had dated some women casually in Monterrey and hadn't felt like this. He had connections in Monterrey. He felt confident in his knowledge of the city. He was normally a very composed man. His problem of nervousness happened whenever he looked at Ana.

He thought she possessed the classic beauty of Mexican film stars. How could anyone not be seduced by those alluring, dark eyes? he wondered. He paused to observe her. She wore bright red lipstick that would look overdone on most women, but Ana's smile required the kind of radiant color you might see on the red carpet of the Cannes Film Festival. David found those perfect oval lips so sensuous that he couldn't concentrate when he looked at them. All he wanted to do was to kiss her. This made him feel green like a young man; but on the other hand, he loved the physical reaction he had to Ana. He got hard quickly. That hadn't happened in a long time. Only Ana did this to him. He knew that with her he could trust his body to perform like a man if he needed.

As if I'll get the chance, he reminded himself.

Still, he was determined to impress her. He had rented just for the two of them the roof top terrace of one of the finest restaurants in Monterrey and one of its best kept secrets. When he reminded Ana where they were going, she knew the area but not the restaurant. She offered to drive.

"Would you like me to drive? Maybe you don't know the city as well as me? It's a crazy place to drive, and I'm a city girl here for so many years."

Now David relaxed and laughed. "Ah, Señora, driving is what I do. In my black Corvette I've already humbled the macho drivers of Monterrey. I can get you safely there."

She admired the black convertible as he extended his hand towards it with a slight bow and said, "Please!"

She didn't know much about cars. She had thought of Corvette only as some kind of gringo car not seen much in Mexico. However, when David sped them, top down, through the dark evening up the winding hills, cutting through the smallest breaks in traffic, Ana admitted that he was indeed a skilled driver.

She breathed in the freedom of the night. She told David, "You drive like a man I could trust!"

The restaurant was in the highest part of the city on this mountain hillside. The Maître D led them through the crowded and romantically dim restaurant, with its glass views of the city below, to a spiral iron staircase ascending to the roof. They emerged onto an open air terrace. On the tables and at the bar the flowers were dancing in the evening currents. David had paid for them to be alone, attended discreetly by their servers. Tall speakers hidden in the shadows of potted palm trees were playing lovely Spanish guitar ballads. When they were seated, David could tell from the amazed approval of her dark eyes that Ana knew he had planned well.

"Oh my God, David, this is incredible! How lovely! Are you trying to conquer me, because it's working!" she said.

His heart jumped. He said, "I'm glad you like it. A friend of mine owns this restaurant. The city lights at night seen from here steal you from your cares and worries. Monterrey looks like an ocean of lights out there with black mountains rising up from yellow waters. This is one of the most beautiful cities I've ever seen. You're the most beautiful woman I've ever seen!" This just gushed out of him, sincere.

She was surprised. She remembered a time when she was fifteen that another gringo had told her the same thing just like that in a restaurant. She unfolded her napkin, then looked up at him and showed him her eyes. In them he saw his reflection. He saw the stars in the sky. He saw something familiar from his time as a young man, like his own face when he was twenty-three and looked in a mirror. She stared into his eyes in a way that invited him to fall inside her, to explore the mystery of what it would be to love her. It's where he wanted to be, inside her, exploring, trusting to her all his emotions as he felt them, giving everything to her, dying over and over to her eyes.

"This is a charmed evening," Ana told him as she saw how he looked at her. "I feel thin layers of magic piling around us." A single chilled breeze kicked up. Ana gave a little shiver and rubbed her arms. She smiled. "It feels like silk scarves falling gently one after another on my skin." Her arms had goose bumps, but her steamy eyes broadcast that she was succumbing to the caresses of the evening.

David was thrilled by Ana's nearness. All his senses intensified. He thought the wind whispered a command that he go to her, so he went and pulled back her chair. He asked her to come with him to the low wall framing the perimeter of the roof. There they had a three hundred sixty degree view of the city, its lights interrupted in a few places by opaque silhouettes of mountains. Above them only the brightest stars managed to shine through the haze of lights. They remained quiet for a while in the peacefulness of the distant noises. David laid his arm lightly across her shoulders, and when he did, Ana pushed back against him so that his arm dropped to encircle her waist.

"I want you to listen," he whispered. "The sounds of the city carry for miles and travel up here. They carry the story of the city. Tell me what you hear. Listen closely, and you'll be able to tell me why I brought you here."

So she listened. She heard the invisible dogs of the city barking their anxious complaints, the laughter of families at a backyard party, the blare of indistinguishable announcements coming from a car with loudspeakers, the whine of a revving motorcycle, the moan of trucks ascending a mountain, some reggaeton music blasting in a distant place, the shouts of teenagers playing a late night game of fútbol in their far away neighborhood, and glass breaking somewhere. It was a symphony of the proudest Mexican city. It played for lovers on distant hilltops.

He watched her as she listened. He saw her eyes close as she drank in the sounds. Her breasts moved up and down with slowing breaths. He knew she would get it. He saw the transformation in her face as she put it together. Already she was understanding him. She was going to open her eyes and look at him with eyes that knew him. She was going to tell him what she felt and what he felt, and when she did, it was going to bind them to a future together. David had already listened to the city and was under its charm. He knew its power and magic and danger. He brought her there to consume the city and fall with him into the abyss. He knew what would come next. She would open her eyes, and there would be triumph in them because she would have the answer to his question.

163

The very fact that you want to please me with the answer tells me you're mine, David thought in his heart.

So finally she turned and looked straight into his eyes. The glow of the city illuminated her face. The wind tossed her dark black hair. She was so beautiful to him that he wanted to take her hand and leap off the building and fly with her over all the life of Monterrey.

"I hear the gunshots," she said. "I hear them in different parts of the city, coming with sharp cracks, rat-a-tat. I hear the cars speeding away and the crashes. I hear the lies and betrayals and hearts breaking. I hear the mothers screaming in anguish the names of their sons. I hear the complete silence of the terrified people. I hear the anthems of our nations falling with their flags. I hear the reason you're here."

The fire in her eyes, the proud outward thrust of her big bosom, the upward point of her chin, the defiant tilt of her wide hips, all framed a picture for him that would remain in his memory forever. She was Mexico enraged; Mexico passionate; Mexico determined to fulfill its glorious destiny. She was fierce and wanted her country. She was fierce and wanted him.

Inside David there was spontaneous combustion. He seized her by the waist and pulled her up to him and kissed her with the hunger of forty years. Her skin was cool from the evening air, but her kisses were hot and drawing. They invited him in. She wanted him to experience her. She tasted his hunger and she intended to deepen it. When he pulled her tight, she drew up against him.

It seemed like they kissed all night, and when they stopped kissing they didn't release each other but instead danced slowly near the edge of the roof. David's body draped Ana the way a lovesick soldier would cling to his foreign lover the night before going into the battle. He felt electrified and prickly. He didn't want to move from her. She bound him there.

The servers watched discreetly from the shadows, and when they saw that the time was right, they brought up their dinner with just enough noise to awaken the couple to the delicious smells of the table. David looked over to see them and smiled, and without saying anything, he led Ana by her hand back to their seats.

They made some breathless small talk as they dined, but mostly they were quiet and warm. They gave each other looks the way new lovers do when there's nothing to see but the face of the other. They had another drink after they finished. They held hands across the table and sat in silence. David leaned over to her and they kissed. She looked at him, then, for the first time since dinner, she looked around at the city and sky again. When she turned back to him, she sat back in her chair, and David saw she wanted to tell him some things.

"I've lived a life that would gratify most Mexican women, David," she said. "My husband and I are both successful business people. We know leaders and politicians and local celebrities. My work puts me in touch with musicians and actors of television and cinema, magicians and comedians, and the people of society. I grew up in a family that had the best of things, thanks to the hard work of my father and the devotion of my mother to raising her children in the right way. We all had education. My kids go to private schools. The thing is, Monterrey has the elite in Mexico, and a very large middle class, but also a tremendous amount of poverty. The poor in this city hustle. They try so hard to work, and when they can't find jobs, they create their own. You see them all the time in the streets selling things.

"I haven't been a woman with a small world of just home and family. I've had the opportunity to travel over all of Mexico, and also overseas, to Europe, the United States, South America, and once to Japan. I love Mexico with passion. You'll find this about Mexicans. We love our country so much. We love who we are as a people, our roots and our emergence from the Spanish imperialism. We have many indigenous people. I think there are actually sixty-eight languages spoken in Mexico. Our history of prejudice and cruelty to them isn't so good, as is true in your country and many others. But I love them, David, I love all the people of Mexico, and my heart bleeds from all the violence and insecurity and corruption that our people endure. The Mexican people are good and don't deserve a life of fear for their children. I've cried a million rivers while trying to understand why we experience this and what paths lead the way out."

She reached in her bag for a cigarette, and this time David was ready to light it with steadier hands.

"We need brave people. Brave leaders, people who know what to do. As I've said, we need heroes. I can hardly stand to read the newspapers anymore. The journalists who have been brave have been tortured and killed. The ordinary person who tries to post anonymously on the web where the drug sales are, and who is doing it, is being killed. Good mayors of cities, as well as bad ones, are kidnapped from their homes in the middle of the night and found beaten to death a couple of days later. People disappear off the face of the earth, and you don't know why. They never return. There has been no effective organized resistance to the narcos. The war on them from the Army has made things ten times worse. The federal government tries to eliminate the top leaders of the cartels, and this only increases the violence as the cartels split up and new people fight for power in the streets.

"One day I saw that video of you in San Antonio. There are heroes like you who, without thinking, just act in the face of some urgency. I saw that you had skills. I smiled so big for days because you were dressed in that amusing costume. I found several YouTube videos of you taken from TV stations who covered what you did. When I saw you jump to save Rafael Jr., I recognized your style of flying from what I saw you do in the San Antonio videos."

Ana took another couple of puffs of her cigarette as she looked intently into David's eyes.

"You're here in Monterrey for reasons besides what you told me, David. I know this. You haven't lied to me, but you only told me part of the truth. You know, I felt the passion in you when you kissed me. I felt how hard you were and the strength of your arms. A man who has that kind of passion knows anger and desperation as well. I think you have a compassionate heart as big as the moon, but something big is behind your hardness. So I'm not asking you to tell me things you can't, but I want you to tell me about the anger that's in your heart."

She caught him off guard. Out of the blue he felt mad, just because she saw this in him: The feelings he tried to defeat, to hide, to ignore. He wanted to die. He wanted to curse. He wanted to throw a temper tantrum and pick up the table and throw it off the roof. He wanted to know how she could say this to him, how she could know, but he already knew. She had locked into his heart and had a clear view of his soul. He felt the words welling inside him, and he wanted to stop them, and the effort made tears come into his eyes. It hurt. He clamped his jaw, trying to keep quiet.

166

She never wavered from gazing into his eyes, and when he didn't answer, she pressed. She was going for it. She said, "You've been seduced by us. You once fell in love with a Mexican woman and now you feel this happening again. You love us, you study us, you devour us, you adore the people you help here, and you're full of rage about what happens here in Mexico. I'm right, aren't I? Who have you lost here, David?"

He felt words jammed inside his throat in a ball so big that he feared a vomit of emotion. He hated that she could see the tears in his eyes. He tried spitting out words one at a time, as each one broke from the jumble. It helped him feel better.

"Roberto. Israel. Myself. Maybe. Others. Some I've worked with. Here. I'm sick of it. I try to help, but nothing I do seems to help. I talk to the victims' friends and their families. I offer support. They look at me with those sad eyes that ask who can help them, who will give them justice. There's no answer. You can trust no one here. Not the police, not the military, not the government. If you find people to trust, they get killed…"

She interrupted him. "Who is Israel?"

"A friend. A beautiful young man who should be able to live the rest of his life. I met him in the condo where I live, and they came and just took him away from where he worked and beat him and burned him to death. I remember his serious face occasionally breaking into his innocent smile, and I go crazy thinking about how scared he must have been when they had him; how he had grown up with a loving family, like your kids, and had never experienced that kind of pain; and how he must have known when they had him that no one would arrive to save him like in the movies."

"Are you trying to help him now?" she asked.

He looked at her, seeing her skills in guiding and soothing the hearts of people. He nodded slightly at first, to indicate he wanted to try to find justice for Israel, but then he began to shake his head, to express the futility of this.

I'm messed up, he thought sadly. *I must never forget how sick I am from the things I've seen. I have to do my daily work, my meditations, my yoga, my prayers. All this anger I have, it comes out any damn time. It's chronic toxicity, that's what it is. I have to keep love in my life. I have to stay concerned for others. If I think too much about how pissed off I am, I'll consume myself in this rage like*

167

fire burns paper. Thank God Eduardo and I have started our work with young people in this idea of the Zs.

Ana reached over and took his hand, and she kept her voice soft and even, soothing him.

She said, "I have a feeling that you know a lot about me, about what I do, about my Tweets and blogs and websites. I've felt as lost and frustrated as you. Listen, David, there are changes in the air. Everywhere groups of people are rising up. They're organizing and protesting the violence. They're reporting the violation of human rights by the police and the military. There are movements for peace and change all over Mexico. Some even have marched in your country to tell your people that they must stop selling the guns here and that they have to do something about the drug consumption. The people beating these drums are intellectuals, authors, poets, actors, the people who have been victims; and they're elegant, and they touch the souls of many." She blew a ring of cigarette smoke to the side. "The government leaders come and pay homage to them. They say their empty words. They do nothing. They're scared, or they don't know what to do. So you know the things I do?"

He nodded. He had just spent a day looking at her blogs, Tweets, Facebook pages and websites exhorting people to action. He saw the pictures of Ana in local newspapers all over the state. When sensational episodes of violence occurred, Ana went with the leaders of the movements to meet with community groups about what preventive and protective measures they could take. She shamed local elected officials and police. He saw that her boldness and militancy through time increased even while journalists and other bloggers were being murdered by the cartels because of what they reported. She was more and more in demand to speak at citizen rallies.

He told her, "You call for heroes, Ana. Yes, I've looked. You're amazing, really. You encourage and help so many people. You embolden them and tell them their rights. I love your favorite expression: 'Ánimo!' I see how many followers you have and who is following you. You should be proud of what you're doing. I'm sure you must worry about it because of your children. Yet you do it, and even if you're afraid sometimes, you act bravely."

She didn't reply. Instead she studied him, as if debating whether or not to ask him the next question. She decided to.

"Tell me, David. In your daily work now, do you taste blood?"

He liked that she asked him questions that were levels deeper than most people probe. He didn't have to ask her what she meant. He understood. She wanted to know if he were on the front lines.

She's checking my bravery meter. She's wondering something more. What is it?

"No," he answered. "I'm on the sidelines. I advise people who are on the front lines. I've taken some risks, yes. I'm good at stealth when I want to be. I'm naïve when my professional guard is down. I worry sometimes that I'm not really brave, but I take comfort from the fact that a few times my natural instincts kick in to make me do brave things without thinking about it. When I think about situations that require bravery, I feel like I'm a coward. Maybe I'm not that, maybe I just know what it is to be afraid sometimes. I always have my guard up."

She brought her lips to his suddenly and kissed him, leaving him breathless for a moment. She whispered, "Was your guard down just then?"

"Yes!" he whispered, and they both drew in nervous breaths. He said, "Now I have to worry that I would tell you too much."

"What would you tell me?" she teased. She kept her lips close to his, until he came quickly to her for another kiss. He didn't want to stop, but when he did, he answered "That you're like crack," and he laughed.

"Mmmm," she responded, and pulled closer to him, and he went to her. He knew he would go to her over and over again, as long as she wanted him to.

When they broke their kiss this time, she astonished him when she said, "David, take me to your condo. I'm going to make you shoot cannons and prepare you for war."

God! He thought. *I'm ready to shoot now!* That was the thing that had been lingering in the shadows. Ana was going to make the decision if she would go home with him.

David shifted the gears of the Corvette back and forth through third and fourth as they zipped down the lower hills of the mountain, around the curves of the city roads, and in and out of the still busy traffic. The top was down and the wind precluded a lot of conversation, for which David was glad because he wanted to stabilize his emotions some, as well as to calm his body. The truth

169

was that he felt tremendously turned on. When they arrived at his parking lot entrance he felt like he had just driven the Grand Prix. He used his card to open the gate and waved to the security guard sitting inside the cement guard station. Everything in Monterrey was made of cement.

They took the small elevator off the lobby to his floor, and being alone inside it, they kissed until the door opened. David thought to himself, *well, so much for my calm body.*

He held his hand as steadily as he could when opening the lock and ushered Ana inside. She had a big smile as she looked around the living room. She walked over to the wall of glass that from the fifth floor gave David a gorgeous view of the mountains in Cumbres and the lights of the city. Directly in front across the parking lot ran the busy street, Pedro Infante. Ana made a brief tour of the dining area and kitchen, and then she asked him to show her his bedroom. She held his hand as he led her. Inside the room she didn't even look more than five seconds. Instead, she stepped into his arms for more long kisses until, in the most natural way, his hands were feeling the skin of her thighs and back and hips. Without the kiss breaking, he unbuttoned her blouse, unfastened her bra from the front, and pulled down her skirt. He became completely lost in her softness and smells. He was so far gone that he didn't realize that he had picked up his naked woman and had laid her on her back on the bed.

That first time David went ecstatic inside Ana's body. Whatever inhibition he had vanished when she kissed him. She set him off. He poured his adoration into a drizzle of light caresses all over her skin. It had been years since he felt so happy or so young. She knew precisely how to tease him to keep him hard. She cupped her huge breasts in her hands and offered them to him when he was raised over her and showed him her eyes. This drove him to lunacy. When he came down on her, crazy-hungry to take her breasts in his mouth, she yielded to him with such softness that he almost came, but he held back with all his effort until he could feel her about to have orgasm. That first time as he shot inside her, she sang out a love song in a foreign language. They climaxed together. His legs quivered from the explosion of his release deep inside her, so she held him tight as if he might otherwise fly into the air. When it was over, they both were so delighted, still hearing echoes of their passion, that they burst out laughing from the sounds of it.

He got up and went to the kitchen and brought them back glasses of water which they took in camel gulps. He fell beside her, took her sideways in his arms, and pulled the sheet over them, and they slept for maybe an hour. When he awoke, he began kissing her again in the darkness, and she responded, and he became immediately hard and put himself on top of her and entered her. He felt at home, at peace.

But when he slept, he had a dream. They were on a battlefield at night, and Ana was beckoning him urgently to follow her. She had a grey bandana on her head, and she was wearing a brown tattered leather dress. She began to run up a dark, grassy berm. David followed, but the ground shook from huge booms of thunder. When they got to the top, as far as he could see along the ridge were cannons on wheel axles. An army of men in black were loading and firing at a cardiovascular pace. A young man running up and down the line desperately shouted commands to the men shooting the cannons. The cannons were pointed in different directions, some even pointing behind, from where Ana and David had come. Once in the distance the young man turned around and noticed David, and then he came running to David and Ana. As he approached, David saw that the young man was Enrique Santos. Ana shouted something to Enrique. He stopped and he removed a flag posted in the ground next to a cannon and then carried it to David. It was a Mexican flag.

David thought about this dream at first when he began to kiss Ana again. Then his member became hard and erect and Ana received him inside her once more. She was wet, so very wet and snug, and David forgot about the cannons and the flag and the Ana in a tattered dress. All he knew was this naked Ana, her softness and smells of vanilla, and her loving kisses. He wanted how she made him feel to last forever. She teased and provoked him, whispering little suggestions in his ear until he was no longer able to hold back what had built up inside him. This time when he exploded in her, he saw flashes of light like cannon fire in the night. He screamed a deep, throaty liberation, and Ana climaxed again, and they shook the bed like a battlefield under siege.

They lay there. Not much later the room brightened from the impending dawn. The time was so satisfying that neither wanted to speak. Finally, Ana sat up and gathered the bed sheet around her like a robe. She paused to tease him, to let him see how her body filled

171

this sheet. She watched him as her curves made him catch his breath. Then giggling she gathered herself up, sheet and curves, and went into the bathroom and showered. David did the same in a bathroom across the hall.

When she was leaving, Ana hesitated in David's doorway, and then she came back inside the condo and brought her big bag over to his kitchen island counter. She reached inside and pulled out a small notebook. She held it in her hands as if deciding something.

She said, "I can tell that you would do anything for me, anything I ask. I never thought I would have a love like this, David. I gave up on having it. I found some life in wanting to help Mexico. I didn't know how to help at first. I've thought I'm just a housewife, a mother of a couple of bright and beautiful kids. They've been my world. Once they got older and went to school, I started following the movements in Mexico, and I started doing my web work. You know, I had this thought for the first time a few years ago when I saw your video that what Mexico needs are heroes. So I've written a lot encouraging that idea, but I know Mexico needs so much more than that. It needs a plan. Our young people need to know how to live.

"Suddenly the other day you literally come flying into my life. You save my son. You look at me with puppy eyes. So I left you and came home. Then that night, I'm up all night with these ideas. They've been inside me. I wrote them here in this notebook. These are my concepts. The next morning, I thought, *oh this looks so silly*. But last night when you made love to me, I knew you were the only person on earth who would understand this. You would see what I miss here. You would read this and take it seriously. So, please, take this and read it. Let me know what you think. And if you think it's silly, I'll come kiss you and make love to you until you're crazy and see the sense in this and help me make this work. You have no defense from me."

She came to David and kissed him long and deep and loving, and when she left he felt, yes, half mad. He poured himself water, and he sat on the sofa with the notebook and began to read. A little ways into it, he stood up.

"Oh my God!" he exclaimed aloud. "How could this be?"

It was as if Ana somehow knew the work he was doing in Mexico! He paced his living room a few minutes, thinking. Then he took out his cell phone and called Eduardo Ortiz.

"Eduardo," he said. "There's someone I want you to meet. I think she has the missing pieces for the Zs!"

Chapter 13: Free Running

Cumbres in Monterrey
Four Years Prior

The brutality of Israel's murder traumatized Enrique. He was surprised by the quick unhinging of his nerves. He thought he was tough and hard, but Israel had been closer to him than his brothers, and someone had taken him and tortured him and burned him, and now his hero was gone. Enrique was a mess. He wondered how the zeal he had to go to law school and then find a way to help Mexico had disappeared so completely, now replaced by fear. Had he just been brave because Israel was always there to fight by his side?

Enrique had grown up as a street-kid scholar: a brooding, defiant, skateboard adolescent in the urban concrete of Mexico City. He hid his intelligence in those days behind silence. He would use his intelligence as a weapon later. When he was twelve, his father died from falling off a building in a construction accident, and two of his older brothers dropped out of school and went to work to help their mother support the family of six children. His mother worked as a domestic helper for not much pay, but her employers loved her and were generous with her when they found out her family situation. Enrique's mom and his older brothers noted Enrique's keenness. The brothers in a very forceful way let Enrique know that his duty in the family was to do well in school and then go to the university. Despite his tendency to go for the edgy and the wild, he wouldn't be allowed to waste his talents. Their family, and especially Enrique's mother and two younger sisters, might depend upon his future success.

The brothers were home in the evenings and made sure that Enrique did his homework and studied. Enrique might have those black, fuck-with-me-and-I-will-beat-you-to-a-pulp eyes, but the brother's eyes were blacker. They saw the dreams their mother had for Enrique, and so for her they became vigilantes to keep Enrique on the straight and narrow. For their younger sisters, they were their two fathers.

Enrique met his classmate, Israel, the year his father died. A couple of afternoons after school, as he walked several blocks home, he watched Israel skillfully pivoting a skateboard and jumping on the sidewalks and zipping between cars of the congested, impatient city traffic. He walked quietly behind Israel at a distance. Enrique's sad, soulful stare never veered from Israel's agile performance. He was observing art in motion. He wanted Israel's style and attitude. Israel looked intense and tough. He didn't say much to people. He didn't connect that he already was much like Israel. Enrique saw that if Israel annoyed anyone jumping out of the way of his rolling momentum, he clearly couldn't care less about it, or what they shouted behind his back. He moved on as if they weren't there.

Enrique was certain that he was watching Israel completely unnoticed, but on the third afternoon, Israel hopped off his board, flipped it into his hands, and suddenly walked over to Enrique.

"Do you have a board?" was his first greeting to Enrique.

"No."

"Get one. Tomorrow I'll bring you my old one, but you'll need something better."

He did just that the next day, and with just a few instructions Enrique was clacking down the sidewalk behind his new friend. Months later Israel told Enrique that, yes, he had seen him watching him and could tell from his look that he had a brother in heart.

In fact, Israel also had a brother in abilities. Enrique was a natural with the skateboard, and in time was duplicating Israel's maneuvers. One Saturday morning soon after meeting, Israel led Enrique to a concrete skateboard park that the city had constructed in the parking level of an abandoned building several kilometers from where the boys lived. Enrique felt electrified by the energy of the kids there, some very advanced in their jumps and flips. He and Israel went there almost every Saturday afterwards and made friends. This was the only place where Enrique felt safe to speak. He conversed because the kids were all there for a specific interest. They spoke the language which Enrique adapted, and they all had a look like him, everything black: torn black jeans, black T shirts, black leather jackets, black sweatshirts with hoods, black gloves,

175

black jewelry, black hair, black eyes, and black stares equivalent to a raised middle finger.

Israel didn't live far from Enrique. One Saturday afternoon when they finished skating with the kids, a thunderstorm came from nowhere and released a temper tantrum of rain and hail just after they left the skateboard park. The city instantly became a flooded chaos, with rivers of water rushing through the streets and the cars grounded in newborn lakes of spring rain. The boys dripped noodles of water, and with people on the sidewalks darting for cover, Israel flipped his board into his hands and told Enrique, "Run!"

That's how it began. They had to cross a street. They were running. Enrique never forgot the joy he felt in his body when he first saw Israel leap onto the hood of a car, then down into the street, then up on the hood of another, and back to the sidewalk, then down the sidewalk on the other side of the street, all in one fluid motion.

"Ven!" commanded Israel. "Come!"

So he did the same. However, when he threw himself atop the second car's hood, he slipped on the wet surface and glided across on his butt into the street. In the noise and mess of the bulleting rain, Israel doubled over in laughter. Then he ran back to pull Enrique up, and next they collected the skateboard which had rolled half a block forward. For Israel and Enrique, this incident marked the beginning of the urban free running which they continued together until Israel's death.

"Padrisimo!" Israel exclaimed breathlessly when they arrived at Enrique's door after running all the way home through the storm. "That was so much fun, hombre! The drivers were so mad, but look how effectively we got home!" Israel was so exhilarated that he kept hopping with adrenaline in front of the house in the dark downpour.

From that day forward, the boys skated, sprinted, leaped, catapulted, swung, and climbed every place they went. At the skateboard park they began to talk to the others about running through the city, and some knew of older guys who liked to do it while committing thefts, and others who did it for the sport. One Saturday afternoon they got introduced to a couple of older boys who led them to an apartment building a few blocks away. The building had cement stairs and landings between sections. As Enrique and Israel watched, the young men began a sprint towards the building. One chased the other. The first ran up a couple of flights of the steps, allowed the second to get close, and then leaped back down to the first landing from the stairway over the other boy's head. That pattern continued, up and down; and then the boys got to the top and came back down to the sidewalk in a series of leaps from one stairway wall to the next flight of steps, up on the wall to the next flight of steps, and pretty much bypassed all the steps.

They didn't stop when they got back down to the sidewalk. From there the chase continued atop cars, on the sidewalks, in and out of buildings, up and down, while Enrique and Israel ran after, watching them from the streets. They lost sight of them for a few moments when both boys ran into an apartment building, but then they heard both of them shouting on the roof above. One was still chasing the other. Enrique and Israel backed to the other side of the street to get a better view, just in time to see one boy leap from the roof across a chasm to the lower roof of the next building. The second young man then came flying across with such confidence that it was obvious to Enrique and Israel that this was a routine that the boys had practiced for some time. They disappeared from view and then emerged from that building on the ground floor in what hardly seemed thirty seconds. Finally they stopped in front of the younger boys, and they were breathless and soaking in sweat.

"Want to try it?" one boy asked.

"Yes!" answered Enrique, but the older boys laughed.

"You'll kill yourselves," the boy said. "You have to practice all the time, and you have to learn how not to get hurt. Come on, you get your first lesson today. You just run up and down steps the rest of the afternoon. If you're serious about this, you'll do it every day this week, and we'll watch you next Saturday to see if you're ready for the next lesson. Agreed?"

"Sure," answered Israel.

They returned to the first apartment building, and the older boys made Israel and Enrique run up and down the steps two hours. It was horribly hot. The air currents rippled mirages and made the steps appear to undulate in front of them. Both Israel and Enrique felt like their thighs had tree stumps attached. Then the pain set in until it passed into numbness. They gasped for air. What began as running up the steps quickly deteriorated into a toiled drag upward and an excruciating plod downward. When the time was over, they were completely spent. They collapsed against the wall of the building, in

177

a patch of shade, until the older boys returned to say their goodbyes. Those went off laughing, leaving Enrique and Israel motionless against the wall. When they began the plod home, they were already so late that both knew they would have trouble from their moms when they returned later than expected. They were numb and exhausted, and neither could even speak of this to the other as they walked.

Their "lesson" the following Saturday consisted of more running up and down the steps of the same apartment building, but it also included some practice time leaping from the stairway wall to the landing below. Each consecutive week added a new skill set. At one point when Enrique and Israel had developed some stamina and a few skills, the older boys announced something new to them.

"You're doing pretty well," the talkative one said. "Today we've arranged something special for you. We have a friend Richii we run with sometimes. He has a taco stand near here. You're going to hit it and steal some items from the counter: an order, some beer bottles, whatever, and run. The thing is, Richii knows you're going to do this, and when you do, he's going to chase you. This is the way for you to really learn, because Richii is a good runner, and he'll definitely catch you. Believe me, you don't want that. Your goal is to keep away from him as long as you can, and we'll see how you do. It's like a test. To make this good, for you to do well, you have to have a little fear. So when Richii catches you, both of you or one of you, he's going to beat you some for the little crime you've committed. You can fight back if you want, and one of you can help the other; it's up to you. Warning: he's a tough guy. If you elude him long enough and impress him, he won't beat you so much. If he catches you right away, well, it can be pretty bad."

"Madre de puta," Israel said, basically meaning "fuck you." He was pissed. "This is a joke, right?"

But Enrique felt defiant and he said, "Yeah, we'll do it. Let's see if the asshole can catch us." He looked at Israel for affirmation, but Israel was just glaring at the older boys.

One said, "We'll go up there and let him know you're coming. Wait about ten minutes, and then come do it. You better just run like your life depends upon it."

"What are we stealing, again?"

"Just grab anything."

178

They waited the ten minutes and walked the couple of blocks to the food stand. Enrique said they should run together since it was a test, and one might have to help the other in a fight. As they approached the stand, they saw the older boys standing with beers and talking to Richii, who was behind the counter. Some people were seated on stools there. Another, older man was behind the counter cooking. Enrique saw a stand of chips, and the customers had food in front of them and some beer bottles. That was it.

"This is ridiculous," Israel said. Then he saw one of the customers pull out some money and lay it on the counter. "Fuck. Okay," Israel said. "You grab the money, and I'll take the two beers there, and we'll run to the apartment building where we practice. I'll stay behind you and keep calling out how far Richii is behind us. You find us places to jump. Be careful that we don't crowd each other and slow ourselves down. Let's run out in the open first, to see if he's faster than us. If he's gaining, we'll do maneuvers."

Enrique felt nervous, but Israel just looked intense and focused as usual. They ran fast to the counter, made their grabs, and started to run.

"Eyyyy, who are those pieces of shit?" yelled the talkative, older boy. "Did you see what they did?"

But the tone in which he shouted it made it clear to Enrique that they had been set up, that Richii wasn't informed about what was going to happen, and that this theft was suddenly a real one. For one brief moment Enrique hesitated, but then he saw the angry customers and Richii already leaping over the counter with a murderous look.

"Fuck, Israel, he didn't know we were going to do it!" Enrique yelled to his friend. The two were running down the center of the street between the opposing lanes of cars. They went a couple of blocks when Israel yelled that Richii was gaining fast. Enrique ventured a quick glance back and saw Richii less than a block away. Behind him, at a distance, ran the two boys who had betrayed them.

"Split up!" Enrique said so that only Israel could hear. "I'll go up the steps of our building. He can only chase one of us! Whichever, the other one stops and watches and helps when the fight begins."

Israel comprehended the directions instantly.

Enrique was taller than Israel and always looked like he had attitude, so he calculated that Richii would come after him. Besides, it was he who grabbed the customer's money. He saw that Israel had already tossed the beer bottles he had been carrying. As for their two personal trainers, Enrique figured that they were going to lag behind and not help either Richii or them in any way. He wondered if they even knew Richii that well.

Enrique saw the entrance to the stairwell of the apartment building where they had suffered so much that first Saturday, and he bolted up the steps. Israel continued down the street. As Enrique expected, Richii followed him. He could hear him bounding the steps a couple of floors behind him. Richii was incredibly fast. Enrique didn't even make it up another story before he felt Richii's hand on his leg, which caused him to go into a running stumble up the steps. There was enough malice in Richii's tug that Enrique found the adrenalin to pull out of his grasp and get up high enough to turn and confront his opponent. He was at head level to Richii. He did a kick to Richii's head that was meant to throw him off balance and backwards. It worked. Enrique took the moment to climb on the staircase wall and leap to the landing behind Richii. He started down and towards the street. He had scored a blow, and now Richii would be doubly furious.

He got as far as the sidewalk, but then some flying man landed on him from the stairs behind him, and they both went tumbling. When they stopped, it was Richii atop Enrique, and he proceeded to deliver rapid-fire fists to Enrique's face. Enrique was trying to roll to his side when Israel jumped on Richii's back and pulled him off and over to the sidewalk. At that moment, Enrique never loved Israel more. Both the younger boys climbed on top of Richii, and then Enrique started to yell something while he held Israel back from hitting Richii, who was bucking right and left in rolls, trying to throw them off.

"Listen, listen, listen, Richii!" Enrique yelled. "We didn't know! Those guys have been training us to run, and they said you ran with them! They said it was a game, and you were in on it, and you would chase us. We were just supposed to take anything and get as far as we could! That's all, that's the truth! We don't care about the money or the beer!"

Upon hearing his name, Richii stopped moving and just looked at them. Then as the boys dismounted him, he jumped up, looking disgusted. He said, "You whores are just lucky you're not dead right now. I didn't know shit about this. Give me that money."

Enrique dug in his pocket and gave him everything that was in there.

"Get the hell out of here," Richii told them. As he stormed off, he added, "I'll deal with those two fuckers. You little mice should run around your house in your own neighborhood. You're going to get shot around here."

As it turned out, Enrique and Israel ran and skated anywhere they wanted in Mexico City as they grew up together after that incident. Before they went to college, they developed a reputation among the skaters and free runners as being the best in the city. While some who did this used their skills for petty robberies like purse snatchings and stealing from street vendors or stores, Enrique and Israel did it for pure athleticism and as a way of getting adrenalin rushes. "Better than doing drugs," Enrique would tell his always suspicious brothers. But Israel and Enrique never veered from the scholastic path to university and graduate school.

Deep inside, Enrique knew that even without his mother's and brothers' constant vigilance that he would study at night and that he would spend the same amount of effort on his own that he did under their prodding. He was smart, and he had a voracious curiosity about the world, and especially about Mexican history. He lived in Tenochtitlán, for God's sake, Mexico City, home of one of the greatest civilizations of all time: the Aztecs! In that city there was hardly a citizen alive who didn't want to trace his genealogy to the Aztecs. Enrique was no exception. It was possible that Enrique had some Aztec blood, but he was tall and looked Mediterranean, and the mixtures of culture inside him and around him pushed him to a love of Aztec and Spanish history. Mexico had been a land of notable civilizations and accomplishments before the Spanish invasion, and the more that Enrique explored his country's history, the prouder he became to call himself Mexican.

Israel was just like him, but a shade more intense, if that were possible. He was every bit as scholastic and very competitive with Enrique about grades. There were just a few occasions when the subject came up, but Israel made it plain to Enrique that both of them would go to one of the finest universities in Mexico together, and then they should become either doctors or lawyers. In addition, Israel commanded, even though Mexico City had fine schools, they had grown up in the city and they needed to branch out in life. Monterrey in the north had excellent schools, and they would go to one of them there.

At fourteen Israel was short but well formed, and Enrique was tall and athletically lean. In the next four years Israel grew maybe an inch and became manly looking, but Enrique topped over six feet tall. He filled out his frame with muscles that turned heads. He seldom smiled in those years. Inside him, he always felt his sensitive heart, but in the mirror he saw how tough he looked. This made for great protection in the poor streets of Mexico City. He adopted a style that made him look dark and dangerous. He used his eyes to express everything he needed to say. Most people, especially girls, didn't feel that Enrique gave two thoughts about them. Enrique had the looks that made girls sigh just because they weren't with him. In truth, he was shy and uncomfortable around them. He won victories over them by giving them a look and not a conversation. On the other hand, Israel had respectful relationships with girl skaters during those years. He only saw them on those Saturdays when they were doing their free running or skating.

The loyalty between Enrique and Israel went unnoticed by no one. Enrique knew that if anyone thought of one, they automatically thought of the other; and he guessed also that everyone knew that Israel usually called the shots. Israel in particular made it clear to Enrique's mother and brothers and to his own family that he and Enrique were a package when plans for the future would be considered. At only fifteen years old, Israel selected the university in Monterrey that both would attend; namely, Universidad Autonoma de Nuevo León, which had an excellent reputation throughout Mexico for the quality of its undergraduate curricula and also its law school that offered Master's degrees and licensure. After showing brochures to Enrique, Israel met with the families and explained that he and Enrique should attend this school together. He showed them the information about the school, the courses required to satisfy the degree programs, and the costs. Fortunately for the boys, public education in Mexico is free, and the costs involved would pertain to the costs of living in Monterrey. All Israel and Enrique had to do was to excel in grades in the high school and then get accepted into the university. They did.

There were many times before Israel was murdered that Enrique thought about the relationship between the two of them and how he measured himself in so many ways against Israel. He was more imposing physically, but Israel had such intense, forward-thinking focus that sometimes Enrique felt Israel was like a father. Israel had "field sense." He always knew who the players were around them in every situation and where they were on the field. He didn't like surprises. He liked to be in control of his destiny. And Enrique's. He would ask Enrique how his older brothers were doing supervising him at night. He would tell him that by the grace of God he, Israel, still had a father, a good man; and that all of them, his father and Enrique's brothers, looked after Enrique like loving dads. Enrique would think, yes, and you too, Israel. He never said it.

So the murder of Israel was a dagger from the shadows shoved into Enrique's heart. For the first few days afterwards he was scared, even afraid to leave the condo. Who were these guys who had whisked his brother of the soul away and deprived him the rest of his life? When he did manage to fall into uneasy sleep at night, he had nightmares. In all of them was the great deceiver, the beautiful young woman who had been the only person ever to crack the pavement in Israel's path of life. Israel had seen her and had completely lost his head from the start. In the couple of weeks that she and Israel were together, Enrique hardly recognized his friend. Israel buzzed around her like a bee at the hive, and Enrique smelled the sex on both of them. They were in that lover's world, looking and speaking only to each other.

Then she disappeared, and Israel became distraught and desperate. He sought her everywhere. Shortly afterwards he was kidnapped and murdered. Enrique found this incomprehensible and he could feel himself falling apart. Would he fall into the same hole as Israel and the girl and become one of the young people disappeared or dead in Mexico? If he even understood why Israel was murdered, that would help him.

He might have fallen apart, Enrique mused, except that David stepped in and took control of things while he was going through his breakdown. When David first came to his apartment that day and learned that Israel was indeed the victim he had read about in the newspaper, Enrique felt wary of him because he didn't know David that well then. David had been a friend to Israel before he became a friend to Enrique. In light of what happened, could he trust David?

God! Enrique thought, *life can be so odd.* Israel had come home to their condo in the evenings and began mentioning this older man, a gringo, whom he had come to know in the lobby. He said the man was showing him how to trade stocks in the United States' stock exchanges. Then Enrique met David through Israel one afternoon in the weight room. David was a friendly man, confident, strong, and astonishingly agile for his age. Enrique remembered wondering what he had done in life to keep in this kind of shape. The condominium gym and weight room was actually a building constructed on top of one of the condominium towers, and that meant it was seven stories up. The cement stairs ran between two of the towers, and at ground level it terminated in a grassy, garden area. Part of the exercise routine that Israel and Enrique did was to time their runs up and down the stairs, with occasional jumps from one landing to another for old time's sake. The gringo did it too! He ran up and down just fine with them, and he had a flying kind of jump that made Enrique laugh, like he thought he was one of the Marvel comics' super heroes. When Enrique commented to David that he worked out like a young man, David laughed and answered that he hurt plenty the next morning, but the key to successful aging wasn't to admit it.

Enrique observed also that David's conversational Spanish was excellent, and he didn't seem to mind switching to English whenever he or Israel wanted the opportunity to practice it. As the three of them got together in the gym, or out somewhere occasionally for a beer, Enrique started having a growing curiosity about David's personal history. The little that David told them seemed like a couple of pieces to a big jigsaw puzzle. He was relaxed and easy about himself, not as if he were hiding anything, but when Enrique thought about it later, he realized David didn't share much that explained what a gringo was doing sitting in a lobby of a condominium and trading United States equities in Monterrey, Mexico.

Then came the moment after he told David that Israel had been murdered, and the man had gently put his arm around him and just sat with him, until Enrique felt his panic and terror dissipate. They were there a good while, and then Enrique got up and went into his bedroom. While he was back there, David called someone in the Mexican Armed Forces, and after that everything began to change.

The thing is, Enrique told himself at the peak of his distress, many times you just disappear or get killed in Mexico, and there is no one caught, no justice, or no explanation for what happened. That was why he wanted to become a lawyer, to do something to help his country. At least, that's what he said all the time when Israel was alive and he felt young and brave. The way it worked is that someone found a body, reports were filed, and attempts were made to identify who it was. News crews might show up and interview bystanders or witnesses, but after that, it was all they could do to move on to the next crime scene and report what happened there. All the reports were the same: when, where, maybe who, guesses as to why, and the how as evidenced by the number of spent cartridge shells on the pavement. Other reports described someone being pursued like Israel, loaded into a SUV, and driven off, never to be seen again, or their remains found some days later in another part of the city.

But…*but*…Enrique thought, *the gringo made a phone call, and suddenly federal police and the Marines arrested three men for Israel's murder and confiscated a SUV like the one described by the witnesses to Israel's kidnapping! Eyyy? Why was that even possible for the gringo to do?*

He might have begun to obsess about that, except that after they arrested the suspects, he experienced the great relief that someone had been caught, and perhaps their motives would be revealed. News of their capture felt like warm balm soothing Enrique's sleep-deprived mind and relaxing him at last. Israel's father had rushed to Monterrey from Mexico City and had spent some time with Enrique as they waited to hear the outcome of the arrest. Under Mexican law, the men could be held ten days while evidence against them would be collected. If that wasn't sufficient time, a judge could extend the incarceration another thirty days, but an indictment with evidence must be presented. So Enrique was busy during this time, and he felt safe.

Then, on the fortieth day, the men were released! The authorities could find no physical evidence that Israel had ever been in that vehicle. The witnesses became unsure exactly what they had seen. Nothing in the homes of the men or their possessions showed any blood or evidence at all that they had Israel with them on that day, or any day. One of the men released was the husband of the beautiful young girl whom Israel had been seeing. He, of course, acted frantic that his wife had disappeared, and he demanded justice. He was twenty-seven years old. She was twenty-two. She was gone; Israel was dead; and he and his companions were free. Enrique knew the score. The fucking husband had killed Israel and his estranged wife for being together, and now he was free. Surprise! Surprise! The newspaper said the husband's connections to organized crime couldn't be substantiated.

In the rage that Enrique felt upon hearing the news, he destroyed the glass coffee table that was in his living room, and he threw his cell phone repeatedly against the wall. While he was doing this, David showed up at his door. His usual relaxed, easy-going appearance was gone.

"We have to stop this shit in Mexico," David said from the hallway when Enrique opened the door. Enrique saw the clinched jaw and the fury in the gringo's eyes. That was the moment when something crystallized for him. David had called someone, and they had found these men, and now the men were released, and David's victory had been reversed.

David was furious.

Enrique opened the door wider to let him in. "Tell me how we're going to do it, David, because I swear I'll kill them all. Come in and tell me. Tell me a lot of things, like who you are and how you know whom to call in Mexico. Tell me what we're going to do, because I'm in. I'm tired of being afraid."

From that moment forward, David's revelations about himself to Enrique came in dribs and drabs. That night he told Enrique that he did training and consulting in specialized intelligence gathering for the military in the United States and Mexico and that he had developed a self-defense program of martial arts to be used in situations where unarmed persons are threatened by armed persons. He threw in that he had a background in gymnastics and he integrated gymnastics techniques into his training. Enrique was thinking, *no shit*, when David suddenly returned to the statements Enrique had made at the door:

"Listen, Enrique, I can't, and won't, forget Israel either. I've been coming to Mexico a long time. I've yet to meet someone who hasn't been touched in some way by death in their family or friends to organized crime. The violence now is stratospheric compared to

186

what it used to be. Mexico has cities and entire parts of states where organized crime is running the governmental services or replacing these services with their own. In my years here I've seen a thousand faces of the dead and ten thousand faces of the grieving.

Israel…Israel… well, this time it's just too personal. We'll get justice for him, Enrique, but we have to be smart, or we'll be dead before we even begin."

"What do we do? What do I do?"

David looked directly into his eyes and answered, "The first thing you do is keep going to school and prepare to be the best lawyer in the country. That is priority one. It's what you and Israel did together. You both worked to get here, and you can't let him down now that he has been murdered. You have to work on his behalf the rest of your life. Comprendes?"

"Comprendo. What do I do right now?"

"Exactly what I tell you, and when I tell you. You are going to have to trust me," David answered.

"I do."

"The first thing is that I want you to meet someone."

"Who is it?" Enrique asked.

"A woman. A homemaker. We'll have a social conversation over some beer and wine. You'll like her. She may ask you a lot of questions. Just roll with it and be yourself. Don't try to figure out anything from the questions, just be honest. I'm sure she'll have a lot to share with you. Can you be at my place tomorrow around 4:00 pm?"

"A little past that, yes. I have a class ending just before then."

"Fine. For now, do nothing else. Neither of us is prepared yet. We have planning to do. While we're preparing what we'll do, you need to keep quiet. Keep your anger about these men being freed to yourself. Otherwise you'll just get yourself killed. I'm pretty sure these guys who took Israel are members of the Zetas who have moved into Monterrey to challenge the Gulf cartel here, as well as Sinaloa, and they're all over Cumbres. You don't know if anyone you speak to is one of them or an informant for them. You can't trust anyone. Keep quiet, be alert, be smart, and work hard in school. You and I'll work together soon."

"So what is this tomorrow?" Enrique asked. "I'm a little unclear about it. Is it an interview of some sort?"

David shrugged his shoulders and answered, "Not really."
But he lied.

Chapter 14: Enrique's Pentecost

Cumbres, Monterrey
Four Years Prior

It was Ana Valdez who answered the door to David's condo when Enrique knocked the next day. He had expected David, not this delicious woman with a dazzling smile. She was extending her hand to introduce herself. It caught him off guard, and he stood there staring before he composed himself enough to take her hand. *Dios, she's beautiful,* he was thinking as he told her his name. He glimpsed David beyond removing something from the oven in the kitchen. It was a relief to be able to look at him there because he was trying not to look at the unbuttoned opening of Ana's white blouse. When he looked down he saw that she wore a tight tomato-red skirt and high heel shoes matching in color. Ana led him inside. She was a pleasant view from behind as Enrique followed her into the kitchen. David greeted him this time with a hug, which relaxed him a little. He smiled knowingly at Enrique as he saw that he had been taken with Ana's sensual looks and hadn't been able to hide his surprised reaction at the door. His look said to Enrique, "Some housewife, eh?"

What Enrique remembered about the early minutes of their meeting was that they ate David's burrito appetizer and drank beer, except Ana drank water. As they talked, the intense, late afternoon sun washed through the living room wall of glass and made the room hot and too bright. David lowered the rolling, translucent shades permitting a hazy view outdoors and blocking views in from the outside. The shades reduced light into the condo by about fifty percent.

Ana skillfully and subtly controlled their conversation, which moved from initial pleasantries to getting Enrique to describe what it was like to grow up in Mexico City with Israel. When Enrique's story caught up to their move to Monterrey, Ana asked him what he knew of the violence before he came and how had things changed as he and Israel settled into life in Monterrey. He was unaware of it that evening, but looking back on it, Enrique saw how smoothly Ana probed him, his heart, his feelings, his intelligence; how she evaluated his body language, and even his body, without making him self-conscious in any way. She was assessing his potential for the role he eventually came to play. David did it as well, sitting beside her and smiling at him, throwing in reminders for Enrique to discuss this or that, while offering more food.

But Enrique had an observation of his own: *These two are in love.*

He saw that David sat close beside Ana on the sofa. They touched each other affectionately without hiding it. When David looked at Ana, he had puppy eyes that looked as if he were recalling what they had been doing before Enrique arrived. Then even as Ana told Enrique about her husband, Rafael, and their two children, she leaned against David in a way that left no doubt her body belonged to him, and for whatever reason she wasn't hiding this from Enrique.

He saw that Ana absorbed everything told to her in minute detail. She asked a lot of questions and later referenced what he said. They were questions like, "What are your goals? Have you ever been in love? How do you keep in shape? What was your friendship with Israel like in Mexico City? What did the two of you do here in Monterrey while you were in law school together?"

The personal questions about Israel in particular were forcing up feelings which Enrique had stuffed inside. It was as if Ana wanted to dislodge them on purpose. At the point in which he felt the saddest, Ana asked him, "And what about you personally, Enrique? How are you feeling about things right now? Are you okay? What do you want to do?"

There was no delay in his response, no thinking required.

"I want Israel back."

His face reddened with anger. "I want him back! We were going to be best friends for life. He's the best friend I ever had. I grew up with him. I didn't have any friends close like a brother to me like Israel. He was closer even than my brothers are to me. But he can't come back. He can never be with me again. They killed him. They're free now, and he's dead, and he was a better man than they are. Those guys whom they set free for lack of evidence…I don't know if they killed Israel or not. But I think they did. It's funny how David called someone, and they picked suspects up so quickly, but now no witness can be sure these are the guys who put Israel in the truck. There's no evidence for a case. But there were reasons those guys were picked up, and now no one is sure about anything!"

"Yeah," David said. "It has been fucked up. I had someone to call and they did their part by finding those guys, Enrique. So the investigators focused on the husband of the young lady. His physical description and those of his two friends with him fit the general descriptions that were given to the police by the employee who saw men put Israel in the SUV that day. The girl's husband had a black Ford 150 truck, which is what the witness said the vehicle was. There are a few hundred of these in Monterrey. Later the witness got nervous and said he wasn't positive about the truck because he was focused on looking at Israel when it was happening. They found no evidence in the husband's truck, and all three guys had alibis with their own witnesses at the time of the kidnapping. Of course, we know how that goes. Everyone in Mexico has an alibi. But these guys are being watched, and they're still tracking down the owners of black Ford 150 pickup trucks like this."

"The employee in the dealership could have been bought or intimidated" Ana said. " I'm so sorry for your loss of your best friend, Enrique. Sometimes bad things happen, and it's all we can think about for a while. Maybe it was thoughtless of me to ask you these questions now."

"No, no, it's okay," Enrique answered. "I want to talk! I feel so damned angry, frustrated and scared. I want justice for Israel. I want to finish what he and I started together. I do want to be a lawyer. I do want to help get our country back from the narcotraficantes. I want security and peace for Mexico. I want to find other people who want this and who are brave. I'm young, just a student. I still don't know too much about how things work in this world. It's scary. I'm afraid for the kids younger than me, and I want to help them. I need to know what to do. No one trusts the political parties, the politicians, the police, or the government. Some people trust the Armed Forces, but there are Mexicans who have been victimized by them too. Even the Zetas came from the Special Forces! We're falling apart, we're falling down, and no one knows how to stop this. I want to make this stop!"

191

When he finished speaking, Ana turned to David and gave him a signal with her eyes. He reached beside the sofa and removed a laptop computer from a black bag. While David powered it on, Ana looked at Enrique and patted the place beside her on the sofa to command him to sit beside her so he could view the laptop with them. Behind them the evening sun had lowered behind the mountains in Cumbres. The long scattered clouds in the west caught its fading rays and refracted them from the red end of the spectrum. Through the translucent shades of David's living room windows the light bathed their skin in red, like blood. It collected in pools amid shadows on David's floor.

What Ana had assembled on the computer was a collage of video clips and news stories of recent protest marches throughout Mexico. These showed the victims of Mexico sending distress signals to a world that didn't notice them. They were women and children and old people limping in the streets from a thousand injustices, and screaming in pain that someone might notice them. The world helped Africa, but no one paid attention to Mexico. The neighbor to its north, which should have been the most compassionate, just wanted to seal the Mexicans inside Mexico so their problems wouldn't infect them, never claiming responsibility for the cancer of drugs and arms that splattered blood everywhere on Mexican soil.

As Enrique watched, Ana narrated for him. "Sometime in the future, Enrique, when people look back at us to understand why things happened as they did in Mexico, this is what they'll see: Indigenous tribes who trooped to the big cities from the mountains to report the starvation of tens of thousands of their people due to drought, while the aid program executives stole the donations to help them. Mothers and fathers who lost sons and daughters to the guns of thugs became activists to heal them of their loss. They all came together in the streets to shout, 'No More Blood!'

"The students of our history will see protesting students shot down by city police. Outside the prisons they'll see wives and small children of murdered prisoners shaking the chain link fences and throwing stones and starting fires on the other side because the guards had let in cartel troops to kill rival cartel prisoners. Mayors and governors and federal deputies being arrested in airports with suitcases filled with cash. Casinos filled with people being incinerated in broad daylight when men doused machines and entrances with gasoline because the owners hadn't paid their protection money. People in rehabilitation centers seeking help for their addictions being gunned down en masse. Tourists traveling on buses being massacred and robbed by pirates with semi-automatics weapons.

"No one stopped these things from happening over and over again. Not the government, not the police force, not even the Armed Forces could stop these brutal horrors."

The light in the room dimmed as darkness sucked Monterrey into the shadows behind them. Now Ana asked for wine which David got for her. She told Enrique to try it. Enrique took the glass and sipped and felt instantly flushed and warm. It felt like he had accepted a chalice in some ceremony initiating him into a secret pact. It was a strange thought, perhaps due to the mood of the evening. He ventured to look at Ana. It was a look intended to review her beauty. He saw her cheeks were flushed a little also, and he thought it was from the wine, but later he realized it was from what she was about to show him.

She wasn't looking at him then, but at the computer as she searched for something on it. She continued her narration, saying, "When governments can no longer protect its citizens or when the governments rot from corruption, the people will revolt, and they'll rise up to reclaim their safety and their rights. In a vacuum of leadership, people of courage come forth to lead. Mexico needs heroes. I want to show you a few things about your friend, David," Ana said.

Beside her, David dropped his eyes briefly and a self-conscious look passed on his face. Ana looked at him and gave a small laugh. She opened a different video file on the computer. The screen said, "Heroes!" A black and white video began to play of little children in another place and time. It looked like a vintage homemade film from years ago. There was a young boy dressed in dark clothing and wearing a mask. The child leaped atop a coffee table in a small house. He fought off some other boys trying to pull him to the floor. He astonishingly jumped over their heads, and then the boys chased him around the room. The kid leaped from table to sofa to chair with agility. He spun as he fought one boy after another. He made a huge leap, and disappeared down a short dark corridor with the boys chasing, then seconds later reappeared with them running behind him. Ana began to giggle.

She explained, "This was fifty years ago, Enrique, and you're looking at young David doing what you do as an urban jumper!" David wore an embarrassed smile and was shaking his head. Enrique looked at the two of them with a confused expression.

"How do you have this video?" Enrique asked.

Ana saw his look of confusion and answered while the video played on. "You must know that David saved my son's life, right?" Enrique shook his head.

"Well, it doesn't surprise me that David didn't mention it to you. He's very humble. I'll tell you about it in a minute, but that's how I came to know him, when he saved my little boy's life. After that I became unbearable in my quest to find out more about him. I got him to share some personal information about his childhood. I found out he had a lifelong fascination with making up imaginary adventures where he used gymnastics to power his escapes! He made the mistake of telling me this! When he let it slip that he had some old home movies of him in the United States that showed him as a child, I made him show me some, and this was among what he had. So I took them and digitized the movies for him, and I kept a few choice selections for my entertainment. But Enrique, my new friend, you haven't seen anything yet," Ana laughed, and she nodded towards the screen.

Her next video was that of David in his costume when he subdued the robbers in the convenience store in San Antonio. When he saw David jump up on the counter from his hiding place behind it, Enrique gasped in astonishment. He shot a look at David and then watched as David took down the first man and then the second man in the doorway of the store with his flying leap.

Enrique fell back against the sofa in amazement of what followed. There were a few brief clips from TV interviews with David about the incident where the commentators described him as a hero. After that, Ana was on the screen with the story of David's jump through the rain of bullets to cover her son in the street. Pictures of her family displayed in the background. Ana said that Mexico is full of ordinary people who act like heroes when the time calls for it. Ana stated that she would like to introduce a few.

When Ana was explaining how David saved her son's life, Enrique threw his hand to his mouth. He looked at her incredulously. "What is this I'm watching, exactly?" Enrique asked.

"This is a video I did for my blog," she answered. "I want to leverage the power behind the various citizen movements by bringing them all together. I want to empower all the people who want an end to impunity and lack of public security here in Mexico. I want victims and their families to know their rights. I want them all to search for leaders with courage. I'm starting a national campaign called the Campaign for Heroes to shine a light on our need for true leadership."

Enrique leaned forward to watch the screen intently. Ana had assembled a series of very brief interviews with ordinary Mexicans who had acted heroically under horrible circumstances. A man opened the door of his house so strangers could run in when two gangs began firing automatic weapons at each other in his neighborhood. Panicked, innocent people darted inside. A policeman refused to take money from a cartel, and they murdered his wife and two children while he was at work. On camera he cried as he told his story, and the next day he was murdered. Many of the people who participated in marches for an end to the bloodshed told their stories of sons and daughters killed. A couple of of them later died as well.

Ana showed journalists who reported and investigated the cartels, and they gave their lives for their efforts. There were people who anonymously posted on websites the locations of sales points for drugs. Computer hackers hired by the cartels identified these people, and the cartels found them and executed them. Ana kept the stories of ordinary heroes coming one after another. The video showed each hero stating a sentence for the camera, describing what they did. In this way the video made its point: In Mexico there was no shortage of heroes. There was a shortage of leaders who were heroic.

Enrique stared into the darkness beyond the light of the computer screen and thought of Israel. He remembered a photograph of him and Israel that appeared in the local section of El Universal newspaper in Mexico City the summer before they left for the university in Monterrey. The article was just a small human interest story about two poor boy skaters going to college together. The photograph showed Enrique standing next to Israel at the skateboard park in the city. In the air behind them was a youth in the middle of an airborne flip with his board. Enrique was holding his skateboard, but Israel was standing on his, which made him appear as tall as Enrique. Neither boy was smiling for the camera. They stared off into the distance slightly to the left, as if looking towards their future.

Israel was the one who looked like a future hero, Enrique thought as he recalled the photograph. *He looked more mature, intense, and focused. He not only knew where he was going, he knew where we were going. But when we walked away from that pose for the photograph and moved into the future, Israel was the one who got killed by the scatter shots of the violence in Mexico.*

Suddenly he felt tears again. He wanted to cry from a welling of rage, and he wished he were alone. His anger felt scorching, and he thought he could actually smell the tears on the skin of his face. They had the odor of burning fury. He had just seen scores of victims and their loved ones in Ana's video. Israel, so important to him, was one more drop of blood in the bucket. It was all so violating. He wondered what David and Ana thought while they were looking at him at that moment. How were they interpreting his tears?

He said to them, "How can our lives have any meaning unless we do something about this? I want to fight! I don't know what army to join. Is that why you brought me here? Do you know what to do?"

Ana leaned forward and kissed the tear on his cheek. She turned and whispered something into David's ear. David said, "We're beginning to, Enrique. If you can make some time Saturday morning, there's a place I would like to take you, and we can talk about this army thing."

Enrique nodded agreement and peered again into the darkness. He was so hot. Something strange rumbled in his chest, and he felt suddenly humid and horny. His saliva tasted salty. It was impossible, but he saw some dark form like an animal leap from his chest and bound through the window behind him. It was carrying something in its paws. Enrique whirled and watched as the form scurried away into the Monterrey night. He got up and walked over to the window. The animal disappeared into the streets.

It was cathartic. He had a revelation: *My fear is gone! That thing was my fear leaving me.*

On Saturday morning David picked up Enrique in his Corvette. He had instructed Enrique to wear jogging clothes. They headed out highway 54 past the Monterrey International Airport. Before reaching Cerralvo Municipality they turned west into the hills and found a narrow private road that sloped upward several kilometers until they came to a ranch. There was an automated gate with a card reader beside a guard house with a soldier inside. David pulled out a card from his wallet and put it in the card reader, and the gate ascended for their entrance to the property. Enrique noticed as they passed that the guard was wearing a private uniform, not one of the Armed Forces. A sign stating, "Los Gemelos" announced the name of the ranch: The Twins.

Near the front entrance of the main house the road forked, and they drove past the house through hills until they came to a compound that Enrique didn't comprehend at first. Part of it was under construction. It was in a clearing about the size of two fútbol fields in a forest, with some paths exiting it into the trees. To one side was a "U" shaped row of concrete houses that were unfinished inside, and steps in between the buildings. The field had steel towers being erected, and there were rope climbing obstacles in several places as well as rows of tires, wooden beams slanting upward, and parallel bars. As they approached, Enrique began to understand that he was looking at a complex for physical training.

David stopped the car in the middle of the field, and they got out into the hot sun. He was wearing dark blue nylon shorts and running shirt and running shoes. Nodding to the buildings, he said, "Race you there!" He sprinted, and by instinct Enrique followed just behind. *The man can run fast for his age*, Enrique thought. It wasn't exactly easy to keep up, and he was impressed.

David led them to cement steps between two buildings, and suddenly Enrique felt at home again, like in Mexico City. They scaled the steps at a heart-pounding pace. Already he was pouring sweat. At the top David entered a door, and then they were in an unfinished room that had a wooden rung ladder ascending through the ceiling. Without a pause, Enrique followed David up, and they were on a roof, but there was no stopping to admire the view. David darted to the edge, and Enrique followed. He observed David's technique as the older man jumped across a divide to the roof of the next building. Enrique leapt right behind him. Then without stopping

197

they went down a rung ladder into another "house," ran out the door to stairs between buildings, leapt down those, went outside again to the next set of steps between buildings, and then back up. That was the pattern, and they visited nine roof tops in this fashion.

At the end, David exited the last stairway and led them into the field. With hands on hips, he began pacing in a circle to let his breathing calm. Enrique chose to stand there, sweat rolling into his left eye and burning. He kept brushing it away. After a couple of minutes, David started walking to the car where he had stored a cooler of water bottles in the trunk. Enrique followed. Neither wanted to speak, but finally Enrique said, "Damn!" They gulped the water, and a couple of minutes later Enrique asked, "Okay, what's this place?"

Before David could answer, his telephone, which he had left in the driver's seat, sounded its phone call notification tune. David retrieved it and tapped on the screen. Enrique could see a text message. David tapped a couple of times again, and a map appeared on the screen with a moving yellow dot.

He said, "Ana and Eduardo Ortiz are almost here. He owns this ranch. Do you know him?"

Enrique was shocked. "Eduardo Ortiz of the cement company?" he asked. David was nodding, and already they could hear an approaching vehicle down the road from the ranch house. "Of course!" Enrique exclaimed. "Everybody in Mexico knows who he is. He makes Presidents and Governors!"

"Well, he's active in his political party, the PAN," David answered with understatement. "I've known him since I was a child. He has been a close friend since I was a young man. He has been a confidant many years. He has helped me in the past with some of my consulting work and some undercover work that I do occasionally. I help him with various projects. And to answer your question, this is a training facility. It's used by the Mexican Special Armed Forces sometimes and occasionally by the United States military to train special units assisting Mexican operatives. Eduardo loans this facility in secrecy to help this country. Lately he has been expanding it under my direction to accommodate a new type of paramilitary force being prepared for Mexico. He does this with his private funds. He's a true Mexican patriot.

"The head of operations for the paramilitary unit, for now, is Ana. She delivered her concept ideas for a public-safety- oriented-youth organization to me over a month ago. She wrote a creed and a discipline of life for this organization. Her ideas and overall concept fit perfectly with what Eduardo and I were already doing. We had been focused more on developing a training facility to prepare young men and women physically for urban combat. So I modified the construction plans here to accommodate many of Ana's ideas, at least with respect to the physical conditioning of the recruits."

"Ana?" asked Enrique, still trying to get his mind around all that he was learning about her.

A white Silverado pickup truck turned off the road and began to drive across the field towards them. Enrique saw a sign on the door of the truck that had a drawing of the ranch house and the words in red, "Los Gemelos." He could make out an elderly gentleman driver and Ana seated in the passenger seat. When they arrived close to them, the doors opened and Eduardo Ortiz spryly hopped down from the interior. Ana was already coming from her side to greet Enrique with a hug.

Eduardo Ortiz had to be in his late eighty's, Enrique thought, and he looked healthy and younger. He approached Enrique with a look of appraisal that converted into a warm smile as soon as he got near. He introduced himself in a natural, friendly way as if he were a new neighbor. As Ana stood smiling, he greeted David, then swept his arm around to encompass the view of the compound and asked Enrique, "So what do you think of our facility here?"

Enrique was trying to recover from his feeling of being in the deep end of a swimming pool before he learned how to swim. "It looks amazing, sir. David and I just took a run through the buildings there."

To his shock, the elderly man said, "Just like old times in Mexico City, eh?"

Enrique kept his composure as if he shouldn't be surprised that this man knew something about him. "Well, yes, my friend Israel and I used to attack the streets and buildings there with our jumps and skateboards." He made a small laugh. Already he assumed that Eduardo Ortiz must know something about this.

"Sí, sí," the old man replied, "many people are surprised that the city boys can be so athletic. You know, the Mexicans, we're a very strong people. We connect with our bodies, and we use them like the words we speak to express what we need to tell the world. The country people who labor in the fields, like I did, get strong backs, but most of our people are in the cities now. The cities have a different kind of landscape to challenge young bodies. These days we're fighting our wars in the cities of this great country. The people who eat the garbage of the cities, who are the garbage of the cities, don't use their bodies; they destroy bodies. They're lazy and use guns and color our country red. However, red is just one of the colors of our flag, Enrique. The others are green and white. The green is our nourishment, and the white is our purity. Did you know that in light, white is the mixing of all colors? So for our Zs, we've chosen black as their color, which in pigments is the absorption of all colors. Most of the Zs that we will recruit will come from the cities. We're building this place for them to strengthen their bodies and to nourish their ideas and fortify their courage."

When Eduardo Ortiz said, "Zs," Enrique instinctively shot a glance at David.

But it was Ana who spoke. "Enrique, Eduardo and David and I and many others believe that the country is heading into turmoil that can destroy our nation. We're already close to this destruction because of the pervasiveness of organized crime in all our governmental and public safety bodies. Literally, our country is being sold for blood money. Our presidents have declared war on the narcos, and the results have been disastrous. The country has been losing the war to a disturbing degree, while the people are being told that things are under control. But the lies are so obvious now, and the people are sick to their stomachs from this disease of drugs and guns sucking the life out of them. We're all losing our sons and daughters, and no one has known what to do. There has been talk of revolution. In some of the rural areas the indigenous people speak of secession. The country is ripe for revolt. This could be good or bad, depending on who the leaders are who emerge from the chaos."

David was nodding. He handed Ana a bottle of water when he noticed the beads of sweat on her forehead.

She continued. "I'll let Eduardo and David explain their participation in our project. For now, let me tell you that through social media sites I've met many people who are fed up with the violence affecting their daily lives so traumatically. At first, I spent

200

most of my time offering encouragement to the people involved in the movements for non-violence: those who were either victims or those who were loved ones of the victims. Through all my research, I came to understand that Mexico has been co-opted by people working for the cartels. The ones brave enough to stand up to them get killed. Worse, the leaders we have in politics, government, and the police forces, that is, the people who are supposed to protect and serve, are the ones behind the crimes. The movements in protest have been scattered and uncoordinated. But what if these became organized? What if they consolidated behind common goals? There would lie the power needed to heal this country. I've been worrying that a revolution of chaos might be the fate of Mexico, but then I came to understand that we have the power to shape our future, and we must do it."

She turned up her bottle above her head and gulped water down as if her thirst could never get quenched.

Enrique looked at her body. *God help me, I want her. It must be the pinche heat,* he decided.

He felt completely unhinged again as if the connections to his former life and childhood had snapped, leaving him to float in space like an astronaut with an untethered lifeline. He looked at the searing sun, which produced a huge dark spot in his vision when he looked away from it. He had a surge of spirit from this trick of the sun's light. He wanted to imagine that when the spot faded, his vision would let him see a future that was good.

He thought, *It's not Ana causing my body to hunger. I'm turned on by the possibility of doing something with my life.*

David took the moment to speak. "Ana is always modest about what she does. The core of it is that she has been cultivating the environment for a revolution that will be won by words and the capture of hearts. That is the only type of revolution that sticks, enduring the ups and downs which immediately follow these. Lasting revolutions are those with its ideals burned into the hearts of those who have won the battles for change. Ana has been working on developing the conceptual framework for institutions of government that would withstand assaults by corrupt powers. Those would be institutions that could be in place after a peaceful revolution, a revolution without violence, hopefully. She has been bringing together people with ideas for this: brainstormers for a better Mexico. She has put collections of ideas for revolution in symbols. For the people of the revolution, she has chosen the fox as a symbol: the 'zorro.'" He began to chuckle, and he shrugged his shoulders. "I love this idea. The stealth of a crafty fox has always been a fascination for me."

Ana took this as a queue. "So, Enrique, we're about to start the first school for 'zorros' here in Monterrey, right here in this facility of Eduardo. It's a leadership school for young people. We're calling them the "Zs". The Zs will live by a code of high ethical standards and will work to preserve public safety. They'll be fit and trained in hand-to-hand combat and martial arts. They'll serve without the use of weapons other than their clever minds, their fraternity, and their physical skills. David and I are hoping you might be interested in helping us with this. We think you're a person with the right heart and the right experience in life to embrace this and to inspire others to join the movement. You said you want to help your country. We realize you have a lot of time requirements and responsibility with the law school, but if you feel called to assist us, we can help you integrate the time you spend with us and the time you need for your studies. What do you think? Are you interested in learning more?"

"Dios, sí, por cierto!" Enrique answered without hesitation. It was the natural answer for what he felt.

("God, yes, you better believe I am," it meant).

The dark spot in his field of vision seemed to coalesce into a silhouette of Israel. Enrique shook his head to shake this hallucination, but the ping he felt in his heart verified to him that Israel was in approval of what he was doing.

They heard the sound of several vehicles approaching, and in the hot sun they all spun to look in the direction of the road. No one said anything. Enrique saw in the face of Eduardo that he knew who would be coming. The first one appeared and turned into the compound: a jeep, and then a truck carrying troops, and then more trucks. It was a small convoy of Mexican Marines. Eduardo smiled and strode forward a few meters to await their arrival and greet them. Enrique saw him standing there, an old guard of the Mexican Republic, with his arms of welcome open. It seemed like a small moment, but a moment in which he himself would step into history.

202

Chapter 15: The Bird's Long Journey

Houston, Texas
Monday Morning

Thank God he was in Texas! He was supposed to be there anyway when the craziness erupted in Mexico. Donald Austin Blair, President of the United States of America, felt grateful that his calendar coincidentally called for him to be there during the time that the Mexican Army initiated a coup against its Commander in Chief. It had been confusing as hell, he thought, to understand just what was happening. He had to admit that all the intelligence reports and briefings he had received didn't make as much sense as what his old and close friend, David Wilson James, told him from his position in Monterrey. Just three hours earlier, while he was en route to Houston aboard Air Force One to attend a convention of the Texas Democratic Party in the George R. Brown Convention Center, he had spoken to David by phone, while Air Force One had begun its descent to Houston. David had told him about the information passed to him: that the Sinaloa drug boss, El Gato, might be in Monterrey.

It was hardly their first conversation about Mexico. The President's first term coincided roughly with the time that David had met Ana in Monterrey. Before that, when the President had served as Governor of Virginia, he had listened, fascinated, as David explained to him the failures in Mexico of the war against the bosses of the drug cartels. Once, on a historic plantation on the James River in Virginia, he had hosted David and his special guest, Eduardo Ortiz, for a weekend holiday. He was finally meeting the father of Annie and Roberto about whom David had told so many stories. The President remembered being impressed by the confident and impeccably dressed Mexican gentleman, Eduardo Ortiz. He had built his family's cement business into an international conglomerate with titanic contracts to building suppliers all over the world. Yet what truly fascinated him was Eduardo's stories of his involvement in

203

Mexican politics. He had brothers and sisters in Mexico who served in state and federal legislative bodies. He hinted that their service might have been helpful to the family business in procuring contracts for construction projects throughout Mexico.

They were relaxing in a screened gazebo on a bank overlooking the James River on a sweaty, buggy summer evening. The hot sun had set, fiercely protesting its demise, but their easy conversation waxed on over cocktails, crackers with smoked salmon, and crab salad. Donald remembered that Eduardo, then in his late seventies, smoked a cigar and spoke English with an accent that charmed him into kicking back and enjoying the man's stories.

"I'm a businessman, true," said Eduardo, "and many years I traveled for our company and spent time away from Mexico and away from my family. But always I kept my hands and my nose in the politics of Mexico. You see, caballeros, I'm a patriot first and foremost. You won't agree with me, but my country truly is the best in the world. Every Mexican knows this. Oh, to each other, the Mexicanos will criticize their leaders and government with their usual cynicism, but when you ask us about being Mexican, we'll puff our chests with great pride and tell you why Mexico is the best."

"And why is that?" Donald asked, as David sat with a bemused smile.

"Ahhh, bueno, here in the United States you know so little about Mexico and our people. Our country, like yours, is rich in natural resources, but Mexico has more of everything. Jungles and rain forests, deserts, higher mountains, more beaches, larger cities. Before the Spanish came we had civilizations among the most advanced of the world for thousands of years. This pre-European history forges our character and runs deep roots in our very souls and bodies. We're physically strong people with passionate, hot blood. Our fire and creativity sets us apart. We create with abandon. We wear our emotions in big, bright colors. This 'pasión' explodes in all that we do. You see the results in our architecture, our literary works, our media, movies, telenovelas; our music and plays, our dances, our great fiestas. We're a people in love, we celebrate love, and we use our bodies to express the sensuality of our souls. We seduce with our eyes. We bathe Mexico in love and the mysteries of sex."

He puffed his cigar and continued, looking at Donnie. "Governor, you've spent your life in politics. Your country is great in its model of democracy. The democracy in Mexico is very new and fragile. Our Mexican Revolution began in 1910 and didn't really end until the late 1920s. Our Constitution of the United Mexican States in 1917 was the first one to set out social rights. But I must tell you, gentlemen, that only one political party won the presidencies, governorships, and almost all the congressional seats from 1929 and for the next seventy-one years, and that was the party now known in Mexico as the Partido Revolocionario Institucional, or the PRI. This happened because of massive electoral fraud, and in truth, each President put the finger on who would be his successor. It wasn't until 2000 that another political party won the Presidency, and that party is the Partido Acción Nacional, or PAN, which is the party that I've supported so many years. This party is pro-business. Theoretically, it's neither left nor right. Its ideology is that the party should adopt policies and platforms particular to the current events that the country is facing at any point in time. We've been called conservative and right wing, although officially that isn't our position. My family has been strongly behind the PAN, and although I had in my earlier years less time, recently I've devoted much time to the PAN candidates. I have through the years given a fair amount of financial support and resources to this party."

The President remembered that he felt surprised by the fragility and newness of democracy in Mexico. He waited impatiently for Eduardo to take a few puffs of his cigar before continuing to speak.

"In the year 2000, Vincente Fox, the PAN candidate became President. He was the first non-PRI candidate to win. In Mexico the presidents serve one six-year term. In 2006 another PAN candidate won, Felipe Calderón, and it was he who declared war on the drug cartels and ordered the armed forces into combat. So as you can see, democracy in Mexico, where the will of the people truly is expressed, is still new and like the blade of grass that pushes up through a crack in the cement." He paused and smiled to see if his companions caught his small joke pertaining to his company's business.

"Still," Eduardo continued, " in Mexico sometimes votes are purchased, and there is much corruption. I may be heavy handed with my money sometimes, I admit, but I push it towards the people who are not working for the cartels and who are strong patriots of Mexico."

"And who are those patriots, Eduardo?" the President asked him, but he was astonished. *Was Eduardo saying he had paid for votes, or did he simply mean that he financially supported the campaigns of candidates he liked?*

"The patriots are the ones jealously Mexican. They fight to safeguard the riches of Mexico for the people of Mexico and to keep the country's resources out of the control of foreigners. They want a better Mexico with less poverty and illiteracy and with opportunity for all people. They want high standards for the Mexican people and to preeminence in the arts, sciences, and technology. They want the country wrested away from the organized criminals in Mexico and in foreign countries. They want to stop the violence that blocks the Mexican people from attaining the goals I just mentioned. They want to eliminate the drug-trafficking and human-trafficking scum who diminish our stature in the eyes of the world."

As the President remembered this conversation, he sat in a secured conference room in the Houston convention center. He could hear the buzz of the Texas Democratic Party meeting in the main assembly area. He was waiting to be joined by the directors of the CIA, the Drug Enforcement Agency, and the FBI, and by the Attorney General, whom he had summoned as the chaos in Mexico intensified. After meeting with them, he would be on a conference call with the Joint Chiefs of Staff, who had been clamoring to see him and who were peeved by his leaving Washington. That conference would be brief, as the President needed to speak at noon to the extremely nervous Texas party members. The citizens in Texas and the states bordering Mexico were particularly nervous and wanted to know what would be the response of the United States besides the "We're in communication with the military leadership in Mexico" type of statements which the President's press secretary had been issuing. Statements that weren't entirely true.

But this conversation with David and Eduardo Ortiz kept playing in his mind because it verified to him all that David told him in subsequent years about the powerful role Eduardo played in Mexican politics behind the scenes. The most interesting pieces of information had a direct bearing on the current military takeover of the government of Mexico. These had to do with Eduardo's secret and close friendships with the top generals and commanders in the Mexican Armed Forces.

"Eduardo is very crafty," David explained to him once. "When he meets someone, he plays humble, like he's simply a retiring cement company executive with a ranch in the country he likes to manage. He doesn't talk about how he lets the military of Mexico and the United States use that land and properties throughout Mexico for tactical training. Unless he knows you very well, he never tells you what he does for Mexico behind the scenes. However, he leaves little clues for people paying attention, and if they look deeper, they'll see that, in fact, he's an extremely powerful player behind the curtains. Eduardo carries a big gun in Mexico. It's a frigging AK-47 to be sure. He's considered a President-maker.

"You can't understand this if you think of him only as a conservative businessman throwing his weight and money to particular candidates of his party. You truly have to understand him as the ultimate patriot. You have to look at his friendships with the Mexican generals to get why so many in Mexico have respected him and feared him. His closest friends are military leaders at the highest levels. The father of the current ranking general, Alfonso Alvarez, was his closest childhood friend. Admiral Tomas also grew up in his neighborhood. I'm sure there isn't a PAN governor, legislator, or President untouched by Eduardo's money and counsel. The truly astonishing thing about Eduardo is that he's a mover and shaker in the backwaters, and hardly any people talk about the role he has played in their being in the positions they are in. Sometimes I think he swears his associates to secrecy."

"And did he swear you to secrecy? Does he tell you everything?" Donnie had asked.

"I think he does eventually," David had answered. "Our relationship is different. We share the bond of loving his daughter who died. Over the years trust has grown, like a close father and son. Maybe I'm replacing the son he lost, the one he asked me to look for, the one who may be dead. He never has asked me to be quiet about anything he has revealed to me. I guess he understands by the nature of the work I've done that I'm used to guarding secrets."

Now in Houston, the President reflected on the information David had shared with him through the years. Eduardo Ortiz seemed to have two great missions that were meant to build a better Mexico.

First, he was strongly in favor of free trade and democracy, which he thought were the best paths to raise standards of living and literacy among Mexico's numerous poor. Second, Eduardo staunchly supported the use of the Armed Forces to find, arrest, or kill the cartel bosses who were growing in power internationally every day. Yet that strategy of going after cartel bosses, strongly coordinated with intelligence agencies of the United States, turned out to be a disaster for Mexico. The soaring levels of violence and corruption in government drove the people into the streets in revolutionary numbers by the time of the current Mexican President's term. That President, a PRI candidate named Pedro Navarro from Mexico's old ruling party, had been elected as a backlash against the failed efforts of the previous President. Though just barely elected.

The President racked his memory as he continued waiting for his parties to arrive. *What else has David told me about Eduardo?*

One extraordinary thing was the strong friendships Eduardo had all his life with the two men who rose to become the ministers of the Army and the Navy in Mexico. On the phone just hours after the coup, David reminded him something that he had told him a couple of times before.

"Mr. President... Donnie... you have to keep in mind something odd about this military coup," David had told him. "Under the Constitution of Mexico, the President is the only five-star general, and he's the Supreme Commander of the Armed Forces. The two principle armed forces, the Army and the Navy, have a four-star general and an admiral, respectively. They are appointed by the President to serve as ministers in the President's Cabinet. The Air Force is embedded in the Army, and the Marines are embedded in the Navy. Consider that General Alfonso Alvarez, the Army Minister in the President's Cabinet, mutinied against the Commander in Chief, with the assistance of the Minister of the Navy! Consider that General Alvarez basically had been functioning as Minister of Defense for Mexico, although officially there's no such position. Consider that both General Alvarez and Admiral Tomas are close, lifelong friends of Eduardo, and that these men were both appointed to the Cabinet by Mexico's President, who isn't even a member of the political party to which Eduardo has devoted half his life, and who, in fact, comes from the political party that Eduardo abhors!"

The President took a long pause thinking how this could have happened, and as it was beginning to sink in, David continued.

"As you know, Mr. President, this past election was very close. Paper thin. Eduardo's candidate was advancing rapidly in the pre-election polls. The unrest in the country had been escalating."

"God, David, are you saying that the election might have been thrown? That a deal was cut? Did Eduardo intimate anything like this to you?"

"No, Mr. President, he didn't say. Like I told you, he's crafty. However, he did tell me that the General and the Admiral were going to be appointed about twenty-four hours before the announcement was made."

He thought about that a few moments and then he said to David, "It sounds pretty strange that these appointments of Eduardo's friends to these positions could happen at the time it did."

"Mr. President, perhaps as strange as an intelligence agent having a life-long friendship with a man who grows up to become President of the United States," David responded with a little laugh. "And the same agent becoming like a son to a Mexican man who lived in Virginia, and who has a lot to do with people in power in Mexico. In this world, it's the connection of people that make mysterious things happen."

The room the President was in had four large flat screen TVs that were now all turned to different channels covering the demonstrations live from Mexico. The sound was turned off on all. One showed a couple of hundred thousand people jammed into the Zócalo, the huge historic plaza in front of the Palacio Nacional, the Cathedral, and the Federal District buildings in Mexico City. The President noted the interspersion of the soldiers among the people, with the soldiers appearing relaxed, as the crowds broke out singing songs and chants. Clearly there was an atmosphere of restraint.

On another screen there was similar coverage of the crowds assembled in the Macroplaza of Monterrey. On a third TV the newscasters were showing demonstrations in cities throughout Mexico, and on the fourth one, the one that interested the President the most, CNN Mexico kept returning to views of the rooftop on which David and Ana stood, waving greetings to the people below.

The President knew from a CIA report that morning that Mexican Special Forces had someone on the rooftop with CNN Mexico. He knew that Ana had requested protection for David.

She apparently knows David quite well, the President mused, *and she understands that David wouldn't want armed protection unless absolutely necessary.* David had wrapped himself in the principles of the No More Blood movement, and the Zs were entrenched in that with him.

The President shook his head, feeling incredulous. His old friend cut a Don Quixote path through life. He had always admired David's romanticism. Somehow his friend maintained the integrity of his character through dark times of spying and intrigue. He had overcome serious depression from profound emotional losses in his life. Now, blooming late, he found love and joy in the middle of civil war in a foreign country!

David, he thought, *you can be such a stone head, and so exasperating. I've no clue why you weren't dead a long time ago. Of all the people on this earth, you're the one I trust most and the one who always seems to understand what's going on. But my friend, what have you had to do with these events happening now in Mexico? Did you get in over your head?*

They were dormitory roommates in sophomore year at William and Mary and continued as roommates the subsequent two years. Donnie was the son of the Governor, and if that was something special for David, he never showed it. David and he had a natural chemistry together, an instantaneous liking from the very first day. Very early in their friendship the two of them entrusted each other with confidences during long walks together. The President listened to David talk about his infatuation with the Mexican girl, Annie, and how he was determined to win her. He heard about their childhood adventures in Richmond; how she and her brother had such an influence on David, teaching him about Mexico, and even how to speak Spanish. Donnie was there during the exciting times later when David and Annie began seeing each other. He was with David in the dark days after Annie's death. He was best man in David's wedding to Julie, and he was there for David also when she died. David had also been involved in many of his own milestones, but as Donnie's life became more public, and David's career was in the CIA, he sometimes couldn't take part in the events.

210

Donnie, being the son of the Governor, naturally majored in political science at William and Mary. Then he went to law school at the University of Richmond. He was, in fact, blue blood of the elite in Virginia. He went to work in the law firm founded by his father and a couple of associates. From the earliest years of his career, he followed his father's footsteps by working in the Democratic Party of Virginia. In his early forties, Donald Austin Blair got elected to the Senate of Virginia and served two terms. He was elected Governor when he was fifty, and President of the United States when he was fifty-six.

It was time for his meeting, and he summoned his aides, who brought into the room the Agency Directors and the Attorney General. They seated themselves at the table at the President's gesture. The CIA Director, Charles Lombardy, looked miffed and stared directly at the President. He was perched in his chair as if awaiting the first signal that one of them should speak, and then he would push a buzzer. Also named Charles, the Administrator of the Drug Enforcement Agency, Carlos Rivera, whose parents had emigrated from Mexico, was a contrast. He appeared relaxed as if he were glad to be in Houston, away from his daily routines. William LaCrosse, Director of the FBI, looked as he always did, skinny in a dark blue suit, white shirt, and red tie. The President noted that his expression seemed the same whatever his emotion, and he even seemed to laugh without smiling. Nathan Williamson, the Attorney General, was there at the President's request because they were old associates who had worked together many years, and he was a lawyer like the President. He had up-to-date knowledge of prosecutions of many of the cartel leaders discussed by the agency directors, and he liked to know the progress of investigations that might lead to future prosecutions. On video phone was the Commissioner of the U.S. Customs and Border Patrol. This was Ernesto Salvidar, who was called to report the latest events at the border with Mexico.

The President made a brief introduction.

"Good morning, gentlemen. Let's jump right in. First, General Alvarez has been requesting to speak to me since yesterday. I've postponed that so far while I receive all the reports from people in the field in Mexico. I didn't want to appear too quick to give legitimacy to the overthrow of a democratically elected President.

211

We first began trying to make contact with President Navarro, but he and all the leaders of government seem to have been quite effectively quarantined by the coup. To our exasperation we've no ability to obtain information as to their condition other than what General Alvarez dispenses. As you know, the General continues to issue statements saying the coup is temporary until public safety can be assured, and the government will be returned to the people of Mexico when honest elections can be held with candidates free of corruption by the cartels. There's still mass confusion in Mexico with the people in the streets and the military there with them. So far we haven't noted the kind of violence by the cartels that was present in recent months, but our great fear is the retaliation of the cartels. We worry also about civil war. We called back the ambassadors and staffs in our consulates a couple of weeks ago when the violence from the cartel wars escalated in Monterrey and some of the border cities."

Then, to the chagrin of the CIA Director, the President opened up the meeting with Salvidar.

"Ernesto, since we're speaking of the border, let's begin with you. We have our troops, National Guard, and your team taking positions along the border. Given that we're in day three of a military coup in Mexico, I understand the situation is quite tense at the points of entry. Since we have pretty effectively sealed the border with little passage through to either country, you can imagine the heat I'm taking from all angles on that! What can you report, Ernesto?"

Salvidar nodded on screen without missing a beat. "Mr. President, I would characterize the situation at the points of entrance, the POEs, as one of high duress. I'm sure you've seen the aerial views of the traffic backups for miles on the highways leading to the border entry points. We've followed orders not to let U.S. citizens pass into Mexico unless they have dual citizenship, and we screen carefully to permit the Mexican citizens to pass. Conversely, we're trying to let U.S. citizens return to this country from Mexico. The language problems and logistical problems in terms of access to the POEs are much more complicated than usual, and the staff is straining under the intensity of the work. The state police in Texas, New Mexico, Arizona, and California are working with the Army and the Army National Guard to clear traffic and turn back unnecessary vehicles. We've tried to permit the passage of trucks carrying essential freight and foodstuffs, as well as any vehicles carrying medical supplies and equipment to areas in Mexico that might need assistance in the case of violence.

"The truth of the matter, Sir, is that we have chaos that seems to be deepening by the minute. There's an increasing problem of the demonstrators who are trying to approach the border points. There are antagonistic groups who shout and push one another. There have been a few minor outbreaks of violence. The problem, of course, is that they're finding workarounds to the road blocks and check points on the highways, coming in off-road vehicles. We have this going on near us while the CBP agents are trying to do their jobs. Not to mention the press, who are managing to have a presence."

"Who are the protestors that you've been seeing?" the President asked.

"There are different groups, Sir. Some are upset over the closure of the border, while others are demanding a complete seal to protect their properties in the states. Some are Mexican Americans who don't like the military overthrow, or who are concerned for their relatives, and they're demanding that our troops go into Mexico! These are opposed by Mexican Americans and other people who don't want the U.S. to intervene in Mexico under any circumstances. It's all very noisy. There are the Zs, the mostly young people in black outfits. They seem to be mainly Mexican Americans who want to enter Mexico to help preserve public safety. They have speakers calling for the cartels and the Armed Forces not to spill blood."

Lord, the President thought, and David's face came into his mind. *Innocent and naïve.* He worried about them. He shook his head, thanked Salvidar, and decided to give the floor next to Director Lombardy of the CIA. The President thought he looked like he would jump out of his skin if he didn't get called on next. He realized that the tension with this man came from the jealousy he had about his relationship with David, a much closer one than the two of them had. It was a sore point with Lombardy. The President tried to make him feel important.

"Okay, go ahead, Charles. I've been anxious to hear from you what the latest information is about the government under quarantine. Proceed."

Still perched on the edge of his chair, the CIA director, who somehow had a voice both shrill and nasal, began to speak rapidly.

213

"First, I want to confirm that there's protection for our man David James. We've been told that Mexican Special Forces are on the building across the street." He nodded to the TV screen which at that moment showed both David and Ana on their rooftop. The President acknowledged the remark.

Lombardy continued, "We have reports that President Navarro was dining at home in Los Pinos with his family when General Alvarez himself and some officers of the Presidential Guard informed him of his quarantine and the simultaneous corralling of virtually all the Cabinet members, Senators, and Deputies of the House. We've been reviewing amateur videos uploaded to YouTube and sites on the internet which show the Mexican Armed Forces massing in the Zócalo and moving into the National Palace and the Federal Buildings in Mexico City at the time of the coup. These have supplemented the reports from our men in the field. There are some videos of the troops rolling into Los Pinos. These videos corroborate the reports coming from the office of General Alvarez that there was an effective and complete quarantine of President Navarro and the government. The videos also show Army transports of government officials from their offices to their homes, where they're guarded. The Armed Forces are regularly addressing the crowds in Mexico City, Monterrey, Guadalajara, and in other cities to provide progress reports. They're assuring them that they'll oversee public services and will provide protection against retaliation by the cartels. They request citizens to go home and to report to their jobs, but there still are huge crowds around government buildings in the big cities."

Lombardy hesitated, and then moved on to a different subject which he knew would fit with the reports of the other Directors. He continued, "Mr. President, our office is concerned about the probable violence and tactical offenses which the organized crime cartels will employ in the next hours and days. We've been sending our analytics concerning Mexico in particular to FBI, DEA, and Immigration and Customs, as well as to your office, Sir, and recently to the Attorney General."

Lombardy looked at the others to queue them to acknowledge agreement. They nodded. He threw a glance to the television again to indicate he was about to talk about David James.

"All of us here are reminded that David James used to work for the CIA for many years, and in recent years he has a cover of his

214

own consulting business. That's a valid cover because he does indeed have such a company, and through it we've contracted his services on a freelance basis. In particular, in the past several years David has worked with us on projects related to international crimes of drug and human trafficking. He has a close relationship with Eduardo Ortiz, who has been working behind the scenes in Mexico with the Mexican Army and Marines, letting them use properties he owns throughout Mexico. Mr. Ortiz has been funding the training of Special Forces for these military branches. More interestingly, he has funded certain paramilitary groups who are supportive of the Mexican military and who are trained specifically to fight the armed units of the Mexican cartels. For example, David James and Ana Valdez have developed with him a physical training program of the quasi-military group known as the Zs. The Zs use their bodies as weapons instead of firearms. They subscribe to a rule of life which has caught fire with the youth of Mexico and with some here in the United States.

"In simple terms, the Zs promote a life of high ethical standards, and they organize themselves to protect citizens from the violence of the cartels. They apparently work in cooperation with the Armed Forces. Many of their recruits are college students. I would venture to say that the Z program has been so successful that in reality it's the Armed Forces who work as friendly units to the Zs. The charisma of David and Ana Valdez, as well as some of their top leaders, has had a lot to do with their success. They have a high trust factor with the citizens of Mexico."

Lombardy paused for a breath. "While that's relevant and important to what's happening in Mexico right now, in the CIA our drug trafficking and trans-national, anticrime sections have been uncovering startling statistics and reports that show an exponential growth of Mexican cartel activity in the United States."

He threw a glance to Carlos Rivera, the DEA Administrator, who nodded pensively.

"Our analysts have been tracking the incidents of violence associated with cartel activity, and cross referencing our findings with those of DEA. The DEA has been tracking specific shipments and individuals and groups of interest to them that are operating internationally and here in the United States. Our mutual findings verify the expanding commerce of the Cartel of Sinaloa.

"However, Sinaloa has moved meth and synthetic marijuana in prodigious quantities into new regions of the United States in the last three years. That cartel has its own meth labs in Mexico, Honduras, and Guatemala. They have moved beyond trafficking and into production, as they have done with marijuana in the past. Meanwhile, the Zetas have extended human trafficking, extortion and kidnappings into the border states of the USA. Both cartels are using Florida and the Caribbean islands as hopping points for the movement of materials to Africa, Europe, and Asia, and the eastern United States. What's really alarming is that all our agencies, including CIA, DEA, FBI, and Customs and Border Patrol, are finding two contradictory things. On the one hand, there is increased corroboration and cooperation by Sinaloa with organized crime and the mafia in Europe, Eastern Europe, and Russia. On the other hand, simultaneously, there has been penetration by Sinaloa in those areas directly."

"You mean competition?" the President asked.

"Yes. So, obviously, trade and merchant agreements in existence now may shortly be in peril, and the likelihood of war soon escalating along the trade routes and in the trafficking hubs like Miami, Houston, New Orleans, New York, and Norfolk is high."

Lombardy looked at Carlos Rivera to queue him

The DEA Administrator said, "Mr. President, if I may?"

The President nodded, after shooting a quick glance at one of the flat screens in the room.

"Charles is using the word 'war.' It's the kind of war that, showing up in the United States like it has done in Mexico the last seven years, will terrify United States citizens. I mean, we could say that this is what happened in Mexico. The people have been terrified, and then they decided to take matters into their own hands when security in their country disintegrated. Sinaloa and the Zetas and all the Mexican cartels have really pushed the envelope of human tolerance with executions and the dumping of dismembered and decapitated bodies on highways and in front of elementary schools and municipal government buildings. I personally think the last straw which set off this coup was the incident in Monterrey a little over a week ago when the fifty-four heads were found in Monterrey. Both the Zetas and Sinaloa left mantas all over the city, each cartel blaming the other. No one knows if they're rival cartel members or immigrants who were captured and taken by the Zetas, but the bodies included a lot of women and children. That outrage put the people in the streets all over Mexico. When the chaos started to get out of hand, some important people urged the Armed Forces to take action."

The President was about to ask, "We have evidence of this?" when Rivera leaned forward and clasped his hands over the table, and peered at the President to indicate he was about to divulge something extremely important. He even lowered his voice.

He said, "The analytics of cartel activity in the USA, and the logistical data that describes changing shipment routes and end points for the drugs in this country, are pointing to this country being on the verge of this kind of violence. Already we've seen the assassinations of people with automatic weapons in new places in the U.S., and extortions and kidnappings are increasing so fast in the cities near the border with Mexico that we can hardly keep up with follow-through investigations."

The Attorney General arched his eyes. Rivera continued. "Before the meeting, Charles and William and I were having a little chat about some patterns we've been seeing that suggest something interesting, something that has been theorized by our friend, David James."

"Which is?" asked the President.

"In the last three years, new distribution centers of Mexican meth, in particular, appear to follow corridors in three sequential time periods. All three trace back to Nuevo Laredo, Mexico, and Laredo, Texas. One line goes to New Orleans and then up the Mississippi to the north, terminating in Chicago, but having branches like a tree into Missouri, Kansas, Iowa, and Nebraska. The other branches reach into Tennessee, Kentucky, Ohio, and Indiana. The second line of new center openings goes from New Orleans to Jacksonville, Florida, then up the eastern seaboard to New York, but with presence in newer, smaller metropolitan areas. The third line from Laredo proceeds north into Oklahoma, Colorado, Wyoming, and the Dakotas. We're encountering new Mexicans with sophisticated understanding of business in charge of these operations. Their methods of operating appear very standardized, almost corporate. Most of these are United States citizens, either with origins in Sinaloa, or family members who emigrated from there. The sources that our agents are able to manage all converse about business in very similar terms. They speak of standard operating procedures."

Rivera glanced at the others, whose expressions urged him to continue. He said, "In our conversation this morning, the three of us agreed that our data is describing an operating environment that's not only businesslike as a corporation but seems to have a stamp of personality on it."

Now the President understood where the conversation was going. He looked at the men at the table and asked, "So you're talking about David's theory that there's one man, someone unknown to us, who has energized the expansion of Sinaloa business in the United States in recent years? The man David calls El Gato?"

"Exactly," Rivera replied. "In fact, as Charles will tell you, it's David who studied some of the analytical reports and traced the pattern of the three routes and put together the time line that supports this idea."

The President felt himself growing uncomfortable. He remembered what David had said about the possibility of El Gato being in Monterrey. He asked, "How new is this information?"

The CIA Director responded. "David made comments about this in a report he sent to me about a month ago. I first shared this with DEA and FBI."

The President was actually thinking, *So this is the man David is expecting to meet on the roof*, when he looked at the flat panel television screen, the one shown by CNN Mexico.

He saw Ana Valdez grab the rope and begin to rapidly descend from the roof at that very moment!

"Jesus Christ, look!" the President shouted. The FBI Director was seated near that monitor. He found the volume and turned up the television. The camera shook very briefly, and then there were shouts in Spanish near the camera, and when it focused again, it showed a man firing an automatic weapon at David. There were two women behind him. The group watched as David took a horizontal leap towards the man. Suddenly three close cracks of rifle fire could be heard, and the camera tilted and gave a view of the sky. There were more shouts in Spanish, and then the camera righted itself. Now David, the man, and the women could all be seen lying on the roof.

"My God!" Lombardy whispered loudly.

The President jumped up. He called for his aides. He turned to the Directors and he asked, "Do we have a bird down there? Do we have something close that can get on that roof if David is alive?"

"Yes!" Rivera from the DEA stammered. They were all standing, stunned by what they had just seen, each quickly trying to formulate what to do. Rivera paused a second, thinking hard, but he spoke first.

"Mr. President, there's a Black Hawk on Eduardo Ortiz' field in Monterrey. The one that the USA gave the Mexican Air Force a few years ago. DEA and their Air Force have been using it recently together doing reconnaissance work together under Project Miralo. We were going to do a mission with them this week, but we put it off because of the coup. I just talked to our team there this morning before coming here as I was trying to prepare myself for this meeting. So I know the copter is there, and so are my men. Eduardo Ortiz is there today also."

"Can we get that thing to fly, like right now?"

"Yes, I think so, Sir. When I talked to them they were actually on the Ortiz property. Our relationship with the Mexican Air Force is very good. I'm sure they would be cooperative about rescuing David."

"Eduardo Ortiz would see to that too. Let's speak to him! Is there a medical team there?"

Rivera thought about the qualifications of the men he had there. "We have medical corps because of the possibility of wounded in the drug operations. The Mexicans have a doctor. Don't know if he's there this morning. The Black Hawk can carry a couple of wounded in bays, one over the other."

The President shot right back, "Yes, make certain Mexicans are on board for the rescue. I want whoever is alive on that roof in the copter. Do this fast! Dead or alive, get David!"

The Attorney General spoke up. "The others on the roof could be Mexican citizens, Mr. President! Their Army will probably get there before we do." He looked confused.

"Where do you want to take David?"

"Right here! Houston! I want David here! Let's see if we can get him! If he's alive, let's do this! We'll decide about the others on the fly."

Rivera had already whipped out his cell phone and punched in a number. All of them were staring worriedly at the screen showing the rooftop.

The President clapped his hands together tightly as he watched.

"Okay," he commanded, "now it's time for me to talk to General Alvarez! Let's get him on the phone. I want to tell him what I'm doing. Damn! Damn! Damn!"

In her sixth floor office on La Avenida Juan Ignacio Ramón, Ana Valdez glanced at her watch. It had been a little over an hour since the helicopter had left with David and the man she presumed was El Gato. Enrique still hadn't sent any word from the University Medical Center. As she worked, she heard a confusion of noises from Mexican soldiers getting on and off the elevators as they accessed the roof from the stairway there. She was too distant to hear their conversations, but from the shouts to one another, she assumed that they were dealing with the bodies of the women on the roof.

From time to time there was sporadic gunfire outside. This made her nervous because she was worried about Enrique and whoever might be accompanying him to the hospital.

She decided to try to text him again. Just as she reached for her phone, she heard hurried footsteps approaching her end of the hall. They were definitely males approaching. She didn't even have time to become alarmed before she heard a young man near her office door announce, "Señora Valdez, saludos! Enrique Santos has asked us to see you!"

Ana left her back office room and entered the reception area and saw three young men dressed in the black Z outfits through the glass double doors. One was carrying a black cloth overnight bag that appeared full. She had seen him before with Enrique, so she relaxed. The men smiled respectfully as Ana stepped to the door to unlock it and let them in. Once they were inside, Ana locked the door again.

One took out a phone at that moment and tapped a speed dial number, while another, the one with the voice she had heard in the hall, introduced himself and stated who the other two young men were. She heard him say his name was Juan, but the conversation of

220

the other young man on the phone was capturing her attention. He was speaking to Enrique! Shortly he lowered the phone and said, "Señora, this is Enrique Santos, and he would like to speak to you."

"Certainly!" Ana answered, seizing the phone. She said, "Enrique, is everything okay?"

"Ana, yes, I'm fine and so far there have been no problems, but I need to let you know something. Please stay calm. I'm sure there's an explanation. It took a while for me to arrive here at the University Medical Center. I had to walk through the crowds, and I came with a couple of guys. I went to the Emergency Room, and the thing is, David isn't here. The staff at my request have been checking all the units in case somehow he was in a different part of the hospital, but the short version of the story is that apparently the helicopter didn't come here! There has been no helicopter landing on the heliport." He stopped to let that information sink in.

Ana stammered. She said, "Enrique! Where else would it go? What other hospital? Do you know any others that have heliports?"

Enrique was ahead of her. "Ana, there are two others in Monterrey, and I've been able to talk to them. I had the guys call while I was turning the medical center here upside down, and we haven't wasted a moment. The helicopter didn't come to any of the hospitals in Monterrey."

Ana gasped. "Then Enrique, who has got David?"

Enrique had had a few more minutes to think about things than Ana. So he replied to her, "I don't know, Ana, but listen. Did you look closely at the medical corps and the soldiers who were on the roof attending David and the other man? I wasn't paying attention. I was so unnerved trying to revive David, and then so relieved that help arrived in the helicopter."

Ana strained to remember. She said, "God, Enrique, they looked like soldiers in uniform fatigues to me. I wasn't paying attention closely either. Just before the helicopter arrived, this huge soldier from the Special Forces came up on the roof and looked at the bodies of the people lying there, but he left quickly. I was watching you with David. I wanted to say something to him, but when I turned around he was gone."

Enrique said, "Okay, this may sound strange. Did they all look Mexican to you? Because I remember seeing one guy whom I

221

thought looked very gringo. The other thing is, and I may be imagining it now, but I think I heard English being spoken once."

"Oh my God, yes!" Ana replied. "I did hear English a couple of times now that you mention it. I speak English all the time to people, especially since I met David and know people in his circle, and I guess it didn't stand out to me as odd. Plus, David is English, well, gringo. God! Enrique, what are you trying to say?"

"I don't know, Ana, but I'm wondering if these were people from the United States on that helicopter. And if that's the case, and the helicopter didn't land in any of the Monterrey hospitals, where might it be going?"

Ana took in a loud breath. "To the United States? Oh my god, Enrique, how could that happen? Who would do this? How would they get to the roof so fast? How would they even know?"

"Think about it, Ana! That helicopter was a Blackhawk. They come from the United States. And think who David has worked with in his career. Think who is his best friend. Do you realize that for three days you and David have been seen on that roof on television, thanks to CNN Mexico?"

Ana threw her hand to her mouth. *David's best friend? The President of the United States!* Her mind was whirring, trying to sort out quickly if this was really a plausible hypothesis, or was there some other possibility that was more likely. While she was silent, Enrique took the initiative to change the topic.

"Ana, I'm a few kilometers from you, and there's an ocean of people in between us. I'm sure you're hearing the gunfire. I don't know what that is. The point is, we don't know what this situation means right now with David missing. I'm worried for your safety. I sent those guys there to be with you and to accompany you to one of our safe places. You know, there's that one not far from your office in El Barrio Antiguo, the one you leased for the Zs. Juan or one of the guys there should have some clothes for you to help you be disguised, and they're going to change into casual clothes so that you can leave and arrive there without attracting attention. I don't know why, but I'm working on gut instinct that I think this is a good thing for you to do until we understand what has happened with David. If necessary, later we can bring Rafael and the kids there if the situation requires. So far the internet, computers, and phones are all working there."

222

"But..." Ana said, and then she hesitated before speaking again. A thought entered her mind. "Not to ask the obvious, but did you try to phone or text David on his cell phone? I guess he had it on him when he was on the roof."

"Yes, tried that, Ana," Enrique answered. "Sorry, no answer, just went to voice mail. No reply to text messages."

She sighed. "Precisely why do you think I'm in danger right now as opposed to any other moment in my life?" She was just letting out frustration.

"It's just gut instinct, Ana" Enrique answered. "But if it was the United States that got David out of there that quickly, and David isn't around, who but me and the Zs are going to protect you? You have to admit, as long as David has been with us, haven't we subconsciously felt like we had some extra layer of protection, just because of his experience and the contacts he knows? Until we find him, more than ever we don't know what we're dealing with. The environment is wide open for mishap, and after David James, you're the person the bad guys would most like to get."

Ana was already thinking that Enrique made sense when he added, "Ana, besides yourself, and I hate to say this, but you have to remember your family has some vulnerability. I think it might be a good idea to get them out of view right now."

She thought of her children and caught her breath. She looked at the three young Zs who were standing there listening to her conversation. She nodded slightly to them as she said, "Okay, Enrique, I'll leave with these guys. Let's spend the next couple of hours trying to find David, please! I'm going to try to reach General Alvarez again to see if he knows what has happened to him. I'll try to reach Eduardo as well. I'm surprised not to hear from him by now. Let's do this, and in the next hour or so I'll make a decision whether to call Rafael and tell him I think he and the children need to join me in the safe location."

She heard Enrique expire a sigh of relief that she agreed with him. Then he told her something she found extraordinary.

"Here is something for you to be thinking about. If you're able to contact General Alvarez or Eduardo Ortiz, you can share this with them. This wasn't hard to find out. I saw it on my phone on the internet here. The President of the United States is in Houston, Texas today to address a convention of the Texas Democratic Party. He's pretty damn close."

There was a loud, warm drone. It was lulling, so David's first struggles to awaken were feeble. *It feels hot in here. Where am I?* His eyes were still closed, and then he realized he was hearing people speak English and Spanish. He strained to listen. He moved a little, and an excruciating pain shot through the right side of his chest. He touched it with his hand and felt skin. His shirt was off. The voices became louder and he realized that he was waking up. He fought to remember where he was, and then the memory of being in the helicopter returned to him. That was the noise. He was still in the helicopter. He had been sleeping and it felt like a long time. He moved his arm over his chest. He felt something rough in his wrist and some plastic tubing touching the skin of his chest.

He listened to the voices. They sounded controlled but slightly agitated. He heard scuffling of shoes around his head and the soft whooshing of clothing fabric *The soldiers*, he remembered. The soldiers in their military fatigues. They were tending someone next to him. They were hurried and anxious and he perceived that things weren't going well with the patient underneath him. *The patient?* he thought. Suddenly he remembered that Roberto, El Gato, was in the helicopter with him. He strained to listen.

He heard Spanish. One voice said, "He's losing too much blood. The wound is too extensive. He's hemorrhaging internally."

Another voice said, "He's not responding to my resuscitation at all!"

"Stay with us! Stay with us!" a third yelled above the noise of the motor.

David thought, *You don't understand! He'll live. This is Roberto! He's going to live because I'm going to live! We have unfinished business!*

There was a pause and then the second voice said, "It's no use! He's gone. I'm not getting a pulse, no vital signs, nothing."

"He's gone?" asked the first. *He's gone?* David wondered.

"Yes, it's over," the second voice answered emphatically. Then the voice turned in a direction away from David and asked, "Are you certain who this is, sir?"

The person answered, "Yes, I'm positive," and this voice was as familiar to David as the sound of his own. David's eyes instantly shot wide open in surprise. In that moment he became fully awake. *How could this be?* His sight was blurry at first, but then it cleared and he saw the interior of the helicopter and the soldiers around him. He could feel the stretcher he was on, and he saw the IV fluid apparatus from which hung the bottle that flowed electrolytes to his wrist. The voice had come from behind the top of his head. It hurt his chest when he moved, but he strained to turn his head to look above him.

"Eduardo? Eduardo?" he called out.

Someone moved and pushed past a soldier and came to stand at the end of the stretcher where David's feet were. David stared at the man for a moment. The image was hard to reconcile with his expectations. He hadn't expected the military fatigues but he recognized the face of Eduardo.

"Sí, soy yo," answered Eduardo. "How are you feeling, amigo?" Some of the other voices from the soldiers greeted him also at that time.

David answered, "Just hot, and my chest hurts when I move, otherwise fine, I think."

Eduardo smiled and nodded. "Good! Your chest hurts because they think you've cracked a rib. You're going to have some nasty bruises on your chest, but otherwise you should be fine. You're one lucky, crazy man."

David felt a thousand questions bottled inside him about to blow. He still was confused. "Eduardo, how can you be here? Where are we? Where are we going?"

Eduardo shook his head a little to express sympathy to David. "We're in a Blackhawk that was at our training facility in Monterrey. This is your rescue mission to get you off the roof after you were attacked. You've been asleep about a half hour. I was there when the excitement began and I insisted on being on board. I obtained the authorization from the Mexican Air Force for this thing to fly. You might not remember right now, David, but we had agents from the DEA at the ranch to do reconnaissance work with us this week."

David felt like he couldn't think fast enough. "Ana?" he inquired. He felt his breath catch as he awaited the answer.

"I heard she did a beautiful descent from the building. A descent you should have made," Eduardo chided. "I didn't reveal myself to her when we landed on the roof to get you. I held back in the helicopter. Before we landed, she was back on the roof with Enrique who did cardiac resuscitation on you because it appears your heart had stopped, probably from the close impact of the bullets on your armor. We're concerned about that. You have some IV fluids to restore electrolytes because you were so long in the sun on that hot roof. Enrique may have saved your life."

Now David remembered Ana's goodbye to him as they put him on the helicopter, and he sighed relief. He thought about Enrique and how anxious he must have been to try to revive him, and he felt a river of gratitude inundate his body. Strong emotions were returning to him in a flash flood. These included the dark one regarding Roberto, and he had just heard the voices say that he hadn't made it. That one was upsetting. It made no sense if he and Roberto had a mutual destiny to resolve. On top of that, he was looking at Roberto's father, and he knew that for him this would be the second time his son had died. David felt tremendously sad, but he knew he had to say it.

"Eduardo, that was Roberto in here, wasn't it?"

Eduardo took a long, deep sigh, and with a look of petition to a soldier next to David, he exchanged places and squatted beside him so he could talk in a slightly less public way. He told David, "I know it looked like him. From the first I thought it wasn't my son, but I took the time to stare at him and try to account for all the years and the aging process. Yet, I knew. Even if there were no birthmark I would be pretty sure who this is. The birthmark on this man here is very similar to Roberto's, but it's different, and I saw this right away. To casual observers, this man could easily pass for Roberto. Roberto was a twin, not an identical twin, of course, because he had a sister. Still, having twin children gives a father much curiosity. I always studied the faces of my son and daughter when they were young. I loved them both so much."

David was shocked. "Then who is this man here? Did he have identification?"

Again Eduardo shook his head, but patiently, understanding that David was recovering his senses. "No," he said, "he didn't have identification. And yes, I know who this man is with all certainty because of his birthmark and the similarity of appearance to my son. This is a man who also had a twin sister. This is my brother's son, my brother who moved to Sinaloa when we were young men. I knew this man here as a child. He was my nephew, called Yog, and he looked so much like Roberto that everyone thought they were twin brothers. This was a great curiosity among our family and friends. This brother and I didn't get along so well. In fact, he didn't get along with anyone in the family. He was a drunk. He moved to Sinaloa and we haven't heard from him during all these years. Yog and Roberto were the same age."

There was silence a few moments while David took this in. A giant worry began to materialize in his mind, a worry about Ana, and he could feel this worry start to transform his face. He was afraid that if he said the worry out loud, it would materialize into reality. Looking at Eduardo, he saw that the man regarded him with expectation, that he knew what must be said next, the logical conclusion. So David expressed it, to get it over with.

"Eduardo, then if this man isn't Roberto, if he isn't El Gato, then I believe firmly that Roberto is still alive somewhere. El Gato lives, and I've baited him. I have this strong inner feeling that Roberto is still alive and behind a lot of things going on in the narco world. I feel his presence in Monterrey."

Eduardo was nodding. "Yes, I do too, David. In fact, if you think about it, the only reason that Yog would be on that roof would be to kill you because Roberto sent him. It wouldn't make sense that Yog would be there otherwise. To tell you the truth, I haven't thought about Yog at all for many years. Now, deep inside myself, I know that this Yog and my son have been working together. You and Ana have become targets."

The worry crystallized and became a heavy weight that sat on David's hurting chest. "My God, Eduardo," he said in a voice nearly a whisper. "I'm here, which means that Ana is alone!"

Eduardo nodded. "But she does have Enrique and the Zs."

David said, "Wait a minute! You said I had been asleep a half hour! We're not landing in Monterrey! Why didn't you show yourself to Ana and Enrique on the roof? Where are we going?"

"You're not going to like this, David," Eduardo answered. "We're on the way to Houston."

"Houston! Why are we going to Houston?"

Eduardo replied, "We're going to Houston at the request of your old friend, the President of the United States. He was there when you were attacked, he saw it on television as it was happening, and he ordered the rescue. He said that you were to be brought to Houston."

David tried to sit up quickly, but a sharp pain made him lie down again. To Eduardo he yelled, "What the…?

And hell hung in the air.

Chapter 16: The Eye of the Cat

Monterrey, Mexico
Sunday and Monday

From under his cap El Gato took in everything as the SUV
plowed into the thick of the city and had to inch its way through
cement powdered streets en route to the safe house where he would
stay the night. Yog became intensely quiet as he drove, irritated by
the people retarding all vehicular movement in the streets. The
women were quiet because they were nervous. They sensed that Yog
and "Sr. Bernal" had formed some conspiracy against them. They
consulted their phones, trying to find ways to be useful to the men,
or at least to appear like they were doing something whenever one
would glance at them.

El Gato was counting. He was counting people in black Z
outfits. He was recording in his mind the location and numbers of
soldiers and police as they approached the safe house. He had done
this for years, always observing the details of the environment
around him, especially police and soldiers, and lately, the Zs because
they could function as hawks to report the movements and locations
of the cartel members. Paying attention to detail is how he had
survived and lived up to the legend of being like smoke, never a
defined shape, never in one place for more than illusory moments.
His eyes sought the one thing that didn't look quite right. Missing
that one detail might result in his capture or death. He could never
relax this vigilance. He didn't even want to. It was fun.

They finally arrived in Anáhuac, and Yog made several
reconnaissance cruises in the blocks around the house. They were
already exhausted from the long trip caused by the problems at the
border and the crowds in the Monterrey streets. He knew El Gato
would order this, and so he did it without him having to say a word.
He knew his cousin would be mentally photographing this
neighborhood of single-family homes built on small lots six years
previously.

Finally, El Gato broke the silence by telling Yog to proceed to the house. From the outside it looked like the other modest neighborhood homes of three stories, with the garage on the lower level and the living quarters above. To avoid suspicion in this neighborhood, one seemingly pleasant man lived there year round. He told his neighbors that he was a tutor of English and math for young secondary and college students and that he managed investments from home. This story explained why so many men and women came to the house. In fact, the man managed the plaza of Monterrey for the Cartel of Sinaloa. He was called "El Contador" (the Accountant). He was in charge of logistics for the shipments of cocaine and meth arriving in Monterrey from South and Central America and other parts of Mexico. He oversaw temporary storage for these in warehouses and approved the transit routes leaving Monterrey to the United States. He had done a good job. He was efficient and reliable, and he had earned enough trust to gain the privilege of speaking directly to El Gato by phone, even though he wasn't sure to whom he was speaking. He only knew that a man of high favor with the boss was coming to head an important summit.

El Gato didn't worry that El Contador would know his physical appearance and voice. He reasoned that with the changes in the air in Mexico and the United States, his days of anonymity should soon come to an end out of necessity for the leadership that would be required in the implementation of his plans. The meetings in the next couple of days would mark the beginning of big changes. As for now, if El Contador did guess that he was talking to El Gato, the man would be smart to keep this to himself.

Yog didn't turn into the driveway of the house. Instead, he drove into the garage of a house on the street directly behind the safe house. The back of this house faced the rear of the safe house. The four emerged from the vehicle and retrieved some bags that El Gato needed. Yog walked to a false wall in the rear of the garage, inserted a key handed to him by El Gato, and pulled at a bicycle rack mounted on the wall. Part of the wall folded down to the cement floor and exposed a door through which the four passed. Yog snapped on a light switch, and they descended a stair case to a illuminated tunnel that led underground to a small anteroom. From there ascended steps to the garage of the safe house.

230

In this anteroom converged two other tunnels from homes on both sides of the one where they had parked. The four houses formed a complex connected by the tunnel system. This had been constructed by a company owned by the cartel just after the houses had been built and before neighboring houses started construction. "Dinero" from the cartel to city officials and other builders in the incipient neighborhood insured that everyone who might have a reason to look at newly constructed houses there took a vacation from that area for a few weeks. The four houses enjoyed the installation of swimming pools in their small back yards, which were put in as a cover for the tunnel construction.

These four urban homes formed a complex for meetings and the receipt of cash that would be laundered through several businesses in Monterrey. The compound was also the payroll center for the envelopes of cash that were distributed to the city police, local politicians, and hawks rendering services to the Cartel of Sinaloa in Monterrey. Although there were offices in the four houses, the most sensitive records and cash were safeguarded in an underground room opening from one side of the anteroom. It also had a small arsenals storage closet. There was one other small room off the anteroom. It was soundproofed and had special plumbing and drains, and it was used for occasional interrogations. Largely, however, the compound was designed for white collar work.

When the four ascended the steps to the garage, El Gato noted that there were two vehicles and three spaces. They went up another flight of steps to a utility room and passed from there through the kitchen into a living area where their host, El Contador, awaited them with cold beers. A burly, inscrutable looking man in dark shades stood at the other end of the living room near the front door to the house. El Gato surmised that these men were the owners of the vehicles in the garage.

Knowing a bit of El Gato's personality from phone conversations and his obsession to be aware of everything around him, El Contador adopted a look of concern and asked him, "How did you find things outside?"

El Gato responded, "There are two ragged kids about ten years old drinking from coffee cups at a table on the corner at that sidewalk restaurant. Seems strange, kids that age drinking coffee in the hot sun this time of day, chatting like girls. They kept looking around them. I also saw four guys in black shirts and pants standing a couple of blocks from here, at four different locations. In this part of the city the crowds of people are moving, going places, but these guys are just standing. Our friends, the Zs. They're there to protect the people, right? Why does anyone need protection in this neighborhood? Your men haven't reported either of these things to you?"

El Contador reddened. "No," he answered.

El Gato glanced at the man by the front door, then he said to El Contador, "Have it checked out. Let's take the little kids off the street and find out who paid for their coffee."

After a nod from El Contador, the burly man began to walk towards the door to the garage. El Gato said to him, "If you're lucky enough to get close to the kids in the black outfits, be careful with them. They might jump right over your head." Then he laughed as if it were a private joke.

El Gato looked around. The others had taken seats on the sofa and chair. "Place is clean," he said. "Ready for our visitors." He looked directly at El Contador. "As we talked about on the phone, tomorrow you're conducting the meeting. I'll be mostly quiet, listening, until I'm ready to speak. I don't want this to drag out. You'll know what to say from my cues. Lay out the current situation succinctly. Describe the three alternatives you and I discussed over the phone. Then I want us to make a decision and have complete commitment which I can take to the boss. We have to act quickly. There's a lot to mobilize."

El Gato found a place to sit, and he took a couple swigs of his beer. He stared a few moments out the window at the lowering evening sun. He felt everyone staring at him. Then he asked, "When are the others arriving?"

El Contador answered, "Some during the night, some early in the morning. I have men in the other houses receiving everyone. We're bunking them there. I have a room for you here set up the way you asked. We can meet in the basement room in the third house. No windows, underground. We're bringing the Zeta here at 9:00 am. Our guest arrives blindfolded and won't know where he is. I assume our ambassador to their hotel will be in the same condition." El Contador paused to see if El Gato had any comment.

He did. He shook his head and sighed. He said, "Human collateral. No trust. But things have changed since the coup. Our common enemies are suddenly powerful. The Zetas and the Cartel of Sinaloa must work together. For a while, at least. There will have to be trust by necessity."

El Gato glanced around the room. He saw that the women looked uncomfortable. Yog, as was his custom, studied El Gato's face during the conversation to pick up whatever signal his cousin might send him. El Gato decided to relax so that the others would. He spent the next half hour reviewing the agenda for the next day's meeting in more detail. Then he discussed a few business problems in Monterrey with El Contador. After that they talked about the demonstrations, the locations of the military units, and which public services were functioning in the city.

Finally El Gato said, "Okay. Time for Yog to head to Cumbres with the ladies. They have a special assignment in the morning, and they'll join us here afterwards in the afternoon. We've had a long day. I'm going to walk with them to the car to have a few last words with Yog, then I'll go to my room here and do some work until I fall asleep."

Yog and the women stood. El Gato followed them to the door leading to the garage and then asked the women to go to the car and wait while he spent a few minutes with Yog.

When they left, Yog and El Gato stood in the kitchen alone. El Gato said, "I've been thinking about tomorrow. They've been televising David and Ana Valdez on the roof the last couple of days. Sometimes the camera is on them while the commentators make observations about what's happening in the Macroplaza. Sometimes the camera isn't showing them, and the TV network is broadcasting from other cities. The point is, if you get an opportunity to make your move tomorrow against them, try to do it when they're not being broadcast. You might not be able to tell if they are or not. You might not have a clear view of the CNN roof. Do what you can. Just a thought."

"Right," Yog answered, "or else the assassination will be on television and we'll be plainly seen. Whoever sees me later may think it's you. Eventually they'll try to find out who I am, who you are."

El Gato looked directly into his cousin's eyes. "Look, primo, I'm not going to bullshit you. We don't know what will happen when you're up there. Tonight I'm going to work out your getaway strategy with some of our men, and I'll inform you either later tonight or very early in the morning what the arrangements are. I want to get you back here after your job as soon as possible to help me with this meeting and the shit we have to do afterwards. I'm not going to sweat it too much if the cameras are on when you're there, but if you can do this without being televised that would be better, is all I'm saying. David is expecting El Gato, so he has informed others that El Gato is coming. Be careful. Take him down quick and get out of there. But let him see you. I want him to know it's me killing him before he dies. But if something happens on the roof..." He didn't say if Yog got killed or captured. "People are going to think that you're El Gato."

Yog nodded. El Gato saw that his cousin understood perfectly well that he might be a sacrifice.

"Who could recognize you?" Yog asked. "I mean, besides David. Who else seeing me on TV might think it was you?"

El Gato sighed. "This is your way of reminding me, mi hombre. You didn't want to say it outright. Yes, we both know that the only other person who might recognize the birthmark, if he were to see it, is my father."

He didn't like to think of Eduardo because when he did, he always remembered their last fight. That made him feel like Roberto again: Weak. Sick. Stupid.

"That wouldn't be so good, verdad?" Yog pressed. "I mean, your father being so connected to the politicians and the soldiers."

El Gato tried to contain his emotion, but he felt spit forming in his mouth just at the mention of his father by his bold cousin.

"What, Yog, you suddenly are so concerned about family history or something?"

Yog didn't answer. He saw the quick anger rise up in his cousin.

El Gato shifted his stance, and an awkward silence held the room. Then he said, "My father is no different than any narco. He pays money to control the politicians. I'm sure he's generous with the military too. The supreme soldiers running our country right now are his fucking friends. Dear old Papa basically got them to slit the throat of the President. You believe any of this "friendly quarantine"

234

shit? I tell you what's going on here, Yog. We have one more cartel now in this country, a big one that's putting in its own government and telling the people it's for their own good. It's a cartel of business interests, you can believe that, and my father is in the thick of it. They have outmaneuvered us by getting control of the military, and so far the people are on their side. Well, some of the people, but they are very misguided. We're going to change this."

He waited a few seconds and then added, "What people really want in life, cousin, is predictability. Predictability went missing in Mexico, and that's why we're having revolution. There has been too much blood in the streets. No one knows if they're going to be alive at the end of the day or if their loved ones are. People can no longer predict how an ordinary day might go. This problem of excessive violence is one of the things we're going to discuss with our men tomorrow."

El Gato seized Yog by the shoulders gazing directly in his eyes. "I need you back here, Yog. I have big plans for our operations in Mexico and in the United States. I've been discussing these with the boss. I got him behind my plan to take a very special package to the United States. I'm going to need the help of the Zetas to get it done. For this to work it requires their resources. I need someone I trust to help me execute this mission with the Zetas if I can get them to buy in, and the only one with balls as big as mine is you."

He saw the look of astonishment on his cousin's face, to think that he would work with their mortal enemies. He held Yog's gaze. They had a communication that had evolved through family DNA and their years of living together in the pressure cooker of violence and blood. Their bond of complete fidelity spanned over thirty years. The command in his eyes said, *Focus tomorrow, Yog. I need you back. Our most important work is ahead of us.*

Yog understood. He decided not to ask any questions about working with the Zetas now. There would be plenty of time for those questions later.

El Gato relaxed when Yog answered, "Don't worry, carnal, we'll get the job done quick and get back to you soon tomorrow."

El Gato released Yog's shoulders and continued, "As for my father and his friends, I know how I'll deal with them. Tell me something. You never talk about this. Tell me about your father. Do you know him? Do you see him? Where is he? He's my father's

235

brother, and as far as I can remember, an enemy of my old man. But what might he know of me?"

Yog released a sound like spurting venom. He answered, "No one knows anything of you. You are El Gato. Roberto died a long time ago, and you want it that way, so I never ask you or tell you anything about our family. You don't need to worry about my father. The truth is, cousin, we don't have any family except each other. My father was a drunk. A pig. He didn't do anything except to drink and to beat my mother and me. She was a mouse, a scared little mouse. She ran to work every day cleaning people's houses for no money, just to be away from him. You want to know where my father is? The reason you never have to worry about him is because he's dead. I killed him. I did it when I was eighteen and came home and found my mom beat to a pulp by him one time too many. He was passed out from drinking. I put him in a car and took him away, and no one will ever find his body. Everyone, including my mother, assumed he just left. She believed that to her dying day."

El Gato nodded and called his cousin "brother" this time:
"Good, hermano. You did good."

He should have felt relieved to know that his uncle wasn't alive, but instead, a sudden sharp pain in his stomach seized him. He had a premonition that this would be the last time he would see Yog. The irony was that Yog would be going to die El Gato's death. He was surprised to feel such a strong sentiment for his cousin. He had been dead to feelings for people a very long time. He grabbed his stomach in a manner to suggest he had a gas pain because he didn't want Yog to see a feeling for him. He said to him, "So you should be on your way. Yog, after your mission in the morning, before you arrive back here, give the ladies their final assignment."

Yog understood this was the command to execute them. It was time to go. Yog gave El Gato a hug of respect, thumping El Gato's back, and he retreated down the steps.

The "summit" didn't go as El Gato had planned. The Zeta, who was second in command and known as Z-30, arrived blindfolded, but he was hardly submissive in any sense of the word. He demanded to meet only with El Contador and persons higher up, including the boss of the Cartel of Sinaloa. He wanted to be with leaders of plazas and decision makers. He wouldn't say a word with subordinates in the room. He made clear that the meeting had better not be a waste of his time. His hosts could understand that any betrayal that cost him his life would be met with quadruple damages.

In effect the Zeta's demands meant that only El Gato and El Contador would be in the room with him. The other Cartel of Sinaloa invitees who had come remained in the other houses. El Gato would meet with them later.

El Gato was grateful that the Zeta even came. In fact, he didn't know that it would be Z-30 until just two days prior when they set up exchange arrangements. The Cartel of Sinaloa sent a son of the boss himself. This was the son who directed money laundering operations for money coming in from the United States. When it was confirmed that Z-30 would meet in Monterrey, the boss let El Gato know that his own son would be collateral. This astonishing fact let El Gato know that his work in the United States and his opinions about the takeover in Mexico had the respect of his boss.

The Zeta said, "I know that the highest command in Sinaloa has sent his own son to be collateral for me. So if he isn't here, then someone very important must be here."

They settled at a table in the windowless basement room constructed for special interrogations. El Gato asked for a couple of guards to be outside the door in case he needed assistance. In the small basement anteroom there were a computer and a television, and the guards had their phones. El Gato instructed them to text him if any urgent news broke of which they should be aware, and he would come out.

Now he and El Contador were alone with Z-30. El Contador offered beer or water from the refrigerator in the room, and the Zeta wanted a bottle of water. El Contador said, "The door is closed and we're here with only one other person in the room, and I'm going to remove your blindfold." He walked to the man and removed it.

The Zeta looked at El Contador, and by his expression El Gato could tell that he knew he was indeed El Contador from Monterrey, as he had been told. Then the Zeta's cold stare fixed on him, and he asked, "Y así, cuál pendejo es Usted? And so, which asshole are you?"

There would be only one way to satisfy this man, El Gato knew, and that would be to answer the question with the one piece of information which would start them off on a leg of credibility. He would cut straight to the chase. For his ideas to be successful, too many important things relied on speed and surprise. He needed the Zetas, their special forces, and their weapons. It would be now or never for the possibility of working with the Zetas to accomplish what he wanted to do.

So he answered, "I'm El Gato." El Contador had returned to his chair, and hearing this he slumped back against the support in amazement, not so much by the revelation as by the giveaway to the enemy. He himself had suspected this but hadn't been sure. The Zeta's face registered surprise as well but converted quickly into a look of satisfaction and relief. He realized that his visit may not be in vain after all.

The Zeta had a slight smile. "Give me some proof," he said.

El Gato didn't hesitate. He answered, "I ordered the execution of your nephew, Jesús Raúl Espinoza." The information was harsh, but he knew the Zeta must be sure who he was. As far as El Gato knew, not many understood that the man executed was, in fact, the son of the brother of Z-30. El Gato knew, and so did Z-30.

The trace of smile on the Zeta's face vanished like smoke sucked through a vacuum, replaced by an odious stare pointing pistols at El Gato's heart. El Gato stared directly back, not blinking. He wanted to show the Zeta that he had made a command of business, and he wasn't embarrassed by it. It was their code of life. The Zeta should understand it. Vengeance for the deed would equally be expected under the code. He held the Zeta's gaze until he saw the slight relaxation in the Zeta's eyes. He saw the man regain control of his emotions as he began to breathe normally. Z-30 wouldn't speak until he could control the tone in his voice. El Gato and El Contador waited.

The Zeta was built powerfully. He was thick and broad shouldered, with a barrel for a chest and a muscular neck. He used his potent body to try to dominate the atmosphere of the room. He shifted his eyes back and forth between his two hosts. He finally spoke when he was calm and in control of himself.

To El Gato he said simply, "Okay. So why am I here? What are we talking about?"

238

El Gato held his gaze as he answered. He gestured around the room, but his gestures meant that he was referring to the world.

He answered, "Everything is fucked up right now. It's all upside down. The soldiers are attacking the government, not the cartels. They've become the kidnappers, instead of us. The people are no longer afraid of us. They have the expectation that we'll lay down. If they have to fight us, they'll do it without guns! We have madness! The whole country is standing in the streets and slowing down everything to a halt. The people we've been buying no longer hold the power in government and services. The military commanders who take our money are no longer the ones in charge. The military leaders behind the coup get their money from somewhere else: big business. The politicians we pay are in quarantine. Jesus! Quarantine! The police who help us are more afraid of the soldiers than they are of us. Half of them don't even dress in uniform. They stand around waiting to see what's going to happen.

"It's frigging impossible to move material across the border and back. The Army and the police of the United States have massed at the border and sealed it. No one knows what the gringos will do. Will they invade? Their troops are right there, poised. You know this about the gringos: When democracy on their back door goes out the window, they come bursting through that back door. The only reason that they don't have troops in Mexico right this minute is that they're still confused as to what's happening. But confusion isn't a good thing where the gringos are concerned. If things get too dicey for them in Mexico, their soldiers will be running all over Mexico City and Monterrey, and we'll have years of their pleasant company, like Iraq or Afghanistan or Vietnam. We don't have much time before this happens. This situation that we, the Cartel of Sinaloa, face is the same one that you face. These facts I just stated are as true for you as for us. We can be idiots and ignore the reality we face right now and continue to kill each other, or we can agree we have problems and try to figure out how to react to them. Better yet, this is what I want to say to you: This mess in Mexico is giving the cartels unprecedented opportunity, an opportunity to expand the business of the Mexican cartels throughout the world at an exponential pace, compliments of the USA. This is what I want to talk about."

The Zeta asked for a cigarette, lit it, then said, "They say El Gato grew up in the United States. Did you know that? They say that he knows the gringos and despises them, and this is why business is so good for Sinaloa in the USA now."

"Those sayings are true," replied El Gato.

The Zeta drew a couple of drags and blew rings in front of his face. El Gato knew that he was studying him the way a poker player observes his opponent for signs of the tell and that the Zeta was thinking.

Finally he said to El Gato, "Among ourselves we've been discussing these current events, of course. We haven't considered that the gringos might invade. I think you're right. This is a mistake we've been making. Mainly our ideas have been to lay low a while, not do so much damage, determine who is really running the country, and make friends with them."

El Gato nodded and answered, "The problem is that old methods are not likely to do any good. It's because millions of people are fed up. All these whores and kids in the streets want changes. They don't want to play by the old rules. We've got new popular leaders out there now. They're not organized, but they're connected through social media. They're charismatic, they have people on fire with the thoughts that there can be government in Mexico without corruption. Eventually, they'll hook up with the ones who have power. We already see this in the alliances like the Zs with the victims' movements, the business elite, and the military.

"It's a mistake to war with them like we have these past years with the military and the federales. We've been thinking with our guts instead of our heads, everything always about blood and revenge and turf. This distracts us from working our business objectives. We kill the soldiers and police, and we, the cartels, fight each other over territory and merchandising. As a result, we move too slowly in our expansions, we miss our opportunities, and our profit margins dwindle. We can keep going on like this, or...." He paused for dramatic effect.

"Go on. I'm listening."

El Gato said, "Tell me something. When the President of Mexico declared war on us, who became the heroes to the people?"

The Zeta snorted. "The Army and the Marines."

"Right. So we cracked their popular armor by buying the generals and admirals, and these heroes began to lose their luster."

"But these protest leaders have started looking good," interrupted the Zeta, to show he was ahead on the trail of logic.

"Yes, and they're talking to each other and helping each other through the internet, while we the cartels have been addressing the people with bloody sheets hung all over the cities at scenes of assassinations and massacres. All these people in the streets are there because they can check their phones and know who is going to be where. They report our activities on Twitter. They investigate the cartels and publish results in blogs. We look somewhat primitive in comparison, don't you think?"

Now the Zeta didn't answer. He only frowned. He waited for El Gato to continue.

"My boss and I've been talking about this coup. Who's behind it? Why did the military do it? What do they get out of it?"

"Well, they wanted to seize control while they had a chance," answered the Zeta. He thought it through out loud. "They say they're going to keep people safe. They say they'll return government to the people. I'm sure they believe they'll be participatory in the new government. They see the chance to enrich themselves in power and opportunity, yes?"

Then he paused and shook his head. "No, it doesn't make complete sense. Someone else is behind this. This is what you believe."

"Yes."

"Of course. So I have an idea who, but tell me what you're thinking."

"The same as you. Big boys in business. The top echelon. Some of these fucking international corporations and big business owners who have vested interest in the economic slavery we have here in Mexico. They can keep wages low because there's so much human capital available to them. Plenty of available labor looking for work. The same reason we can expend people. But these guys are our own customers. They have been paying us, and now they're turning on us.

"They don't want to pay our piso for protection," the Zeta agreed.

"And the violence is scaring investment and companies out of Mexico. We did, in fact, create the problems we have right now. Some of our lines of business have scared our most powerful and wealthy customers into an alliance against us. The business community united behind the Armed Forces is a powerful enemy. Together, they have access to capital, control of money flows and the firepower to fight the cartels."

"Ok, I get it," said the Zeta. "You mentioned that we have opportunity to convert this situation into one that helps us expand in the United States. So you're far ahead of us in your thinking. I would be pleased to hear what's on your mind."

El Gato was about to speak when he felt the cell phone in his pocket vibrate. He looked at it and saw that he had a text message. It said, "Urgent. Come out here." He kept a calm demeanor, and he said to the other two, "Pardon me just a moment." He rose from the table and went out the door to the anteroom where one of his guards was sitting in front of a screen and indicated he should look at it.

It only took a moment for the image to register in El Gato's mind what he was viewing. He recognized the roof top. He saw the bodies on the roof: two men and two women, and then the door behind them bursting open and soldiers rushing out.

The guard said, "It was the craziest thing you've ever seen. That woman, Ana Valdez, jumped off the roof and went down the building on a rope, just as she and the gringo, David James, were being attacked. The gringo jumped at the shooters, but then it looks like someone shot all of them from somewhere else!"

El Gato frowned and stared at the screen. He felt cold. The guard continued, "It all happened so fast. The commentators were talking and showing scenes of the Macroplaza. Then they switched to the roof where you could see the gringo and the Ana woman, but within a couple of minutes everyone got surprised by what happened!"

El Gato watched. He recognized the shapes of his cousin and the women on the roof. The soldiers were standing over the bodies and checking them, as if checking for vital signs. One was talking on a radio. A soldier squatted beside Yog's body and checked him. The door to the roof blew open and a young man rushed over to the gringo's body, David's, and pushed a soldier away. He pressed on David's chest and then began unbuttoning his shirt. He was hurrying, and he rolled David a little to pull the shirt off, and El Gato could see that David wore something underneath. It was a bullet proof vest. He watched the young man begin removing that as well.

El Gato turned to the guard and said, "What do you mean Ana Valdez jumped off the roof and climbed down?" But even as he said it, the door opened again, and a soldier and a woman ran out, and the woman immediately ran and knelt beside the gringo. The young man was looking up at the soldier and talking, and then he straddled David's chest.

Before the guard could answer him, El Gato said, "Well, for someone who went off the roof, Señora Valdez looks very uninjured." He felt inside him a rage now, but he struggled to concentrate to see if there were any clues that any of them were alive. Two soldiers were now squatting beside Yog. El Gato was guessing that both David and Yog were still alive.

El Contador appeared in the doorway, but El Gato gestured that he should go back inside and not let the Zeta come out. "I'll be back in a minute," he told him. However, the Zeta stepped forward from behind. He had been watching.

The Zeta said, "They are lovers, you know. The gringo and the Valdez woman."

Inside El Gato felt stunned. He had heard jokes, people calling them the love birds, but he always assumed it was no more than an unusual and unlikely friendship that they had. Ana Valdez was married to a successful Mexican business man. She had come to popular power with this close ally, David Wilson James, and she had adopted him as a symbol, and she had turned the Z movement into a peace movement that the young could identify with. Yet somehow he never considered that the two of them might be lovers. That would be so incredibly risky. The Zeta was saying this like he knew.

He thought of David and his twin sister Annie. He thought of David and this woman Ana. He thought of Yog. He felt anger inside him like he might explode. He steadied his breathing so he could retreat within himself, to enable himself to focus his thoughts. When he looked back at the screen, there was a commentator in the studio in Mexico City. He was saying that they had lost the feed from the transmission from the rooftop in Monterrey and that they were trying to find out what was happening.

El Gato turned to El Contador and said, "I'll resume the conversation with our friend," nodding towards the Zeta. "You stay out here and put our men into action. Find out who is dead and alive on the roof, and if any are alive, where they go. We have people all around that building. Get most of them out of there, get the weapons out, but assemble the team who will find out what's happening on the roof and where they go. The Mexican man up there is Yog. If he's alive and you can do it, get him here. When you have news, come in here and tell me."

El Contador was listening and already picking up a radio to call someone. El Gato motioned that he and the Zeta should go back to their table, and he closed the door behind him after they reentered the room. They sat at the table again.

"What you told me about the gringo and the woman, you have knowledge this is true?" he asked the Zeta. He nodded. El Gato raised his eyebrow, as if to say, "And? Why did you never take advantage of that report?"

The Zeta understood and said, "This just recently came to light. A couple of our men saw them intimate. But in these last days we had too many other fucking things to think about."

El Gato was tapping his finger on the desk. "I should have known it," he said quietly. He thought about David, how he spent his life in inappropriate relationships. *Beginning with my sister, Annie, and then late in life, the piece of shit is in Mexico with a Mexican house wife!*

He envisioned David in the years in between, being with women he should have no business with. He hoped now that Yog had failed to kill him, and that David would live, so he could kill him personally in a painful and humiliating way.

And then. And *then*. He knew exactly what needed to be done! God, he felt a burst of excitement that made him feel like he would explode from the pure joy of the idea! He grabbed a bottle of water from the table and nearly emptied it in gulps down his upturned throat. He saw the Zeta regarding him curiously.

El Gato put down the bottle and told the Zeta, "I apologize to you for killing your nephew. After we do any business together, you may need to try to kill me. I understand this. So let's get this said and out of the way so we might continue with important things."

The Zeta nodded. "Okay."

El Gato began to talk to the Zeta about the world of the gringos. He asked him first where in the United States he had been, and the Zeta replied he had only been to Texas. El Gato said, "To understand how to do business in the United States you need to know what they fear and what they love. Don't think that all the gringos are like the people in Texas. Half the people in Texas are Mexicans, and this isn't true in most of the other states. In many places there are other Latinos and some of those hate Mexicans. Some states have practically no Latinos. It's important to understand that you can't predict how a gringo in New Jersey will act compared to one from Virginia or one from Texas."

The Zeta nodded again, deciding he would be patient and listen.

El Gato continued, "The gringo land is a melting pot. The gringos speak proudly of this, but they don't understand how their diversity has deepened in the last thirty years. Some might speak of the melting pot, but they don't like anyone different from them. They think they're a democracy, but they're not this. They have a government run by lobbyists. The lobbyists buy their Senators and Representatives. That country is no different from Mexico, where the cartels are the lobbyists. They're a republic, and the representation for them by Senators and Representatives are determined politically. There really are only two political parties of any consequence. These have their politics and origins from a time when the country was more homogenous and mostly white. That isn't the case now. The two political parties have become impotent under the demands of a more culturally diverse population. The platforms of those parties don't address the needs of a culturally diverse country. In that respect, the USA is a lot like Mexico. There are so many people who feel alienated, hopeless, and unheard. They're cynical about their government. They're ripe to seek the people who can help them. "

Now the Zeta caught a glimpse of where El Gato was going.

"Really," El Gato challenged, "does anyone think that even the Democratic Party is going to meet the needs of the Muslims in the USA? And the Eastern Europeans? And the new Africans? The ones a little franchised in the system are the Asians, the Hispanics, and the African Americans. The ones losing grip are the white Anglo Saxon protestants, and the ones who lost all from the very beginning are the first Americans, the native Americans, just like the indigenous tribes here in Mexico."

He gulped some more water and continued. "That big middle class in the United States has shrunk. The point is not that the number of poor is growing. What's important to us is that the number of people who feel fucked is growing. Here in Mexico, these are the kind of people who supply the manpower for our cartels, who come to us for protection, and who pay for our services. These same kinds of persons now form the largest classification of people in the United States. The people who feel fucked over. I've made the Cartel of Sinaloa successful in the gringo country because I give them what their government and economy can't."

The Zeta snickered and said, "Like jobs?

"Pues, sí," replied El Gato. "And the drugs they want. That country has had a voracious appetite for drugs a long time, mi hombre. What's good today is the openness of their young people to try new synthetic drugs. I've jumped all over that. I got labs built both there and in Honduras. I know the USA, I know the gringo mind, and I'm accepted easily because I understand the culture. I give good jobs and good pay in distribution and sales. These jobs are going to ex-policemen and city workers, to unemployed factory workers, to new college grads who have big student loans to pay."

The Zeta nodded and offered a cigarette to El Gato. He wanted the man to keep talking. To tell him things. He said, "I see news articles all the time where the gringos talk about breaking up a drug ring having ties to organized crime."

"Mierda!" said El Gato. "They know shit about organized crime. When they say Mafia, most of the gringos still think of the Italians. They don't think of the Eastern Europeans, the South and Central Americans, the Africans, and the Mexicans. They don't know because all they do is watch movies and TV and internet celebrities. Their ignorance has been good for the Mexican cartels. Sí, very good, but our window of opportunity can close suddenly. What would really help us is an open border. The goods we move depend on that. Once over the border, the merchandise gets moved by U.S. citizens. My hires. These are not Mexicans. These are people working for the Mexicans. We're moving the stuff to new big cities. Our plazas. We have to move fast to open new plazas before the gringos wake up."

El Gato felt himself getting restless. He wanted the Zeta to understand how important he was in the United States operations because he was going to request big assistance from the Zetas in moving very important merchandise there. He was trying to establish credibility with the Zeta because he knew he would blow his mind with the request.

But before he could continue, the door to the room opened and El Contador rushed in.

He said in an apologetic tone, "We couldn't get anyone to the roof. There were soldiers and Zs everywhere. We couldn't get across the street where the cameras were. We got a man to the roof of the building next door, just in time to see a helicopter land. Soldiers came out of it and took the two men on the roof. They left the women. The bird just flew."

"What kind of helicopter?"

"It had Mexican Air Force lettering, but it was one of those gringo black hawks like we've seen in the mountains."

El Gato said, "Did it fly to the University Medical Center? Or to Doctor's Hospital?"

El Contador shook his head. "He didn't think either one. Said the thing flew up high and headed northeast."

"Fuck!" El Gato replied. "Heading to Nuevo Laredo?"

El Contador shook his head and said, "Who knows if it will change direction? But if it were to stay in a straight path, it was flying much more northeast, like towards Reynosa."

El Gato felt angry again. "And if it kept going, it would be to the United States. What's that way?" He thought for a moment. *Houston!*

El Gato stared at his hands a moment as he concentrated. Then he asked, "Were the soldiers Mexican?"

El Contador felt relieved that he had anticipated that question and had posed it to his source on the cell phone.

"Our man says some of them had gringo bodies. Couldn't be sure, but he didn't think all were Mexican. Some were."

"Yeah, fucking military whoring with the gringos," El Gato said. He was pissed. David was alive and might be going back to the USA. Yog was apparently alive and the gringos had him. What information could they get from Yog? He had to think about this quickly.

And if they have David back home in the USA, how long would it be before the gringos invade? The son of a bitch is a friend of the President of the United States! Wouldn't David love to come with the troops storming into Mexico to make sure his girlfriend is safe?

247

He now knew that there were two persons he needed to get into his possession as soon as possible.

He looked back at the Zeta sitting at the table in the room. He had to get this deal closed now.

He told El Contador to get the word out in all the plazas, cities, and towns to be on the lookout for the copter and where it lands. Then he closed the door and returned to sit with the Zeta. He felt distracted. He had to focus. He would have to make recommendations to his boss very soon, given this development of the failed assassination and the rescue of one of the USA's favorite sons from the battlefield in Mexico. The Zs in Mexico and the United States would be screaming within minutes, demanding to know where David was. The voices in favor of an invasion by the United States would get louder.

It was all an unpredictable mess. He had to become a player in the game now. He had to hold some cards and have say in what would happen. He needed a stable border through which he could pass people, weapons, drugs, and money. He didn't need U.S. troops massed at the border and sealing its two thousand miles. He for sure didn't need those troops pouring into Mexico and putting curfews in the cities.

The Zeta in the room with him was a bitter enemy. Both of them had been responsible for horrible deaths in the other's cartels. He had seen to it that the Zeta's nephew had been killed; and not just killed, tortured first. It had been personal down to bones, raw nerves, and blood. It wouldn't be surprising if the Zeta took an opportunity to wring the life out of him in that solitary room. He couldn't worry about that. The stakes were too high, and he needed what the Zeta had.

"We have a situation," El Gato said to the Zeta. "A helicopter took David James from the roof where we had a team attempting an assassination of him and Ana Valdez. The men from the copter took away our man as well, so he must have been alive. The copter belongs to the Mexican Air Force, but it was one of the Blackhawks given to Mexico by the United States. The Air Force and the DEA have been using these to hunt our poppy and marijuana fields in Mexico. Some of the men from the helicopter appeared to have been gringos. It lifted and flew out of Monterrey. It didn't fly low to land in a hospital in this city. It may have been heading to the USA."

"The woman was unhurt," the Zeta said. "On the television, I saw her on the roof. Did she board the helicopter?"

"No."

"So they took a USA citizen and a man from Mexico," the Zeta mused. "They needed medical treatment. Maybe not enough room for others on the copter. If the woman didn't try to get on the helicopter, she must have believed it was a medical mission. If there were any other intent on the part of the rescuers, she probably didn't know what were the plans."

"That makes sense," El Gato replied.

"But if they were flying to the USA, why would they take this Mexican man for treatment? That seems like it would be trouble for them."

El Gato paused to think before answering, but then he admitted, "They might have believed he was me. We look alike. The gringo, David James, has been hot on my trail in recent weeks. I don't know for sure what his friends in the CIA and DEA know about me, but possibly by now through David James they have some idea of my appearance."

The Zeta raised his eyebrows in surprise. Then he said, "The woman is leading the Zs, and she's free, and someone has taken her man. How long do you think it will be before she knows who and where?"

"Shit," El Gato answered. "She probably knows now."

Maldito! he thought. *The Zeta is thinking quicker than me.*

He saw the Zeta looking at the door as if he already knew El Gato would be going out to issue an order to get Ana and bring her to him. She was one of the two people that he wanted, but the Zeta helped him understand that he needed her fast. El Gato was already thinking of her now as a bargaining chip with David James, and by his friendship with the President, possibly with the United States. Yes, Ana Valdez would be an important chip to play, but the other chip would be even more valuable.

He jumped up and left the room to speak to El Contador. He gave him the order to seize Ana Valdez. When he came back, he asked if the Zeta were hungry, and he ordered sandwiches and beer. When he sat down again, the Zeta asked, "You really think the United States would invade Mexico?"

249

"Definitely," responded El Gato. "The gringos have a vested interest in the old order in Mexico. We, the cartels, are an important part of the old order. We buy the guns and arms from the gringos. We're a big, big customer. Our purchases support a lot of families in the United States. We can say "Gracias" to the National Rifle Association and the gringos for their obsession with the right to bear arms. It means plenty of guns get made, and we can get any kind of weapon we need.

"We also supply their drug habits. In Mexico, the old order includes the Federal Government of our Republic. In the gringo mind, all commerce, legitimate or illegitimate, depends on democracy in Mexico. Anything other than business as usual scares the hell out of them. When they see this military coup, they'll think of Mexico as a banana republic or a "failed state." They're reactionary. They'll call for international intervention, trying to legitimize getting their noses in here. They'll go nuts worrying about who is really in power. Yes, they'll seal the border completely. Then they'll bring troops in. Then they'll control the border on both sides. We have to make sure none of this happens."

"But General Alvarez says there will be new and free elections."

El Gato responded, "First, you have to believe that fairy tale. Second, even if you believe it, how long will it take to organize elections? Too long. The USA won't agree to recognize the legitimacy of the military government here. But the generals will try to hang on to what they have started as long as possible. In the meantime, the border is sealed or controlled by the United States. We can't wait that long "

"What is it you want to do?" asked the Zeta. "What do you need from us?"

"Your skilled manpower and your heavy weaponry," answered El Gato. "A lot of you guys came from Special Forces. For the mission I'm envisioning, we need the talent that some of your men have. Deployments from helicopters. Storming and assaulting classified and fortified targets. We need some of the weaponry that you have. Maybe a couple of tanks. Planes that can shoot. Grenade and rocket launchers. Armored and blinded vehicles. Fast drivers. Communication equipment with encryption. We're going to need to capture some special merchandise from a well-equipped enemy and move it fast and with stealth."

"Madre!" responded the Zeta. "Are you planning to attack the United States or something? Some of what you want we have scattered all over Mexico. It will take a while to coordinate getting all this. I need to understand what the mission is to get everyone to buy into it. How much time are you planning for this?"

"We need to move like lightning because things are happening too fast and are out of our hands. The quicker the better, and I don't think we have more than two or three days to plan and put this in place."

The Zeta looked skeptical. He said, "Where is this special merchandise that we need to obtain?"

"Mexico City," answered El Gato.

That surprised his companion. "And where are we taking it?"

"To the United States, of course," El Gato responded.

The Zeta shook his head. "So tell me what the fuck we're talking about. What exactly is it that we would be delivering to the United States?"

El Gato studied the face of the Zeta. He assessed whether the Zeta would take his answer seriously or not. Then he realized that the Zeta had come to the meeting. He remained even after discovering that the official murderer of his nephew was El Gato himself. He apparently agreed philosophically with most of what El Gato had said. Apparently the Zeta did believe that they the two cartels had common enemies, common purpose, and common urgency. He was going to offer the Zetas a fortune in money for their services.

It was time to put it out there. He leaned back in his chair and folded his arms.

He answered, "The merchandise I'm talking about taking to the United States is Pedro Navarro, the President of Mexico."

Chapter 17: The Agony of Captured Hearts

Houston, Texas
Monday Afternoon

David felt it again, a moment balanced on the tip of a needle: one of those rare eclipses of time when some unexpected, extraordinary awareness stops the universe. You can look at the still scene surrounding you and observe with astonishment details in high resolution. In the midst of all the detail, there might be one thing screaming for you to see, and to miss it would be to incur a cost too painful to bear.

The thing is, he reminded himself as he looked around him, *you have to see with your heart. You have to feel what you see.*

He sat in a brown folding metal chair near the open door of a hangar at the George Bush Intercontinental Airport in Houston. Earlier it had been raining hard as it always does in Houston, but the afternoon sun fought its way victoriously through low, skulking clouds. Now steam rose from the tarmac outside. In the distance Air Force One shot glints of reflected light, while closer, the Blackhawk helicopter that had transported him there perched like a dark vulture anxious to leave. Furor had given him strength to disembark the helicopter and make his way into the hangar, where nurses and doctors attended him, but he dismissed them as soon as he saw the limousines arrive. He wanted to be standing up when the President would enter. He had a few words for him.

Yet after the tense emotion of their encounter, fatigue betrayed him. His knees almost gave, and he collapsed into the chair. Perhaps he fell through a hole in time on the way to his seat, because now he was experiencing that moment on the tip of the needle. Or maybe this was induced by one of the medication drugs they gave him.

All around him were Mexican and U.S. soldiers, secret service agents in their dark suits, and medical personnel. David couldn't see him, but he felt the presence of Yog's body somewhere nearby, and this was like feeling Roberto in the building. All these people faded into the background in David's mind, not as relevant to the scene as he and the President, who stood before him in sharp relief. He saw that he wasn't being the President at this moment, but Donnie, his friend. The look on his face was caring, and also stressed from the scare that his best friend might have been dying. There was frustration in Donnie's expression to because of the argument that he and David had had. Eduardo, still in fatigues, sat in a metal chair scant feet away. In this moment Eduardo's worried, tense face transitioned into relief as he shouted into the cell phone, "Enrique? Enrique! This is Eduardo speaking!"

David snapped to attention. He thought, *Thank God! We're in touch with Enrique! Now I can know about Ana!*

That was when David realized that Ana was the thing screaming not to be missed. He focused to feel her. She was a wild, beating heart inside a cloud of cool mist, but he felt her warm body in his chest. Her heart beat so strongly inside him that he felt new energy. He thought he heard her speaking a message to him:

Cariño, I know how much you love me. Your love is sweet and at home in me. You're the greatest gift of my life. I call for you and you hear me. Forever you'll hear the call of my heart! I need you now!

His body jumped. He heard time begin ticking from a slow start, and the world began to move again.

Forever you'll hear the call of my heart.

He heard this in his head even as he heard Eduardo speaking to Enrique by phone. The urgency to be with Ana stressed his feelings to the max.

When Eduardo put the phone down and began explaining the call to David, he immediately understood why he felt Ana's desperation in the pounding of his heart. Eduardo told him, "David, Enrique has lost touch with Ana! He went in search of you in the hospitals after the helicopter took you from the roof. Ana remained in her office. Enrique spoke to her by phone when he couldn't find you, and then he sent some Zs to accompany her to the security house downtown. They arrived at her office; they began to leave; but since then he has not been able to talk to Ana or the men with her by any means, phones or radio. He says this was about a half hour ago. No one responds to the calls."

David already knew. He could feel inside him Ana's heart, screaming with indignation.

They had her. She had been taken!

He felt the frustration rising again inside him that he had vented against Donnie minutes earlier, when they had argued. Now he turned to the President, and he couldn't help it, but his eyes were burning and accusing. His look said: *You should never have taken me from Mexico!*

He might have said too much to him when the President first arrived in the hangar. He had wounded his old friend with words. He had to remain calm if he were to have any hope of returning to Mexico right away. He had to find the words and the logic that the President would understand so that he would help him. Besides, the President needed his loyal support even in the middle of personal anger. The man had been catching huge flack for perceived slow reaction to the events in Mexico. But the President had been trying to be cautious in the midst of confusing and conflicting reports. And he had called to ask David's assessment.

He needs me. He trusts my judgment.

To calm himself David took deep breaths.

He saw that the President was listening to Eduardo when an aide came up to him and whispered something in his ear. While the aide was talking, the President stared at Eduardo with a look David had seen many times in his friend since college days: He was assessing Eduardo with a question mark.

David stood up and walked over to the President. His chest still hurt some and he still felt a bit unsteady on his feet, but he had found a vein of energy because of the urgency of Ana's disappearance. He whispered to Donnie, "Follow my lead while I talk to Eduardo."

The President nodded and told his aide, "Please excuse us." When the aide walked away, David called for Eduardo to join them. The old gentleman bounced up from his chair and strode spryly to them.

"Eduardo," David began. "Just now the President told me that he has ordered more troops to the border. He's got a lot of people crawling up his ass to send the Army into Mexico to help stabilize things. The problem is that no one in the United States really understands what's going on in Mexico. Most of the President's advisors see the military coup as a takeover by the Right. The issue scaring everyone in this country is the apparent sudden disappearance of democracy in Mexico."

The President added, "Yes, and it doesn't matter that General Alvarez claims Mexico had to be saved from civil war and that the goal of the coup is to restore free democracy. What people see is that the Armed Forces sequestered the Federal Government of Mexico and are holding it hostage, along with some governors, state officials and mayors. What this looks like to the world is a military purge. Mass kidnapping."

Eduardo nodded, acknowledging that point of view.

David continued, "Eduardo, you have a great affection for Ana Valdez. She's an enormously charismatic leader. She has captured the hearts of the Mexican people. All of these protest movements these past years: the peace movements, the people demanding non-violence, the victims' groups, the No Más Sangre supporters, the Zs…each with their own leadership, but all of them aligning with Ana's ideas for Mexico…you've seen this; you've advised her; you've helped her emerge."

"Sí, go on," Eduardo said.

"And you, Eduardo, you are known as the number one patriot of Mexico! You've got powerful friends. You're always backstage in the major political dramas. You're connected in the highest levels of the business world. You provide facilities and vehicles to the Armed Forces using your own resources. The highest ranking military leaders are lifelong friends of yours. And you've earned the respect of the Mexican people because of the stands you consistently have taken against organized crime."

Eduardo didn't reply to the assessment David made of him. David had seen many times the impassivity of his crafty old friend's face.

He thought to himself, *How rare, this Mexican octogenarian standing here with the President of the United States in the aftermath of a military coup in Mexico!*

Even as he thought it, he realized that was the crux of the thing: A popular revolution might have been in the making, but some minority of people… military leaders… had hijacked it and had turned it into a coup. Eduardo was dead center among those people.

"But," David continued, "now we have all sorts of problems. There's an international involvement beyond Mexico that must be taken into account. Here is what I think, Eduardo: I think you were holding good hands of cards in the game playing out before the coup. Now you're keeping a poker face with us. But we don't have a game. We have danger of tremendous loss of life and possible outcomes over which you really have no control or say. Time is running out on us if we're going to have any possibility of determining the outcome. We're all going to have to work together, and that includes taking help from the United States."

David studied Eduardo's expression. He saw a light of understanding in his face. He knew Eduardo needed a little more push. So he turned to the President and asked some leading questions which he knew Donnie would exploit: "Mr. President, what's happening right now at the border, with the Zs, with the Mexican citizens, with the people of the United States? If you saw what happened on the roof with us on television, then so did many people in the world. What are people saying about my disappearance and the whereabouts of Ana?"

The President got it and played it perfectly.

He answered, "Everyone wants to know who took you, who shot at you on the roof, who shot the attacker, who, who, who? And yes, everyone is screaming for Ana to come forward. The Zs in the United States are pushing up against the troops and the news crews at the border points, and they're demanding information about both of you. We have chaos, and it's getting worse quickly. It's happening in Mexico also. Amid all the reports of demonstrations and gunfire in the cities, people are demanding to know what happened to you. Where did the helicopter go? On this side of the border the nervousness is growing exponentially. As a result, my administration is talking to the United Nations about possible intervention in Mexico."

The President turned to Eduardo and continued, "I did speak with General Alvarez after I saw the attack on the roof on television. I have to tell you, Eduardo, I think the Mexican military is stretched too thin to manage the governing of the country. We don't know what response will come from the cartels, but there will be response, you can believe it. We tightened the border points of entry. The cartels certainly don't want the border sealed. How will the Mexican military be able to provide public safety, govern the country, and at the same time deal with attacks from the cartels? With millions of people in the streets, the fatalities can go stratospheric, and the Mexican people will be worse off than before. They don't deserve that; the world doesn't want that; the United States doesn't want that; and I personally can't stand for it. It's too close to home."

David glanced at his watch. He felt desperate for time. All he thought about in the background was Ana. He fought to keep control of his emotions, but he needed to keep this moving quickly. He looked at Eduardo and saw on his face that Eduardo was ready for his question.

So he put it out there. He asked, "Eduardo, are you largely behind the coup?"

The man didn't hesitate. "Sí."

"Did Ana know?" David held his breath.

"I gave her no direct information about what I was doing, but I think she understood that there was a plan in place by powerful people, including the military, to take some action that would regain public safety. I protected her from details so she could be innocent and could continue her work in the peace movements, and with the Zs, with no compromise to her integrity."

"You did that for me, too, didn't you?" David asked.

Eduardo ignored the question. He continued, "Ana has her own friendship with General Alvarez, and she has influence herself among many in Mexico, including politicians and business leaders. Entertainers adore her. She's popular with the liberals and with the poor in Mexico."

He paused and shook his head, measuring what he was about to say. Looking directly at David, he said, "She gave you an image in Mexico, you know. And you are this popular gringo who brings the magic of the Zs to a real paramilitary group that actually has roots in the peace movements. The Mexican people are delighted to have a gringo of importance who loves them so much. I think this is true of you, David. Ana saw how young people relate to you, how you inspire young Mexicans precisely because you're an outsider who has heart for them. They can look at you and say, "If this gringo believes in us, and wants to be a zorro fox with us, then there's hope. There are roads out of the barrios."

David felt moved and also relieved that Ana's involvement in the coup had been peripheral.

Eduardo told David, "Ana loves you and is fiercely protective of you. If you want to understand Ana, that is all you need to look at."

David nodded and answered, "She's in trouble, Eduardo. We have to help her."

He looked at the President, and calling him by name in a low voice he said, "If we help her, Donnie, we help you."

"Okay, David, tell me what you're thinking," his friend answered.

So David turned to Eduardo. He thought that Eduardo was primed now to hear the request that he had prepared for him.

He said, "I think what we need is for Eduardo to propose to General Alvarez that the General should announce the appointment of an Interim President of Mexico. This idea needs the support of the business community and the people from the Right who helped the coup of the Armed Forces behind the scenes. The Interim President must be someone very popular and with a clean image among the poor and the middle class of Mexico. It's probably best if this person isn't someone who has been heavily involved in politics. I think what would give confidence to people would be the idea of an Interim President who works to help set up new elections in Mexico as soon as possible, with a date specified at the time of the announcement. This would give credibility to the statements by leaders of the coup that they want to see the country returned to a free republic. It would be best if the Interim President isn't a military commander. Such a move as this would come as a great relief not only to the Mexican people, but also to the international community. Certainly there would be a lot of questions and concerns, but probably an intrusion or invasion by foreign powers such as the United States, or some United Nations forces, would be a possibility that's taken off the table."

The President's jaw literally dropped. Eduardo raised his eyes to stare at the ceiling as he thought. David waited patiently for Eduardo to answer. When the old power broker brought his eyes down and turned them to David, he saw in them a look he had seen only once before, so many years earlier, when he told Eduardo that Annie had died carrying his child. It was the look of a person who comprehended the complexities of raw, simple truth.

"Well, David," Eduardo said, "I think I agree with you." He paused again, clearly assessing his thoughts as he was speaking. "Indeed, the type of person you've described is probably someone Ana knows, more so than me. I think anyone I know would be considered too 'old boy' by Mexicans now. And you're right. It can't be a military person either."

He paused again, and David held his breath. He knew what needed to be said, and if Eduardo said it, it would make more of an impact on the President.

"So obviously we have to get our butts back to Mexico and find Ana and talk to the General. We should leave now," Eduardo said.

When David looked, he saw to his great relief that the President was nodding agreement. "We need her help," he said to them.

David jumped in. "Mr. President, we have Enrique Santos and the Zs; we have the Mexican Armed Forces; and maybe some of the DEA agents we have in Monterrey can help us. Mostly, we just need to get back there to find Ana."

Their moments of tension earlier had been because David was carried out of Mexico, and he never would have wanted to leave Ana. Now he realized that his friend, the President, had been in Houston and had demanded that he be brought there because the man cared about him and wanted him to be safe and alive.

"You believe she's in danger at this moment?" asked the President.

David almost choked on his words. He knew it as certain as he knew where he was and what day it was.

"Mr. President, she would have contacted me, or, at least, she would have tried to by now. Enrique would know exactly where she was. He would be talking to her. Something bad has happened. They have her, I'm sure of it." Before the President could ask who, he said, "Sinaloa. The cartel. El Gato."

"Roberto," added Eduardo, in a voice bitter and disappointed.

The President looked with intense sadness at his friend. "Then you better go, David."

That was what David needed to hear. He felt love for his lifelong friend. He grabbed him in a quick hug and slapped his back. He saw a secret service agent tense and stand more upright.

He smiled at this, but he was overcome with a sense of urgency. "Let's crank up the bird," David shouted, and he turned to Eduardo, saying, "Vámonos! Let's go!"

"We can return to my ranch," offered Eduardo.

"The first place we're going," answered David, "is back to the roof of Ana's office building."

Jesus, what a day, he thought.

His name was El Chico, and he was someone El Contador trusted. At the time he received the call from El Contador, he and four others in the cartel, all in their late twenties, had just parked a stolen Nissan Armada in a parking lot in El Parque Fundidora at a place close to the river walk along the Santa Lucía River. While he received his instructions, El Chico eyed a city policeman who was in uniform and was sitting in his patrol car in the parking lot. El Chico recognized him as paid muscle for the cartel. At the time, the river walk was full of persons filing along the river towards the Museo de Historia Mexicana. Their destination was the Macroplaza, which already overflowed with people.

Across from the museum on La Avenida de Juan Ignacio Ramón was the building in which Ana Valdez had her office. El Chico told his men to take their radios, walk along the river, cross over to the front of Ana's office building, and post themselves there to see if she might come out. There were exits from the lobby in the front and the rear of the building, so two of them could stand near each exit. He explained the business which he was about to conduct with the policeman. He ordered them to follow Ana if she came out and to inform him by radio. He would come to their location in the police car.

El Chico got out the GMC and walked over to greet the policeman. He gave him thirty thousand pesos for the use of his car and uniform for the remainder of the day. Nearby was a building that was a public restroom in the park. El Chico got the policeman to break the lock, and the two went inside and exchanged clothing. El Chico gave a warning to the policeman that he was going to punch him in the face a few times so the man could have an alibi that someone overpowered him and while he was knocked unconscious took his uniform and police car. He ripped the shirt that El Chico was wearing to make it appear that there had been a struggle. El Chico took the cop's pistol and went out wearing his uniform.

The policeman remained in the hot building in his underwear with El Chico's crumpled clothes nearby. When he heard someone

260

entering, the policeman went through the charade of appearing that he had just awoken from being unconscious. It looked good. There was blood all over his white T shirt from a hard punch to the nose which El Chico had delivered. Feigning outrage, he grabbed El Chico's pants and put them on and then played the charade of a cop running outside to radio assistance from his patrol car. He had already hidden the 30,000 pesos inside his shoes. The police car, of course, was gone.

El Chico had decided to find another parking place nearby out of view until he heard from his men. The radio in the car seemed remarkably quiet. He suspected that not many of the city's police were working because they assumed that they might not get paid. He found a space on La Avenida de Juan Ignacio Ramón several blocks from where his men were stationed.

Fortune was with El Chico and his men that afternoon. The two guys by the front of the office building observed three young men dressed in black enter. One carried a large handbag. The cartel men studied the faces of the youths to remember them. About a half hour later these same three young men came out dressed in colorful T shirts. One carried the same bag. With them was a woman dressed in a jogging suit. She had her dark hair pulled back in a pony tail that extruded through the back of a baseball cap. She wasn't wearing makeup, but the men knew that she was Ana Valdez. One of the cartel men radioed El Chico. He told them to follow Ana and her escorts and to be prepared to take down the young men at the moment that the police car appeared. They should grab Ana and all get in the police car.

El Chico's men followed Ana and the three Zs, who headed into the park directly below the Macroplaza. They walked along the path that passed the City Theater and the Justice Department and Congress for the state. As they approached one of the emblems of Monterrey, La Fuente de Neptuno (Fountain of Neptune), it became apparent that their destination might be in El Barrio Antiguo, the historic part of Monterrey with shops, restaurants and hotels. Most of its streets were closed off to traffic. The men radioed El Chico, who knew that part of the city well. He started the patrol car and began to drive towards the old historic center.

He knew that some of the streets there were always closed to traffic, so it was important that he be informed exactly where they

261

were walking. He stayed on the radio with his men. He wanted to intercept all of them at an intersection at one corner of the old neighborhood, but he might have to adjust his plan quickly, depending on where they were heading He needed to get to them. Traffic was crawling, so El Chico had to maneuver tight spaces between vehicles in order to advance. He had operated city police cars many times in the past because he had once been on the force and had accepted money from the cartel. So when it was necessary, he sounded the siren, flashed the lights and forced drivers to inch aside so he could pass.

He clawed his way through the people and the vehicles to Diego de Montemayor and made a left there. The traffic was actually moving, so he zipped along and turned right onto Fr. Servando Padre Mier and then arrived at its intersection with Ignacio Zaragoza. He was just in time to see his four men crossing the street behind Ana Valdez and her three escorts. They were at an entrance to El Barrio Antiguo where poles blocked vehicular entrance into the streets. He could see that the old sector was packed with people in this late afternoon.

This would have to be the time and the place for interception. He quickly radioed his men. He saw that it was unnecessary. They had already seen him in the police car and were drawing the pistols that were tucked in their pants. He cut on the patrol car lights, lurched into the intersection, and pulled up to the sidewalk just ahead of Ana and the Zs. He jumped out the car and ran to the rear passenger side and opened the door wide.

Ana was tense and nervous when she left her office building with Juan and the other two Zs. She relaxed after a few moments as they strolled through the park on the way to the security house in El Barrio Antiguo. No one seemed to be paying attention to them. No one recognized her. The afternoon was very hot, but in the shade of the trees and shadows in the park it was comfortable. On the first part of their walk, most people were strolling in the direction of the Macroplaza, but as they got deeper into the park, the groups of people ambled more in the direction of the old sector. She had a

262

feeling that the environment in there, even in this time of disruption, was going to be more social, with people seeking friends and family. In normal times during the day, the old neighborhood offered its shops, hotels, restaurants, and plazas to residents and tourists. Because much of El Barrio Antiguo was closed to traffic, the ambience was much more relaxed than the urgent, business-like rush in the rest of the urban Monterrey area.

In the park at La Fuente de Neptuno, Juan halted them a couple of moments while he looked in the bag he was carrying. He found the radio to try to communicate with Enrique. The attempt failed. The radio just emitted annoying static and a cacophony of human voices. Ana checked her pocket and pulled out her cell phone, and that was when she discovered that it was dead from lack of battery charge. Juan had the same problem; so, frustrated, he urged that they should hurry to the security house where there would be communication. Ana was glad that she had had the presence of mind when they were changing clothes to pack her phone charger in the bag.

She thought about the security apartment where they were going. She had leased it through a straw agent over a year earlier and had paid a lot for an agreement to modify it to have a hidden entrance. The apartment was on the second floor of an old red ornate apartment building near Sanborn's store and restaurant. On the street floor of the building was an Italian restaurant. She had the landlord build a storage closet in the rear of the kitchen of the restaurant. Inside this locked closet, they put in an iron spiral staircase which ascended to the master bedroom of the apartment above it. Therefore, it was possible for authorized persons to enter and exit that apartment unnoticed by any of the other residents of the building. One could exit the bedroom, descend the spiral steps into the false closet, and leave the building from a door in it into an alley. The apartment itself had three bedrooms, two baths, a small kitchen, a small dining room, and a decent sized living room equipped with computers, printers, cable television and internet. It would serve fine, Ana thought, if her children and Rafael needed to stay there temporarily.

They were crossing the intersection from the park to the entrance to El Barrio Antiguo when Ana noticed the police car that suddenly put on its lights and lurched to the sidewalk just ahead of them. She saw Juan tense. In the middle of the intersection, the three Zs in casual clothes stopped, looking around in all directions. There were just so many people. Then they moved to the corner's sidewalk and paused again. It was that moment when Ana saw the four young men pulling pistols from underneath their shirts! They were approaching quickly from the intersection, and Ana shrilled a warning to the Zs.

She saw that Juan had noticed them. He dropped his bag and jumped high along the side of a lamp post near the advancing four men. With his left leg, he pushed himself forcefully to the closest man with a pistol. He delivered a kick to his head that sent the man crumpling to the ground and the pistol scooting across the cement. A second Z threw himself on the sidewalk at the feet of another man. The guy fell forward on his stomach. The Z then straddled his back and got his hands on the man's pistol to wrest it from him.

A movement in the corner of her eye made Ana look back at the police car. The policeman had emerged from it with his pistol drawn, and he was opening its back door.

Suddenly, she heard a shot, and to her horror Ana saw that one of the attackers had shot Juan in the face! Another fired at the third Z, who had been slow to react to the rush by the four men. The policeman advanced a little from the car and shouted to her, "Señora! Señora! Venga aquí! Aquí!" He was urging her to run to the back seat of the police car.

Ana's first instinct for safety was to do just that. The gunshot had shocked her. She ran to the car and jumped into the back seat. From there she saw the rest of what happened. The people nearby were screaming and running for cover after they heard the gunshots. For a split instant, Ana thought of David, and inside she screamed, *My God, David, look what's happening!*

She saw that Juan was down and probably dead. The second Z shot had fallen, and he wasn't moving. The attackers ran to the Z who was straddling their comrade and struggling with him for his pistol. They pulled him off and then fired their pistols into him.

Ana looked at the policeman, who was just watching and doing nothing to stop the outrage. Now the full understanding of what was happening dawned on her:

They don't want to kill me. They want to take me! The police car is a trap!

Just as she realized this, Ana saw three of the attackers begin to run towards the car as the policeman started to return to the driver's side of the car. The fourth, assaulted by Juan, lay motionless on the ground.

They were directing themselves towards her open door. Ana jumped out and ran to the rear of the vehicle. She noticed the approach of a sedan in the lane beside the patrol car. She timed her move so that she would jump on the hood of the car just as it passed. She was counting on not being shot. She executed perfectly, crouching on top of the car's hood for the few seconds that it took the surprised driver to understand that he had a woman on his car.

This set her pursuers into a run down the sidewalk in the direction of the sedan. But when the driver finally slammed his brakes, Ana jumped to the hood of a car traveling in the opposite direction. She got enough distance on that car, about fifteen yards before the driver reacted, to leap off on the opposite sidewalk at the entrance to the park that she had just walked with the Zs. She sprinted into it, heading to the densest areas of people. She heard the cursing of the men chasing her. Without looking back, she sensed that she had put a little distance between her and them as they tried to cross the intersection of people and cars to pursue her.

Running and shoving people whom she passed, Ana tried to attract as much attention and to generate as much chaos as she could. "Ayúdame! Ayúdame! Help!" she shouted as she ran, but she didn't stop for the people trying to ask her what was wrong. It would be too dangerous for herself and innocent people. She had to keep her pursuers moving. She wanted to get to the Macroplaza and the stage area in front of the Governor's Palace, where Zs and soldiers and people might know her. She chanced a quick glance back to the intersection behind her to see if the police car had moved. She saw the policeman standing beside the car, and it looked like he was talking on a cell phone. At least, that was the quick impression she had. She couldn't slow down. She also saw that the men chasing her had made it into the park.

The park was packed with more people as she got closer to the Macroplaza, but they were concentrated more along the concrete pathways. Therefore, she ran through green areas of the park where sculptures had been placed so she could run faster. Up ahead were the steps that ascended to the area of the Macroplaza. She liked the opening on the left. She made a sudden crisscross in that direction to keep her pursuers confused, passing a sculpture of a reclining naked woman nursing her baby. Then she made a zigzag towards the steps, and at the top, to her great relief, she saw some soldiers standing. She bounded the steps, shouting to make a great commotion. At first the soldiers didn't hear her because of the blare of the loudspeakers from the stage in front of the Governor's Palace, but they turned and saw her just as she was upon them.

Ana caught the gaze of one of the soldiers who seemed to be a leader, and she shouted, "Help me! Help me! Men with guns chasing me! They killed my friends! Help! Help! Men with guns!"

The soldiers drew their weapons instantly, and Ana put herself right in the middle of them. There were five soldiers. She pointed in the direction of the three men who had chased her below. They had hidden their weapons and were now merging into the crowds individually, pretending to be casual walkers. When the soldiers descended a step or two looking to discern whom Ana meant, Ana ran away behind them. She pushed her way into the Macroplaza to disappear into the crowd. She needed to find some Zs. She had to contact Enrique.

When the soldiers turned to look back at her, she was gone.

El Contador cut the call, feeling sick instantly from the fear in his stomach. El Chico had just told him that Ana Valdez had escaped near the Macroplaza, even though all her escorts had been killed. He tried not to comment aloud as El Chico told him, because El Gato was sitting across the living room and staring a hole into his head. It felt like a bullet hole. Just minutes before, his men had driven the Zeta away; El Gato had laid out a plan for the next few days; and he had dispersed the rest of the men. He was alone in the house with El Gato.

Even after he pressed the "end call" button on his cell, he held the phone and stared, just to give himself a few seconds to think how to break the news. But, finally he had to look into the soulless black eyes of the man known as the Cat.

266

He swallowed and said, "She got away. She saw the trap as she sat in the police car and watched the Zs get killed. She jumped out the other side of the car, did leaps and jumps across the traffic, headed into the park across from El Barrio Antiguo, and ran to the Macroplaza. She found some soldiers, who started coming into the park to look for our men, so they turned back and returned to El Chico. Our men didn't shoot at her because the instructions were to take her alive and in good condition. We lost one of our men. El Chico wants to know what to do now."

He hated the expression on El Gato's face. It looked like cold shadow on dark stone. He couldn't decipher that El Gato was thinking that Ana was perhaps more savvy than David and that he wanted to have Ana to torment his old nemesis. David, his ulcer, his cancer. He didn't want to read in El Gato's expression the disdain that he felt for the accountant of the Monterrey plaza. But he did know. He saw that El Gato was thinking that El Contador was poor in execution of simple personnel actions.

"This has not been a good day for me," El Gato said with controlled fury. "Yog is gone, but David and Ana are still alive. And you are a pinche fool. El Chico wants to know what to do now? It's pretty obvious, isn't it, asshole?"

He heard the clenching of El Gato's jaw as the man growled a low, dry command:

"Get Ana's family! Now! Bring them here, at least her fucking children. Kill the father if you have to. Who cares? Don't fuck this up. And find this out: Why were Ana Valdez and her Z fairies going to El Barrio?"

El Contador saw El Gato look at the cigarette burning in an ashtray in front of him. He knew what the man was going to do, and he prepared himself for it. He sat still and kept silent as El Gato arose, picked up the lit cigarette, and and pressed it into his cheek. He held it, and the accountant didn't move a muscle as it burned his flesh. He closed his eyes to hide the tears from the burn. He was receiving his documented disciplinary warning from the human resources department of El Gato's criminal corporation. There could be no more mistakes.

Chapter 18: A Rooftop in Rome

Monterrey, México
Monday

Enrique tried to keep panic out of his voice when he reported to Eduardo that he had lost contact with Ana and Juan, but the truth was that he had never felt more shattered and scared than at that moment when he ended the call. All the people in his life who helped him were now gone, and everything suddenly rested on his shoulders. Eduardo and David were in the United States, for God's sake! Ana was missing. The queasy feeling inside him filled him with dread. Someone had her. The cartel. Or worse, she was dead!

He saw her body in his mind, which increased his anxiety. It was because he had seen the pictures of Israel. The reporter for El Norte had arrived ahead of the forensic officials and had taken photographs of his friend's charred body lying there in that vacant lot. They published two photos in the newspaper. He had stared at the pictures repeatedly, not wanting to believe that the strange carcass there was his friend. His soul brother. His rock. His leader. In the context of his life and years with Israel, his friend's death made no sense. From that moment in which he learned the news, Enrique felt the world unravel into the present chaos and madness. But he found footing in shifting sand when David, Ana, and Eduardo began molding him into the Z leader that he became. When they were around, he felt like a man. He was making great strides, and he would be a man of character and skills, a molder of a more civilized world.

However, in these moments in the street, just after he finished the call with Eduardo, he felt desperate, a total fuck-up, and he was the only one on the scene now who could go and find Ana. How could this turn of events have happened to him? She had told him to go find David, and he went. He should never have left her alone. He didn't find David, and now Ana was missing. On top of that, David turned up in the United States! At least he had guessed that as a

268

possibility, but he himself was in Mexico uprooted. The distance from Monterrey to Houston seemed infinite when measured in time against the present urgency of finding Ana.

Finding her alive!

Pushing people out of the way at times, he and two young Zs jogged to this location just a couple of blocks from Ana's office building. He tried to contact Ana and Juan en route to Ana's office but had no success. He was nervous and stressed. Then suddenly Eduardo's call somehow came through! The call kept breaking up, but he was able to let Eduardo know that Ana, Juan, and the others weren't in communication and that he was going to find them. Then Eduardo said that David was summoning him, and the phone cut off. So Enrique at least knew that David was alive and communicative. He could summon Eduardo. That was it. He didn't know anything else about them.

The two Zs waited while he looked down at the sidewalk and focused his thoughts. He closed his eyes and drew a long breath. For a moment he slipped back in time to a day in Mexico City when Israel was skating ahead of him and pulling away. Israel looked back at him and gave a rare smile, shouting to him, "Adelante! Sígame! Rápido!"(Onward! Follow me! Quick!) But then in his vision, Enrique wasn't in Mexico City, but here in Monterrey, and Israel was skateboarding on a sidewalk he knew very well. It was the walkway that Ana and Juan would take from her office to the safe house in El Barrio Antiguo. It was as if Israel pointed out that the most logical thing to do would be to trace the route Ana and Juan would take from her office. Enrique decided to do a quick check in her building and then follow the path through the park as quickly as possible.

Be alert for clues along the way. Stop anyone who might have noticed anything unusual.

He told one of the Zs with a data phone to check for any reports of incidents involving a woman or the Zs in the last half hour in this vicinity.

He felt his inner tension increasing. His churning stomach threatened to release in his pants.

Dios! Again he thought it: *I might not find Ana in time.*

He broke into a jog and led the other two through the mass of people on the crowded sidewalk. The young Z with the phone bumped his way along, tapping the screen of the device. Sometimes to pass people, Enrique fell to old skills from the early days with Israel: running to the side of people close to a building and then using momentum to run along the wall beside them and propel ahead of them. The Zs followed suit. Enrique imagined them as three black spiders scooting along the buildings. Israel would have smiled.

They made it to the sixth floor of Ana's building, and Enrique discovered that her office was locked. He peered through the glass door into the suite. All looked in order. A good sign.

So now I know that Ana and the guys left the office to start their trip to the safe house, he thought. *Any intruders who might have intercepted them in the office wouldn't have taken the trouble to lock the door behind them. Probably I would see some signs of struggle if a confrontation had taken place.*

He looked up and down the hall. Everything appeared normal, so he would waste no more time here. He told his men they would now go through the Macroplaza on the way to the safe house in El Barrio Antiguo.

This little bit of action helped steady Enrique's nerves, but he still knew that he was racing time. He hoping that he had not already lost the race.

So he announced to his companions, "We have to make time! We're jumping!"

So he led them, and they went Z-style down the stairs. They leapt over the railing from the middle of the top set of steps to the middle of the one below it, and the ones after those, with a cadence that put the three in the lobby in just seconds. They hustled outside to the sidewalk. The Z with the phone began tapping again, and when they had proceeded a short distance towards the Macroplaza, the young man suddenly shouted with excitement, "Wait!" He waved the phone in the air for Enrique to see.

The three came together. The young man showed Enrique on the phone that there were four consecutive "tweets" from Zs in the central zone of Monterrey. These reported the shooting of three young men on the street Ignacio Zoragoza at the Old Barrio. A woman with them had escaped, fleeing into the park. The last message said that a policeman on the scene didn't fire at the armed attackers who ran in pursuit of the woman.

God! Enrique thought. *It has to be Ana! She's alive! Oh my God! Are Juan and the guys dead?*

Enrique looked at the time of the messages. The latest had been posted just two minutes prior. If Ana had run into the park, then she would be scrambling towards the Macroplaza now.

Of course! Enrique realized. *She would be running to where she would find people she knows! A person like me!*

"Vámanos a la Macroplaza!" Enrique shouted. As they rushed he tried to think about time. They were about three blocks away. There were heavy crowds in the Macroplaza, and it would be difficult to move quickly. Ana would probably try to advance towards the stage. She might even be in the Macroplaza now. This made Enrique push harder. He led aggressively, grabbing people by the shoulders as he ran forward and shouting for people to make way.

Focus, Enrique, he told himself. *What would Ana be thinking? She just saw her three protectors shot, and she's being pursued.*

Of course! He realized that she would be worried about the safety of her family! If the attackers were chasing her and didn't shoot her, then obviously they wanted to capture her alive. Ana would know this, and she would know that her family was in grave danger if she escaped. She would be looking to find safety quickly to warn her family.

They made it to the plaza in front of the Museo de Historia Mexicana. Enrique decided on a course to a point halfway between the stage in front of the Governor's Palace and the far end of the plaza that descended to the municipal park. He searched for Ana in the throngs as they pushed in, but he realized that it would be nearly impossible to find her in a crowd like that.

I need for her to be able to see me! he thought.

Desperately he looked around. When he noticed one of the statues at the rear of the plaza, he saw a kid standing there holding a skateboard.

Thank you, Israel, he thought to himself. Now he knew what to do.

He told his two companions to nab as many black-shirted Zs as they could to join them while they pushed through the crowd. "If we get separated, your destination is that statue in front of the fountain at the rear of the plaza, near the entrance to the city park," he said. He pointed to the statue of the man on a raised horse, which towered over the crowd in the distance. In the low late afternoon sun, they

271

saw the silhouette of the horse and rider, the horse rising up with its front left leg off the ground. The statue was mounted atop a column of stone blocks. It was protected from tourists by an iron fence surrounding its perimeter, but in the overcrowded Macroplaza young people were standing inside there.

By the time they arrived at the statue, they had gathered eight other black-clad, young men and women. The people inside the low iron fence climbed out to oblige them space. Enrique went to the stone block column serving as the base of the statue. He reached for the ledge at the top and used his feet to help him climb. He had to reach for a leg of the horse as he lay on the ledge, but soon he was upright. Once on the narrow ledge around the statue, he helped some others up to stand with him. They managed to get five up there surrounding the base of the statue. They were now an obvious mass of black Zs visible on the statue above the hordes of people.

Enrique had a good field of view. He scanned the crowds of people slowly, looking for anyone pushing or approaching resolutely towards them. He didn't have to wait long. She was behind the horse when he saw her coming, gazing directly up at him as she made her way. Her black hair tossed back and forth behind her from under a cap. She was dressed in an athletic outfit, but Enrique recognized her instantly. He knew her body. He remembered a day (it seemed like a hundred years ago now) when Ana turned her head up to guzzle down a bottle of water in the heat of the sun on the training fields of Eduardo's ranch. He was dehydrated from his run with David and dying of thirst, yet the silhouette of Ana's body in front of the sun had set off a charge of desire in him that he never forgot. He had attributed it to the heat.

But there she was! She was his miracle! He had done well; he had found her; and he felt huge relief. He could feel Israel congratulating him with a clap on the back, and he could imagine David jumping up and down with "alegría!" He wanted to whoop for joy and leap from the statue!

So he scurried down, yelling for the others to follow him. He climbed over the little fence, ran to Ana, and gathered her in a huge, brotherly hug. When Ana said, "Gracias, Enrique, gracias," he couldn't stop the tears in his eyes. The young Zs in black encircled them and faced outward to the crowd around them. The circle was more than a ring of fraternity. The Zs were being protective and

272

vigilant to give their leaders, Enrique and Ana, time to discuss next steps.

"I think soldiers scared off the men chasing me," Ana said. "Oh, Enrique, things are so horrible. They shot Juan and the others. I think they're all dead!"

Enrique didn't even give her the opportunity to say the next words on her lips. He knew her thoughts, and he said "God, Ana, I'm so sorry! We have to warn your family! We have to get them to safety!"

"Sí, sí, Enrique, now please!" Ana agreed. "Have you…"

But he interrupted. "I haven't had time to call to them. I found out what happened to you just after we got back to your office. It was on Twitter, Ana. After I left the medical center, I lost contact with you. On the way to your office, Eduardo got through to me by cell phone. He was with David, and they're in Houston as we guessed. David is okay, Ana. I haven't heard more from them. We've been on the move to find you. We saw tweets about Juan and the others being shot and that you escaped. Well, the messages reported that some men had been shot and that a woman fled into the park, so I thought it must be you and that you would be coming here."

Enrique already had the phone in his hand. He punched a speed dial number that would ring Rafael's phone.

"I'm calling Rafael now," he told her.

Every ring seemed to take forever. He noted Ana's impatient and worried face. The call went to voice mail. He tried again. While the phone was ringing, she asked him about David. Did he know any more? Enrique shook his head.

"He'll come here, Enrique. I know him, he'll find his way to Monterrey, and fast. He'll want to be with me," Ana said.

Enrique nodded agreement. The phone went to voice mail again. Ana noticed, and she said, "Oh, God, my kids!" She threw her hands to the sides of her forehead and held them for an instant, stressed, and then Enrique saw the lightbulb in her eyes flash. She said, "Call Paula's phone!" She rattled off the number.

But when Enrique dialed the number, it went directly to voice mail too, which meant that either the phone was turned off or that it was out of battery power.

"Mierda! Shit!" Enrique said. Then anxiety hit him and Ana at the same time:

"Ana, we have to get you out of here! This is important too! I'm sure they're still looking for you."

"I have to go to my house!" Ana answered.

Enrique shook his head. "Not safe for you there!" he said. "We have to get the kids and Rafael. We can't go to El Barrio Antiguo now. It will blow the cover of that place. The ones chasing you are probably wondering why you were going to that neighborhood before."

He paused. He was thinking, *If we get Ana's family, where do we take everyone?*

Ana said, "I can tell you where we need to go. David is going to come for me, right?. He'll come, and he may come with troops. We can try to get in touch with him, but I know first he'll go to Eduardo's ranch. That's where we all need to go. Whether we get through to him or not, he will end up there."

"You're right!" Enrique agreed.

But still he thought, *Damn, damn, we're running out of time. It's always a fucking race against time! We have to warn Rafael, and we have to get him and the children out of their house. What's the quickest way? Who can help us? Shit, where is Rafael? Why doesn't he answer the phone?*

Then that word Ana had used hit him: *Troops.*

He said, "Ana, should we call the Army and the Marines to find Rafael and the kids?"

"Yes!" she replied. "Give me the phone. I know the numbers. You talk to our guys here who have phones. Get them to find Zs in my neighborhood. Tell them to get Rafael or Paula to call your number. Tell them to get them inside somewhere, not our house, until we can arrange to take them to the ranch, either by Zs or by the soldiers. They are to trust no police!"

Enrique handed her his phone.

"Where is your car? Has anyone got a vehicle to get us out of here?" Ana asked.

"Mine is parked behind the Arena. Pretty far, given this crowd. I'll try to find some better way."

Enrique saw that Ana was already punching numbers into the phone from her memory.

Maldito, this isn't like racing a deadline in law school, he thought. *Lives are hanging in the balance.*

He looked at the Zs encircling them. Two of them were young girls. One was Ana's size. This gave him an idea, but first he instructed the three guys to call Zs in San Nicolas where Ana lived. While they did that, he asked the girl who was Ana's size to exchange clothes with her. If they were going to be on the move to a vehicle, they needed to go in a small group and not attract attention. Ana needed to blend in, dressed in black. Someone looking for her in that vicinity would be looking for a woman in the athletic attire and cap. Luckily the young lady had dyed her hair blonde. She could put on Ana's clothing, minus the cap, and let her pretty blonde hair fall to her shoulders. She would look nothing like Ana and couldn't be mistaken for her. The girl agreed without hesitation. She wanted to help.

He noticed that Ana had failed to contact someone on the phone her first two or three tries, but now she was speaking to someone in the Army. He deduced from her conversation that it wasn't General Alvarez or one of the commanding officers whom Ana knew, but a lower ranked soldier taking emergency calls.

He asked the Zs if any had a vehicle close to them. One said that his car was in a parking lot not too far away in El Parque Fundidora. Enrique calculated that the car was approximately the same distance as Ana's office. They could make their way to the plazas in front of the Museo de Historia Mexicana and then walk the sidewalk beside the river into the park with decent speed.

One of the Zs now told Enrique that he had on the phone a guy who was in San Nicolas with two other Zs. They lived in that area, and one had a car. What should they do?

Enrique gave him Ana's address and a description of Rafael and the children and their ages and names. He told them to find them, get them into the car, and to drive to la Avenida Universidad and head north.

"Just get them out of that neighborhood, then phone me for further instructions. Do anything you need to do. Use any trick! Just get them out of there!"

Ana returned the phone she had been using to Enrique. She sighed and said, "I didn't reach anyone I knew. I spoke to someone who promises to have a convoy go out to my neighborhood as soon

275

as possible, but he couldn't tell me when that would occur. He said it could be very soon, or it might take a couple of hours!"

"Ok, Ana, we'll keep trying! We have some Zs in your neighborhood now dispatched to find your family. We need to get out of here and get to the car. I want you to change your clothes fast."

Ana cocked her head with a question mark on her face. Enrique smiled for the first time in hours, and he pulled the young blonde girl in with them. He told the Zs to circle tight, with the young lady and Ana in the center, and put their backs to the women.

"If any of you turn to look, you'll be decommissioned Zs!" Enrique told them.

The men, always dutiful and serious in their roles, contained half smiles and did as commanded.

Enrique looked at Ana and the young blonde girl, and he said, "Go ahead now. No one will see you do this."

Ana replied, "Okay, Enrique, and you have to turn around too. I want to see your back." She let herself grin.

But soon they were on the move again, Enrique, Ana, and the two who had been with Enrique earlier, Oscar and Richii, and the young man who had the car in the park, Alex. They walked directly in front of Ana and Enrique. They headed across the Macroplaza to the broad sidewalk that ran next to the river from the museum through El Parque Fundidora. They were tense. Ana had kicked them into full-throttle thinking, and she spoke her own thoughts to Enrique as soon as they came to mind, with no filter.

"Enrique, everyone must be worried about David."

"Yes, Ana, the internet is full of rumors and questions. I've been looking on my phone."

"Publish a tweet from me now. Get on my account. Report that David is fine, that he's receiving excellent medical care, and that he'll shortly make his own announcements."

It slowed them down just a little, but Enrique tapped the message on the phone while they walked. Next Ana instructed Enrique to send a text message to the phones of Eduardo and David that they were en route to "the farm" to be joined by family and friends. She wanted to clue them that they were heading to Eduardo's ranch and that Ana's family would come there. She added to ask them when they were coming back from their vacation. It was code, of course, an obvious one.

"See if you get an answer from either," she told Enrique, "and if you do, we'll phone them."

Next she said, "Now see if you can reach the Zs who are trying to find my family. Have they gone to the house yet? Is my family okay?"

Ten or fifteen minutes had passed since someone had spoken to the Zs going to Ana's house in San Nicolas. Enrique had marked the number. Now as they approached the parking lot where Alex's car awaited, he managed to connect to the young man in San Nicolas.

He told Enrique that there were three of them; they had just gotten into the car; and they were starting out to Ana's address.

"God," Ana said to Enrique. "This is taking so long! I'm so worried."

The five of them arrived at the car in the parking lot. It was a small, older model Nissan Sentra. They had a quick discussion about what to do. The location of the training facility behind Eduardo's ranch was relatively secret to those outside of the Z circle. Enrique thought that if only he and Ana drove to the ranch, it would attract less attention and that Ana could lie down in the back seat so it appeared he was driving alone. No one would think much about a lone driver inching through the crowded city streets to get to the roads where traffic flowed more fluidly. The young man who owned the car, Alex, agreed to let Enrique and Ana borrow it. Enrique told him to use his vehicle, which was parked behind the Monterrey Arena.

They had less than a minute's talk, and then Enrique was backing the car out of its space. Ana was low, unseen in the back seat.

She had Enrique's phone. There were still no messages from David or Eduardo.

Rafael hadn't seen any of the video clips of his wife descending from the roof when Enrique's phone call had reached him earlier that morning.

277

"Ana is fine," Enrique told him. "David took some hits from the shooter on the roof, but he was wearing a ballistic jacket. He needed some medical attention. Ana performed a trained descent from the roof to safety when the shooting began. Now Ana wants to post some announcements that she's okay. She has been working with the Mexican Army and Marines in an undercover operation to capture a cartel leader. She's going to do some work in the office. She asked me to bring her home in the afternoon and to let you know she's all right."

It didn't make sense to Rafael. *Did Enrique say that Ana climbed down a building from a roof?*

"This was what she trained for, Rafael," Enrique told him. "This was why all the ropes and trampoline work. She did it perfectly. As a result, we have the cartel leader and two associates he was with, women. The women died on the roof. I'm not sure the condition of the man. A helicopter is now transporting him and David to the university medical center."

Enrique cut the call short before Rafael could even think to ask more questions. Rafael didn't realize that Ana was doing any kind of undercover work with the military! He tried to call Enrique back, but there was no answer. He tried to call Ana, but she had turned off her phone.

What the hell? Rafael thought. God knows, the relationship between him and Ana had become very non-communicative, but he thought he should have known this! He really hadn't paid enough attention to the work that Ana was doing. More and more in recent weeks, she had been involved with the different protest groups and victims' groups. She had been gone from home frequently, giving speeches and making public appearances. He was just beginning to understand that his wife's fame now spread far beyond Monterrey. She did a lot of her work from her office, but, yes, recently she was traveling to other cities. She hired a nanny to help manage the activities of the children while she was away and while Rafael was working so much. They already employed a cook and housekeeper.

Then later in the day the children began hearing reports. His kids, who inherited the technology genes of his wife and who were all over the social media, saw the first ones. His daughter Paula came running into the living room and told him, "Mom climbed down from the roof of her building while some cartel members shot at

David James! A helicopter took David and the man who shot him away! No one knows where they are! Have you heard from Mom?"

After that, the news became more and more bizarre. People were worried about the United States invading Mexico, or doing it with some international force. The border points were very tense, and demonstrations were breaking out on both sides of the border. He and the kids had the television on, and the kids kept getting on the internet, on Twitter, on Facebook, on blogs of their mother and of David James, and on websites of the Zs in Monterrey and other cities. (His children adored the Zs.) The children were pulling in as much information as they could as fast as possible.

Then in the early afternoon they heard gunshots. Automatic weapons firing. From a window, they saw their neighbors in the street scurrying inside their homes. Paula and Rafael Jr. got their laptops and joined Rafael in the kitchen. He told them to keep away from the windows. The shots sounded like they might have been a couple of blocks away on la Avenida Universidad. They only lasted a few seconds. At the kitchen table, the kids couldn't find any reports of what had happened on their laptops.

Just part of daily life in Mexico, Rafael grumbled to himself. *So many times you hear these noises, and you never find out why.*

So after a while the neighbors came back out into the streets. Most congregated in a neighborhood park just a block away. Rafael saw them out the window. He felt antsy, so he said to the kids that they all should go to the park.

"Maybe someone will know what happened. Besides," he told them," we've been cooped up in the house all day. We may as well do something until your mother arrives home and we can get some information from her first-hand."

But they made mistakes that changed their destinies. When the three of them walked to the park, none had their cell phones. At the time, they assumed that they would be out of the house just a few minutes. Paula left hers charging in her bedroom.

To Rafael, things looked normal in the park, no different than before the coup overthrew the government. The adult neighbors gathered in small groups to chat and share information, and the younger kids either hung around the swings and playground equipment or played fútbol in the field in the center of the park. Rafael met up with a couple of men of the neighborhood, and he watched Rafael Jr. run to join some kids on the fútbol field. Paula spotted some girl friends on the opposite side of the park, and she sauntered over to them. Rafael saw her standing and laughing with them. Rafael's two friends reported that they heard the shots, but no one seemed to know what they were about. There were no reports of anyone hurt.

That was the scene in the park when the madness broke out. While Rafael chatted with his friends, he glanced occasionally across the field to observe Rafael Jr. playing. Beyond him, almost in a straight line, he could see Paula.

The first unusual thing made just a small impression on him: A car double-parked a block away on the far side of the park. Three young men in black Z outfits exited the car and ran to the side of the fútbol field. They stopped there, hands shielding their eyes from the sun. They turned back and forth as if they were looking for someone.

I wonder if this has anything to do with the earlier gunshots, Rafael asked himself as he listened, distractedly now, to his two friends.

But then occurred a more ominous disturbance. On the side of the park, to the left of him, three men dressed in khaki pants and buttoned, short sleeve shirts appeared and began to run towards the kids playing in the fútbol field. Rafael glanced over to the Zs. They clearly had noticed. They began walking towards the men, slowly at first, but with a coiled aspect, like they might break into a run in a moment. They seemed to be sizing up the situation and deciding something was wrong.

Next, on the opposite side of the park, on the street that ran parallel to Rafael's, a police car came scurrying to a stop near the group of girls where Paula was. It had its lights flashing and siren sounding. This seemed to confuse the Zs. They paused for a moment to observe. A policeman emerged from the car and began running to the girls.

And...towards Paula! Rafael realized.

Rafael glanced back to Rafael Jr. He saw that the boys playing fútbol were involved in the game too intensely to notice any of this yet. They were still yelling to one another as they passed the ball. Rafael turned to view the men running. Now he saw that two of them were sprinting full speed towards the boys playing ball, and that the third one had turned towards the group of teenage girls where Paula was.

Suddenly the sense of danger punched Rafael's body. He felt everything at once, his heart thumping noisily, adrenalin burning in his chest, arms, and legs, a scream choking in his throat. Rafael sputtered, and then he emitted the loudest shout of his lifetime:

"Paula! Rafael! Watch out!" He didn't even notice that he was already running, but his overweight body was moving at a pace it had not experienced since high school. He was about a quarter of the distance to Paula when he noticed two things:

The two men who tore onto the fútbol field ran among the boys and came up behind Rafael Jr. and took him by surprise. One picked him up and carried him in the direction of the police car. The other pulled a pistol out from under his shirt and ran backwards, intermittently pausing to wave the gun in the direction of some of the adults near him. Those had finally noticed that something was amiss and had started to advance towards the boys.

Rafael was gaining ground on the men who took Rafael Jr. In the corner of his eye, he saw a couple of black clad Zs also darting towards the man who had his son. They were coming from an angle that was drawing them closer to Rafael, but then they split apart to form a pincer approach to the man.

The second thing he noticed was that the policeman had run up to Paula. She looked confused, and she was answering something that he said to her. The other man from his left was now almost there. When the girls around Paula saw him coming, they screamed and ran. The policeman grabbed Paula and pulled her towards the police car. His accomplice drew up to them and pulled out a pistol. He shot it in the air three times. This drew screams from people all over the park.

They're not going to take my kids, Rafael thought as he ran. *They're not going to take my kids!*

He was three quarters the distance now, all fear, rage, and spit. His legs pumped like pistons. His chest constricted. He made huge gasps for air. His chest suddenly hurt like hell, but his eyes took everything in. The policeman pushed Paula into the car. The man carrying Rafael Jr., who was kicking and yelling, arrived at the police car and stuffed his son in as well. The two men with pistols

281

now noticed Rafael running towards them. They began to advance in his direction!

They came towards him side by side. Rafael saw that their eyes had locked on him and that they were coming for him next.

But no, they stopped. Still looking him directly in the eyes, the men began to raise their weapons and point them at him!

Rafael couldn't stop running. He was raw. He was one hundred percent emotion. He was desperate. There was only one instinct powering him, and that was to get to his children, who were now in the police car. Then suddenly he got light headed. His lungs couldn't suck in air fast enough. Black spots swirled in front of him, blotting his view. He saw red and blue lights flashing everywhere, as if the lights from the police car were spewing all over the park. The siren filled his ears. The heat of the day broke out fires on his skin. His legs went heavy and rubbery, and with horror he realized that he was going to collapse. His legs shot out of control. They were running, but they were spastic, making him fall forward. Through sheer will power, he kept his eyes on the gunmen.

He saw something he couldn't make sense of at first. There was a large, black object flying close behind the gunman on the left. There was another black object sailing behind the guy on the right. They were oblong and head level. As Rafael pitched head forward to the grass, he struggled to understand what he was seeing. The jolt of his chin and the sting on his palms slapping the ground jolted his vision to normal. His eyes had stayed glued to the men who were going to shoot him. Now he was witness to his salvation. The black Zs had run behind them, coming from a wide berth. Suddenly they were airborne, having taken spiraling jumps that enabled them to deliver lethal kicks to the backs of the gunmen's heads. Rafael saw the light in their eyes extinguish immediately, and they went down as quickly as he had. Their drawn weapons went sailing from their hands.

He heard screams and men shouting and car doors slamming. He pushed up with his arms so that his head could see. The police car was screeching away, its lights still flashing and its siren unbearably loud. Yet that noise didn't obliterate another, insistent vehicular groaning increasing in volume on his left.

What is that? Rafael wondered. He tried to stand and see, and then a young man in black took his arm and helped him to his feet. He got up just in time to see the police car speeding away.

Fear and panic made him grab the arm of the young man who had helped him stand. "My children are in the police car!" Rafael screamed, shaking the boy's arm.

He got distracted by the shouts of people yelling at the new vehicles arriving. He turned and saw two military trucks with flat beds full of soldiers riding in standing positions. People from the park ran towards them and pointed at the police car and screamed that there had been an abduction of children. They pointed to the bodies of the gunmen lying on the park ground. Someone indicated Rafael and shouted, "There's the father of the children!"

The trucks paused. A soldier of rank jumped from the cabin of one. He ordered four of the soldiers to come down from the truck and to secure the park. Then he commanded the drivers of the trucks to chase the police car. They started with lurches. The officer sprinted beside his vehicle and jumped back into the cab. They all accelerated away.

Rafael felt stunned. He realized fast that he had to calm himself and focus. He needed a phone. His hands felt his pockets.

Fuck! he remembered. *I left mine back home! I can run there. What would save time?*

His kids were speeding from him even as he thought.

This is Ana's fucking fault. What has she done? A revelation hit him. *Ana! She knows everyone in the world! I have to reach her. How? I need to think... Enrique! I have to call Enrique! The kid next to me here is a Z. He must know Enrique!*

Rafael didn't have his number, and even if he knew it, he was too upset to remember.

"Do you have a phone?" he asked the kid.

"Yes, sir." The young man pulled one from his pocket. The other two Zs, the ones who had flattened the gunmen, arrived to join them.

"My wife is Ana Valdez," Rafael told them. "I need to reach her immediately. They have our children. I haven't been able to reach her by phone all day. Do you know Enrique Santos? Do you have his number?"

"Yes, sir" replied the young man with the phone. "Enrique is the one who instructed us to find you to warn you that your family is in danger. Your wife is with him now."

Rafael couldn't help it, but he danced with impatience and excitement.

"Please! Call Enrique now, and pass me the phone!"

In the back seat of the car that Enrique was driving, Ana was having attacks of anxiety over the silence of the phone. She sent some more text messages to David and to Eduardo, and no response came. She tried to reach Rafael and Paulina again, without success. She had some second thoughts about going to Eduardo's ranch and challenged Enrique about that plan.

"We should head to my house! I don't know if anyone is going to get there in time to warn my family!" Ana anguished to Enrique.

"No, no, no!" Enrique responded. "They're out there looking for you, Ana! Of course they'll go to your house! They'll succeed in getting you there, for sure. Listen, we have the Zs and the Army going to contact Rafael and the kids. Let's keep trying the phones. We should stay away from your house. Maybe we're even being followed right now. If we are, we would lead them straight to your family! Let's stick to our plan and get to the ranch and get in touch with David. We'll have your family join us there. Let's hope for some luck with this! Stay down, please!"

Suddenly the phone in Ana's hand rang, and she jumped. Instinctively she answered it, not remembering that she was holding Enrique's phone. The caller ID on the screen listed a man's name she didn't recognize. There was a hesitant pause on the other end of the line, and then a young man's voice asked, "Is this Enrique's phone?"

"Yes, it is," Ana answered.

"I recognize your voice, Señora Valdez" said the young man. "I …"

But then someone near to the young man said, "Is that Ana? Give me that phone!" When the person put his mouth to the phone, Ana recognized Rafael immediately.

"Rafael!" she shouted.

Rafael's voice broke right away. He was intensely excited. Ana could tell that he was talking through tears at that moment.

"Ana! What have you done? They have taken our children!"

She sucked a big gasp of air. Her own voice trembled with sudden panic. "Rafael, who took them? Where?"

"Some sons of whores with guns, and a policeman! We were here in the park on our street. It just now happened, like two minutes ago! A police car pulled up, some men ran across the fútbol field. A couple got Rafael Jr., and the policeman and another man got Paula, and they put them in the police car. Then two of the men came at me with their pistols, Ana. The fucking assholes were going to shoot me! They were going to kill me! But two of these Z guys came behind them and kicked them in their heads, and it looks like they're dead. They're right there on the grass. The police car sped away, but these two army trucks with soldiers suddenly pulled up, and people yelled at them what happened, and the soldiers gave chase with the trucks. They're chasing them now!"

"God, Rafael, why haven't you answered your phone? I've been trying to call you and warn you! I called the Army, and Enrique called the Zs and that's why they are there…"

Rafael interrupted her. "Well, they're here too fucking late. The sons of bitches have our kids! What the hell have you been doing, Ana? The kids are showing me all day things about you jumping off a building and David being shot, and I'm finding out you've been involved in undercover operations with the military, and I don't know shit about this! Now they have our kids!"

"Rafael, please, calm down! I'm upset too! We need to focus and think!"

"Calm down? Calm down? Are you crazy? This is your fault, Ana! Your fault! Ever since you got mixed up with that damned gringo, I have no idea what you're doing. Look what it has done!"

She felt a dagger in her heart, not so much from Rafael's words, but from knowing someone had her children. If anything, at this moment when she might have begun to panic, Rafael's attacks on her made her steel inside. She felt a surge of anger. No, it was rage. He wasn't going to talk to her like this! He needed to be helping her. They needed to figure out what to do. But she knew this wasn't going to happen with Rafael. He wasn't the man to put this together

285

with her now, when they needed to focus on action to save the children. They would talk about blame and differences later. Besides, she knew exactly what needed to be done.

"Rafael, listen to me! Listen to me. I'll fix this. These men don't want the kids. They want me. You're not useful to them. They would have killed you for interfering. They're not going to hurt the kids because they want to use them to get me. I'll fix this!"

On the other end of the phone, Rafael clearly had become even angrier. He responded, "You damn right, you'll fix it, Ana! You get our kids back. They want you? Then give yourself to them! I want our kids here, right now, and out of danger. So you do that, you hear? You give yourself to them, and make sure these children get safely out of this mess you made! I can't believe you put them in this kind of danger!"

This was language Ana had received for years and years, an idiom of recriminations. This was the end of the line. If she were guilty of putting her family in mortal danger, she would face that truth and deal with its consequences and justice after her children were safe. Now she truly understood that this would happen by her own choice, and that she didn't want Rafael's involvement in anything she did. She didn't want it. She hadn't wanted it for a long time. She didn't want him.

"Shut up, Rafael!" she told him. "I'm going to fix this." She cut the call.

She looked up at Enrique's face in the rear view mirror. His face was pale. She said, "You heard it all?"

He nodded sadly.

The kid was screaming in the back seat to let them out, please. His sister was crying quietly. El Chico's accomplice, Tito, the one who wasn't killed by the Zs, rode in the back and had his gun in his right hand.

Jesus, what a fucking bad day, El Chico grumbled to himself. It was unbelievable, really. The woman had actually escaped from them, and now this kidnapping of her children was a disaster. The son of a bitch little kid had been kicking and screaming and making

286

such a noise while Tito carried him that none of them noticed the two Zs who had run to the sides of them. *How in the hell had they been able to kill two of his men with single kicks like that?*

He had seen that they were dead. He could tell by the sick way they crumbled to the ground. He and Tito had barely got the boy and the girl in the car when the fucking army trucks appeared out of nowhere. Now they were right behind him as he sped up La Avenida Universidad. The Mexican police car he was in was a Dodge Charger. It should have been very fast, but the streets were congested with cars, and he could barely keep forty miles an hour at best. He had to avoid any situation that would make him stop, because if the trucks were close enough behind, the sons-of-whores soldiers would jump off and run for them.

Tito had dialed the phone and had operated the radio for him, his own radio which he brought. Tito held these to his mouth so he could talk while driving like a maniac, while still focusing on the street in front. He needed the soldiers to be intercepted. He talked to El Contador on the phone to confirm that he had the kids. El Contador wasn't pleased to hear the news of the two dead. He passed the information to someone else in the room, someone important, because then El Contador told him to put some distance between them and the soldiers. "They" were arranging for men to help them. He should bring the kids to the safe house where El Contador stayed. He could hear the man in the background giving instructions.

Ten minutes went by, and then El Chico hit a stretch of road where he could open up the Charger. He had an advantage now of a couple of blocks over the Army trucks when he pulled up on an intersection that had SUVs and pickup trucks everywhere.

Mother of God! There they are! he thought happily. He saw three men frantically waving him to pass through. He could tell that these were specialists of the cartel in clearing people out of the way very quickly and efficiently, because suddenly in this area he wasn't seeing the sedans and minivans that had been on the road before. El Chico blasted the siren and sailed through a hole in the lineup of vehicles. As he passed through, he saw two men running with grenade launchers to get in position to attack the soldiers coming in the trucks. The three men who had been waving for him to pass ran and jumped into the bed of a pickup truck. In his rear mirror he saw them and others already pointing their Ak-47s.

"God, I wish I could hang around and see what happens," he told Tito, feeling a big smile stretch his face. Tito was looking out the rear window. He was bouncing with excitement.

"What a fucking party the Army is coming to!" Tito laughed.

But El Chico knew he had his job to do, to get these kids to El Contador, and fast. He felt so happy with relief that he let out a big whoop of joy. *Those guys back there are saving my life,* he thought to himself. The day had been such a screw-up that he had felt the weight of a tombstone on his forehead. But with the guys from the cartel stopping the army trucks, he was home free, mission accomplished. He would get these kids to El Contador, and he would live another day!

Enrique whipped the Sentra into the parking lot of a small strip mall and parked. He and Ana needed to talk and figure out what to do next. He kept the engine running, because they found a phone charger in the glove compartment, and they used it to charge Ana's dead data-phone, which she had been carrying in her pocket. They chose the strip mall because it had a coffee shop that provided wireless internet, and the signal was actually on.

Ana felt frantic, but she willed herself to remain calm so she could think clearly. She thought that there would be a good chance the Army would catch the fleeing police car, but would her children be hurt? She wanted to believe in that possibility, that the Army would catch the false policeman and his accomplice. She thought for a moment about the horror she had witnessed just a couple of hours earlier, when her three Z protectors died trying to save her. Her heart cried for them too. She remembered the faces of the young cartel men who ran to the police car she sat in, and wondered which two of them were killed by the Zs who saved Rafael. She then realized that she had been sitting in the back seat of the same car where now her children probably were sitting. That was too disturbing to think about.

God, I've got to do something!

"So I escaped, and they got my kids," she said to Enrique. "I don't think they want them, of course. They want me. So if this is true, someone is going to contact me. God, Enrique, I don't think I can wait much longer!"

"Okay, Ana," said Enrique. "Let's think this out. How are they going to contact you? What they know is that you got away from them in the city, and you probably are accessible by phone or computer. So you did a good thing by finding the phone charger and getting your phone up and running. Who would have your number?"

"Well, I've always put my personal cell number on my websites, to make myself accessible to so many groups, especially women's groups, so that I could help them."

"If they don't use your phone number but want to communicate with you, how would someone do this?" asked Enrique.

"I suppose on Twitter, Facebook, or on one of my blogs. People can send private messages there."

"Okay, Ana, then let's start there. Since no one has called you yet, let's monitor your sites for messages until either we hear from them or we receive some information about the children from someone."

They spent about twenty minutes using the browsers on their smart-phones to look at the many Z Twitter sites. Ana tried to reach David and Eduardo by phone again, but with no answer from either.

A little more time passed by when Enrique asked, "When was the last time you blogged?"

To Ana it seemed a million years ago, but she thought and remembered. "Last night, on my Stopping the Bloodshed blog," she told Enrique.

"Look there," he suggested.

She pulled up the website on her phone. There were seventeen responses to her blog, and the most recent one had been three hours earlier. She read a few and then hit the refresh button. A new message suddenly appeared. The sender was Empresas Felinas. It didn't hit her at first, but then Ana caught her breath. Feline Enterprises.

Nervously she said, "Enrique, I think this might be something!"

She looked at the body of the message, and it said simply, "6748-0911 Feline Enterprises. Tu gatito está listo."

Your little cat is ready.

Enrique was reading it on the screen with her. "El Gato," he said. "I think you better make the call."

David sat staring blankly at the windows in the sliding side door of the Blackhawk helicopter during the three hour flight from Houston to Monterrey. Eduardo was to his side. He felt hot and "fatally exhausted," as he described it to himself. The flight was too long. There was too much for him to worry about. His last news about Ana was that she was missing. The cell phone service in flight might have worked under normal circumstances, but with the events taking place in Mexico, being able to use a phone was hit and miss. He hadn't been able to reach her or Enrique by phone, and he had heard nothing from them.

So David only had one way to hear Ana right now, and that was to become quiet and listen to his heart. He felt her there. He felt that she was in trouble, that someone had taken her, and from experience he knew that this feeling was something he could trust. He called what he did "going internal." He had done it since childhood, when deep in his imagination he created adventures with his girl partner. Later in life he understood what he did was a form of meditation. He first became very quiet in his body, he breathed slowly with long breaths, he blotted out thoughts and visualized a single point of light and nothing else, until he was left only with awareness of his heart. He might "see" pains he felt in his body or see the colors of anger or grief in his heart, or he might see the truth about another person. This is what happened in the helicopter when he was so frustrated over his separation from Ana and the lack of news. He went in search of her heart.

David floated through his meditation. He was like a person asleep who is aware that he is dreaming but who watches the dream and experiences it as real anyway. He pulled up Ana's face, her lovely, transcendental face. He looked in her eyes as he always did, and, in an instant, he saw again her face of Mexico. She showed him mothers, mothers who had lost their children, mothers who were working through their grief by giving up their lives to follow causes. For peace. For the end of bloodshed. For virtue and courage. He saw them marching through the cities, across Ana's map of Mexico, until they arrived at the border of the United States. Through the fences they reached for the hands of the gringos on the other side.

But then Ana's face swam suddenly into view again, and she screamed, Come to me, David! Come quick!

David jumped, startled. The cell phone in his pocket was vibrating. He fished it out and saw that messages were arriving all at once. They were coming from Ana and from Enrique. Eduardo jumped as well because his phone also vibrated. David's hand shook while he stared at the screen, trying to find the most recent messages. The first ones were asking him to call. He saw one that informed him that Enrique and Ana were together and heading to Eduardo's ranch!

Thank God, is it possible Ana is safe?

He scrolled nervously. He checked his watch. They were almost three hours now into flight and were approaching Monterrey. It had taken almost an hour to prepare everything for the flight back. It had been maddening. They had refueled and had reloaded Yog's body on the helicopter. So there had been a total of four hours since his final words with the President.

Finally he found the most recent of Ana's text messages, which had just arrived, in fact. There were three consecutive ones that formed one continuous message:

David, so you'll know this is me, I remind you that we've always dreamed of having the chance to dance desnudos fuera on a rooftop in Rome under the stars of a midnight sky. This afternoon the cartel of Sinaloa, under the direction of El Gato (you were right), attempted to kidnap me and I escaped. Three of our brave Zs were killed trying to defend me. To bring me in, El Gato ordered that Rafael and the children be taken. Despite the efforts of me and Enrique to warn Rafael, the cartel succeeded in getting the kids. They were about to assassinate Rafael, but two Zs saved his life. El Gato exchanged the children for me. They were freed in the parking lot of a shopping mall, and when I saw that I gave myself up. El Gato is reading what I write here. He plans to keep me until he contacts you. He's going on a mission and he'll take me with him. You'll not be able to contact him or me. You must wait until he contacts you. Be alert to his call. Enrique is returning the children to Rafael. Enrique can give you more details about today's events.

Reading this delivered a savage blow to his gut. It was brutal news. David's arms fell to his side in despair. Then he handed the phone to Eduardo, and he watched his face as the old man read the message from Ana. It was irrational, but David somehow thought that looking at Eduardo's face while he read would change the situation, that Eduardo would hand him back the phone and say, "I'm so glad Ana is safe and is awaiting our return at the ranch." Instead, the old man's skin turned a deeper grey. He seemed to age five years before his eyes. Then David remembered. El Gato wasn't just a leader in the Cartel of Sinaloa. El Gato was Roberto. David was looking in the face of Roberto's father. The man to his side was a man who had seen his bright and handsome little boy grow into a monster. The man had also lost his precious daughter. David had lost the love of his youth. Now El Gato had the love of his life.

But Eduardo looked directly into David's eyes, and he said with the greatest sadness David had ever heard, "I'm so sorry, David. You love Ana so much. She's like a daughter to me, like the daughter I lost."

The defeat David felt lasted only a few seconds. Eduardo's words brought him strength. He saw how closely life bonded them. In Eduardo he had a brother, a father, and a comrade of arms.

You're right, Ana, he thought. *I do know it's you by what you wrote, and you wrote the message in English, which is what you always speak to me. What we dream is to dance "naked outside" on a rooftop in Rome under the stars of a midnight sky. Why did you put those two words in Spanish when we always speak in English of dancing naked outside?*

They changed their destination to Eduardo's ranch now that they learned that El Gato had Ana. As they approached the training fields, David saw that the bulk of free space was taken up by military vehicles, including trucks, jeeps, and three tanks. There was another helicopter near the entrance to the fields from the road that led to the ranch house.

Eduardo saw it too as their helicopter approached, coming in fast.

"General Alvarez is here," he told David.

Chapter 19: The Longest Day's End

Monterrey and Washington, D.C.
Monday Afternoon and Evening

Enrique saw how quiet Ana became after she made the call to El Gato. "We have a date with destiny, Señora Valdez," the man on the phone told her. She had followed instructions to put the phone on speaker and all occupants of the car must identify themselves. Enrique stated his name, and that was all. El Gato made no comment to him. "I'm El Gato, and I believe you might know a little of me. Of course, this call isn't about me. We'll have plenty of time to discuss our personal histories later. Right now, there's a more pressing concern, that of the release of your children, which will be possible only by your agreement to exchange yourself for them."

He went on to name a shopping mall parking lot in the north of the city and gave them twenty minutes to be there. It was a fishing statement, meant to give El Gato some idea of where he and Ana might be. Enrique knew he could be there in twenty minutes, even with the complexities of the traffic at that time and the pedestrians everywhere in the streets and sidewalks.

"Identify your vehicle with a brief flash of turn signal when you see our cars. Not lights, so the children won't notice. They'll be released and will be told to run from there to the pharmacy at the intersection where Enrique Santos will meet them and take them to safety. It's probably best they don't see you. After the children leave, walk straight to our car. My men will give you your ride to be in my company. At that point, Señor Santos should leave to rendezvous with the children."

They drove as instructed down the ramp leading to underground parking at the rear entrance of the mall. It was closed, but most of the parking spaces were filled for God knows what reason. There was no sign of anything unusual, so they found a spot several rows back from the entrance. From there they could see vehicles entering and leaving the ramp. Ana got into the front seat beside Enrique.

293

They were about five minutes early. Ana wasn't saying anything. Enrique saw that she was containing a cool, controlled rage. She was plotting. He had seen her analytical mind take over in the past. This time her whole body was tense and focused. He thought she wore a patina of sharpness. She was a dagger that would plunge a heart. He, of course, had that familiar feeling that he should know what to do but didn't have a clue. He didn't know what to say to her. He was scared, but bravely sitting on top of his fear.

When the vehicle arrived with the children, he knew immediately. He had wondered if it would be a police car, but no, two black SUVs entered the ramp. They cruised in, looking sinister. Enrique flashed his turn signal twice. Suddenly he felt like someone decisive woke inside him and took the wheel. Ana looked at him when he did it, but she didn't say a word. She turned and focused on the SUVs.

She waited until the two vehicles pulled to a stop in front of the mall entrance before speaking to him. They saw the children get out of the back seat of the first, and then some men who had emerged from the second vehicle prodded them and shouted for them to run up the ramp. One of the men ran alongside them until they were half way up, and then he stopped and watched until they disappeared. The driver of the first vehicle sat in place with the window rolled down. He had seen them in their car, and he stared at Ana.

Turning to Enrique, Ana spoke quickly. "I'll be fine, Enrique. Remember, they want me alive for a reason. You have to be strong now and make good decisions. David will come. He'll help you. I'll see you again, I promise." She gave him a quick kiss on the cheek and then opened the car door. "Please go get Paula and Rafael Jr. now."

He watched her stride determinedly towards the men standing beside the car. One opened the rear door of the SUV, and Ana boarded. The windows were darkened, and the driver rolled up his window, so when all were in the two vehicles, Enrique could see no one. Enrique started his car and backed out and then roared up the ramp before the SUVs began to move. He wanted to leave ahead of them so Ana could see him going for the children. He remembered that on the way to the mall parking lot he had called for some guys to come meet him at the pharmacy so he would have more protection for the children. He estimated that they should be arriving there soon.

The kids were standing on the sidewalk in front of the entrance to the pharmacy. When Paula recognized Enrique, she tugged on Rafael Jr., and they both ran towards Enrique's car and jumped in. Rafael Jr. wasn't even settled in the car when he asked, "Where is our mom?"

He threw himself into the back seat. Paula took the passenger seat beside Enrique. It was, still warm from her mother.

"She gave herself up for us, didn't she?" she demanded.

He wasn't going to lie. It would be pointless, and it would be all over the news anyway soon enough. So he looked directly in her eyes and then in Rafael's.

"She did do that," Enrique answered. "But she told me that she's going to be fine and she has a plan. These men want your mom for a reason. I don't believe they're going to hurt her. She said to tell you that she'll be with you soon and to please be brave. She told me to be brave too. So let's do that for her, and we'll figure out what to do now, okay?"

He waited just a few minutes and his associates came, some Zs. He asked them to follow him in their car to the children's home. He wanted them to remain with the family to guard their house. When they were driving, he thought about what he had just said to Paula, that the men wanted their mom for a reason. He was fairly certain the reason was David.

Jesus, where are David and Eduardo right now? he asked. It was a prayer.

David sat feeling small on an immense dark red leather sofa trimmed with old-world wood in Eduardo's fully-Mexican ranch home. Normally there was clutter from Eduardo's lifetime of achievements and travels, but now in this grand sala most of the furniture had been pushed aside for the addition of big tables in the center of the room. Computer equipment, monitors, and laptops were everywhere, along with radio equipment and transmitters. There were soldiers, as well as men in civilian clothing, and agents of all types, including some from the DEA who had been staying at the ranch when the government coup took place. Some staff from the kitchen brought David, Eduardo, and General Alvarez food which they set on an oversized, rectangular oak coffee table in front of the sofa.

The General reported that President Blair from the United States had reached him twice, first to inform him that he was using a helicopter to bring David and any victims on the roof that morning to Houston for medical attention and later to report that Eduardo and David were on the return to Monterrey. Now General Alvarez had talked almost non-stop for a half hour, bringing the two of them up to date on what was happening in Mexico, while the business of the coup went on in the center of the room. That is what David thought of the scene around him. It looked like "Revolution, North East Branch, Monterrey." General Alvarez had flown to the ranch from Distrito Federal by helicopter to meet them and had arrived just minutes before Eduardo and David. They all took a truck from the training fields to the ranch house.

On the way, David phoned and confirmed that Enrique had returned Paula and Rafael Jr. to their home. He asked Enrique to be on standby until he called him again with instructions after they met with General Alvarez. When he told Enrique that he had received a message from Ana, he could hear the relief in the young man's voice. He knew Enrique was afraid that something horrible might befall her. David was afraid of the same thing.

"Hang in there, Enrique; we're going to need you," David told him. "We're getting Ana back! Are you up for that?" Enrique's voice cracked a little when he answered yes.

Now David looked about the room. General Alvarez was talking about the Army, Navy, and Marines working together. While he was explaining how military staffs of the Armed Forces were taking control of governmental public services, David let his mind wander a few minutes. Mentally, he felt anxious about Ana, especially in the hands of Roberto. Physically, he now felt alert and strong, which was ridiculous considering the hellish day it had been. It was because some genius during the day had put steroids in his IV fluids! So now he felt good when he should have felt exhausted. He felt like he could now jump off a roof with Ana, like he should have done when Yog burst out the door and opened fire on him! Had he known

296

that someone would shoot their assailants, he would have gone down with Ana.

The day seemed like it was book length. In between the early morning drama and now, he had been wounded; the President of the United States had kidnapped him to Texas with the complicity of Eduardo; Ana had been captured and escaped; her children had been captured; Ana had exchanged her life for them; and now…Roberto had her! God, this was insane! Roberto, from a million years ago!

But it was true. Roberto was El Gato. David fleshed him piece by piece as he tracked drug routes and Sinaloa cartel activity in the United States. He had put together a blurry image of a man and was developing a profile of him.

Now the portrait is crisp and clear, and it's Roberto? I never saw that coming!

His mind turned to what Ana texted him over the phone. Some things about Ana's message were bothering him a lot. In the noise of the helicopter and in the subsequent commotion of the landing and arrival in the ranch house, he hadn't been able to turn his full attention to it. They had given David's phone to a communications expert when they arrived in the house so he could try to trace or find information about the phone of origin for Ana's message. He had taken the number, and as all of them expected, he soon reported that the cell phone originating the message had been reported stolen weeks before. With every arrest of cartel members, always was discovered a cache of stolen cell phones, taken to be used for short periods.

As General Alvarez was talking, David studied the message again. In a few minutes he interrupted the other two.

"I think Ana is sending important information in this message," he said, brandishing his phone. Eduardo and General Alvarez hushed immediately.

"Eduardo, have you ever known Ana to speak in language like this, even in English?" David asked.

"No. I assumed that the language was stilted because she was writing it in front of El Gato, who would be reviewing or censuring it."

"True," David answered, "and Ana would know we would expect this and not think it was that unusual. She began the message by giving me a sentence to identify her. It's an intimate and personal

297

message, so I think she chose this to gain the confidence of the person reading it, to make him believe that she was cooperating with him fully, agreed?"

The other two nodded.

"Okay, let's break this down. It's a text message. Why did she choose to send a text message?"

General Alvarez answered this time. "Because they tried to phone you and couldn't reach you, so they wanted to leave a message and they texted it. Hmm, did you check voice mail?"

"Yes," David answered. "And there was no message from Ana there. So my guess is this. Ana wanted to make sure I could detect hidden messages, so she put this in writing so I could look at it again and again."

"You could listen to a voice message repeatedly," said General Alvarez.

"Yes, but some things stand out in writing that might not in sound. In this case, the most obvious clue is that she chose an intimate saying we have, but she put two of the words in Spanish to highlight them. I've been puzzling over the choice of these words but haven't been able to figure out what she might be trying to say." Then David repeated the words. "Desnudos fuera. Naked outside."

Both General Alvarez and Eduardo frowned in puzzlement.

"Let's get back to that. The other thing is that Ana tells me I'm right about El Gato. She doesn't know that El Gato is Roberto, I don't think, so she must be telling me I'm right that he's a major leader of the Sinaloa Cartel. Then she says he's keeping her until he contacts me. This is to say that she's alive and will remain alive at least until I'm in play. Maybe she's saying that she'll be exchanged for me. I'm not sure about that. What's important is her choice of words next. She says that El Gato is going on a mission and will contact me later. Some time is going to pass, and I have to wait. Clearly El Gato wants me to suffer the silence. The not knowing."

Eduardo said, "The choice of word 'mission' sounds military."

"Yes," General Alvarez answered, "and it's going to take some time. He'll be busy. He's taking her with him. Why would he do that? Ana is clever. She has contacts throughout Mexico. She's an easily recognized public figure. This seems like a risky move."

David nodded as he listened. "Okay," he said, "he's taking her with him because it's going to take time, and they're going out of

Monterrey. Maybe he feels it's more of a risk to leave her behind. Whatever he's doing, it must be important or he would be dealing with me right away, don't you think? What is it he would be doing that's so important?"

"The cartels should have their hands full trying to move merchandise while the border is effectively sealed," answered Eduardo. "It must have something to do with cartel activity during this time. It has been surprisingly quiet so far." He took a bite of salad. "What would be the mission?"

"Desnudos fuera?" answered David. "The two words in Spanish?"

Suddenly General Alvarez sat up straight. "Gentlemen," he said, "What's the first thing a person does when trying to analyze a code? The first thing is to consider initials, right? Desnudos fuera: D.F. Distrito Federal!"

The simplicity of this idea slapped David in the face with its feeling of truth. Immediately he thought, *Oh God, yes, this is so Ana!*

"Are we sure about this?" General Alvarez asked, breaking the pause. "Would El Gato have revealed so much information to Ana so soon? Would he be including her in talk about a mission?"

"Are you shitting me?" he exclaimed. "Mexico City?" Then he asked the question, just to help them focus. "And what's in Mexico City?"

General Alvarez answered it: "The Supreme Court. The Senate. The House of Deputies. The President of Mexico!"

"Ex-President," Eduardo corrected. "If El Gato is leading the Sinaloa Cartel on a mission to Mexico City, then he'll be arriving there with troops. Maybe with a whole lot of firepower."

They became silent, each man thinking.

"Are we sure about this?" General Alvarez asked, breaking the pause. "Would El Gato have revealed so much information to Ana so soon? Would he be including her in talk about a mission?"

"You know Ana pretty well, right, General?" David answered. "All El Gato would have to say is something like, 'You're coming with me to Mexico City,' and Ana would be figuring a lot of things out. She's a smart lady, and she's a map of Mexico. I can guarantee you that she heard something to make her choose the word 'mission' in her message to me. You don't know how she can get information out of people. Then there's this: I remember Roberto. He'll definitely want to play with my mind and torture my soul. He's gloating that he has my Ana. He wants me to know that he's taking her away with him, on a mission, almost as if she'll play a part in it. I'm worried what he has in mind."

Eduardo hung his head and nodded. He said, "I'm too afraid this makes sense." He turned to the General. "Alfonso," he addressed him. "We both know about Pedro."

He was referring to Pedro Navarro. General Alvarez gave Eduardo a look that said to continue.

Eduardo elaborated, perhaps for David's benefit.

"Pedro is a very wealthy man. He comes from the state of Sinaloa. His life of public service in that state and later in the federal government has benefitted him privately in enormous ways. The man has always been a puppet for the Cartel of Sinaloa. He has favored them with public booty. He has instigated investigations of rival cartels. He has protected their private airfields and transit routes. He has found jobs for cartel members in all branches of government and in the police. In return, he has received so much: money, property, vehicles, and special gifts- like misfortune falling on his opponents at opportune times. The network of protection for Navarro has been such that no one has ever been able to pin a thing on him, even though the cries of foul have dogged him scandal after scandal. However, many people voted for him this past election because his past regimes provided civil and economic stability in Sinaloa. During his terms in office there wasn't so much of the violence there, like what has plagued the country in the last decade. He promised a reduction in violence, and this is why he got elected. Many voters in this past Presidential election stopped caring that Navarro's victory would mean turning over government to organized crime. They just want the bloodshed to end, to be able to go to work and enjoy their daily lives without worrying about being killed or kidnapped. In a stable world, impunity doesn't stand out, but in a world where violence wreaks havoc in the daily landscape, impunity stinks like garbage. It can't be ignored."

David felt a chill. He looked at General Alvarez, then at Eduardo. "What are you saying, Eduardo? Do you think El Gato is going to Mexico City for Pedro Navarro so they can have their man back?"

"I'm not sure, David," Eduardo replied. "But we think that El Gato is going to Mexico City on a mission, and he has his reasons. Pedro Navarro and many of the quarantined government officials are there." When he used the word "quarantined," he shot a glance at General Alvarez.

David turned to him and asked, "General, the government leaders who are quarantined in Mexico City are heavily guarded, verdad? The city is well defended?"

The General didn't answer the question directly. Instead he said, "I need to go there right away."

"What if we could find El Gato here in Monterrey before he leaves?" David asked. He tossed the question out there before he had taken time to consider it.

"Based on the message, he may have already left, especially knowing you would be seeing the message and would be extremely anxious to resolve things quickly," responded the General. "I need to get my madre-de puta-ass back to D.F. and Los Pinos and assess our readiness for an armed attack that might have some muscle behind it. Most of our activity to date has been to preserve order and to try to run public services. We need to be ready if someone tries to start civil war."

"Take me," David said quickly. "If the action is there, if Ana is there, I need to be close. Ana may be able to help us, especially if she knows I'm close."

General Alvarez had doubt written all over his face about the idea, so David continued, "Think about this: you may need me on the spur of the moment to talk to the President of the United States. Who knows what help you might need? I might be able to procure it for you quickly. The President needs reliable reports and good recommendations from his men in the field. He knows I'm his best man. He trusts me the most. We've been like close brothers since college. What if you need me, and I'm distant, and there's a failure in communications? You need to take me."

"Sí, bien," sighed the General. He saw that Eduardo was about to speak, but he beat him to the punch. "I know, Eduardo, you want to come."

"El Gato is my son."

"I know. We'll all go."

"And one other," said David. "I have a right hand man of my own now that Ana is out of commission. I'm bringing Enrique Santos."

The men blindfolded her in the car and taped her wrists together behind her. Ana focused and listened to the sounds of the city as the car moved, and she estimated distances. In her mind she had an idea of approximately where she might be. She heard them driving through a residential area, and then they pulled into a home which had a garage door opening. When it shut behind them, one of the men helped her from the car. Then there was a strange trip. They went down some stairs, and after that they passed through a long hallway, then they entered some kind of large room. She could tell by the sounds. From there, someone led her into a room that felt chilly and had her sit in a metallic chair. She was left alone there for a few moments. Then she heard the door to this room open and shut, and someone came in quietly and paused. She felt like it was a man looking at her and assessing her. She decided to say nothing so she wouldn't betray fear or nervousness. The man walked towards her and lifted the blindfold from her eyes.

He was a handsome man approximately David's age, but he still had solid black hair. He appeared physically fit. His skin was a little weathered as if he had spent a good part of his life in the outdoors. It made him look rugged. He had dark eyes, Mexican dark, but darker still, and they were fixed on her in a curious way. Yet Ana's eyes went directly to his most distinguishing physical characteristic: an almost perfectly star-shaped, bluish birthmark on the left side of his forehead, at the hairline. Something rang in her subconscious about that, but it eluded her.

He nodded to her slightly before turning to walk back around to the other side of the folding metal table in front of which she was sitting. He took a chair directly across from her. As he walked, Ana observed that she was in a cool room with no windows and one shut door. There were fluorescent lights staggered across the ceiling of the room, but they weren't lit. The illumination at this time was coming from a household lamp sitting on a small table near her. It appeared as if it had been moved there from some other room. There was no other furniture except the folding metal table, six folding metal chairs, the small table against the wall near her, and, laughably, an artificial plant about five feet tall near the table. The

302

floor of the room was tile, and its surface slanted slightly to a drain in the center of the room. The opposite wall had a long industrial wash basin attached, separated into three stainless steel sinks: one for soap, one for rinse, and one for sanitizer. There were metal shelves above the basins. A series of rubber tubing ran from a mounted panel over the sinks, which dispensed the soap and the sanitizer. In the opposite corner of the room there was a smaller panel, and this had controls to dispense either soap or sanitizer through a long garden type hose that had a spray nozzle. There were no dishes, pots or pans to be seen. The whole scenario to Ana was just macabre. The room felt refrigerated and evil. No household lamp or artificial plant was going to dispel her feeling that horrible things had happened in this room.

The man spoke to her in English. "Well, Señora Valdez, it's a pleasure to make your company. Please let me introduce myself. I'm El Gato. I apologize for the accommodations. This is somewhat of a multipurpose room. We bring furniture in as needed. We'll bring a mattress for you tonight. Fortunately, we'll not be staying here very long. We have a trip to make, and I'll enjoy the honor of your company. I expect that you'll be quite a help to me, actually. I hope that you enjoy Mexico City this time of year. We've quite a lot of activity ahead of us, so you'll need your rest. We'll be leaving early in the morning."

"Do you promise to leave my kids alone?" Ana asked, looking at him steely. She intentionally ignored what he said to show him she had different priorities than he.

"Yes, you kept your end of the bargain. Your children will be fine. No worries. We had a little too much tension this day, don't you think? Enough of that. Let's be very focused in the next days so our mission will be successful and there will be no unnecessary accidents."

She ignored this again. She thought that if she didn't seem curious about what he was telling her, he might keep providing more information, either to impress her or to frighten her.

"You almost left my children fatherless."

If her tactic annoyed him, he didn't show it. He kept an impassive face while he lit a cigarette. He offered her one, but she shook her head. He blew a puff, and then he finally responded, "My reports are that he was charging towards my men."

303

"He was unarmed," Ana retorted. "Could your men have been so frightened by him that they would shoot an unarmed man? Yet that's what the cartels do all the time. They execute defenseless persons while shooting them from a safe distance. It isn't manly."

El Gato wouldn't be baited. He wasn't smiling, not even suggesting a smile on his lips, but there seemed to be a hint of amusement in his eyes, which remained focused on Ana's. "Ah, yes, you're all about nonviolence, I know. However, I believe we've seen that men…or women…do not need to be armed in order to be lethal weapons, Señora Valdez. Throughout Mexico your Zs now appear to be making their mark."

"The Zs have rules of life. An important one is that they'll seek to preserve life and safety of citizens through means of self -defense, and whenever possible, without the use of firearms or excessive violence. Because of their intervention today, my husband was spared his life. I would like for him to continue to live for the wellbeing of our children," Ana answered.

"He has no worries at present, Señora. He isn't in the crosshairs." He continued to stare at her as he smoked, pausing a couple of minutes, still assessing her. Then he said, "We have a lot to do. Right now we have a pressing matter. We need to contact your friend David James. I'm sure he's quite worried about you. I have a phone here. I want him to know that we're enjoying each other's company at present and that in the near future we'll be contacting him about some business we can do together. I'm sure he'll be quite surprised you're with me, and he'll no doubt be very upset. The thing is, I can't be distracted right now by small, personal dramas. I must remain sharp for the days ahead. He also will need to think clearly to be able to work with me, so we'll communicate with him via a text message as the best way of checking emotions at the door. I'll help you compose a message to him, so that he hears from you and feels relieved on that score. I need for him to know it is truly you sending the message. Do you have some way of identifying yourself, some intimate detail perhaps that only the two of you share in your friendship?"

God, Ana thought, *this might be my only opportunity to pass information to David!*

She replied to El Gato, "Yes, I have a way of doing that, of course, and it's intimate. When I write it, he'll know I'm the only person who knows this other than him. Let me have the phone." She knew he would have to untie her.

El Gato laughed. "I can see we're going to have so much fun because you're so clever. Yes, I'll untie you, and I'll sit beside you while we construct this text. I knew I would like you. I have had some time to learn about you through your blogs and websites. You're smart and have many friends. You're beautiful. You remind me a lot of my sister. Her name was Ana too, but everyone called her Annie back then."

Ana almost inhaled air in a loud whistle. Every alarm ringing in her body told her that she must remain absolutely calm. She shouldn't give any indication at all to this man that now she knew exactly who he was. After all the things that had happened that day, she didn't suspect she could experience any more shocks, and yet this bomb shell just exploded in front of her. She saw El Gato studying her face, as if looking for her reaction, but she kept an impassive look. She hoped she gave no flash of recognition whatsoever. She turned this information over in her mind at hyper-speed.

Think, Ana, think! Didn't David tell me when I first met him that he loved a girl named Annie, and that she was the twin sister of his friend, and, oh my God, these were the children of Eduardo Ortiz! Think! What was the name of Eduardo's son, the one who died? God, I know this…the day has been so long…what is it?

Ana knew she couldn't delay any seconds, or El Gato would know she was processing the information he had just given her. Her instinct told her this would be a mistake, perhaps a fatal mistake. So quickly she responded, "Okay, come over here and untie me and sit beside me, and let me type my identifier in the phone. I'll show it to you. Then you can tell me what to say in the rest of the message."

He has given me clues about his identity to test to see if I realize who he is. This is why he has been speaking to me in English! He wanted me to know he has been in the United States. This is a clever man too. I'm going to have to be so careful!

His eyes studied her a few moments more, and then he walked over to her and freed her wrists. He pulled a chair beside her and handed her the phone.

His name is Roberto, Ana remembered. *Roberto Ortiz!*

President Donald Austin Blair took a moment to sink back in his executive chair and emit a sigh. He was back in Washington, in the Oval Office in fact, and an aide was arranging a secure call to David at Eduardo's ranch. The aide had contacted David on his cell phone, and David had suggested a conference call on speaker on Eduardo's land line. Apparently they were arranging that now in Monterrey, setting up in a private room for David, Eduardo, and General Alfonso Alvarez. This seemed to be taking a few minutes, and the President welcomed the bit of time to relax and to think.

It had been an exhausting day. In Houston, despite the interruptions concerning David's transport there, he managed to address briefly the conference with the Texas Democratic Party and to have a video conference with the Joint Chiefs of Staff. They were pressing about developments in Mexico and recommending more troop movements to the border and discussing ship arrivals near Mexican ports. On the flight home to Washington aboard Air Force One, he received a chaos of reports about demonstrations and rumored gun battles everywhere in Mexico. In the middle of those, he gobbled information about the structure of the Mexican government so he could have an idea of the extent of the coup in the country.

He felt embarrassed not to know that Mexico has no Vice President. The position most similar to that was the Secretary of Government, whose office was denoted SeGob. The bureaucratic structures of the Mexican federal and state governments easily rivaled those of the United States, the President decided, and changed often with each Mexican President's six year term. He was still trying to get a handle on how the Armed Forces in Mexico had come to form this strange alliance with the myriad protest groups of the Left and the conservative patriotic groups of the Right. For now, he accepted that he couldn't understand this completely. His gut told him it was an unstable alliance that might lead to civil war. He should be prepared for possible entry into Mexico to stabilize border regions.

He wanted to avoid armed conflict with the Mexican neighbors if possible. He worried that the longer the Mexican military held control of government, the more entrenched it would become, and the more challenged democracy would be to return to Mexico. His other concern was what the Mexican cartels within the United States might do in reprisal for the sealing of the border. His agency heads had been warning him of violent reactions not only along the border cities, but also in the large metropolitan areas where so many of the cartels were now entrenched.

In his conversation with General Alvarez that morning, he brought up this subject, that the international community (he avoided saying in particular the United States) would feel the need to take action in the face of an illegitimate takeover of government in Mexico. They must continue to dialog and to work towards a quick resolution in favor of the restoration of democracy, he told the General.

In spite of everything, the General made a good impression on him. He wasted no time assuring the President that Mexico was a democratic republic, and his every intention was that democracy and free elections would be restored.

"The problem, Mr. President, is that the organized criminal elements so undermined and corrupted the federal, state, and local governments that government didn't serve the people, didn't protect the people, and horribly abused the privileges of power against the people. The citizens had enough. Every day the demonstrations became bigger and more virulent. We were just days away from people storming the government buildings. Eduardo and many conservative businessmen, patriots for justice, saw this coming. We in the military witnessed corruption weakening our own ranks. This is why we took control, so we could impose order in Mexico and avoid huge amounts of bloodshed and loss of life. We're treating the government leaders humanely. We're working with their staffs and those people employed in public services so that we can reopen governmental services to the public as soon as possible."

Those were the words of the General in the morning, when the President reached him via phone to let him know that the United States was going to fly David and the wounded attacker to Houston for medical treatment and debriefing. The General already knew that David was an almost lifelong friend of his. But what really impressed the President was the fact that when he called to make contact with David and Eduardo, the General was already there in

Monterrey with them. He had flown from Mexico City. This showed the importance of Eduardo in the movement, and perhaps also, the importance of Monterrey as a strategic northern site for the coup. Whatever the reason for the General's presence, it was perfect. He was there with David, and the President could communicate directly with him, David, and Eduardo at the same time.

His aide broke his train of thought when he said, "Sir, Mr. James, Señor Ortiz, and General Alvarez are on the line." The aide waited to be sure the four could hear one another and then left the room.

David took the initiative and he quickly informed the President in sparse words what the situation was:

"Mr. President, we're here at Eduardo's ranch home. This place has been set up as a communications command center for the northeastern region of Mexico for their Armed Forces. Staffs representing all four military branches are here, as well as some Drug Enforcement Administration agents from the United States. When we arrived here, we were informed that Ana Valdez turned herself in to one of the top capos of the Cartel of Sinaloa in exchange for the release of her children, who had been kidnapped from their neighborhood earlier in the day. Ana sent a text message to my phone, which probably was reviewed before she sent it by this cartel boss who calls himself, 'El Gato.'

"In the message Ana wrote a phrase that only the two of us would recognize. She did this as a means of proving her identity. We believe that her message contained coded meaning. We think that Ana was telling us that El Gato is going to lead the cartel on a military-style mission in Mexico City, particularly in the Federal District. We think the target of the mission is possibly Pedro Navarro. Eduardo and the General have described to me the career of President Navarro and his career long connection to the Sinaloa cartel. Ana stated that El Gato is taking her on this mission, and that there might be some days before I would hear from him or her again. Apparently he's taking her to Mexico City with him. When you called, Eduardo and I were making arrangements to travel with General Alvarez to Mexico City. He feels the urgency of us leaving immediately so he can assess the readiness of the Armed Forces should there be an attack by the cartels. President Navarro, as you know, is in Los Pinos, right in the center of Mexico City."

Wow, President Blair thought to himself, *David, as always, is professional even under great personal duress.*

He emitted an audible sigh so David would understand it was a personal condolence meant for him. Then he said, "Okay, thank you, David, for so succinctly summarizing some news that must be particularly painful for you. This is what we feared. I need to tell you, gentlemen, that if the Mexican cartels unleash waves of attacks, then the world will look at the coup in Mexico as one deteriorating into civil war." He paused a moment, and then he asked the group, "What would be the purpose of the cartel making President Navarro a target at this time?" He referred to him as President on purpose.

"Unknown," David answered. "We don't know if he would be subject to assassination or liberation. The motivations of the cartels are often very murky."

"General Alvarez," asked the President, "are the positions of President Navarro and other government elected officials whom you've quarantined secure? Can you protect them?"

"My belief is yes, Mr. President, but I want to return to Mexico City and meet with my commanders to determine what changes in troop deployments we might need to make in light of a large scale attack by the Cartel of Sinaloa. David, as you're aware, was the one who built a case that a powerful lieutenant who calls himself, 'El Gato' is determining much of the strategy of the cartel internationally. He has insight into the character of this man. Eduardo is his father. They can help me decide strategy in Mexico City."

The president thought, *Jesus, David really is in the center of this mess in Mexico!*

"Are there any ideas about the force of fire power this El Gato could bring in armed confrontations with the troops in Mexico City?"

This time Eduardo answered. "Mr. President, I think it could be very significant, on the order of a small army. In Mexico, the former President had a strategy of attacking the cartels by going after its leaders personally. However, the one cartel that benefitted from this strategy and found itself in the strongest position is the Cartel of Sinaloa. You recall that the head of this cartel escaped from a high security federal prison and eluded capture while he directed the activities of the cartel. He has been protected not only by common people, but also by corrupted officials in the government and in the military. I believe that whatever attack might occur in Mexico City, it will be very strategic and focused and well supported by fire power."

"Ok, gentlemen, is there any possibility of alliances by cartels for the purpose of armed confrontations with the Mexican Armed Forces?"

Again Eduardo responded. "Yes, there's a history of cartel alliances from time to time, usually short lived because of the competitive factions. These people are hijos de putas and criminals with no respect for human life. They use everyone to achieve short-range goals. There are very few sacred cows to them."

The President addressed his next comment to the General.

"General Alvarez, this is a very dangerous scenario that deeply concerns me. There are people climbing all over my ass here in the United States that we have a fast resolution to this unacceptable situation in Mexico. Congressmen. The Chiefs of Staff. My agency directors. We have the news media and public interest groups and human rights people all up in arms not only here in the United States, but globally. I would like to make a couple of suggestions to you after thinking about our earlier conversation this morning and some of the comments you made to me."

"Thank you, Mr. President" answered General Alvarez. "Go on."

"First, it stands to reason that the United States should offer assistance to you in the form of military weaponry and troop support to help maintain the public peace and to strengthen public safety measures. We should do this especially in the face of the possibility of civil war with the organized crime cartels in Mexico. There are too many guns and weapons down there in their hands. I know what you're thinking, that most of these came from the United States, but it is what it is, and it's a reality we must confront now.

"Second, we need a coordinated strategy between Mexico and the United States regarding how we handle things at the border between our two countries, and what measures we take if there's civil war in Mexico, particularly if there are attacks upon the border by the cartels or any other armed groups.

"Third, I think it would be a good idea for you to call upon certain international organizations to lend assistance with public

310

services, public safety, and emergency preparations for regions that might suffer if armed conflict and broken food supply chains occur.

"Finally, it's extremely important that you announce a date for elections to take place in Mexico and to make preparations for those elections. If I were in your shoes, after making so many assurances to the Mexican people that this military coup is for their public safety and that the purpose is to restore democracy that isn't co-opted by the drug cartels, I would get this date out there now. Give your people a hook they can hang their hat on. Otherwise, you're going to have worse nervousness not only within Mexico, but also internationally. Your small Armed Forces won't be able to handle millions of Mexican citizens climbing all over your tanks and trucks. You understand what I mean by all this, I'm sure, General."

The General answered immediately, "Yes, Mr. President, and I basically am in agreement with what you're saying." He paused to collect his thoughts. "I'll return now to Mexico City with David and Eduardo. This is the first urgency. I would like to continue this dialog with you over the next hours and days as we come to understand what El Gato is up to. I'll discuss with my advisors your recommendations, and with David and Eduardo, and we'll see if we might need military assistance from the United States. We would try to avoid that, of course, but I can assure you that we'll do whatever it takes to protect the Mexican people. I thank you for your offers and for your suggestions. Give me these hours, and we'll talk again and share latest developments and intelligence. With respect to setting a date for elections, that has always been my intention, but I'm hearing you suggest this as a means to calm the international community and also people within Mexico, if this is done very soon."

"Yes."

Eduardo spoke now. "I've had some thoughts regarding government structure while the electoral processes are decided, and I'll share these with the General." He said this to let the President know that he and David hadn't had time to breach the subject of appointing an Interim President, and that they would follow through with this.

"Excellent, Eduardo," answered the President. Then he said, "David, on a personal note, I know you're concerned about the safety of Ana Valdez, as we all are, and I assure you I'll be attentive to any actions or resources you might need for her liberation."

David responded with his thanks, but the President heard behind his words what David was truly thinking:

Thank you, Donnie, I hear you, and you bet your ass if you have a way of helping me, I'm calling on you, and I don't give a shit about international protocol. This is my Ana.

Chapter 20: Preparations

Monterrey
Early Tuesday Morning

"Enrique, este hombre está muy encabronado," the Z on the phone said to Enrique as Enrique headed to Eduardo's ranch. "He's one pissed off man." He was speaking of Rafael, who had received the children and then withdrew behind the walls of his house. As Enrique requested, some Zs stood guard outside Ana's home, and this one stayed inside the house. Already a couple of reporters appeared there, trying to locate Ana to get some statements from her regarding the protests that suddenly were strengthening again. Her absence from her blogs and Twitter account was noticed.

Rafael refused to talk to anyone. He hardly spoke to the Z inside the house, the one who talked to Enrique on the phone.

"All I can tell you is that the man is in fortification mode, dug in his trench," said the Z. "He's making the children stay in one of the bedrooms; he has shut off all the electronics; he doesn't want anyone near the house; and the only thing he said when I told him that the cartel now had his wife was, 'Well, then let David James get her out of there. She likes him so much. Let her see what he can do for her. I'm going to keep my kids safe.' He then went back in the bedroom with the children."

David told Enrique to pack some clothes quickly in a bag for a trip of a couple days and then to come to the ranch as soon as possible. Enrique hardly recognized the place when he drove up. It was dark and now about three in the morning. Military vehicles of all types were stationed in front of the house. He saw the dark silhouettes of soldiers everywhere. One of the guards at the driveway entrance examined his identification. He obviously was expecting him, told him where to park, and had a soldier escort him to the main sala where David greeted him with a hug replete with emotion. *We share the urgency of freeing Ana,* Enrique thought. He also felt David's love. When he broke away, he saw the water in his eyes. The man looked exhausted.

It's too much too fast, all this that is happening.

David brought him to a study that was free of people. He glimpsed General Alvarez conferring with some officers in the grand sala. David told him that Eduardo had retreated to a bedroom for a few hours' sleep before they would take a helicopter to Mexico City. David had dozed a couple of hours on the same sofa where he had been talking to Eduardo and the General, in the midst of all the lights and noise of the command center set up in there.

Enrique felt fidgety and wired from drinking coffee and from the pure exhaustion of trying to calm his nerves so many hours. Inside his skin, he felt a manic boxer dancing. It would help his jitters to throw punches, but instead he punched out sentences in English:

"David, it's loco out there. It's getting harder to find internet. I drive and find a few spots but they need passwords. I still had internet in my apartment. The social media are all lit up about Ana. Where is she? Why isn't she posting? So I've been posting, making calls to the Z cells, trying to be visible. I can't do it fast enough. Everyone asks about Ana. Her blogs are saturated with comments and theories about where she is. Mothers for Peace are begging her to come out of hiding. They're urging her to lead the nation! No Más Sangre, same thing from them.

"What's happening with the demonstrations? Any violence?"

"The Zs are reporting more confrontations between demonstrators and soldiers in several cities. Some of the demonstrators have pistols and may be hired by the cartels. Others are civilians yelling at the soldiers and throwing rocks. People are starting to turn on the soldiers. It's not so bad here in Monterrey yet, but Mexico City is very tense. The Zs there are reporting troop movements, and they also see narco vehicles arriving in caravans. In the outskirts, guys are shooting automatic rifles into the air from the back of pickup trucks!"

"I'm concerned about that in particular, Enrique. It's the middle of the night. Isn't it quiet in the Zócalo?"

"It's packed in there. Seems to be student groups. Some are shouting about freeing the government, and others are demanding immediate elections. The soldiers have to keep pushing the kids back from the National Palace."

Enrique took a breath, and David pointed to a chair for him to sit.

When he did, David asked him, "What about the area around Los Pinos, where the President's home is?"

"There are soldiers completely surrounding and patrolling the streets around Los Pinos, Chapultepec Forest, and Chapultepec Castle," Enrique answered. "The soldiers have cordoned off the roads around there. Still, there are many people lining the streets across from the soldiers. There are armed men going into buildings in the blocks around the cordoned zone. Tonight a lot of the military vehicles have been moving around, entering the grounds and the little roads in the forest."

Enrique remembered this area of Mexico City well. He could visualize, even in nightscape, the grounds of Los Pinos with its Presidential House occupied by Pedro Navarro and his family. He remembered el Bosque Chapultepec, the forest, with its little roads winding through to the massive castle on a high hill from which can be seen much of Mexico City. It was el Castillo de Chapultepec. The castle had served many purposes since its construction, notably as the Military Academy in 1833, and later modified to be the home of Emperor Maximilian I of Mexico and his wife Empress Carlotta in 1864. Perhaps most importantly, the castle was the site of the glorified deaths of Mexico's six "Boy Heroes," who died September 13, 1847 defending the castle from the siege of the United States forces in the Mexican-American War.

He saw David staring off, thinking. He felt the boxer dancing anxiously inside him. It made him breathless and nervous. He couldn't wait longer to ask what was on his mind.

"David, what are we going to do about Ana? Tell me where we're going!" he demanded.

The distant look in David's green eyes focused and turned on him.

"We're going to Mexico City, Enrique," David answered. "Your home town. You, me, General Alvarez, and Eduardo. El Gato has a mission there, and it will be the place where we get Ana back."

El Gato had slept lightly, so when the alarm on his cell phone sounded at 2:00 a.m. he was awake and thinking in bed. He shut it off, and as he did, a text message arrived. The light from the phone illuminated the bed around him as he read. It was simply a phone number with "3:00 a.m." written beside it. It was from the Zeta. He got up and went to the bathroom, then opened the door to his bedroom and saw light coming from the kitchen. He smelled new coffee. He ambled down the hall and encountered El Contador pouring a cup near the sink.

He told him, "Go wake up our prisoner downstairs and escort her to the shower. Tell her to prepare for the flight. We leave soon. She has to hurry. I want to be at the plane at 3:00 am. Have a bag for her with some of our ladies' clothes in it. Meet me in the garage in fifteen minutes."

He got his coffee and returned to the bedroom and switched on the light. He saw his own bag at the foot of the bed. It was open, and inside on top of the clothes was the journal that he carried everywhere with him still. Annie's writing. He thought about her. He considered how strange it was that Ana Valdez reminded him so much of her. It wasn't the way she looked physically so much, but her mannerisms were very similar to his sister's. Talking to her brought memories of Annie alive that he had long forgotten.

He retrieved his toiletries and went into the bathroom and began to shave at the sink. He thought about Ana again.

The famous Ana Valdez. Maybe the Joan of Arc of Mexico. Frigging beautiful whore. Did I really deceive her with that message?

He felt confident that the message would have the intended effect. He had picked the word "mission," and she put it in the text to David, just as he wanted. He had told her about going to Mexico City before. It took him a few minutes when the two of them were writing the message to figure out how Ana was alerting David to the location, but then he noticed the words, "desnudos fuera." She put those words in Spanish, while the rest of the message had been in English. This puzzled him until he realized the "d" and the "f" were the code for Distrito Federal. So he was right about Ana. She was clever and definitely would try to clue her lover. So he thought about what he wanted her to send. She did it perfectly. From "Distrito Federal," it would be a simple crossing of a mental bridge to deduce

316

that Pedro Navarro was the objective of the mission. He wanted David and the Army to know that.

El Gato had had several conversations with the Zeta since the previous morning. The man sent text messages with a different phone number each time, letting him know when to contact him. He was clever also. He was working with an enemy who wanted to kill him, but so far he trusted what the Zeta did. He was rounding up equipment and manpower.

From the very beginning he told El Gato that the time frame for the logistics of attacking the Army at Los Pinos was too short. The Zeta said they couldn't move enough of their crude armored vehicles to Chapultepec, and they didn't have enough time to round up the ex-Special Forces Zetas with the talent to drop from helicopters onto the roof of the Presidential home. El Gato had been overly optimistic. Still, he pushed, and each call from the Zeta brought news of more gunmen and armored trucks arriving to add to the growing numbers in Mexico City. All El Gato wanted now was enough fire power to keep the Army busy when he initiated the strategic operation to take the President and his family.

He was lost in his thoughts when suddenly he noticed himself in the bathroom mirror. He was aroused. Thinking about guns and winning always excited him. He reached in his pants and held his cock. It enlarged more. He pulled down the jeans he had slept in, and then his underpants. *I have a big one and still useful even at this age.* He took off his shirt and admired himself. *Not bad. I still have muscles. I'm still guapo, verdad?* He thought about the photos of himself he used to leave for his sister Annie to see, and he laughed. *I'm a bold man. I bet Señora Valdez would be impressed. Haha, she wouldn't like me, but she would be impressed. Well, maybe I'll just impress her.* He laughed again. He finished shaving with his pants bunched down at his feet.

He had to think about what to tell the Zeta at 3:00 am, and that was in only forty minutes. They had to leave now to get to the plane. The Zeta was already in Mexico City.

He quickly slipped back into his clothes, threw his razor in the shaving bag, tossed it in the overnight bag by his bed, and hastened to the garage. He checked the car trunk for weapons. He retrieved a 9 mm pistol, hung it on his belt, put on a jacket from the trunk, and slid into the driver's seat to wait for El Contador and Ana.

He became pissed because they were taking too long. He checked his watch for the third time. It was already twenty-nine minutes to 3:00 am. *Shit!* He would have to talk to the Zeta in the car in front of Ana Valdez.

He got out the car to go inside to find them, but at that moment the false door to the garage opened, and El Contador and Ana emerged from the steps. Ana's hair was still wet from the shower. She was handcuffed and blindfolded. El Gato shot a look of irritation to El Contador for taking so long, then he got back in the driver's seat. El Contador helped Ana get in the rear seat, and then he took the other side.

At this time of the morning the streets were relatively clear. El Gato drove a few kilometers and took a secondary road leading out of the city to a little used country road. Several kilometers there he would pull over and park, and then the three of them would cross a dark field where the small plane awaited them. This was a field the cartel had used for a couple of weeks. It was necessary constantly to find new places suitable for landing in Monterrey when the cartel didn't want to use the hangars in the smaller airport there. At times those were watched by rivals, Federales, DEA agents, or by God knows who.

El Gato checked the rear mirror to see Ana in the back seat. She pretended to be sleeping. He looked at the time on the dash. Just a couple of minutes before 3:00 a.m. and he was just at the beginning of the secondary road. His boss scheduled the plane for him and wouldn't like it that he was late. He'll know too. He checks everything. He could pull over and talk to the Zeta away from the car, but that would take more time. He considered whether to talk in front of Ana.

Shit, what difference does it make? I'll be watching her every move. She can't communicate to anyone unless I let her.

At 3:00 am he punched the number of the Zeta in his phone while he continued driving.

The Zeta had asked him how he planned to get the Army guarding the President to move him. Always the most vulnerable moments are those in which someone is being moved to another place. When El Gato realized that they wouldn't have enough weaponry and manpower to defeat the Army in a head on battle at Los Pinos, he came up with the idea of forcing the Army to move the

318

President. He thought it would be perfect to have Ana Valdez send a message to David that certainly would be shared with General Alvarez. He needed David and the General to know that Pedro Navarro was the object of the mission at Los Pinos. If they expected an attack there, they would move the President to safety elsewhere.

So now when he told the Zeta about Ana's message and its design to get the President moved, the Zeta asked, "Where will they transfer him?"

"I don't know yet," responded El Gato. "I have an insider who will find that out. It doesn't matter a fuck where, hombre. We'll get him when he goes anywhere. They'll try to move him either by air or land. Either way, they have to get the family out the house. They can't keep them safe there, so close to the roads in the city. If they choose to move them by car, it's possible that they'll put the President in one and his family in a second. He'll come with us cooperatively because he knows us and that we're rescuing him, and the lives of his family depend on cooperating with us. Once we go for them, we have to make sure that none of them gets hurt."

"What about the Castle?" asked the Zeta. "They may move the family there. It's right there and it's defensible from its high ground. Wouldn't that be the simplest thing to do?"

"It's the National Museum of History now," El Gato answered lamely.

Damn, I sound stupid. That would be a natural place, close by, and hell, yes, they can put living quarters in there. It's not like tourists have been able to go there these past few days.

He quickly added, "But you're right. That would be a smart place and the move could be done with lightning speed."

He glanced in the mirror again at Ana as he continued driving. She was leaning against the window. El Gato shook his head at the thought that she was pretending to be asleep.

Careful, Roberto, she's a dangerous woman. He straightened. *Roberto? Why did I call myself that?*

He remembered that Ana had come out of the back of the police car and had leapt from one car to another and then outran his men into the park. He glanced in the mirror while the Zeta spoke on the phone. He looked at El Contador. At least he looked awake. He shot a glance back at Ana. Her hair was drying and falling over her face. She looked harmless, blindfolded, and with her hands cuffed behind

319

her back. In his view of her in the mirror she was sexy, erotic, a woman in bondage.

Yes, Gato, remember she's dangerous. She created the Zs. She took the Z training. She knows how to kill without firing a gun. She's the voice of hope for all the protest movements in Mexico. Everyone looks up to her. I can never release her. She has become too dangerous a leader.

He heard the Zeta talking: "Okay, assuming we successfully capture Navarro, your plan is to deliver him to the President of the United States. How exactly will you do that?"

El Gato had withheld information from the Zeta. He fed him bits of information with each call. He was as vague as he could be for as long as he could be. Now it was time for a direct answer:

"We'll be helped by David James, the Z leader who is a close friend of President Blair. He'll help us because we have Ana Valdez. He'll do anything to save her. He'll want and need his powerful friend to help him."

"I suspected as much," answered the Zeta. "Listen, my new friend, we're running out of time. This border situation is creating problems for us more quickly than we anticipated. That border fence is bulging with people losing their tempers. In Laredo some truckers began crashing their rigs into Border Patrol vehicles and moved closer to the International Bridge. Everyone wants those check points opened up. A lot of people think the United States will invade. All these things that we're doing, shooting in our towns here in Mexico today, paying people to harass the soldiers: it's working quickly, like you told me it would. Too quickly. You wanted to make it look like we're having a civil war here. Well, it's working. It's scaring the shit out of the gringos. We have to deliver Navarro to the United States fast."

Shit! thought El Gato. The whole idea was to make people think that there was no popular support for the military coup! Then the United States would accept the rescue of Navarro, and the cartel would look heroic for accomplishing it. More than heroic: they would look like players on the international stage. But the Zeta was right again. The mission to free Navarro from the coup had to be done before anyone else attempted it. Someone, for example, like the United States!

El Gato tried to reassure the Zeta. "I'm positive they'll try to move the President within the next several hours. If they want to do it in darkness, they have run out of time today. It will be light in a couple of hours. So they would have to wait another twelve to fifteen hours for darkness again. They won't wait that long. They'll attempt the move in broad daylight. So let's review what we'll do when this happens:

"We feint an attack on the Army and then take the Navarro family when they try to move them out of the battle zone. I have responsibility for getting them to the United States by working through David James. Once we have liberated Navarro, we do our public relations work, showing who is boss down here in Mexico, who really wants the Republic restored, and who will take action to do it. We do our press and marketing releases. We hang our mantas in all the cities and villages of Mexico. The world already notices the demonstrators we put in the streets to demand the government of Mexico be freed. The people of Mexico are watching. These groups who have been protesting the violence, the impunity, the lack of security, they all see this. Everyone begins to understand that the people of Mexico don't want the military coup. Those people who have been uncertain that the coup is a good thing will decide that it's wrong for the Armed Forces to overthrow the government, even if it was a corrupt one. They'll say that the voters should replace the leaders, not the soldiers.

"What will they see when we attack and rescue the Presidential family? We show how weak the military is, once again. They could never defeat the cartels before, and they can't do it even when they run the government. The cartels are the ones who determine whether the country has stability or not. We decide whether there's violence or not. We completely discredit the military and the leaders of the coup. We humiliate them. The United States and the countries of the world have sympathy for Navarro and want him restored.

"When I contact David James, I'll condition Navarro's release to the United States on their opening of the borders and the promise by their President not to invade. When the coup fails, the generals and officers and all those having responsibility for the coup will be arrested. While President Blair is deciding what to do, as Navarro and his family are received into the United States, we, the Cartel of Sinaloa, will unleash a wave of violence in large gringo cities to show them that we're a force even there. We can pull the triggers in Chicago, Atlanta, Houston, Los Angeles, New Orleans, Norfolk and so many cities. The gringos will be shocked how their own government and police forces have been asleep while we worked. They'll see they're no better than Mexico. I'll promise the President of the United States to end that violence when he keeps his promise to open the border and not to invade."

The Zeta didn't say anything for a minute. El Gato knew he was digesting all this. The Zeta was a smart man. El Gato had told him a lot in a few sentences. He would understand. During the pause, El Gato began to think about the information the Zeta had given him at the beginning of their conversation: How many men the Zetas had available in the city. How many vehicles, guns, grenade and rocket launchers. Their locations and availability for fight. He calculated the size of their growing army by adding what the Cartel of Sinaloa had in Mexico City.

"If I follow this logic," said the Zeta finally, "then you believe that when President Navarro is in the United States, he'll publicly clamor to return to Mexico, and he'll have the support of that country. You believe then the coup will crumble. Don't you think Navarro will want the United States' forces to invade to defeat the military here? He should be hot for revenge."

"We'll have him a little while to explain things to him," replied El Gato. "The thing is, once he and his family are there, you know Mexican sentiment will be for the Armed Forces to give up. I'm sure there will be defections even among soldiers. They'll see the futility of the coup, and they'll fear what will happen to them when the coup fails. The United States doesn't have to invade. Diplomatic pressure, plus just the possibility of the United States or an international force coming in, will be enough to obtain surrender. Mexico is a republic! Who in their right mind in this country will trust the military to restore the Republic when the President of Mexico and the strongest republic of the world constitute a better guarantee?"

El Gato felt an adrenalin rush from his own speech. He thought the Zeta was eating from his hand.

He continued, "Look, things will deteriorate quickly here. As it stands now, the Armed Forces need time to learn how to run public services. They have to instill confidence in the banking system here quickly. What experience do they have to do this? The markets, the economy, and the employment of people are all in great peril right now. Even if the generals are allied with some of the wealthiest business leaders in the country, who is going to reassure the common man? Every day the people of Mexico will wake up and be anxious as they think of these things and what isn't going so well in their lives. They'll believe that their government may not have always served or protected them before, but they had a country running nevertheless. What people really want are stability and predictability. With the military and the government off the backs of the cartels, we can give Mexico the stability that the people crave. Hombre, as I've told you before, once we scale back the violence and run our businesses in smart ways, then we have a world of unimaginable riches awaiting us."

"Sí," the Zeta agreed. He paused again and then changed the subject. "Okay, we have our special vehicles in Mexico City now to help with this mission. They're incredibly effective. They overcome blockades and resist very strong firepower, including grenades. Only direct hits by rockets would be problematic. I was able to get these here to Mexico City. Our custom made Zeta specials."

"Good," replied El Gato. "We'll probably need one copter also."

"I have one. It can take some hits. It's here in Mexico City now. We borrowed it recently from the Jalisco State Police," the Zeta answered, and he laughed. "Es una madre! What a mother! S-70i Black Hawk. That state is out 6 million dollars. This bird can take El Presidente and his family up north easily, in the style to which they have become accustomed. So contact me when you arrive here. When we hang up, I'll text you a number you can reach me from this time forward. Answer it so we know we're in touch. While you're traveling here, we'll continue to set up for the attack and to monitor activity in Los Pinos. Let me know of any urgent intelligence you receive, and I'll do the same. Otherwise, we'll talk when you're here and decide next steps."

When they hung up El Gato was turning on to the little country road that ran alongside the field they were using as an airstrip. He felt exhilarated by what lay ahead and so happy to be working with a partner of quick comprehension like the Zeta, enemy or not. The thrill in his pants returned. He couldn't resist one last look at Ana in the mirror before he would have to "awaken" her. He had no doubt she had listened to the entire conversation.

He saw how fetching she looked in her bindings. He couldn't help thinking: I wonder if I'll have opportunity to fuck her before I kill her, like David did my sister?

The thought made him get harder.

Chapter 21: The Battle of Chapultepec

Monterrey and Mexico City
Tuesday

David knew that before Enrique arrived he must have dozed a few times, because the evening seemed to have passed so quickly into the pre-dawn hours while the General conferred with officers both in Monterrey and in Mexico City. Eduardo had slept in his bedroom. Then suddenly the General was ready to go. Quickly they grabbed their things and piled into the truck to carry them to the training field where the helicopter awaited. As David bounced in his seat, he stared at the Mexican black sky doming Monterrey. There was no moon, only stars, and not enough atmospheric disturbance to set those twinkling. He took time to look into the heavens even in the day, when occasionally the moon surprised, posing dimly in the blue refraction of the sun's light.

He remembered a rare peaceful afternoon with Ana, when the two of them lay on a hilltop after a private picnic in the springtime and gazed from the grass into a cloudless, azure sky. He realized something as they lay side by side, and he remarked to Ana, "One of the big differences in the sky I see here, compared to the sky I look at in Texas, is that often here I see no jets or planes. Mexico has nowhere near the flight traffic volume of the United States. When I look up back home, I always see jet trails drifting and crisscrossing overhead and almost always glimpse a plane, helicopter or jet. Look now, Ana, there's no trace of aircraft at all in the sky! There are no vapor trails, no moving sparkles of light from a passing jet, and today not even clouds. Nothing is blemishing our blue Mexican sky!"

He was pointing upward, and Ana took his arm and wrapped it around her shoulder. She noticed that her gringo had used the word, "our."

"If only our land were so unblemished," she answered softly.

Now as they reached the field, David saw the dark silhouette of the Black Hawk that would transport them. They would have nearly a three-hour flight. He imagined them in the dark, flying southwest, a moving, black, block of noise obscuring stars, with blinking lights to entertain anyone awake and looking from below. Soon the approaching dawn would crack the night sky. When they descended into Mexico City against the palette of sunrise colors, what an impressive vision they would be! The Black Hawk was as long as two first downs on an American football field, and its wingspan almost the same. What would the Mexicans on the ground be feeling these days to see this gigantic mechanical vulture swooping down with the words on its side, "Fuerza Aérea Mexicana"? The Mexican Air Force, a branch of their Army.

The thought of them soaring through the night sky caused him to wonder, *Would he and Ana both be flying in the same air space this night, rushing to Mexico City?* He glanced at his watch. It was nearly 4:00 a.m. He felt her somewhere close.

But El Gato was the one with her. As he, General Alvarez, Eduardo, and Enrique retrieved bags from the truck and began to walk to the Black Hawk, David turned his thoughts to El Gato. El Gato was taking on a mission possibly to do battle with the Army, and Pedro Navarro was his objective.

What is it precisely that El Gato wants to accomplish? he wondered. *Think, David. You know this man. You spent a youth with him, and you loved his sister. How does he rationalize? What would he be up to now?*

David's eyes were wide open as they boarded the helicopter. No one looking at him would realize that he was in another time and place. He was reviewing memories of his days with Roberto. He went back to the things they liked to do together; the bicycle rides, the horse rides, the board games they played with friends, the foot races, and, of course, the gymnastic meets. Immediately he recalled how competitive Roberto was, how he liked to win. No, it was more than that. He had to win, and when he didn't he became sullen and very quiet. He was older and physically more imposing than David in those days, and this had given Roberto...control over him. *I liked to please him,* David thought. *Why?* Then as the years went by, David saw Roberto become increasingly possessive of his sister. He thought that the lengths Roberto would go to in order to control access to her was sick. In the last year of high school Roberto began taking drugs and drinking. He became dark and even more sullen: someone present but emotionally distant and, increasingly, very cold.

Think, David. What was Roberto's primary characteristic in the dark side of his soul?

It came to him: *Control.*

He must have exhausted himself trying to control everything on the stage of our lives, David realized. *It did become crazy, didn't it? That was it!* Whatever the situation, Roberto was slave to his compulsion to observe and process the environment around him and then manage all of it: the game to be played, the players of the game, the rules of the game, the selection of game strategy, the order of execution, the minimization of chance.

There was a year in which a group of the kids, including David and Roberto, used to love to play the board game, "Risk," where the object is to conquer the world with your armies. Roberto always talked others into forming alliances to attack and defeat a strong enemy. He was good at getting people to do what they didn't want to do. When the enemy was sufficiently weakened, Roberto double-crossed his partner at the perfect strategic moment to remove both of them from the game.

Of course, the victor of this game ultimately has to break all alliances to be the sole winner, but Roberto's knack was to do it at a surprising time when his ally would still trust in the alliance. His allies would become upset, but Roberto would laugh and tell them that you have to do what it takes to win the game, and that loyalty was an expendable quality relevant only in times of opportunity. David had witnessed this behavior a thousand times, and so he never allowed himself to form alliances with Roberto in the games.

Roberto loves to fuck with people's emotions and betray them at a personal level, to disarm them and break them, David told himself. *That's why he took Ana, so he can put me on an emotional playing field that he has chosen, one to upset me because of its cruelty. If he reduces my reasoning abilities, he can better predict my behavior and control the outcome of the game. He wants revenge because I loved Annie at a time when he wanted her and couldn't have her. But this isn't just about revenge. There's more. He wants power over me to make me do something I wouldn't want to do.*

The engines started warming up as soon as the four of them seated themselves, along with several soldiers. They sat near each other so they could talk. As the noise increased, they had to shout. They were tired, and this taxed their voices.

During the brief truck ride, General Alvarez was busy on the radio, but on board the helicopter now, he summoned the attention of Eduardo, Enrique, and David. He announced, "In the last few hours, there are a lot of weaponry and men coming into the central area of Mexico City in the vicinity of the Zócalo all the way to Los Pinos and Chapultepec. These men are disappearing into homes and businesses in that area. I've ordered that some troops do reconnaissance in the city blocks surrounding Los Pinos to determine if these are cartel men, how well equipped they might be, and how many there are. However, I can't leave remaining troops protecting the grounds of Los Pinos and the Forest spread too thinly. Just a few kilometers away, near the Palacio Nacional, there are student activists creating a lot of noise and disturbance. It's strange that they're out and organized so late. Not being there, it has been difficult for me to get from my men a reading on the degree of problems that might be developing, but my gut doesn't like it at all."

"How many soldiers do you have there, General?" David asked.

"About fifteen hundred are in the central downtown area," he responded.

"Doesn't seem like a lot," David said. He thought he recalled that the Armed Forces only had a total of a couple hundred thousand troops in all Mexico. Their organizational mission was to preserve peace in Mexico and to assist localities in times of national disaster, and, historically, to combat the drug trade. Mexico's policy of non-involvement in foreign affairs and wars rendered large military bodies unnecessary.

The General responded, "In total around Mexico City there are about eighty thousand troops in the brigades. I'm speaking of the number now in the historic district. The problem is that the city is very dense and congested, and the area we're concerned with is highly concentrated," replied General Alvarez. "It's a problem also for the cartels if they're trying to move men into the area. When we took over, we didn't anticipate that there would be any large scale effort to free the President or to assassinate him. We wanted him to be comfortable with his family in their home while we organized to take the reins of government and to provide public services."

"Then what were you planning to do with him?" Enrique asked. He had been quiet, and his question startled the General, who turned to his right to face him. David softly chuckled to himself. Enrique was like a naïve kid asking the question the adults were too polite to ask.

"To free him and his family, and all the ones we've quarantined, just as soon as we have a handle on things and we're set to announce elections. We plan to have electoral commissions set up in the cities of Mexico under the aegis of a national organization that establishes the rules that will ensure an honest, safe, and secure electoral process," the General answered. The General looked at Eduardo, signaling him to make some comment.

David listened to Eduardo's response, hearing him, but also thinking again about Roberto. Eduardo went on to talk about the elite team of business owners and public servants behind the military coup, and that all of them had intended to upend what they considered fraudulent elections of corrupted cartel cronies to positions of public trust. People who had ruined Mexico, Eduardo said.

But David was working logic in his head:

If it isn't entirely revenge motivating El Gato, then what is it that Roberto wants me to do? He's on the way to Mexico City with Ana on some mission to encounter Pedro Navarro. The President of Mexico has a history of close ties to the Cartel of Sinaloa. Does Roberto want to take him or to assassinate him? He strained to think of a reason why El Gato would want to kill Pedro Navarro now during this time of turbulence and international attention and could find no reason where it made sense to kill him.

So let's rule out killing him. If he takes him... David felt something dawning inside him... *it would be to pressure the attempted legitimacy of the coup by its leaders in the court of public opinion...that of the Mexicans...and that of the world...and in particular, that of the United States... which is controlling the border...and, yes, of course, El Gato knows that I'm a completely trusted friend of President Blair... and...oh, God...oh, God...then he has Ana and Navarro, and he has me front and center to help him!*

*He wants to have Navarro free to lead a rebellion against the coup!
He wants the United States to back him!*

He could feel the blood draining from his face as his body went cold as a dead heart. He realized the revenge part of Roberto's plan.

*After he uses me and things are going his way, he'll kill Ana.
He'll make sure I'm alive to know it.*

They were about to lift off. He heard Eduardo telling the General that to take control of events which were now spiraling out of control, the General must secure public trust by announcing the appointment of an interim government with civilian leadership, and that this civilian interim government must be supported by the Armed Forces. But David couldn't concentrate on that because inside him he felt desperation rising like a black-clad assassin.

He tried to calm himself. As soon as Eduardo finished saying that Mexico needed an Interim President, he reached over and grasped the General's right forearm and shouted, "General, please stop the helicopter! I have to stay here!"

The General looked totally confused from the sudden interruption. David repeated, "I'll explain. Please order the helicopter to stop!"

While the engine was shutting down, David reached for a memory when he had caught Roberto off guard. He remembered the afternoon when he walked the distance to Roberto's and Annie's house and found Roberto caring for his horse in the stable in the back. He made surface cuts on their fingers and announced that they were blood brothers as the red made little streams on their hands. He mixed their blood, and when he looked into Roberto's eyes, he had the satisfaction of seeing brief tears there. He had wanted to get to him. He had wanted Roberto disarmed completely by doing this unexpected thing, something Roberto would never anticipate. It was a moment when things were good and neither of them could foresee the divergence of their paths ahead, when Roberto later would fall into the abyss that eventually transformed him into El Gato. David knew there was no salvation for him now.

But I know my only shot to save Ana is to trick Roberto into a game where he plays on my home field. I need him to come in with one cat eye blind, still thinking that everyone is in his field. I was caught off guard on the roof. The next time there can be no failure, or this lady, the love of my life, is gone! The consequences to history of Ana's absence from the world...Jesus, I can't let this happen!

The engines died, and the only sound on the Black Hawk was the soft creaking of soldiers shifting in their seats. David heard the night breezes cuffing the sides of the helicopter. Eduardo, Enrique, and the General were staring at him with *what-the-hell-is-going on* faces. Nevertheless, he breathed long and deep and took the time he needed to complete his ideas.

Finally he told them, "I'll explain this. Enrique, Eduardo and I need to remain here near the border. El Gato isn't going to assassinate Pedro Navarro. He's going to kidnap him and try to get him out of the country to the United States! He'll use me to help him. I know what we need to do."

He paused several long seconds so the other three could digest what he had said. Then David looked directly into the General's eyes.

"General Alvarez, it's very important you tell me how you're going to safeguard Pedro Navarro and his family."

The General had enough experience with David to trust him completely and didn't hesitate to answer. First, he ordered all the soldiers off the helicopter, and when just the four of them remained on board he said, "I've spent the last several hours discussing with my officers different alternatives, but we settled on moving them to El Castillo Chapultepec. The castle is the museum now, but it's easy to convert a section into living quarters that are easily secured. As you can imagine, the castle is a much easier place to defend the security of the Navarro family. It's a short distance from where they are now, and that transfer bears the least risk in moving the family. At this very time, living spaces for the family are being created in the castle. We can move them through the roads passing through the forest to the long access ramp that climbs the cliff to the building."

"Is there any possibility there's anyone in Los Pinos working for the cartels who can find out the plans and pass on this information to them?"

"David, this is Mexico. We've been taking all precautions, and, of course, I wouldn't think so, but I've learned not to be surprised by anything," answered the General.

David nodded. He respected the General for being honest. He observed the curious expressions of Eduardo and Enrique and then continued speaking to the General.

"Let's assume that you do have an informant who leaks information. Let's assume that the cartel becomes aware you're going to transfer the Navarro family to the castle. Their best chance of success in getting them is to try to take them when they're being transferred. To minimize loss of life, because the cartel will attempt the kidnapping, the transfer should be done soon, within hours, before they have more time to bring even more weapons and men to the area."

Looking at everyone, David said, "Ok, gentlemen, here's the thing. Trust me on this: We must let the kidnapping be successful! We have to let them succeed without it appearing that we're allowing this to happen. At the same time, it has to be done in a way that few people are hurt, to the extent this is possible. So when the transfer of the family to the castle takes place, and that's when they attack and succeed in kidnapping them, we let them implement their plan. They'll have an escape planned, and that plan must work. I'm one hundred percent certain that the first person El Gato contacts after this will be me. For my ideas to work, we're going to need the help of President Blair. I know he will help us. I have to be near the border when El Gato contacts me. The border is the next place El Gato will go."

The expression on the face of the General said, *David, have you lost your fucking mind?*

But David knew that very shortly he would completely win the General's confidence. He had a plan that the General would like. All he had to do was to ask the General a few questions, and the General's own answers would bring him right on board. He started with this one:

"General, bear with me. Let me ask you a few questions. I'll start with this one. Do you agree that Ana Valdez is an icon of leadership and integrity in Mexico?"

The General nodded gravely and signaled with a slight raise of his hand for David to continue.

He was so creepy, El Gato, and if she had an opportunity to kill him, she would do it knowing that she had rid her country of a cancerous tumor that had sapped so much of its vitality. In the past day, El Gato had kept Ana beside him continuously, except for the brief hours she had been allowed to sleep before they departed Monterrey. On the flight to Mexico City, he let her cuffs be removed, but he had the seat beside her. Sometimes he brushed her hair from her face and tried to rub the back of his palm on her cheek. He just stared at her before he did it, and three times she pushed his hand away, and he stared at her again with disgusting smiles. He did it to violate her, she knew, and he would do far worse later when he had the chance. Now they were on a flight back to Monterrey after the most shocking twenty-four hours of her life in Mexico City. She realized how revolted she must be by this man. After all that she had seen and experienced in the past day, when she settled in her seat on the small plane for the return trip, it was El Gato's malicious caresses that she hated the most.

They lifted off, and as they rose, she thought of him beside her in the plane, and she wanted to vomit. He had kept her with him even in the fury of the battle in the Forest of Chapultepec, in that damned armored SUV which made her so motion sick while El Gato maneuvered across the grounds with bullets pinging everywhere and grenades exploding nearby, and then later as El Gato made their escape through the city. There were three gunmen in the back. One remained with her when El Gato left the vehicle and directed the men who were charging the limousine that carried the President of Mexico and his family through the Chapultepec Forest. It was shocking what she saw. The army trucks immediately before and after the Presidential car were in flames, hit by launched grenades. Blocked in the front and the rear, the Presidential car had to halt. It was broad daylight but the fires were bright orange. What was scaring her as she observed all the commotion was that the trees in the forest around them seemed to be exploding and catching fire. That made an impression and also the metallic sounds of the bullets thudding against the car she was in. It was all loud and terrifying.

Cartel members firing their weapons went running from the trees towards the soldiers who had come from their trucks and lined the road behind their vehicles. But then firing started from the forest behind the soldiers, and they were caught in a vice. Ana saw several of them fall. El Gato and the men in her car jumped out and joined their compadres. El Gato began leading the charge. Ana heard a larger battle behind her, coming from the rear of the Presidential Residence. It sounded like a bombardment. At the time that El Gato ran to the Presidential limousine, she was alone except for one gunman behind her whom El Gato commanded to remain to guard her.

"If she tries to escape, shoot her," he had told the man.

El Gato looked fearless. She saw that he was an expert marksman. In fact, the men shooting with him were doing a good job picking off the soldiers. The soldiers had to fire in two directions, and they looked desperate. There were two trucks ahead of the limousine, and she counted four behind it. The soldiers from the rear two vehicles saw an opening for retreat down the President's Way, in the direction of the President's Residence. They began backing and firing as the cartel shooters shot the soldiers ahead of them. As far as Ana could tell, only two or three from the cartel's forces took hits. Once the soldiers began retreating, El Gato's men pushed forward, firing their automatic weapons furiously. Then, incredibly, when El Gato reached the Presidential limousine, he opened the front passenger door. Ana glimpsed through the opened door the astonished look of the President, and then the two of them had a conversation that must have lasted at least forty-five seconds, an eternity after the thick of gunfire. Ana saw something else, and the impression it made on her was so forceful that she heard herself think it: *Navarro knows El Gato! He recognized him!*

The gunfire there stopped, but Ana still heard battles in different places around them. Suddenly the President got out, and in a very animated way he motioned to his family in the seats behind him to follow. What Ana saw next was the weirdest sight of her life, that of the President of Mexico, his wife, and two pre-teenage sons running, bent low, towards the vehicles where she was. Men directed the President's family into an armored SUV beside them, and Pedro Navarro climbed into the front of the one Ana was in, next to El Gato. El Gato returned to the car running backwards, sweeping his weapon from left to right. Several of his men moved in a similar fashion, ready to provide a cover for the President's family and themselves should it be necessary. From the trees in the distance there came no firing, and Ana supposed it was because someone had the presence of mind to think about the safety of the family and had ordered no shooting.

Later, in the grueling getaway, Ana had the distinct displeasure of throwing up behind the Mexican President. She remembered this as the plane ascended. Ana tried to stop the memories of those moments because she really felt like vomiting again. Next to her, El Gato smelled like day-old sweat and nausea, combining with new body odor caused by the heat in the plane, which had sat in the torrid sun in the small airfield outside Mexico City. He had that same smell in the SUV when they left the field of battle and went tearing through the congested and deadlocked city; lurching, braking, running up on sidewalks and medians, reversing, and turning. El Gato's men had maneuvered the SUVs through the trees from La Gran Avenida and had attacked the Presidential caravan while it was on the straight road, Calz del Rio, in the forest. Other cartel troops had already come into the forest on foot, and they were waiting for El Gato to signal the ambush. After the President and his family were in the SUVs, they made their escape by crunching their way through the trees to La Gran Avenida on the other side of Calz del Rio. On the way, the men fired at soldiers from the windows. The remaining cartel members retreated from the field of battle again on foot, returning in the opposite direction from where they had come.

The SUVs made it to Avenida Colegio Militar, and from there found the Peréfico Boulevard. At the turn onto this expressway, Ana saw behind her a visage of war: burned buses and trucks that had been set on fire in the middle of this expressway around the city to impede the Army's chase. Their escape had been facilitated by a ferocious moving shield of bullets and launched grenades coming from hundreds of men shooting at the soldiers in the complexes of Los Pinos. She saw two thickly armored dump trucks with oversized tires and lowered dirt movers in front, and she guessed that these were the special vehicles the Zeta had referred to in his conversation with El Gato. Beyond them was a pile of several civilian and military vehicles that the trucks had cleared out of the way so the kidnappers could access the Peréfico and make their escape. To the south and behind them, the Zeta's forces were waging war with the Army to keep them pinned in while El Gato and the driver of the other SUV got safely away.

The SUV was pitching violently as El Gato drove in the direction away from that mess, due to the debris and vehicles everywhere, and Ana did vomit. Some of it went out the window which El Gato had electronically lowered when she shouted she would get sick; but she was cuffed and could lean so far, so some of the sickness lumped along the crevice of the window and dripped down the inside of the door. The ride was merciless, punctuated by El Gato's non -stop obscenities. He and the gun man showed their weapons out the windows from time to time as an encouragement to get people to move from their path.

Pedro Navarro said nothing. He looked nervously around as if to spot someone who might fire a bullet into their SUV. He looked behind sometimes to try to see the other SUV carrying his wife and sons. Perhaps only ten minutes had passed when they arrived at a corner vacant lot several blocks from the Peréfico, but to Ana it seemed like she had passed an entire afternoon in nausea. In this area of the city were mostly rundown, concrete, single-story, small businesses. There were tire shops, produce markets, barbacoa stands, and cheap clothing stores, all marked up with layers of graffiti that documented the annual passages of gangs. But in the middle of the lot was a huge black helicopter surrounded by several old and dented minivans.

El Gato pulled the SUV into the lot and then turned to watch out the back window. About a minute later, the second SUV arrived, and when it did, Ana saw several men run to both vehicles to direct the President and his family into the helicopter. As they were boarding, El Gato suddenly appeared at her door and opened it and pulled her out so they could transfer into one of the minivans along with four gunmen who had come out of other cars. From there they had a more controlled ride to the air field where their plane awaited, along with the pilot who had brought them to Mexico City just twelve hours prior.

Thankfully, the air conditioning of the plane was kicking in, and its freshness let Ana collect herself somewhat. She began to put together what she had seen with what she had heard through El Gato's conversations on phones and radios. Being with him continuously, she heard everything. There was no doubt in her mind that if he were letting her hear everything, then he planned to kill her when her usefulness to him was over. There was only one occasion

336

on which El Gato had left her alone, and that was after he had put her on the plane. He stepped off, and she saw him outside on a cell phone, one that had been handed to him by a man standing by the plane. He had his back to her, and she couldn't see his face as he talked, but when he returned to the plane, he looked tense. He sat in his seat and immediately closed his eyes. He didn't say a word to anyone. She saw that he had enclosed himself in his anger.

There could only be one reason for that, she believed, and it was because he had just spoken to David over the phone. El Gato was just across the aisle from her, a very short distance away. She kicked his leg with her left foot to make him look at her. He opened his eyes like he was furious.

She didn't care. She had had enough. She told him, "I know all about you, Roberto Ortiz!"

His eyes filled with fire, but Ana continued. "You just talked with David on the phone, didn't you? Do you really think you're going to be able to outsmart your old friend? He's a full man. He's a gringo who has done more for his country and this country than you've done trying to destroy Mexico. I'm also a close and true friend of your father. Now there is a real patriot of Mexico! He doesn't know what happened to his son, his son Roberto, who died to him long before he disappeared. Now he knows about you, coward! Your father carries the honor of bearing the flag of Mexico, and all you have is the disgrace of destroying good lives, thousands and thousands of lives. He has no children, but he has the memory of a beautiful daughter who would have followed in his footsteps to build a legacy for our country. You're nothing but a coward who lives behind a mask and tries not to appear real."

Roberto bolted from his seat and swung his arm in a furious slap to the right side of her face. "Shut up, you complete whore!" he thundered, his own face redder even than Ana's. "Who the fuck do you think you are? You ..."

But Ana felt defiant, and the slap emboldened her, and she interrupted him, screaming her words.

"I won't be any good to you dead or hurt, imbecile, and you know this! Don't dare to touch me again! You really think David is coming to exchange his life for mine? Then be smart in the way you think you're smart. I'll tell you this. David isn't coming to give you his life. He'll come and steal yours!"

337

El Gato looked as if he could rip the seats bolted to the floor and hurl them out the windows of the plane. He raised his hand for another slap, but instead he stopped and let out a growl, and then spit in Ana's face. He threw himself back in his seat and closed his eyes and put his hands on his ears.

Ana felt herself shaking in rage. She was so angry that she wanted to cry, but she steeled herself. She forced herself to take long deep breaths.

I have to calm down. I have to observe and pay attention. I have to be able to alert others, and I have to be able to move if I get an opportunity. Tranquilo, Ana, tranquilo!

She wanted to think hard about the past few hours to understand it as best she could, because in those recollections might be the clues that would save her life or David's. Now the horrible noises of the battle were gone. In the whistling hum of the airplane cabin, El Gato was trying to doze off. Ana's vertiginous body began to stabilize and her nausea passed. That's when she examined what had been nagging her:

The successful kidnapping of Pedro Navarro and his family had been too easy.

Although it appeared that the cartel men around her, with their earlier jubilation and back thumping and hugging, didn't share this doubt. They obviously believed that they had implemented a well thought out plan to catch the Army by surprise.

Was it easy like I think? she asked herself. She gulped deep breaths of the fresh air blowing from the ventilation nozzle above her and reviewed what happened.

Someone inside the Presidential home in Los Pinos had leaked that at two p.m., Pedro Navarro's family would be moved in a caravan through the grounds and forest to El Castillo Chapultepec. El Gato had been in multiple communications after that with "El Zeta" and others in his command. He also spoke with his boss by phone, and that had been for Ana an eye-opening conversation. They talked about coordinating mass shootings in different cities in the United States after Navarro's kidnapping, and they discussed the possibility of using those attacks to leverage the President of the United States to open the border and defer sending troops into the north of Mexico. The top Sinaloan boss decided that commitment to an action like that could be made later. He wanted to see the outcome of the kidnapping first. During all the conversations, El Gato had referred to the plot as "la fiesta en Los Pinos."

When it was finalized, the plan seemed simple enough.

At fifteen minutes before two p.m., forces directed by the Zeta would begin a battle with the Army behind the Presidential Residence to create enough mayhem to hasten the departure of the President and his family a few minutes early. The theory was that the officers and troops in charge of the President's security would be caught off guard, would hurry, would make mistakes, and would ride directly into the trap being set by the forces directed by El Gato as they tried to get the President to el Castillo Chapultepec from the front of the Presidential Residence.

The Zeta was going to bring an impressive number of men to confront the Army, who were positioned along barricades lining the city highway that passed close behind the Presidential house and the grounds of Los Pinos. The Zeta had elite forces of men who had gone through Special Forces training in the Mexican Army. They had taken over buildings and houses nearby, in areas south of Constituyentes, near where this boulevard intersected El Peréfico and Molina del Rey, the street that passed just to the rear of the Presidential Residence. Ana knew what the opening tactics would be. She had seen this in Monterrey when the cartels paid men to steal cars, trucks, and especially buses at gun point in the city, and then take those vehicles and line them perpendicular to the traffic in the streets. They would block all lanes and set fires to the larger vehicles. In her mind she could see the Zeta's men causing havoc by going into the traffic and shooting guns, pulling men and women and children from the cars, taking the vehicles, and shutting down the city's arteries. His small army of men would have then run from across Constituyentes up Parque Lira and Molina del Rey, as well as the part of the Peréfico which ran parallel to Molina del Rey just behind the Presidential Residence. They would have found their positions just around quarter to two p.m. to launch their hail of bullets and grenades behind the Presidential home. The whole point would have been to make the President and his family flee. This battle wasn't an effort of the two cartels to defeat the Mexican Armed Forces. The brilliance of the plan lay in its small scope.

Still, things seemed to have been so easy, Ana thought. *And why wasn't David here?*

That question resonated within her. She knew, just knew, he had understood the message she sent him. So he would know that El Gato had her, that he was on a mission, that the mission was in Mexico City, and that it had to do with Pedro Navarro. God, she missed him, and knowing how he was about her, she knew that David painfully missed her, too, and that he was half crazy that this creep from his past possessed her now. So the whole time that the preparations were underway for the kidnapping, and even during the kidnapping, Ana expected that David would come. Certainly, he and General Alvarez would have been doing everything in their power to strengthen the security around the President and wouldn't have allowed the kidnapping to take place. Had they been so far behind that the cartel really beat them to the punch?

David had to know what was going to happen, she thought. *So why didn't he come?*

He knew what was going to happen.

He knew what was going to happen.

Her breath caught, and she sat upright in her seat. Her eyes went wide with the dawning of her realization.

He knew what was going to happen. They knew what was going to happen. And they let it! God, she thought, *that explains everything, including why soldiers made such a light response to the attack!*

The air conditioner by now completely refreshed her. She sighed lightly, feeling as if she had just been freed from a wall of worry of several hundred pounds. If David wanted the kidnapping of Pedro Navarro to be successful, then it had to be because he knew El Gato meant to contact him and bring the President of Mexico to him. David would be the ticket to the United States for Pedro Navarro and his family.

So David has his own plan, Ana thought. *He wants to meet El Gato on the roof for real this time. It won't be the roof of my office building, but it will be a setting which David controls.*

Ana settled in her seat. She realized that she was flying to David, and she felt a spark of hope in her heart.

Chapter 22: Circles Have No Beginning nor End

Mexico City and Monterrey
Tuesday Afternoon

The real name of El Zeta, Z-30, was Jesús Raúl Espinoza. It was the same name as that of his nephew, the one ordered to be murdered by El Gato. The Zeta knew that El Gato didn't understand exactly whom he had killed. In Mexico, "la familia es toda," family is everything, and this includes the extended families of uncles and aunts not truly related by blood but by affection. Family includes also special friends, the ones who would be invited to share "carne asada." Even if El Gato knew that his nephew was close to the Zeta, he wouldn't have understood how special was their relationship. The Zeta's brother was eighteen years older than he, his brother being the eldest of the family and the Zeta being the youngest. His older brother had his son when he was seventeen years old, and he still lived in the household with the mother of his child in Puebla when the Zeta was born. The Zeta was named after his older nephew in a bit of family irony. They were a year apart and very similar in resemblance, and they grew up together like close brothers. Many people thought that they were fraternal twins.

Puebla was the town in which the Mexican Army defeated the French invaders on May 5, 1862, and this date came to be celebrated as el Cinco de Mayo. During the annual parades of celebrations on this date, The Zeta and his nephew would stand together in awe when the Armed Forces passed, especially the Special Forces. Both the Zeta and his nephew went on to become members of the Special Forces and learned the skills of urban combat. It was the Zeta who later introduced his nephew to organized crime. Until the moment of his nephew's death, they had spent a lifetime together. When El Gato had his nephew assassinated, the Zeta felt like El Gato had assassinated his twin. A big part of his heart lay open and ragged from a wound that never stopped bleeding. So when irony played a big hand in the Zeta's life by giving him the opportunity to avenge

341

his nephew's death in an unusual way, the Zeta believed that God had put the sheath of justice in his hand. He would exercise it in an imaginative way, so that El Gato would suffer the consequences of a perfect vengeance.

The Zeta had heard los corridos, the songs about the mythical El Gato's early days, years before. Those songs had come from that damned state of Sinaloa which for generations had its sons laboring in the mountains to grow marijuana and whose businessmen on the coast were so good at smuggling meth and cocaine from South and Central America. Of course, the native son who really put the Cartel of Sinaloa on the map in the most international way was El Chapo, now El Gato's boss. The Zeta studied the methods of that man and came to see how El Chapo disdained anyone who acted like a showboat and drew attention to themselves or others in the cartel. As he came to know El Gato, he saw that El Gato clearly understood his boss well. He had been successful in establishing the cartel's strength in the United States precisely because he worked intelligently and quietly in that country. However, at this time when the Zeta was coming to know El Gato, he saw that his enemy was letting things go to his head. With a little push, El Gato might slip into a world of miscalculated delusions. He saw also that something about his history with David James and Ana Valdez was making him excitable and sloppy. The Zeta intended to exploit that.

It wasn't that he disagreed philosophically with El Gato on many things. In fact, El Gato caused him to rethink how the violence of his own work and the ruthlessness of the Zetas in expanding their territory in Mexico might lead to their downfall. He believed that El Gato was right. The fortunes and power of the cartels would rise with their abilities to function like corporations in a world now dependent on mass production and efficient networks of distribution and real time information. El Gato preached that violence should avoid being spectacular, that it should be one tool in the tool chest, with the correct implement being applied to the right task. Yet in the strangeness of the days just after the military coup in Mexico, El Gato spoke in grandiose terms of wars and kidnappings of world leaders, extortions from heads of state like President Blair, and the subjugation of governments to organized crime. The Zeta thought that some of this grandiosity had to do with El Gato losing his head over his recent encounters with David James and the Valdez woman.

But he did think that a well-executed plan to kidnap President Navarro would work, and he knew how to help with that. In fact, Navarro's kidnapping would provide the Zeta the perfect opportunity to avenge the death of his nephew. The cat would encounter the end of his ninth life. The death he would suffer would be a slow and painful one of the soul.

So the Zeta did collaborate with El Gato on his plans for the kidnapping because they fit perfectly with his own.

It's easy to manipulate El Gato, he thought. *Let him believe he's in control. Simply ask him leading questions and feed him what he wants. Let him dig his own grave. It's working. He takes bigger and bigger chances. He makes many independent decisions that shouldn't be made at his level, decisions that should be discussed with his boss. Certainly by now El Chapo is taking note. What does El Chapo really think about El Gato's idea to splatter gringo blood in Yankee cities to pressure President Blair to meet the demands of a Mexican drug cartel? Isn't that just a bit mad? The gringos would call this terrorism and go crazy!*

Yes, the Zeta had a hunch that El Chapo was becoming concerned about his trusted lieutenant. He was becoming a loose cannon.

The Zeta saw that discrediting the military coup early in its regime was the right strategy to boost the prestige of the cartels. El Gato was right about that. The Zeta also feared invasion by the Yankees. The gringo Armed Forces had over one hundred years of experience in invading foreign countries, bombing them into oblivion, and occupying them for generations. If the United States thought that a civil war in Mexico would spill across the border, its troops would be in Mexico within days. The gringos invaded Mexico three times since the Mexican American War, only a little more than one hundred sixty years earlier. So this idea of an occupation of Mexico by United States troops wasn't so farfetched. Under an occupation, the receipt and movement of supplies would be much more difficult for the cartels. The effects this would have on revenues would be incalculable. The ability to conduct business would be very challenging if the United States had soldiers patrolling the streets and enforcing curfews in Mexico.

It hadn't been easy to help El Gato with the plan to free President Navarro. The man spoon fed him information and he had to guess what he intended. The expenses to the Zetas of getting all those men and material quickly to Mexico City were enormous. Usually the Zetas operated in small cells with contract services in the plazas and cities which they ran. They got most of their revenue from "piso," a percentage of revenue fee. So in Mexico City, The Zeta contracted a lot of human resources, especially the poor and hungry young men who stole the cars and blocked the traffic while the trained soldiers of the cartel ran to their positions in Los Pinos. Therefore, the Zeta made El Gato pay handsomely, in cash, in advance. How had El Gato been able to do that so quickly? The Zeta kept rushing the man to make cash decisions on the fly, independently. El Gato was taking big chances that his scheme would work and would pay off huge for the cartel in the long run. It was the Zeta's good luck that external events were forcing El Gato into hasty decisions as well. The way things appeared, the Cartel of Sinaloa was running the show and contracting services from the Zetas, and this was just what the Zeta wanted. When the stage fell, it would be the Cartel of Sinaloa lying in the destruction, and the Zetas would be gone, their faint footprints covered by the dust and debris.

El Gato actually referred to the intervention in the forest as "the Battle of Chapultepec," like the historical battle there in September, 1847, when the United States Army put the castle under siege and stormed its cliffs. The Zeta thought that was El Gato's way of feeling a perverse sort of patriotism for Mexico.

Still, he had to admit that El Gato's plan had gone very well. Here he was now in the lot where El Gato and some of the Sinaloa men had just arrived in their specially armored SUVs with the freed President of Mexico and his family! He acknowledged inwardly that this was an astonishing event. He sobered quickly, recalling that Navarro was himself a man from Sinaloa in more ways than one. Not good. Besides, there was much to do now that they had arrived.

In the confusion on the day of the military coup, the Zeta cell in Guadalajara, Jalisco, had seen an opportunity to steal the S-70i Black Hawk helicopter which had been delivered by its maker in the United States, the Sikorsky Aircraft Company, to the state police the previous year. The state of Jalisco began using it to fight organized crime, and they soon found a use for it in emergency natural disasters. This helicopter came equipped with external auxiliary fuel tanks, giving it a 600 mile range in cruising speeds around 100 to

120 miles per hour. The Zetas in Guadalajara had been giving bribes and favors to two of the pilots for a few months, and finally they intimidated them into joining them. The Zetas took particular glee from knowing that they had stolen the expensive aircraft which had been ordered to fight organized crime. *Oh, the deliciousness of life in Mexico*, thought the Zeta. The Black Hawk could accommodate twenty dressed and armed troops. The cartel kept it hidden in several hangars in different locations in Mexico.

On this day, one of the pilots had flown the huge vehicle earlier to a private hangar near the airport in Mexico City where it was fueled for the flight it was about to make to Nuevo Laredo. Now the pilot was here, standing beside the Zeta in the lot as El Gato arrived. Somehow the Cartel of Sinaloa also had a pilot who could fly Black Hawks, and he was with them now as well to go on the flight taking the President and his family to this city on the Mexican side of the border from Laredo, Texas. The Zeta understood completely that El Gato wasn't entirely comfortable with the President being only among Zetas on the helicopter, and so he agreed to let the pilot from Sinaloa fly it. The pilot from Jalisco had been showing the instrument panel to him in the few minutes they had after the helicopter landed and the Battle of Chapultepec began.

When the Zeta realized that he just referred to the battle as that, he laughed to himself.

There wasn't a lot of time now. The men who were involved with the objective of the mission, to liberate the President, had to escape in the stolen minivans that had been brought to this vacant lot. The mad exchange of vehicles was now taking place. The Zeta made a quick nod of acknowledgement to El Gato when he ran with Ana Valdez and his men to their dented blue minivan. The Zeta boarded the Black Hawk. The pilots had climbed in ahead of him, and the men had directed the President and his family on board. He thought about the journey El Gato and company would make, first to their plane, then to Monterrey where El Gato was going to have David James picked up, and then finally to the airfield near Nuevo Laredo, where they themselves were about to fly. Their plane would be much faster than the Black Hawk, but their car journey to Nuevo Laredo would cost them time. By calculation and agreement, El Gato and the Zeta should arrive at the airstrip near Nuevo Laredo approximately the same time, about 7:30 or 8:00 pm. All the pieces would have to fall into place, including that of David James agreeing to the demands about to be made upon him, but the Zeta knew that all of this would go well. The most difficult part of the scheme had just been accomplished.

The S-70i Black Hawk had range and speed, but by plan it was supposed to fly low and slow to avoid detection by the Mexican Air Force on its trip north. However, the Zeta provided a flight plan to the pilots that would get them to the air field in Nuevo Laredo about an hour early. This was his own plan. They would take some chances.

Enrique Santos pointed to his watch to show David that it was almost 12:30 pm, the time when General Alvarez would address the nation in a press conference from Mexico City. Enrique had the large screen television on in the grand sala of Eduardo's ranch, and he pulled a chair in front of it so he could hear it. There was loud noise from the military personnel in the room, and the television was on low volume. David was in an ample-sized study off the side of this room with Eduardo, and he was still talking to the President of the United States on the phone. David nodded to Enrique that he understood and to go on and listen. Enrique had come from the study minutes before. He had heard enough of the conversation between David and President Blair to know that the President also would be watching General Alvarez's address. David, Eduardo, and Enrique already knew what the General would say.

Enrique observed that the General was pretty much sticking to the script that they had discussed. The General began with a quick report on the level of cooperation the new government was receiving from bureaucratic staffs of public services. He ticked off a number of coming meetings with Treasury, members of the banking community, and the Mexican stock exchange. He made statements of reassurance that the Armed Forces would work tirelessly to preserve public safety and that the incidents of resistance against the military had so far been relatively mild. He stated for the umpteenth time that the coup occurred to protect and strengthen the Republic, and now, towards that end, he wished to announce the formulation of an interim government. This would administer the country until new elections could be held in the following September, just seven months away.

The interim government would have an appointed President, who would be a civilian, and a body similar to a Cabinet that was composed of both military and civilian members. He and Admiral Tomas would serve on that body as Secretaries of Army and Navy as they had in the Cabinet of Pedro Navarro. The main responsibility of the Interim President would be to create a national commission which would establish the rules and regulations of national elections and to work with appointed governors of each state, all from the military, to undertake similar commissions at the state level. The Armed Forces would continue to administer police duties at the national, state, and local levels, but would work with the existing bodies to purge corrupt or inadequately trained or educated personnel, and to standardize training programs and requirements for police forces throughout Mexico.

Enrique saw David commenting on the phone to President Blair as they watched the General's address together. He knew that the General was getting close to the announcement that would be the most surprising to the listeners in Mexico. He felt the beginning of nervous excitement. David and Eduardo and the General had argued this back and forth, and it was clear that all three of them were worried about whether or not it was the right thing to do. As far as the world knew at this point, Ana Valdez was simply quiet somewhere. No one had reported her as kidnapped or missing, not even her husband.

Enrique was the one who had put in front of the others that something needed to be done about Rafael quickly because at any moment he might reveal that his wife was a captive in the arms of the Cartel of Sinaloa! David agreed and asked Enrique to to break the news to Rafael by phone so that he wouldn't be surprised when he or his children heard General Alvarez's announcement.

"You're the only one he'll even come close to trusting, Enrique," David explained. "He certainly won't accept anything coming from me, and for our plan to work, it's important that Rafael is on board with it. You're absolutely right. He could spill the beans at any moment. You have to do this."

When he was first on the phone with Enrique, Rafael was palpably tense. Enrique asked about the children as he searched for the entrance to Rafael's heart. He effected a calm and soothing voice so that Rafael would relax. He decided that going directly to the subject would earn Rafael's trust. The man was suspicious.

"Rafael, I'm calling you so that you won't be caught off guard by some news announcements and reports that you or the children will hear very soon," Enrique began. "First, let me tell you that as far as we know, Ana is alive and in the company of a top commander in the Cartel of Sinaloa. We're convinced her freedom will be ransomed in exchange for certain political demands on the United States."

"Such as exchanging her for David James," Rafael said bitterly.

"Probably bigger than that, Rafael," Enrique answered. He thought downplaying David would be agreeable with Rafael. It worked. Rafael paused, sighed, and replied, "Okay, go on."

"I have to be honest with you. We have a lot of concern that Ana won't live through her captivity. The cartels have a history of killing their captives even after ransoms are paid. Add to that the volatility of the situation we're all in, and you can understand why we're worried. Rafael, let me ask you something."

"Go ahead."

"Do you really want Ana to die? Are you really so angry that you don't care if she lives or not?"

Maybe it was the way Enrique asked the question, but he heard the change in Rafael's tone immediately, from anger to sadness. "Of course not," he answered. "I can't want that. She's the mother of my children. What kind of man would I be to want this?"

"What kind of human being as well?" answered Enrique. "Well, I'm glad to hear this. Do you understand why? Not even talking about the personal reasons, all of Ana's friends, your kids, your family, me…all the persons who love her…there's something else, something extremely important, and we must keep Ana alive for this."

"I think I know what you're going to say, Enrique" Rafael replied. "I'm late to the party, but my children have been showing me these last hours what Ana has been doing. I knew she had been busy and was receiving a lot of recognition for her work, but I had no idea that so many people of different backgrounds in our country

348

have been calling for her leadership. I've been so angry and focused only on her Z work. That seemed to be consuming her, but now I see that she has been involved in so much more. This is why you're telling me it's important that she lives. You want to say that Mexico needs her."

"Rafael, Mexico trusts her. Do you realize that she's close friends with the people who brought about the military coup? Not just the top leadership of the Armed Forces, but also the business community and patriots of the Right who've been funding and planning the coup with the military."

"No. I didn't really put it together. We haven't been so close. I've been angry with her a long time. We don't talk that much. This is incredible to me to start to know this. All these women's groups, the peace movements, the Zs; all these activists who have been in the news; all have been brought together by Ana's work. The kids have been showing me today on the computer the news websites and blogs and messages about Ana. I've been living with a politician and didn't even know it."

"A politician of sorts," Enrique agreed.

"What do you want from me, Enrique?" asked Rafael.

"Your silence. Your silence, because when General Alvarez has his press conference today, he's going to make an announcement that we're calculating might keep Ana alive. The man who has her is called El Gato. He has a personal history with David James that leads us to believe he might kill Ana after he forces David to take certain actions based on his close friendship with the President of the United States. We want to make it difficult for him to do this in the eyes of the people of Mexico. In the press conference today, General Alvarez is going to announce a joint military and civilian interim government with an Interim President of Mexico. This appointed government will rule Mexico until new national elections can be set up, elections with procedures in place to minimize the chances of corruption in the elected leaders and in the voting process. Because of his relationship with Ana and that of Eduardo Ortiz, and because many people in Mexico are already shouting for Ana to lead them, the General will announce that Ana is being considered for the job of Interim President. This is a good thing. Ana is an icon of truth and courage. People have faith in her."

Enrique knew this was going to shock Rafael. He heard him whisper in the phone, "Dios mío!" He repeated this several times. Enrique could just imagine what thoughts might be rushing into the hole in Rafael's brain caused by that bombshell, including the realization that he could be married to the President of Mexico!

He finally spoke again, barely above a whisper. Perhaps he didn't want the children to hear.

"But…no one has discussed this with Ana, right?"

"No, of course not," Enrique answered. "But Ana is smart. We're sure on her end, when she hears this, she'll know how to play it to keep herself alive."

"And you want me to keep quiet about this?"

"Yes, and the children also, because right now Mexico isn't really aware that a drug cartel has Ana. We want El Gato to have all the options available that he needs to release her. It gives him more options if he believes that no one in Mexico knows the Cartel of Sinaloa has her. He can let her go, and the cartel doesn't have the blood of its most cherished and trusted leader on its hands."

Rafael protested, "But, Pedro Navarro is the man connected with Sinaloa! Wouldn't they want him to be President instead?"

Enrique saw that Rafael had gone straight to the heart of the debate which David, Eduardo, and General Alvarez had. The man was quick.

"Yes, obviously they would prefer that. This is a calculated risk. However, we feel it increases Ana's chances if El Gato is faced with the dilemma that his captive is expected by the people of his country to lead Mexico out of the military coup. To kill her would be a horror maybe too costly for the leadership of the cartel to claim. That's our logic. That, plus the fact that Ana truly is the person General Alvarez and others want to be the Interim President. Everyone trusts her, Rafael. She's a capable and experienced administrator. She wants transparency and honesty in government, and she wants to end the violence that has wounded the hearts of the Mexican people."

There was another pause, and then Rafael asked, "What is it I can do to help?"

"Sit tight. Keep the kids close. Watch the news, the internet, and stay tuned. The media will be hounding you, wanting to know where Ana is. Go out once and make a statement that she's away in hiding

350

for a couple of days to think over the things that have been put before her, that she wanted to be away from the pressures so she could think clearly what she should do and how she should position herself to help Mexico the best. Don't worry too much about doing this, Rafael. You know how it is in Mexico. Families with a member kidnapped often negotiate privately without the help of police because so many of them work for the cartels. We want to get Ana free and alive. Will you help us with this?"

"Yes," Rafael answered. "I can do this. Obviously, there is much I have to think about myself. I'll talk to the children. They have been frantic about their mom, and it will be good to be able to give them some news that there's a plan in place for her."

"Perfect, Rafael, thank you" Enrique replied.

When he hung up, he couldn't resist the emotion that hit him suddenly and swelled his chest. For Ana he had acted like a man and had done a man's job!

On the television screen, the General had just finished announcing that he and his advisors were considering Ana Valdez as Interim President. He was giving reasons for this when a strange look appeared on his face and he became quiet. He put his hand to the earphone in his left ear and clearly listened to someone telling him something through the ear piece. Then he abruptly brought the speech to a conclusion. After asking the nation for their trust, confidence, and support, he ended. The screen went to a static bulletin stating the time of the press conference. Off camera the viewers heard him say, "Implement Operation Omega," and then television commentators appeared on screen, looking confused, trying to adapt to something unexpected.

The General had been advised that at Los Pinos, the Battle of Chapultepec had begun.

It was about 2:40 p.m. when David's cell phone vibrated and an unknown number appeared on the screen. He was back in the large room with Eduardo after they finished the conversation with President Blair. Enrique was also present. David jumped from his seat and ran to the military aide who was in charge of

351

communications in the command center that was set up in Eduardo's main living room. The aide recorded incoming number and input it into a computer. He hoped to trace the cell phone location through GPS or by network. It was the same man who had attempted to trace the origin of the phone used to send Ana's text message without success.

David answered the phone quickly after he provided the aide the number. He simply stated, "This is David James."

Even though David expected the caller would be El Gato, the words of the responder threw a cold chill over him.

"I'm El Gato."

David looked for familiarity in the voice.

"You have Ana," David said.

"I have Ana Valdez, yes; and now I have Pedro Navarro, his wife and two sons."

They were speaking English. David tried to remember Roberto's accent, and he thought that he detected a similarity to this voice on the phone, but this man had a mature sound, that of a man who had aged.

"You are Roberto," David said, imposing a tone of certainty. "I know who you are."

"Roberto is dead," came the quick response, and then "We don't have a lot of time, David James. I'm moving very quickly at the moment, so please pay attention. I want you to help me deliver Pedro Navarro and his family to the United States. They need asylum, and President Navarro must meet with President Blair on United States soil, in a safe place, to discuss the unlawful overthrow of our government. This has to happen immediately. We'll allow no time for delay or consultation with advisors. Nada. We're en route with President Navarro and the family now to the border of the United States. We'll land near the border, and then we'll want air escort to the United States by the U. S. Air Force or the Air National Guard. Our range is about a thousand miles, and we want to enter the United States through Texas. I know that you have the ear of President Blair, and you're the one who can cut through the red tape to make this happen now. We're speaking of a matter of the next few hours. This must be done in the utmost secrecy. Your cooperation will guarantee the safe release of Ana Valdez. Once President Navarro is in conference with President Blair, the points of access along the border must be opened so that international commerce can resume. The current mess at the border is insufferable. Once President Navarro is in the United States, you'll turn yourself over to me in exchange for the release of Señora Valdez."

David looked at the aide who was attempting to trace the call, but the man just shook his head to say there was no luck. David realized El Gato was using a phone with no GPS chip or the service turned off, and probably it was stolen, but it had been worth a shot.

His heart was thumping from the mention of Ana and because he had been correct in all his assumptions about what El Gato wanted. He kept his voice even and confident. During the past hours he had rehearsed so many times in his head what he would say.

"Listen to me, Roberto. I pretty much guessed what you were up to and that you would call me for this very reason. So I've already had some conversation with President Blair. The release of Ana is highly important, maybe for reasons you don't know, and you must start to consider this now. I'm sure you were quite busy executing the escape of President Navarro and don't have the latest news. This afternoon, just minutes before the attack on Los Pinos, General Alvarez announced in a televised press conference that he was appointing a joint civilian and military interim government to administer the country until free elections are arranged for next September. He stated that an Interim President of Mexico will be appointed, a person who isn't a "politico" nor a military person, and the person he has in mind for the job is Ana Valdez. The country is screaming to know where she is, and I'm sure after your little stunt in Los Pinos a while ago and this announcement that everyone is expecting Ana to make a statement. So you're absolutely correct that we need to work fast, because there were plenty of witnesses also of the Navarro family running to the vehicles that facilitated their escape. This country will be going absolutely nuts, and so will the world, and we'll have to provide answers for them immediately."

"What the fuck?" El Gato screamed into the phone. "Are you frigging kidding me? How the hell is this Mexican housewife going to run Mexico? No one has talked to her about this! She has been with me! What are you mothers of whores trying to pull?"

"Calm down. The whole country wants Ana's leadership. General Alvarez recognizes that Mexico trusts her, and he wants her to supervise the electoral procedure. I'm sure he's making a calculated move to win support for what the coup is trying to do. The point is, no matter what, it's important that she be released to freedom. Mexico wants to hear from her and wants to know where is President Navarro. So, yes, I'll help you get Navarro out of Mexico; and yes, I'll exchange myself for Ana as you request after the Navarro family is in the United States. We have to do this quickly."

David could hear the incredulity on the other end of the line. He had taken El Gato completely by surprise. He heard the barely contained rage in El Gato's voice when he spoke.

"I've got the legitimate President of Mexico, asshole! Ana Valdez as an Interim President? What a joke! She won't do the country any good if she's dead, right, my old amigo? She's beside the point to me, whether she lives or dies. This will be up to you. I have old scores to settle with you. So you are damned right you'll be the one to redeem her. Where are you?"

"Monterrey."

El Gato muttered a short obscenity.

David could practically hear El Gato thinking, *Yeah, the son of a bitch figured everything out and stayed near the border. So he has been talking to Blair. What the hell is this Ana Valdez move?*

El Gato said, "When I'm close to Monterrey, I'll text you the coordinates of where to be. Some of my men will pick you up there. Be certain you're alone. If there's anyone following, or any tricks whatsoever, Ana Valdez dies immediately. Have the arrangements completed, because when we get to the border, we'll put you on the flight with the Navarro family. Then that meeting with President Blair must be immediate. Have preparations begin for the border opening. Have the air escorts available. Once the Navarro family has disembarked in the United States, you'll return to Mexico with my pilot. When you arrive to my custody, Ana Valdez will be released."

David tried to remember how Roberto was when he was mad. This older El Gato sounded furious on the other end of the line. It made David nervous for Ana. He tried to be as placating and as calm as possible when he spoke.

"I understand you completely. I have already begun these things before you called, and now I'll execute everything else just as you state. I want to be sure that Ana is freed and unharmed. So I'll do as you wish. I'll be where you want me to be as soon as I receive the coordinates and can get there. I'll be completely alone."

"One more thing," El Gato said. "We're coming right now to Monterrey. No interference from the Mexican Air Force or things will be a mess in so many ways."

David sensed El Gato was about to cut the call. He still had something important to say, so he spoke up quickly.

"Yes, there's one more thing, Roberto. The Mexican Air Force is the least of your worries if anything happens to Ana, if one hair of her head is touched. With me you think you're avenging the death of your sister. She was a fine woman with dreams and ambitions, and she would have done great things for Mexico. I loved her deeply, first as a friend, and then as someone I wanted to cherish and support all her life. I loved and admired you as my friend, the closest I ever had, and I would have been loyal to you to the end of our lives. Something happened to you, Roberto, something dark. Ana Valdez has nothing to do with these things. If there's something personal between us, be man enough to deal with me and not take it out on her. If anything happens to her, I, not you, will be the crazy one. And I'll send your soul to hell for eternity. Me comprendes?"

David thought that he must have enraged El Gato because he didn't answer, but David heard a very heavy breathing like someone trying to contain himself. So he spoke again and simply said, "Ok, we both have to get busy. We have quick work to do." He hung up the call.

David slumped back in his chair and let out the nervousness that he felt in a long audible sigh. He hoped desperately that the decision to announce Ana as a possibility for Interim President was the right thing to do and that El Gato would react to this in the way they had gambled to keep her alive. But he wasn't certain at all.

Enrique had listened to the entire conversation. He saw Enrique staring at him, but David was too distracted to read the expression on his young friend's face.

But Enrique was thinking *I know exactly what I'm going to do.*

Eduardo sat stone-faced. David momentarily forgot that the man had just listened to his conversation with Eduardo's supposedly dead son. When he became focused and pulled himself together again, David reached over and patted him fondly on the shoulder. Eduardo looked at him and nodded slightly.

Eduardo said, "You really loved my daughter. She was a treasure. I grieve her every day. The two of you would have done great things together."

David was astonished to see tears in his old friend's eyes. He searched for something to say, but just sat quietly.

In a few moments Eduardo suggested, "Okay, David, I believe you want to get the President back on the line." They all arose and walked over to the aide in charge of communications.

Chapter 23: Omega

Washington, D.C. and Nuevo León, México
Tuesday Evening

The President took David's call, and David recounted for him his conversation with El Gato. After he hung up, he mulled an idea that David had presented, and he called Charles Lombardy, the CIA Agency Director, to describe it to him. He wanted to know if Charles thought the idea was feasible. It seemed simple if it would work. He ventured his idea after he brought Charles up to speed on the conversation he had just finished with David.

"There's no way we're going to give up David James to this El Gato slash Roberto Ortiz, Charles," the President said. "I think the easiest thing to do would be to escort the Navarro craft to Houston. David will be on it. It wasn't said the type of craft, but David and I are sure it must be helicopter because El Gato mentioned limitations on range and speed. It's probably one of our own Black Hawk copters coming back to haunt us."

Lombardy sighed. "Damn, all our hardware and weaponry are down there."

"I can go to Houston and meet with Pedro Navarro, no problem," added the President. "That will make it look like full cooperation and put El Gato at ease. He may relax a little so we can do what we need to do without him becoming suspicious and unpredictable. I certainly don't want the President of Mexico in Washington right now, around all the members of Congress. Jesus, can you just see it?"

"What's the idea you're so curious about?" Lombardy asked.

"It involves GPS tracking," answered the President. "If we can get a tracker on David, then we can know where he is when he turns himself in to El Gato. That's exactly what David will do. He's fiercely loyal to and in love with this Mexican woman, and there's no other plan in his mind other than to turn himself in and be where she is when he does it. This is a big opportunity for us, Charles, to get this El Gato guy. He's the one who has been deepening the supply channels for the Cartel of Sinaloa in the United States. What I'm wondering is how we get a tracker on David without it being found on him. When he's in the United States it should be easy to put it on him. When he flies back to Mexico, I'm sure he'll not go directly to where El Gato is, but they'll take him to a place where he'll exchange himself for the Valdez woman."

"Why do you think that?"

"Because they won't want us to know where El Gato is. After David is back in Mexico, our guys will leave, and then they'll take him in the exchange."

The President paused a moment as if thinking.

Then he said, "Certainly they'll search David when he arrives in Mexico before taking him anywhere. It sounds like El Gato wants everything to happen fast, so we won't have time to do anything surgical. I was wondering…"

"Yes, Mr. President," Lombardy interrupted during the slight pause. "You're wondering can he swallow a GPS device. Yes is the answer. We have small models that can be ingested, and we've done this before. He just needs to make sure he doesn't go to the bathroom until he gets to El Gato."

The President said, "Excellent! We can have some of our own agents already in Mexico track him to El Gato at the time if we're lucky. I'll talk to General Alvarez to see what they can do and how we can work together on this. We can't mess this one up. We have to get Ana Valdez and David out alive."

"You have a complicated situation there, Mr. President. General Alvarez apparently wants to appoint this woman as an Interim President of Mexico, but you'll have the elected President of Mexico in the United States. How do you intend to reconcile that?"

The President sighed. "Charles, I don't intend to reconcile it. I'll let the court of world opinion speak about this. I have to do the right thing at the time things happen and make the best judgment under the circumstances. I certainly can't refuse the elected President of Mexico entry to the country when he's escaping from a military coup that overthrows him, and incredibly, General Alvarez was convinced by David to allow him to escape here. The General apparently believes he has the people of Mexico behind him. David has told him that Ana represents the movement for no violence and those

358

who want to confront the cartel problems in Mexico by offering alternative choices to the young people there through education and opportunity. He says Ana supports the coup and the right wing patriots of Mexico, primarily the business elite, because the coup was necessary to rid the country of corrupt government bodies and police forces. She's wildly popular there, and the General apparently is casting his bets on the Mexican people supporting what he's doing and believes she'll help him. If I help both Ana Valdez and Pedro Navarro escape their captivity, then it doesn't look like I'm taking sides. It just looks like I'm on the side of Mexico."

"Very good, Mr. President, then let me know as soon as you can where our operation will be, and I'll be preparing something edible for our friend David in the meantime."

The President laughed. "Okay, Charles, I'm sure in the past you might have been tempted to poison him, but I'm going to trust you on this one."

The CIA Director chuckled as well. "Yes, you can. Sometimes I have to do the right thing too."

From the air Ana recognized the landscape as they approached Monterrey, including individual mountains of the Sierra Madre that surrounded and poked through the huge metropolitan area. The city was spread out. Compared to Mexico City's twelve million population it looked small, but still one could sense its importance in this northeastern region of Mexico. Even from the air Ana thought the city looked electrifying and beautiful and worthy of the many songs about it.

El Gato had spent the trip completely silent and with eyes closed. She could tell he was still extremely angry. Something about the phone call just prior to the trip had gotten to him, and then she and he had their volatile confrontation. It was all so personal. Now El Gato was inside a wall to keep others from speaking to him. There was no doubt in her mind that he was thinking and planning something that had to do with her and David. It made her tense. She still felt nauseous and clammy despite the air conditioning of the plane, and she was sure she looked ragged and unattractive.

She looked at Monterrey below and wondered if David was in her field of view. She worried about her children and how they were doing with Rafael, who was so enraged with her. She tried to locate her neighborhood, but then the plane banked and headed to the northwest, where apparently they were going to land in the same field in the country from which they had taken off. In the fading afternoon sun of this mid-winter day, the shadows below cast long exaggerations of ordinary objects. In an hour and a half the sun would set.

The plane dropped low and passed over countryside and then doubled back. She could see ahead what appeared to be fútbol fields in the middle of nowhere, with a building that might look like an athletic field house off a small, faint road tip-toeing through trees. The fútbol goals were pulled to one side. There were six of them, as if there were three playing fields. The field was surrounded on three sides by forest. She thought about it and then guessed that the building actually hid a fueling pump, and this was the field where they would land. In a minute, she found out that she had been correct. When they bumped on the ground, she saw El Gato open his eyes.

In the helicopter the Zeta leaned forward and squinted his eyes because of the setting sun hanging low on the horizon. They were twenty kilometers to the west of Nuevo Laredo and the border with the United States in an area marked off by Highway 2 in the state of Tamaulipas. Below, he spotted the small lake and the forest next to which was the landing field for their helicopter. He saw that this field was modeled like the one in Monterrey to resemble fútbol fields from the air, and there was a medium-sized utility building which masked the fueling pumps. He was certain that the men from Sinaloa had stolen the fuel from the national oil company of Mexico, Pemex. Theft of natural resources was a big source of income for the cartels.

During the flight they made good time. The pilot from Sinaloa had flown, given direction by the one from Jalisco with the Zetas. They had varied their altitude, dropping low in the countryside whenever they spotted suspicious aircraft, but they arrived here at the time the Zeta wanted. About an hour into the trip, the Navarro family finally relaxed and began to chat. The Zeta had put on the charm and had joked with them about having a vacation in the United States until the mess in Mexico was settled. He asked the children what places they might like to visit while they were in the USA. The youngest boy asked who he was, and he told him that he worked with a friend of his father's, and that he was glad to have this opportunity to help them escape from their captivity in Mexico City.

Now the pilot from Sinaloa called out, "We're here, but I don't see anyone below."

The Zeta made a show of looking at his watch and then searching the terrain below. It was about 6:30 p.m. He said to the pilot, "It's okay. We're just a few minutes early. Land, and we'll wait. It's better than being up here in the sky where anyone can see us. Land close to the fueling station, that building near the woods."

"I know what it is," said the pilot. He brought the helicopter down fast, hovered a brief moment, and then touched ground. They were making a lot of noise so the pilot shut down the engines quickly.

The Zeta retrieved a nine millimeter pistol from his bag and got up and walked behind the pilot from Sinaloa and shot him in the back of the head. Blood splattered the cockpit, and the Jalisco pilot jumped with fright. The Zeta pulled on him to get up and told him, "Block the door."

Pedro Navarro was unbuckling himself and hastening to stand. His wife and children were screaming in horror. The Jalisco pilot passed in front of the Zeta as he moved to the door, momentarily stopping him, but they disentangled, and the Zeta reached the elected President of Mexico just as he stood. He put the gun barrel on his forehead and pulled the trigger, and the President slumped backwards. More blood. His wife was convulsing with hysteria, and the Zeta calmly shot her in the head, and then one of the boys. By this time the oldest boy had arisen and had thrown himself against the pilot from Jalisco as if to pull him away from the door. The pilot looked at the Zeta, saw that the others had been shot, and handed the boy to the Zeta. He moved him around by his family and shot the child in the head.

Now the Zeta saw the pilot from Jalisco standing there, looking at him expectantly, as if he would be the next to be killed. The Zeta told him, "I'm not shooting you. The world will think this family has been shot by the Cartel of Sinaloa. I've avenged the death of my nephew by destroying the dream of El Gato. Help me move the bodies. We'll put them inside the fueling building. We're leaving the pilot from Sinaloa on the helicopter with us. I have a place for us to go in Nuevo León not far from here, about fifty kilometers, where we can fuel. Do we have enough fuel to make it there without refueling here?"

"We can go about fifty kilometers, then we're on reserve," answered the pilot. He was visibly shaking.

The Zeta nodded. "I thought as much. Good, then let's hurry. We need to get out of here. We'll clean up later."

Enrique Santos had heard that El Gato wanted David to meet his men at a place in Monterrey and to come alone, but he couldn't bear the thought of David going alone, without help, to put himself in the hands of this monster. He would die of anxiety wondering how David was. He had had enough, feeling like all the dramas of his life were being scripted by others and that he had no control over anything. Some men had come and taken Israel away, some had taken Ana away, and now he wasn't going to let this happen with David. When David was busy occupying himself, Enrique found Eduardo and confided in him his idea. He would need Eduardo's approval because he needed some equipment from the military, and Eduardo would be able to get it for him. Enrique was thrilled and relieved to find that Eduardo had the same anxieties as Enrique about David going alone to El Gato, and the old patriot embraced Enrique's plans. Enrique thought, *Okay, these ideas have merit if Eduardo is on board with them.* He knew that both of them realized that one mistake would cost the lives of Ana and David.

It was the military aide trying to trace the cell phones that gave Enrique the idea about using GPS. Eduardo and Enrique talked to him about their needs, and the man produced a GPS device the size of a cell phone that was strongly magnetic and would attach to the underside of an automobile. It transmitted location in real time. It was a device made for the Army and intelligence operations in Mexico. It didn't rely on cell phone towers to triangulate a position. This device used satellites that had been put in space by the United States and which Mexico had been permitted to use. He provided him also a viewer, a box-like, battery-operated computer that showed a map like a car's navigation system. Enrique realized also that some of his actions would occur outside in the dark, so he requested a pair of night vision goggles and a couple of illuminating flare guns, just in case.

When the text message came with the coordinates where David was to drive to meet El Gato's men, he and David and Eduardo looked the location up on a satellite map. Enrique saw that David was to drive to a position a little south of Nuevo Laredo, where he would park at a cantina and then join El Gato's men to go to meet the aircraft that would take him and the Navarro family to the United States. He was to be there at 7:00 p.m. By this time David had determined with President Blair that their destination from Nuevo Laredo would be Houston again.

When David wasn't present, Enrique said to Eduardo, "You have to give David a vehicle to use that has a trunk. It should be dark by the time he gets to the rendezvous point. I'll be in the trunk. I'll be dressed in black. We're assuming that they'll transfer David to their vehicle so I'm not going to have much time to try to get the GPS device on their car without being seen. I'm not sure how I can do this. If they see me, it could be all over with. I'll have to try it when they're checking him out or when they're starting to leave."

Eduardo replied, "You have enough time to get some other Zs to the cantina or in that area now, ahead of time. Whatever happens there, it might be possible that they can help you. They could be dressed as patrons of the establishment; maybe hanging around the parking lot and drinking. Think about it."

Enrique grinned a giant smile. "Not bad, Eduardo!" he said. He looked around the room and made a slight nod towards the men in there. Then he said, "Do you think the soldiers are really going to let me do this?"

Eduardo shook his head. "I don't know, Enrique. Once you have the GPS fix on that vehicle, I'm sure the soldiers will have it too. I'll try to reach Alvarez to have him hold them at bay, but I'm not the General."

"You are in my book," Enrique said without smiling, "and I think you're running a lot more of the show than you let on."

There was a faint smile on Eduardo's face. He was amused. "What more do you need?" he asked Enrique.

"A flashlight or lantern for the trunk; some rope; a small pillow; and an extra set of car keys in case David leaves and takes his set with him. What's my ride going to be?"

"An old white Toyota" answered Eduardo. "It has nice trunk space and if it gets banged up I won't be having a fit."

"Okay," said Enrique. "Be sure it has a full tank of gas. Keep David distracted and help him get in the car. Make sure he has no reason to want to open the trunk before he goes. I'm going to go try to get in touch with some of my compadres to set things up at the cantina, and then I'll change clothes and get in the car trunk. When it comes time for him to leave, just tell him I was too emotional to see him off." Then Enrique laughed and added. "He'll believe that. He knows my antisocial ways."

At 7:10 p.m. El Gato felt the vibration of his phone. He pulled it out of his pocket to read the text message that said, "Passenger on board. We're en route."

They were in a SUV on the way to the field where the Black Hawk was going to land. El Gato wasn't driving this time. He had a driver and a man in the back seated next to Ana. Already they had turned from the outskirts of Nuevo Laredo and were headed west to the rendezvous point. El Gato said to the driver, "They have David James and are on the way. They shouldn't be far behind us." He turned and looked in the back. Ana was being quiet, but El Gato knew she was listening, as always.

A couple of times he sent text messages to the Zeta or tried to phone him or his pilot, but there was no service. He didn't really expect to have the luck of reaching them. They should still be in the air but already close to Nuevo Laredo.

364

About 7:15 p.m. they turned onto the two-lane country road that approached the athletic fields, which was really a landing field for the cartel light aircraft. They drove a couple of kilometers and turned onto a dirt entrance to the fields and drove across the sparse grass towards the utility building. It was dark, and the vehicle headlights put color in the earth in the swaths of light. El Gato noticed and said to the driver, "Shut off the lights." They stopped not far from the side of the building and shut off the engine. El Gato and the driver rolled down the windows. It was completely quiet. There was no sound, not even the sound of a distant helicopter. The air was still, and then there was a crack from the noise of a small branch falling from a tree in the forest behind the building. El Gato listened, but there was no other sound. He drummed his fingers on his thigh for a few seconds and then he said to the driver, "Let's get out. You go check the building."

The complete silence and the darkness of the place was making him feel anxious. He didn't like not hearing from the Zeta. There were reasons why he wouldn't be hearing from him, but still, he had a weird feeling. He leaned against the passenger fender and lit a cigarette. Ana and the back seat companion weren't saying anything, and the driver was walking around the building. Then the driver came back to the SUV suddenly and opened the door by El Gato, reached in the glove box, and pulled out a flashlight. El Gato tensed.

"What's wrong?" he asked.

But the driver didn't say anything right away. He went in a hurry to the glass window in the front of the building and shined the light inside. El Gato followed him.

Now El Gato heard a vehicle approaching from the road that came to the field entrance. He expected that it would be his men bringing David James.

But his driver now yelled, "Mierda! Shit! There are bodies! A man, a woman, a couple of kids!" He was a big man, and he handed the flashlight to El Gato and then he ran to the double sliding door of the building. He shot the lock and beat the door with his body until the lock gave, and he pushed the doors apart.

El Gato looked in the window with the light, but he already knew who the bodies were. Inside the building the driver shouted out, "It's the Navarro family. The whole fucking family has been murdered!"

365

The vehicle was turning onto the field now, and El Gato squinted into its headlight beam. By the configuration of the headlights and the shape of the vehicle he saw that it was the SUV that he was expecting with the delivery of David James to him. He ran to the door and shouted to the driver, "Get out of there and shut the door behind you! Come back to our car!"

The ride to the cantina in the trunk of the Toyota hadn't been fun. Once David began to drive, Enrique pulled the plastic lever that opened the trunk. Holding it to keep it from flying open, he wedged a piece of the small pillow and held the trunk down. The pillow was to prevent the trunk lid from making a noise that David might hear when they bumped along the roads. Then he wanted to be sure that at the cantina when he got out of the trunk no one would hear the sound of the trunk opening. From time to time he turned on the lantern and checked his supplies, mostly to break the monotony of the ride, but also to think of situations in which he might use them. The flare guns were there, and they were metallic Very guns that looked like normal pistols. He had the GPS in the magnetic case and the computerized viewer for following the car once David would be taken, if he had to follow the car.

He had spoken to the Zs who would already be at the cantina, and they had discussed several courses of action for different scenarios of what might occur in the parking lot. What actually happened couldn't have been more perfect.

He felt the car slowing, and he heard the sound of the norteña music blaring from the cars in the parking lot of the cantina. It sounded like a bunch of young people partying. David pulled in the lot and made a sharp turn and stopped; then he began backing into a parking place against a fence on the side. Enrique opened the trunk lid ever so slightly to peek. He saw that David had backed into a space next to a car blasting music. There were a couple of young men sitting on the side of the hood, drinking beer. The back door of their car was partially open. A young couple was making out in the back seat. Enrique shook his head. He knew the guy. One thing he could say is that the young Zs were enjoying their work.

366

He listened. David was remaining in the car. He checked his watch. Three minutes until 7:00 pm. He heard another car pull into the lot and then begin to maneuver near the Toyota. He heard a couple of doors of the new vehicle open in front of them. It was show time.

A voice said, "David" in Spanish. "Da-veedth."

When David opened his door, Enrique picked up the GPS and the two flare pistols and rolled silently out of the slightest opening of the trunk that allowed him. He could hear two men standing and making sounds near David, and he assumed that they were searching him. One of the Zs sitting on the car hood looked at Enrique, who was crouched behind the Toyota, and flashed three fingers.

Three men.

The two young men got off the hood and began laughing and talking nonsense and clanking beer bottles and dancing towards the SUV with the blackened windows. The youth making out in the back seat of the car abruptly stopped. He got out the car and extended his hand towards Enrique. He reached for the GPS device, took it, and started walking towards the SUV. This left Enrique with the flare pistols. He kept below the window line of the Toyota, but crabbed his way to the passenger side fender so he could see where everyone was. The youth with the GPS walked casually behind the SUV, bent quickly, and slapped it under the rear bumper. Enrique saw the two laughing boys getting themselves into position for kicking the heads of the men who were involved with David. They were standing just to the side of the left headlight. Enrique looked, and the back door of the SUV was open behind the driver. He saw that after the driver had watched his companions searching David, he started checking something on his phone. Enrique nodded at the two young men to go, and then he ran and jumped into the back seat of the SUV. He put the barrel of a flare gun to the nape of the driver's neck.

"Not one move! Not a single movement except for releasing the phone, then hands on the back of your head!" Enrique commanded. The youth who had put the GPS on the vehicle now jumped into the seat beside the driver and quickly grabbed a pistol that was at his side. He began to rifle through the clothes the man was wearing to look for more weaponry. Enrique glanced and saw two semi-automatic weapons on the floor of the back seat.

At the same time that Enrique made his move, the two beer-drinking Zs jumped and delivered kicks to the backs of the necks of the men who were searching David. Enrique heard bones crack. The men crashed against the Toyota and slumped to the ground.

"David, get in this car!" Enrique shouted. "Take the front seat!" He barely had enough time to witness the astonished look on David's face in the glare of the multicolored fiesta lights decorating the cantina and the fence. But David reacted quickly and ran to the front passenger side of the SUV.

"Move them!" Enrique shouted to the two young Zs who had subdued the men of the cartel. "Take any weapons and wallets. And their shirts!"

The Zs dragged the bodies of the men to the ground by the fence and searched their clothing. When David was coming to the front passenger seat of the SUV, the other Z got out and climbed into the back beside Enrique. He set the pistol he had taken from the driver down by the automatic weapons. He had the driver's phone in his hand.

"Give the phone to David," Enrique said to him. The young man did this, and David started looking at the messages on the screen. He found a series of recent messages, and he showed them to the driver.

"Are these to El Gato?" he asked. The driver nodded.

David typed a text message: "Passenger on board. We're en route." It was 7:10 p.m. He showed it to Enrique and pressed "Send."

"I guess we know how this will go down now," said Enrique. "You taught me everything I know, David. So we're the replacements for these guys to take you to El Gato."

"Jesus, Enrique" said David. "We don't know how anything will go down. We don't know how many men will be there. I'll have to go with the Navarro family to Houston. How will you guys get away?"

The two other Zs now ran over to Enrique and handed him two more pistols and two shirts. Enrique told them to get the GPS viewer he had left in the trunk of Eduardo's Toyota and lock up the car. They did this and got into their car. The girl was still sitting in the back seat of their vehicle.

"We have a lot more coming to the party once we know where it is," said Enrique, finally responding to David. "I'm sure our driver here will let us know this. Let's get going, señor Driver. I expect there's an airfield around here somewhere."

"El Gato has Ana!" David protested. They started to drive. "And who knows where?"

"David," Enrique said. "Think about this. How do you know she's alive?"

The question silenced David. Enrique said, "You would have thought of that by the time you got there tonight. You're going to the USA, then return in exchange for Ana, right? You want to know that she's okay. El Gato will have her there to show you tonight, so you'll cooperate."

David kept quiet, thinking. Then he said to the driver, "Where are we going exactly?"

As the driver spoke, Enrique and the other Z in the back seat broadcast some text messages to Zs, giving the location. Enrique thought of one other thing, which he didn't mention. The GPS on their car was broadcasting their movement to all interested parties. However, he did say to David, "One thing about the local Zs. They know this countryside pretty well."

It was part of Z training to know all the terrain of their home area.

It was now dark. When they turned onto the road that began the couple of kilometers to the field where they would rendezvous, Enrique commanded the driver to stop for a moment. When he did, he leaned forward and applied a pressure to the driver's neck that caused him to lose consciousness. The Z in the back jumped out, ran to the driver's side, and pulled the man into a ditch. He then got into the driver's seat. He put on one of the shirts of the men they had subdued at the cantina. Enrique put on the other one. They began slowly up the road and looked for the entrance to the field.

"It's 7:30," David said. "We're right on time."

They turned in the entrance, and they could see a dark SUV parked near the utility building, but they saw no aircraft.

"The plane or copter isn't here yet," David said. "Thank God, I only see one car up there. Drive slowly towards them and keep the

369

headlights on. Keep the lights pointed on them even when I get out the car, so they can't see well. Enrique, I'll stand by the car just near the headlight beam. Stand behind me and have a weapon as if you're covering me. Use one of the flare pistols. We need them to think it is their man holding me."

He looked at the Z driver.

"Roll your window down and hang your arm out and let your shirt show, in case that helps. If they yell to cut off the lights, fumble and do it slowly; maybe keep on parking lights, whatever. Try to keep them blinded somewhat by the light."

Enrique said, "David, if we have a good shot of getting Ana, we'll do it. Delay as much time as you can. We have more guys coming, and they'll be Z quiet. When the aircraft arrives and things work out that you get on it, we'll do next whatever is expedient. That would be the time to put the drop on El Gato. If somehow they try to escape, we'll follow El Gato home if we have to."

"Enrique, this is messed up," said David. "You should have let me do this alone. What's done is done, but let's keep our eyes on Ana! El Gato wants to kill her in front of me, I just know it! He isn't expecting to have to do it now. He thinks he'll do it when I return from escorting Pedro Navarro to Houston."

They rolled up about thirty yards away from where El Gato was standing. They saw one other man beside him. They were shielding their eyes from the headlight beams. Enrique got out of the car. He opened the front door and made a show of pulling David from the vehicle and jerking him into position just near the headlight beam. El Gato started to yell something. Clearly he was agitated, but he got interrupted when from the back seat of the vehicle near El Gato, Ana screamed, "David, the Navarro family is dead! Their bodies are in the building!"

El Gato turned around in a fury. "Fuck! Get her out here!" he yelled to the man in the car with her. "Keep your mouth shut! Say one more word, and you and your boyfriend are both dead!"

The back car door opened. A man pushed Ana from the vehicle and she stumbled a little as she got out. He came out behind her. Enrique and David could see that Ana had her hands behind her back.

El Gato had a pistol in his hand, and now he waved it at the driver of the SUV that Enrique and David had just exited. "Shut off those fucking lights, idiot!"

But David knew they all had just received shocking information, so he tried to keep El Gato mentally busy, to buy himself some time to figure out what to do. So as if El Gato had said nothing about the lights, he jumped in with a question close on the heels of the command El Gato had given.

"Gato, what's going on here? Where is the plane? Or helicopter? Where is the Navarro family? Are they really dead?" He chose to call him that.

El Gato sounded highly distressed. "I don't know what's going on, asshole! Yes, they're dead. I'm trying to piece this together. I just got here and we found them!"

"You didn't do this?" David knew it was a stupid question, but he just wanted to keep El Gato jumping. He kept his eyes on Ana. Her body was tense, coiled. She was ready to jump at any hint of a command that David would give her.

El Gato responded, "Of course I didn't do this! I rescued them personally at Los Pinos!"

"So they came by air separately from you, and that aircraft has come and gone then. Helicopter or plane? These were your men who flew the Navarros?"

"No, fuck!" El Gato said. Enrique and David saw that El Gato also was trying to figure out a new strategy, but David's questions were indeed slowing him down. "It was a helicopter. No, they weren't my men."

"That's confusing, Roberto," David said, intentionally switching to that name. "It doesn't make sense. You had the Navarro family with men who weren't yours? Who were they?"

"Jesus, don't call me that! They were Zetas. They had the helicopter. I had the pilot that flew it."

The man standing next to El Gato, a huge guy, shifted on his feet and advanced a couple of steps. The car lights were still on, still blinding them. The man was trying to see the driver. He yelled out, "Hey, asshole, cut off those fucking lights! What's the matter with you?"

David sensed that El Gato next would command his men or at least the driver to come over to them, so he quickly interjected by shouting, "Please cut the lights! We can't see anything." He was telling the Z driver it was okay to cut the lights and they would still have a few moments of light blindness working to their advantage. He also hoped that after that it would be too dark to see well, and they were far enough away. The driver cut the lights. Then to keep Roberto from having a chance to issue any other command, he quickly addressed him.

"Okay, Gato, we do have a situation here that we need to make the best of," said David. "You still have the same demands you want satisfied: That of the border opening. That of no invasion by the United States. Now we have a stabilizing force for Mexico right here in our presence. This Ana Valdez. And you and I had a deal. My life for hers. So yes, this Navarro assassination is a mess, but if you have me, the President will still need to listen to what you have to say. And he'll believe me if I tell him you had nothing to do with the assassination. You would be the one who rescued the President of Mexico. I can vouch for that. So we should make this deal, Gato. Set Ana free, take me into custody, keep me alive as long as I'm useful, then do what you need to do."

The movement in the dark was so faint that both Enrique and David in the first moments weren't certain that they saw anything. Yet a couple of seconds later both of them saw shadows moving from the forest behind El Gato and his men.

"She'll never be completely free, you gringo fuck. All her life she'll have to look over her shoulder. She has made herself an enemy of all the cartels. And you! You believe you're valuable enough that your country won't invade us?" He made a derisive laugh.

"Listen to me, Roberto!" *Back to that name. Keep him emotional, distracted.* "You never understood the importance of blood. You and I were blood brothers. The President and I are blood brothers. It's like that. He's Donnie to me! I know the worst mistake the United States could make is to invade here. I know why. I know the President trusts me. He'll listen to me."

David could see a little better in the darkness now. That meant the others could as well. He looked over at Ana. She was still coiled in her body, ready to make a move at the first advantage. She was studying David's face.

The shadows had slinked closer now, coming from the forest into the field on both sides of the utility building and getting into position.

Then suddenly there was a complication.

They could all hear the sound of motor vehicles coming up the road towards the fields. They were trucks. They were the distinctive sounds of a military convoy.

El Gato pretended not to hear, but his head had turned slightly towards the sound. Next something changed about his body. Enrique saw it. David saw it. There was some signal of resignation, of some fated act. Then El Gato waved his pistol towards Ana, who was watching intently.

"Señora Valdez, walk forward towards their SUV. David, walk towards me. We'll make this exchange."

She hesitated just a moment, but then Ana started walking. At that second both David and Enrique knew what El Gato was going to do. They saw it in his body language. They heard it in his lie. He was going to shoot Ana in front of David and let him see that for a moment, and then he was going to shoot David. David felt a furor of desperation like none he had ever experienced.

The truck sounds were loud now, and headlights were showing around a curve in the road before the entrance. The shadows behind El Gato and his men were in place.

David realized that time was slowing down again as it always did in very intense moments. Looking at El Gato, he suddenly could read everything that the man's body communicated. He realized that he had recognized him right away when he first saw him because he looked like Yog.

He's willing to die now as long as he knows I see Ana die. He thinks I killed Annie. He thinks I killed Yog. He hears the Army. He'll go down in a blaze. But I'm going to be the one to kill this fucker.

In the lowest voice that only Enrique would hear, David said, "Give me the flare pistol."

David began the walk towards El Gato as if he were going to do the exchange for Ana. In his first stride he swung his right arm behind him and Enrique thrust the gun into his hand.

Just as El Gato began to raise his arm, David shouted, "Ana! Drop!"

373

She threw herself solidly to the ground. There wasn't a microsecond of hesitation. She had never taken her eyes off David's face.

The first Army trucks rolled through the entrance and now their headlight beams began to illuminate the field. Soldiers standing in the back of the flat beds jumped down and began shouting to drop weapons.

El Gato fired quick shots towards Ana on the ground and then turned his arm to shoot at David. David was in stride. He pointed the flare gun at El Gato and with a confident pull of the trigger fired the flare directly into El Gato's head. He had wanted never to fire a weapon again in his life, but he had done it plenty in his career, and he was an expert marksman. For Ana, he would shoot. For the rage he felt inside him, he would kill. This Satan of a person thought he would take away the most beautiful love of his life, and for that alone, David would send him to hell.

David saw El Gato fall backward as his head seemed to take a direct hit. His nervous men had already drawn pistols, and in response to the firing of the flare began to fire shots furiously. But the Zs were already jumping on the men from behind so the weapons popped haphazardly into the air and across the field towards the soldiers. A couple of soldiers returned fire.

Now David did what he always did. He jumped and flew, straight to Ana, and landed on top of her and covered her body. "God, Ana! Are you okay? Are you okay?"

He felt her moving underneath him. She said, "I'm fine, darling, I didn't get hit!"

They heard the sounds of infantry boots rushing towards them across the field. Someone among the soldiers was shouting, "We have two men down!"

Enrique began jumping up and down shouting frantically to the Zs, "Manos arriba! Manos arriba! Manos arriba! Hands up!" He shouted for the car driver to get out of the car with hands up. He called out desperately to the soldiers, "Only Zs remain! There are no shooters! Hold your fire! Don't shoot!"

The infantrymen ran towards them with weapons pointing and sweeping, but everywhere they saw hands in the air and no weapons, except for the ones beside the bodies on the ground.

David rose to a sitting position on his knees, straddling Ana, and he put his hands up high. He felt the presence suddenly of a man standing beside him, a man who had his left arm up in the air, but whose right hand held a pistol lowered to his side. He turned to look, and it was El Gato. He looked grotesque, with blood streaming down his face from a wound in the top of his head. His eyes had a satanic look, and he raised his pistol just inches from David's face.

"Yeah!" El Gato said. "We're all going, the three of us." His eyes shot briefly down to Ana. Then his gaze returned to David for the moment to pull the trigger. The soldiers were almost upon them but none had noticed or understood the situation yet.

And then there was a Voice.

To David, in a frozen moment of time, it sounded deep and distorted, like a voice recorded and played at low speed. It said, "Roberto! Don't!"

David saw El Gato hesitate in confusion. Someone had called him by that ancient name from another life, and it disoriented him. It dislodged him not because of the name he was called, but because of the sound of the Voice. It was the voice of his father. It was Eduardo.

David focused his attention, and he recognized in the weird light of shadows and silhouettes the man he had loved like a father for forty years. Eduardo was there in his camouflage uniform again, small but full of spit and vim, and standing beside him was one of the soldiers, a giant of a man raising his weapon to fire.

In the next horrifying moment, David saw Roberto suddenly sweep his arm to point the pistol at Eduardo. He heard Ana scream, "Noooo!"

"You Fuck!" El Gato screamed, and he fired at Eduardo point blank. But Eduardo also had a pistol which he raised just as El Gato turned, and he fired at the same time.

The giant blasted El Gato with his automatic weapon and propelled El Gato's body several yards backward. From the riddling of the bullets El Gato's body did a convulsive dance.

But Eduardo was lying on his back on the ground. He had a large stain of blood around a hole in his shirt. Both David and Anna scurried beside him. Enrique, in a state of shock, recovered his senses and ran from the automobile to join them.

"Eduardo! Eduardo!" David shouted. He opened his eyes slowly when he heard his name, and when he did, Ana slipped her cuffed hands underneath his head and raised it slightly. She put her head close to his face, and she whispered, "Eduardo, please…"

They could barely hear him, he was so weak, but he said looking at David, "Is he gone?"

David nodded, holding his gaze, thinking if they could keep eye contact, somehow Eduardo would live. "Yes, Eduardo. The soldier shot him." His voice cracked a little. "Roberto shot you! But he's gone." He didn't want to cry, but if he did it would be from frustration and rage.

He saw that Eduardo was holding his hand.

Eduardo slowly shook his head in Ana's cuffed palms. He struggled to speak, and they heard him say, "No, that wasn't Roberto!" He paused to take a wheezing breath. Then he added weakly, " My son died a long time ago. That man was El Gato."

His labored breathing rattled as he tried to muster the strength for more words. "David," he said, "it's time for me to be with Annie now. You still have important work to do. Don't grieve my life. I'm proud of what I did. Finish our work. Vaya con Dios, mi hijo."

Go with God, my son.

He didn't have the strength to do another thing in life. He died holding David's hand.

The three of them knelt beside Eduardo. The other soldiers from the convoy all arrived. They swept their weapons as they surveyed the scene. The young Zs kept their hands high and remained silent while the soldiers evaluated them, and then one of the soldiers gave a command that the Zs could lower their arms.

The giant went to view the corpse of El Gato, and then he returned and extended an arm to help Ana to her feet. She was sobbing silently. David rose and put his arm around her and drew her close. He kissed her cheek, and she composed herself enough to tell the giant, "Whoever is in command here, you need to know there's a terrible situation. In the building there are the bodies of President Navarro and his family. They were dead when I was brought here."

There were gasps. One of the soldiers issued a command, and they went running to the utility building.

Except the giant remained. David saw Ana look up at him, as if studying his face intently. David saw a Special Forces insignia on his uniform.

"I recognize you," Ana told the giant. "I saw you on the roof. You came and looked at the body there of the man who shot at David. You didn't say anything. You just looked at him and walked away as the medical corps came."

The giant nodded. "Yes, Señora. I was the one who shot that man from the other roof. Eduardo knew me, and he asked me personally to be there to protect you and Señor James. I wanted to be sure I had hit him; I wanted to see him; and I knew when I saw him that he wouldn't live."

The giant looked down at Eduardo then and put his face in his hands. Ana turned to David and buried her head in his chest and let herself cry. Enrique came to the other side of her and put his arm around his two best friends. His sigh joined the night winds.

Epilogue

Ana didn't believe she knew how to run a nation, but she knew how to heal a nation. She knew the power of touch. Symbolically, she kissed and rocked in her arms every person in Mexico who had lost someone to the drug trade, or human trafficking, or kidnapping and extortion negotiated by bullets and torture. She put the disappeared persons back into their homes.

So despite the fact that it felt ridiculous to her being appointed the Interim President of Mexico, she immediately agreed to the job. She had work to do, and she didn't trust anyone else to do it better.

She couldn't think of a more horrific act than the murder of the Navarro family. Rumors abounded throughout the country about who had done it, some blaming the Cartel of Sinaloa, some the Zetas, and some even the military. Ana told the nation what she thought happened, what she had heard and seen, and eventually most believed her because most trusted her. That was good, because it was a skeptical country. What was more important in Ana's eyes was that the nation should properly grieve for every victim brutally sent away from their lives.

She moved quickly. As a condition of accepting the job, Ana insisted that the Armed Forces release all the Senators and Deputies of the legislature, the Governors, the Supreme Court Justices, the Cabinet members and any of their families whom had been quarantined. She knew that in the eyes of the world the coup most likely wouldn't be recognized as legitimate, but her hyperactive work in those first days of her presidency dazzled everyone. She understood that no one in Mexico liked the government that had been, nor did they trust the coup, but everyone could see that people trusted her. So she worked weeks without sleep to establish a legitimacy of government deriving from the hard work of people who thirsted for justice and security.

There was a beautiful mass celebrated in the Metropolitan Cathedral in the Zócalo in Mexico City for the Navarro family several days after their murder, and this was televised throughout the world. Ana and Rafael and her children attended and sat with the Navarro relatives. Images of Ana's genuine grief and kindness towards that family unleashed tears from a nation that needed to be seen crying by everyone watching on television, computer, cell phone, or tablet.

Ana knew she had the ears of important people: General Alvarez, Admiral Tomas, the leaders of peace movements, the elite of the Right, and young people like the Zs. All saw that Ana was extracting the best from the fractured segments of Mexico. She was finding the leaders to move the country forward. She was doing it at lightning speed.

But Ana in the earliest hours of her new position understood that she had to capture the trust of the people to the north, the people who were like David, the gringo she loved. This man she adored had been the college roommate of the President of the United States. Could the gods have smiled any more sunshine upon her?

"Mr. President," she told him, "I invite you to meet me half-way on the International Bridge between our two Laredos."

And that's what happened. Three days after the funeral of the Navarro family, the newly appointed Interim President of Mexico walked at the head of hundreds of Mexican citizens across the Juarez – Lincoln International Bridge towards the United States, over the Rio Grande. The bridge had been cleared of vehicles for the ceremony. The border had reopened two days after the death of El Gato, the day Ana accepted her appointment.

Rafael and the children walked beside her, Paula carrying a large flag of Mexico. Behind, cheering crowds and marching bands and grinning, black outfitted Zs fell in, having a wonderful time with the novelty of this symbolic act. They were cheering because walking directly towards them from the United States' side were President Donald Austin Blair and his wife and an Honor Guard of Marines carrying a large flag of the Stars and Stripes. Thousands of persons had climbed over cars which had backed up in Laredo for two days to join the party as it moved to meet the Mexican delegation. As the two groups got closer, the cheering and shouts grew even louder. In the center of the bridge was a small area roped off with a podium and microphones, and some television crews waited. Overhead, news service helicopters circled to record the historic moments. Both Ana and President Blair gave short speeches.

To Ana, it was a simple ceremony to relieve days of ungodly tension at the border points between Mexico and the United States. President Blair recognized the public relations and political value of doing this as soon as Ana suggested it to him. He had planned to make a trip to Houston, if necessary, to help save David, but to come to Laredo for a ceremony to celebrate the reopening of the border with Mexico was much more a happy outcome. The images of Ana and the President speaking on the bridge, then exultant Mexican and United States citizens hugging each other over the Rio Grande did everything to reassure people in the United States that there was absolutely no reason to invade Mexico. Besides that, the relief that international commerce was returning to normal put everyone in a good mood.

Ana often relived that day. She always believed it was her finest time. Even though she marched across the bridge with Rafael, she felt David not far behind her as he walked beside Enrique. She wanted to be with him, but both knew that what was important for Mexico at that moment was the complete healing of families. Ana and her family represented the wholeness that the victims once enjoyed. David and Ana were intensely sad, but their time, if any, would have to be in the future. As for Rafael, he thought that being married to the President of Mexico would be very good for business, and he was right.

Ana put together an electoral commission which worked exhaustively to set up procedures for new state, city, and federal elections in conformance with existing state and federal constitutions as much as possible. She lost weight with the long hours of fatiguing work and travel. Just before the elections, she was so run down that she became very sick with pneumonia and had to be hospitalized. The country, of course, had wanted her to run for the Presidency, but Ana declined. She understood what her role was, and she knew she was the shining symbol for the moment. She knew that she didn't want to run a country six more years.

Two years after the election, Rafael died of pancreatic cancer.

When Eduardo died, he left a tenth part of his considerable estate to David and a tenth part to Enrique, and the rest went to the foundation to fund the operations of the Zs. Ana was present at the reading of the will, and one of the most interesting moments came when Enrique handed David a journal that he had taken from Eduardo's home.

It was the book that El Gato carried around all the years since taking it from his parents' house the day he left forever. Soldiers reviewing the car El Gato was using the day of his death found it in the trunk and took it back to Eduardo's ranch. Enrique saw it there and removed it. Enrique knew after a few minutes of examination that the journal would be meant for David.

It looked like a diary, but when David opened it, he discovered that it was a book of poems that Annie Ortiz had written between the ages of thirteen and fifteen, some fifty years earlier. The poems were the work of a bright and sensitive young girl who marveled at horses and developing breasts and the wonders of friendship in springtime. She wrote about love, and David thought that a couple of poems might even have been about him. Then when he realized that Roberto had kept it with him at such personal close range for all those years, he thought that perhaps Roberto had thought those poems were about him.

There was one very strange entry at the end of the journal, and it was written in Annie's handwriting. This entry was dated when Annie was near the end of her senior year in college, and it was totally out of place with the young adolescent reflections of years prior. It was as if Annie had found her old writings one day and recorded a new entry that reflected much more mature and prescient sentiments. David cried when he read the entry. He thought to himself that Annie truly had been Eduardo's daughter.

Annie had written, "Is life truly cheap as it appears to be in times of greed, or is it so dear that it can never be priced in the hearts of love? I think the question is answered differently on each side of our border. Mexicans believe that the gringos assign value in dollars to everything in the great market of the North, including people. They believe that the gringos don't assign value to people south of the border. Those bodies floating in the river of blood from Colombia, Central America, and Mexico have no materiality in their financial statements. But once the red river begins to inundate the great Yankee cities and sweep victims from their lives, suddenly the value of lives will be computed. Zero value south of the border, but life insurance value north of it, plus "opportunity cost," or maybe the

381

present value of the stream of future cash flows lost from lives cut short."

After Rafael died, Ana and David fell into bed together in utmost secrecy for a year, and then Ana permitted herself to have public dates with David. It was a traditional way, to pass a year in mourning. When the year passed, and immediately Ana flew to David's arms, no one in Mexico really was surprised. The rumors had been there for years. Ana was a celebrity in the country, and when she and David married just six months after their first public appearances, the nation celebrated their happiness. Ana and David chose to live modestly. They selected a new house built in a suburban community in the heights of Cumbres. It had a rooftop terrace with furniture and soft lighting and large speakers for music. Occasionally, at two or three in the morning when neighbors were asleep, David and Ana would emerge there from their bedroom which opened to it. It took David a couple of months to convince her, but soon Ana joined him dancing naked under the stars.

One night David drew Ana to the edge of the roof top and they looked at the lights of Monterrey below. He held her close in the dark shadows of the mountains. "Tell me what you hear," he whispered in her ear.

She listened with eyes closed a long time. Finally she spoke.

"I hear the winds passing the future to our children and to young men and women of heart like Enrique. I hear the sound of our footsteps going to the North."

She had fought a long time, but right now she was hungry for him. She needed the strength that he gave her when he shot cannons inside her. She wanted to electrify him and keep him young as she always did. So she turned her dark Mexican eyes to him and kissed him with just her look, and she saw how she made him hard, and she celebrated her victory as he picked her up and carried her quickly to the bedroom. Her soft laugh remained behind, floating in the night breezes of Monterrey.

####

Prologue to the Sequel: *Corvette Nightfire*

Rogelio Nightfire
Just Outside Bridgetown, Barbados

Rogelio wondered exactly how they were going to kill him. He had received a five-minute warning from a poker friend by pure chance. The phone call in the house hadn't awakened Madeline or his son. He had happened to be in the kitchen when the wall-phone rang. He got the news, didn't ask questions, and ran to the bedroom trying to be light on his feet and quiet. It took him forty-five seconds to do this and slip on the pants he had left on the floor. His wallet and keys were in the pockets because he had simply dropped his pants earlier, playing with Madeline, who was teasing him from the bed. She had fallen asleep after their sex. Rogelio, as usual, lying beside his wife, had fallen into his recurring post-midnight state of anxiety and hunger. So he had gotten out of the bed to go to the kitchen to make a sandwich. Then the phone had rung.

He had always heard that your life passes before you in the instant before death, but he thought that he had about ten minutes before they would catch up with him. He wanted to spend this time reviewing where he had been, what he had done, and whom he had loved.

That should be ample time, he thought, *but, then again, I'm speeding on a motorcycle in the middle of the night on this dark island road to keep my killers away from my family sleeping at the house. I'm a little distracted.*

Over the course of a lifetime, "whom he had loved" boiled down to a handful of people: the old Texas rancher couple who had raised him when his parents got deported to Mexico (never to be known again); a few friends through the years (all living back in San Antonio); Madeline, his

383

long-legged wife whom he had worshiped since their first
dance on the cruise ship; and Corvette.

Always Corvette.

Since the moment of his son's birth when the kid had
snatched his heart and had made it his own, Rogelio lived
for him. Rogelio could talk Madeline into anything when it
came to giving to Corvette. Even more than Madeline,
Rogelio liked the child to be dressed in style. That is to say,
he shopped for his clothes to give the boy the flair of the
father: little caps, ties, striped shirts and knee shorts, and
wool scarves. To go with the clothes, Corvette had the
smile and winning mannerisms all his own. He grew up tall
like his British mum and Latino-looking like his Mexican
padre. There were two things the boy could do:

He could dance.

That was a genetic no-brainer. Madeline and Rogelio
stopped the show when they got on the dance floor, so
smooth-stepping and rhythm came naturally to Corvette. In
addition, Mum kept him in dance lessons until he was
seventeen.

And he was one hell of a poker player.

God, forgive me. I did that to him, Rogelio thought, *in
the backrooms of Texas and Barbados. Those led to my
downfall. Corvette, though…he's just an eighteen-year-old
kid, but Dios, what a head he has for probabilities! I'm
sorry, Lord. It's just that he's always dying to play, and he
can seduce anyone at the table into thinking what he wants
them to think. Even I can never resist him! The thing is, he
adores me. I know this. He thinks I'm something I'm not.*

Rogelio came up suddenly on a curve and downshifted
two gears with his foot as he braked. Just before he rounded
the bend, his side mirror caught the flash of headlights
behind him. He gunned the throttle, and his engine
thundered coming out of the curve. No one would be on this
road at three a.m. unless he was there for him. He was
ninety-eight percent certain that he knew who it was behind
him. Probabilities again. A lifetime of those! These
calculations told him that his pursuers were employees of
El Gato, the capo in the Cartel of Sinaloa. Like Rogelio,

they were a long way from Mexico. The cartel had global reach.

Well, I'll give them a run for the money.

The irony of that expression made him chuckle.

He had many regrets, but what now surfaced from a hurting place in his heart surprised him: He should have learned Spanish. He should have taught it to Corvette. That would have helped his son confront what certainly would come to his life: the necessity of reconciling the sins of the father and probably those of the grandfather. That wouldn't be possible unless Corvette knew who he was. Corvette would discover that the key to his redemption lay hidden in the canyons of Chihuahau. Somewhere in those places were either the footprints or the graves of Rogelio's parents. Corvette's grandparents.

Rogelio had failed to find them, and now he had run out of time.

The headlights behind him separated in his mirror, and he saw that these weren't from a car at all, but from motorcycles. Suddenly he understood how he was going to die.

He made a deal with God:

Give me eternity, Lord, in some limbo or some barren plot of heaven. Just not hell. I want to watch after my boy. I want to love him forever. I want to scream his name through the impossibilities of his hearing me from the faraway place that you put me. I want him to know that I'm always close. For this favor, I'll accept an infinity of penance for the wrongs I've committed. I'll guide him to you.

In the blinding flashes of light, Rogelio couldn't see. He wasn't sure what he had hit, but his last sensation was one of flight.

####

385

Acknowledgements

Two lifelong companions, both teachers of English, through their literary criticism and encouragement provided me the courage to publish this novel. They own large parts of my heart.

My editor, Robert Selfe, known as Bob, has been my best friend since kindergarten. He had a distinguished career teaching high school English literature and grammar for over thirty years. His continuous encouragement and laborious hours of detailed review through the numerous drafts of this novel made it possible for me to complete it. His enthusiasm for the story and his contribution of ideas greatly enriched the final product.

My brother, Stephen Wetta, the author of the award winning novel, If Jack's in Love (Amy Einhorn Books/G.P.Putnam's Sons/The Berkeley Publishing Group), likewise asked challenging questions and made suggestions based on his lifetime history of writing novels and short stories. I've been in awe of him as a writer since we were both young, and his encouragement and literary criticism meant the world to me.

The generous, affectionate and creative people whom I came to know and love in Monterrey, Mexico, when I lived there in 2009 and 2010 put the passion in my heart to start and complete this novel. I wanted to do it especially for my friend, Israel, who was murdered when I lived there. I couldn't rest until I could tell the story of the daily horrors the Mexicans endure while living lives filled with close and loving families and friends. They don't deserve the atrocities that occur in that wonderful and beautiful country.

Finally, I want to acknowledge my wife Judy, who never complained about the countless hours I spent tucked away writing in the two years it took to research and finish this novel. Her support and encouragement have been beyond measure, and I'm so grateful for her patience with my selfish indulgence in this project.

About the Author

Daniel Wetta grew up in Richmond, Virginia. He loved to imagine adventures, invent lies for his friends, write short stories, and pretty much exaggerate and embellish everything in his ordinary life, especially to get laughs. He ended up graduating from The College of William and Mary with a B.A. in History. Later he became a Certified Public Accountant after completing the accounting curriculum in the Graduate School of Business at Virginia Commonwealth University. While serving as CFO and CEO of a Virginia hospital, Mr. Wetta obtained his Master's in Business Administration from the University of Dallas. He currently lives in Williamsburg, Virginia, with his family.

In 2009 Mr. Wetta's restless spirit led him to Monterrey, Mexico, where he leased a condominium in the beautiful, mountainous community of Cumbres. There he made a great young friend named Israel, with whom he enjoyed working out in the gym and discussing international business over beer. To his horror, Israel, a bright and ambitious young professional and law student, was tortured and murdered by members of a drug cartel when he happened to meet the wrong person at a party. Mr. Wetta had other friends who also were victims of crime, including home assault and car theft at gun point. One morning as he observed all the minivans and SUVs of moms driving their bright, uniformed children to their bilingual schools in Monterrey, the thought hit him: How would the suburban moms and dads in the United States feel if on the way to school their children witnessed horrible and traumatic events in the streets due to the bloody fighting of drug cartels? Or worse, if they were victims? He knew that none of his friends in Virginia had a clue what their good neighbors south of the border went through or that so many of the problems there were due to unresolved social problems in the United States.

Fired up with love for his engaging friends in Mexico and with a passion to tell a story both entertaining and chilling, Mr. Wetta wrote The Z Redemption. He did it for Israel, who would want justice for all victims of organized crime worldwide, justice that Israel did not receive.

For more information or contact:

Website: http://www.danielwetta.com

E-mail: cursillo86@gmail.com

www.ingramcontent.com/pod-product-compliance
Lightning Source LLC
Chambersburg PA
CBHW071645260626
47170CB00001B/237